SIXES WILD

Professor Kurious Whitedimple was an unassuming teacher of archaeology at Space-Home University. Possessor of a boring life and a boring future.

Junior Badille was a 20-year-old wrinkled gnome with an improbably high IQ, living with his parents in an isolated research station orbiting Saturn at 3.5 million kilometers. Possessor of a lonely life and a short future.

The odds of these two meeting, sharing high adventure, and forming a lasting friendship were astronomical—on the same order, for instance, as the accidental discovery of an alien artifact on the surface of Iapetus. . . .

"A very distant descendant of *Treasure Island*, but the 'treasure map' and the action it stirs up are thoroughly different from anything Robert Louis Stevenson could have imagined."—*Analog*

GRANT CALLIN

SATURNALIA

BAEN
SCIENCE FICTION
BOOKS

SATURNALIA

This is a work of fiction. All the characters and events portrayed in this book are fictional, and any resemblance to real people or incidents is purely coincidental.

A Baen Books Original

Baen Publishing Enterprises
260 Fifth Avenue
New York, N.Y. 10001

First printing, January 1986

ISBN: 0-671-65546-9

Cover art by Alan Gutierrez

Printed in the United States of America

Distributed by
SIMON & SCHUSTER
TRADE PUBLISHING GROUP
1230 Avenue of the Americas
New York, N.Y. 10020

Dedication

To the memory of my father, David Callin.
He was the midwife at Junior's birth.
I'm sorry he didn't remain to watch him grow.

1

"... caused the priests of Ptolemy V to inscribe the slab in hieroglyphic, demotic *and* Greek. Napoleon's troops found it near Rashid, at the Rosetta mouth of the Nile, in 1799. But it wasn't until after 1801, when the British captured it, that Champollion and others were able to ..."

That's how I used to sound performing my profession, teaching SpaceHome University's one required course in archaeology. I remember that particular lecture because it was precisely then that something unprecedented occurred: A clerk came into my classroom bearing a message on a slip of paper. He whispered that it was quite urgent, then left with an exaggerated tiptoe.

Feeling like a participant in a drawing-room comedy, I said "Excuse me a moment" to the class, then bent to read the note. It was from Mr. George Ogumi, president of the SpaceHome Corporation. It requested my presence in his office as soon as possible.

Notwithstanding the fact that the corporation was a principal subsidizer of the university (and consequently my salary), there was my professorial dignity to consider. I was a bit miffed at the idea that Ogumi's wishes might be considered more important than the course of higher education. Therefore, I wadded up the note, stuffed it into a pocket and continued to describe the struggles of Champollion and others until the end of the period. Besides, there were only three minutes until the bell.

After class I went to my office and punched my home number. Heather answered, of course:

"Whitedimple residence."

"Hello, honey. I'm afraid I'm going to be late tonight; better not hold dinner for me."

"Why? Where are you going?" she demanded. Heather and I weren't married, but she liked to keep tabs on my movements. I told her about the note.

"What do you think he wants?" she asked.

"I haven't the slightest idea, sweetheart."

"Well, try not to be gone too long, Whitey," she said. "And be careful about what you say; Mr. Ogumi is a very important man."

"Of course, my darling." I said goodbye and hung up the phone. I went outside and looked spinward, trying to decide whether to walk through the residence level to the SpaceHome head offices, or to go down to the shop level and take the loop lorry.

'Home III is a torus, with the residence level being the "top" floor. There was nothing above me but the inner walls curving gently up to the shiny-surfaced cosmic ray baffles sixty meters overhead. Looking straight up, one would be turning his eyes toward the geometrical center of the torus, which contained the hub and the complex, directable set of mirrors which supplied sunlight to the colony. It was currently "daylight," so the mirrors were positioned to reflect the sun's rays through the chevron baffles to the residence level.

I liked this level much better than the lower portions of the doughnut. Man is not troglodytic by nature; his soul food includes at least a partial diet of open spaces. Up there on the residence level, there was an unobstructed view of over half a kilometer before the upsweeping horizon cut off the views up- and down-spin. The houses, flower gardens and small farm plots made a pleasant, if unexciting, landscape. But twenty meters below, at the shop level, or another twenty meters below that at the maintenance level, the light was artificial, there were no long views and the feeling was closed in.

SHU occupied several degrees of all three levels, with windowed classrooms and offices topside—which is one reason I liked teaching. The head offices of the Space-Home Corporation were one hundred and eighty degrees around the torus, almost two and a half kilometers as the colonist walks. I'd almost decided to go on foot when my common sense got the better of me—and my curiosity, to be honest. I had no clue as to what Ogumi wanted, and was anxious to find out. I turned back inside and took the elevator down to shop level.

I've no idea how the loop lorry got its nickname. It wasn't really a truck—just a simple field-effect open trolley. Or four trolleys, rather; they ran every three minutes and stopped at four points around the circle. It was only a few seconds until a car arrived; I swung aboard and sat down.

By the time the lorry started up I was lost in thought. I barely noticed the food and clothing shops and cheap restaurants flashing by. I even failed to notice the feeling of exhilaration as the midpoint velocity of the trolley canceled some of the 'Home III spin and lessened gravity by a third. I was trying to remember everything I could about George Ogumi; it wasn't much, as I was almost totally disinterested in both economics and politics. They're both dirty occupations.

I ticked off the few thing I knew on my fingers.

Pinkie: Ogumi had been president of the SpaceHome Corporation for about ten or twelve years.

Ring finger: During that time, SpaceHome had wormed its way out of total economic dependency on a complex, intertwined group of Earth-based cartels and consortia, and was now approaching an autonomous status.

Middle finger: To do this, SpaceHome had bought out

several firms which had voting control over various SpaceHome operations. To do this, the corporation had gone heavily into debt; it was paying the bill by charging Earth stiff-but-competitive prices for everything from beamed power to telescope observing time.

Index finger: This strategy carried an additional price of some hard feelings and a growing estrangement between us colonists and the Earth peoples. The Earthers, led by the moods of their giant cartels, grumbled about the high prices of "services" charged by the Colonies; while the colonists began more and more to feel the chauvinism of the high ground—only natural for 80,000 close-knit people committed to living 400,000 kilometers from the home planet.

Thumb: So far, Ogumi had been steering us through this socio-politico-economic morass with an acceptably deft hand.

By the time I had run out of fingers and thoughts, the lorry was pulling into the SpaceHome Corporation complex. I hadn't even noticed the stop at the Theater.

You're not going to believe this, but I'd never been inside the corporation complex.

My parents emigrated from Earth when I was only four years old; I grew up on 'Home II. Mom and Dad were industrious; they paid my way through SHU by working overtime building 'Home IV. After getting my bachelor's degree, I stayed on 'Home III for graduate work. I got my doctorate shortly before old Professor Jensen died; it was natural that I stay on as the ranking (and only) member of the archaeology staff. So except for a grueling nine months on Earth doing my doctoral research, I'd lived in 'Home III for over twenty years. And in all that time beating around on a hundred-odd hectares of area—of which the SpaceHome Corporation occupied a substantial fraction—I'd never set foot inside its buildings. Maybe it was an inborn uneasiness with any kind of non-academic authority. Or maybe something else; I'd never stopped to figure it out. But I knew that I was distinctly uneasy as I swung off the lorry and surveyed the lower level of the complex.

The elevator looked invitingly plush, but I decided to take the stairs to have time to compose my thoughts. Then I changed my mind when I recalled that the executive offices were tiered well up the wall of the residence level, and I'd have to climb more than forty meters. I wouldn't exactly say that I was in *bad* physical condition, but the thought of climbing two hundred steps and arriving at Ogumi's office out of breath struck me as being somewhat out of character for a dignified member of the university faculty. So I turned back to the elevator—then lost some of that dignity anyway, by rushing to get in before the doors closed.

'Home III is built like a bicycle tire with six spokes. All of the spokes are structural and of sufficient volume to house offices, labs—and even residences—all the way up to the low-gravity hub. Three of them contained freight elevators; the other three boasted two passenger elevators each, one of which I was riding. It was much fancier than either the SHU or Auditorium elevators, both of which I'd taken to the hub many times.

I rode the richly appointed cubicle up to the level of the corporation offices and debarked on an elevated breezeway. The walk across to the office complex was a long one, since that structure was built up along the sloping wall of the torus some forty meters laterally from the elevator door. The vista from the walkway was intimidating because of the dangerous fall to the gardens down at residence level. I stopped gawking when I noticed that none of the people bustling back and forth were paying the slightest attention to the height.

The complex was complex. It contained rooms and offices which were indoor/outdoor, terraced, split level—and in general artistically arranged with no thought as to how a stranger might find his way to a specific location. After getting directions from a good Samaritan I finally found my way up a flight and a half to the president's suite.

The door was simulated wood—very expensive—with a small, tasteful plaque beside it at eye level which stated simply: Office of the President. I entered, feeling unfairly intimidated.

I was totally surprised at the room's size; it must have been all of five meters square. Along with the ubiquitous aluminum, slate and glass were touches of what looked like real wood, brass and leather. Easy chairs, end tables and wall decorations were strewn around the room in eye-pleasing arrangements.

I was even more surprised that the room contained not the president, just his secretary. She was the decorative-but-professional type; she appeared more than sufficiently competent to use the complicated desk/computer console wrapped around her. At the moment I walked in she was dictating a letter, which was being reproduced on a CRT to one side. She flipped a switch and looked at me over a small arrangement of flowers on her desktop.

"Yes, sir?"

I may have been intimidated, but my tongue rebelled: "I'll bet the secretary to the president of International Power down on Earth has an office twice this big."

She awarded me a thin, frosty smile. "I wouldn't be surprised. Do you have business with Mr. Ogumi, sir?"

I told her my name.

"Oh yes, Dr. Whitedimple. Mr. Ogumi left instructions that you're to go right into his office." She gestured at the double door which I swear was made of wood. I tilted my head back about five degrees and pushed my way into the inner sanctum.

The office of the president was only slightly larger than that of his secretary. It was dominated by a large desk strewn with charts and papers, over which three men were bent. The shortest of them straightened up to greet me.

George Ogumi was not physically impressive. He was small, round and flabby. His white hair swept down to a pair of black horn-rimmed glasses—an oddity in an age when simple surgery could permanently correct almost any visual defect. Epicanthic folds covered the inner corners of dark brown eyes which were penetrative—disconcertingly so; he seemed to be able to look at my face and read my mind. His first words tended to confirm this:

"My astigmatism has become quite pronounced in the past ten years. Unfortunately I can't seem to find time for a corrective implant. And you, I presume, are Dr., uh, Curious Whitedimple?"

That final query, unfortunately, was one I'd heard many times before. I sighed to myself before replying: "That's *Kurious*, Mr. Ogumi. *Koor*—ee—us." I reached across the desk and took his outstretched hand.

He was relentless. "My, that certainly is an unusual name. How did you come by it?"

"It's a long story, Mr. Ogumi. I'm afraid we'd both be bored by the time I finished it." I looked pointedly at the other two men straightening up from their work. One was Tim Buffington, a colleague who taught cultural anthropology; the other I'd never seen before.

Ogumi shook off the snub effortlessly: "Later then, perhaps. Let me introduce you to Brent Grism; he works in the Hub communications department, and is the only person in the Colonies with any training in cryptology." I shook a hand damp with perspiration and manfully resisted the impulse to wipe my own on my pants.

"And of course you already know Dr. Buffington. He's the one who recommended that you be included in this work session."

Wondering if Buffington had done me a favor, I took his hand. "Hello, Timothy." Surprisingly his hand, too, was sweaty. That made me look carefully at them again; they both seemed strained—excited and apprehensive at the same time, somehow. But I didn't have time to wonder because Ogumi was continuing:

"Dr. Buffington says that you have done research involving the deciphering of ancient writings." He stopped and waited for a reply.

Surprised, I answered: "Why yes, I did some digging in a fresh pre-Etruscan find in northern Italy about twenty years ago. Dissertation reserach." I shuddered at the memory of that enforced stay in that ridiculously deep gravity well. "But surely you're not interested in obscure pottery glyphs. . . ."

"No, not exactly." Ogumi smiled. "We're more interested in your *talent* in interpreting, uh, obscure glyphs, as you call them." He motioned to the desk over which the other two were standing. "Come around here and tell me what you think of this." He pointed to a large sheet of paper on the table.

I walked around, inserted myself between the other two, and looked. The paper displayed a computer drawing of what appeared to be a perfect hexagon about a third of a meter across. In the center were several concentric circles; further out were arcs, each arc ending on individual circles of various sizes. The innermost circle was about five centimeters in diameter; it contained five spokes radiating from the center, each with a symbol at its tip. There were also groups of symbols nestled in five of the six apices of the hexagon.

"Well," I said, "it looks like a hexagon with circles and other markings inside."

Ogumi frowned. "Please, Dr. Whitedimple, don't be flip. This is a serious matter."

Belatedly I remembered that Ogumi held SHU purse strings. Bridge mending was not my forté, but I tried: "I was not attempting to be humorous, Mr. Ogumi. That artistic style is totally unknown to me; and without understanding the context in which it came to be here, I couldn't even begin to make intelligent speculations."

Ogumi looked hard for a moment at Buffington, who nodded imperceptibly. Then it was my turn for the horn-rimmed stare.

"Very well, Dr. Whitedimple." The little man spoke without once taking his eyes from mine. "This is a picture of an artifact recently found on the surface of Iapetus. It was discovered by two repairmen out on a job to replace a malfunctioning navigation transponder about four hundred kilometers from I-Base."

My eyes almost crossed. "Do you mean that this image was not designed by a human culture?"

Ogumi nodded. "Yes. It is absolutely certain that this is a non-human product."

"Do you have an extra chair I could use for a moment?" My legs weren't exactly *shaky*, you understand; but they did feel funny, and in such circumstances prudence was dictated. I sat for a second and breathed deeply twice before speaking again.

"Pardon me, please. I needed a little time to get used to the idea. Now, could someone please describe the exact appearance of the artifact, and tell me the exact circumstances under which it was found?"

The other two looked to Ogumi, who answered again: "It was found in a box, just sitting on the surface. The container looked kind of like a hexagon-shaped hatbox. It was very light in mass and appeared to be almost a perfect insulator.

"The artifact itself is made of some kind of metal or alloy; it's about one centimeter thick and very heavy, according to the message sent by the I-Base manager. It's blank on one side; the other contains very fine lines forming a picture. This piece of paper," he tapped the drawing in front of me, "is a true-sized replica of the picture, taken at high resolution, scanned and transmitted by encrypted digital imagery."

He smiled thinly, which seemed to be the only way he could. "The I-Base manager also encrypted his explanatory message. Thank goodness. He also mentioned that the actual image was formed by hair-fine, etched grooves, and that he had to side-light the image and boost contrast drastically to form a transmittable picture. Now, if I may repeat myself, what do you make of it?"

The president's matter-of-fact monologue had helped steady me, so that I had some thoughts collected.

"Well, I'm a bit uncomfortable about seeing just a picture . . . but it's obviously a message, and meant to be found by strangers. And as such, it shouldn't be too difficult to interpret. We should probably begin by assuming that it was produced by a highly sophisticated civilization which would understand in advance that there might be no common cultural referents on which to draw for deciphering."

I put my elbows on the table and pressed my spread fingertips together. It was one of my best affectations. "In which case, the referents should be scientific or analytic only. All of which I'm sure you've deduced already."

"Precisely, Whitey," Tim Buffington said, bustling into the conversation, "and we'd like your insights to help us to continue our interpretation of the message."

Then it was Ogumi's turn again: "And I'm afraid we're in a bit of a hurry, Dr. Whitedimple. The message came in from I-Base about twenty hours ago, and we sent one back almost immediately, ordering the personnel there not to discuss it in any form of broadcast. We've also clamped down on loose talk among the Hub comm shack people. But," he gave me that ten-kilovolt stare, "we can't keep this under wraps forever."

I looked at him curiously. "Why should you want to? This is the greatest event to hit humanity since ... since ..." I couldn't think of a referent with sufficient hyperbole, so I just gave up and raised my eyebrows at him.

"We fully intend to release the news, Dr. White—do you mind if I call you Whitey? We're going to be in close quarters for a while, and formal titles are so cumbersome."

"Not at all, sir."

"Very well, Whitey. We will release the news in good time. But first we would like to translate the message, if it is indeed a message. We are of the hope that it might lead us somehow to technology or information which SpaceHome could use to economic advantage."

He looked me in the eye again. It made me nervous. "Are you aware of the current economic situation of the Colonies, Whitey?"

I admitted to a global ignorance—not in those exact words, of course.

"Hmm, well I suppose we can't expect an ivory-tower

academician to be overly interested," he said. "Let's just say that our credit is finally good, but we're still several years away from running in the black. If we could somehow gain economic leverage over our creditors with this find, it would be an enormously good thing for SpaceHome. For all of us."

He saw my mouth opened to reply and held up a hand. "I think I know what you're going to say. But please, put yourself in my position for a moment, Whitey. Given that this is an enormously important find for all of humanity, I still ask you to consider this: The Colonies contain thousands of people engaged in a remarkable struggle to make a home away from the multitude of oppressions existing on the homeworld. I think we're winning that struggle, but it's not a sure thing. But if this discovery leads to some means for assisting that victory, then it's surely worth the wait to open it up to the entire race. It has been there on Iapetus for who knows how many thousands or millions of of years. A few more days or weeks surely won't make any great difference on its impact or timeliness.

"Besides," he finished, "the board of directors of SpaceHome Corporation has voted in favor of a temporary suspension in releasing the news, and I am under that obligation as a matter of course."

Though I had my doubts, I could do little but nod my head. It wasn't until much later that I remembered that Ogumi had most of the board members completely under his thumb.

"All right, sir, I'll do what I can. I'll be here first thing in the morning to start work; I don't have a class tomorrow."

"Perhaps I haven't made the urgency quite clear enough, Whitey," he said. "We'd much rather you help us in working out the translation now—tonight—before you leave these offices."

"Well—"

"Please, Whitey," he said earnestly. "I'd consider it a great favor if you would inconvenience yourself for this purpose." He smiled. "I'll try to make amends any way I can."

"Could you let me call home to tell a friend not to wait up for me?"

"I'll do you one better, Whitey. I'll call myself. Perhaps the message will be a little more believable coming from me." He smiled. "What is your friend's name?"

"Heather Lynn." I gave him the number. "And thank you."

Ogumi excused himself and, except for brief appearances from time to time throughout the night, he left us alone. We got down to serious work, and before long the import of the thing became a background issue to the puzzle it presented.

As I began to examine the drawing carefully for the first time, the cryptologist came to life. "It's obviously a picture of the Saturn system," he said. "You see, the central circle is the planet itself, and the tight concentric circles are plainly meant to be the ring system." He pointed to a pair of them. "See this gap here? That's certainly a representation of Cassini's Division."

Planetography had not been my strongest subject in college; nevertheless it was obvious even to me once he'd pointed it out. I felt bold enough to chip in: "In which case, the outer circles represent Saturn's moons?"

"Precisely, Whitey," said Buffington. He pointed to a small circle way out near one of the angles of the hexagon. "This would be Iapetus. Then thirty degrees clockwise and further in toward the center is Hyperion—see how small and irregular it is." His hand continued to move as he catalogued the moons. "Then another thirty degrees around the edge, and even further in, is the largest one—Titan. You see, it's opposite another apex of the hexagon.

"Then Rhea, and Dione opposite a third apex here; next comes Tethys, then Enceladus opposite a fourth apex. And this is Mimas; it's the closest major satellite to Saturn—see, it's only about a centimeter from the outer edge of the ring system."

"What are these arcs extending from the moons?" I asked. "Are they supposed to represent orbital paths?"

"Precisely," said Buffington for the third time in as many minutes. One thing about Tim: Once he found a phrase he liked, he stayed with it through thick or thin. This habit forever barred him from the ranks of brilliant—or even interesting—conversationalists.

By then I'd noticed something else. "There's an arc here in the middle of Saturn's rings; looks like it corresponds to the fifth apex of the hexagon. What do you make of that?"

"Obviously there is something within the B-Ring that holds a major significance," Grism said, then frowned. "But we don't know exactly what it could be. I know of no major bodies embedded in the ring system of Saturn. . . ."

By then I had another question. I started to ask it, then changed my mind and said: "Why don't you just tell me everything you've observed and deduced. That'll save us some time."

"Not much more than you already know, I'm afraid," he said. "Those spokes in the center of Saturn's image each point to an apex of the hexagon. The symbol at the tip of each spoke is repeated here," his finger swept outward, "at the corresponding apex, along with two other symbols."

He pointed to one of the groups of symbols at an apex. "You can also see that two of the three symbols here—this one in the middle, and the small hexagon— are identical for all five groups at the apices. The only symbol which changes from apex to apex is the third symbol, the one repeated at the tip of the corresponding spoke in the center of Saturn."

"What about this little hexagon?" I asked, pointing to the group of symbols in the apex opposite the unknown point in the B-Ring. "It has a symbol inside, but the rest of them are blank."

"I'll get to that in just a second," said Grism. "But first, notice that the symbols which are different at each apex are very regular; only these two vertical lines change position." He pointed to each symbol in turn. "This system makes an ideal counting method. We could assign the values one, two, three, four and five to these because of the changing positions of the lines. If so," he continued with animation, "then the number of the symbol inside the little hexagon—the one you asked about—would be the number six.

"Outside of that," he finished dolefully, "we're stuck. We don't know why that symbol is inside the little hexagon at one apex and not the others—though obviously it calls attention to some special importance—and we don't know why the sixth spoke is missing from the center circle, or why the sixth apex of the hexagon has no symbols."

"That's why I asked Ogumi to call you in, Whitey," said Buffington. "We're hoping you might come up with something which will get us unstuck."

I looked hard at the drawing for two minutes, then began mumbling under my breath. I didn't even realize what I was doing until Buffington broke into my thoughts: "What are you talking about, Whitey?"

"Huh? Oh, excuse me Timothy. I was saying 'relationship and correspondence.' " I turned to the cryptologist. "Brent, have you noticed that every straight line on this picture appears to be the same length?"

"Why, no," he said, "I haven't given much thought to it." He rummaged through a pile of instruments on the table, found a pair of dividers, and proceeded to compare lengths.

"You're right, Whitey. But what does it prove?"

"Well," I said, "unless the culture responsible for those markings evolved in some weird, orderly manner, those symbols are no part of it's natural language. Which makes sense; they wouldn't try to communicate to aliens with their native markings. Exactly what *is* the length, Brent?"

He got out a reticle and placed it over one of the symbols. "Just shy of one centimeter," he said. "Call it nine point two four millimeters." He looked up. "But what good will that do us? Surely our units have no meaning with respect to theirs."

"Relationships within the drawing," I said. "Now let's check the diameter of Saturn's image in the center."

Grism performed the labor. "Fifty-five point four three millimeters," he said, then bent to his calculator for a minute. He looked up with a light in his eyes and said: "Bingo. Exactly six times the line length."

They were looking at me expectantly, with a markedly elevated degree of respect. Noblesse oblige required a word or two: "An educated guess, gentlemen. Now, does anyone know the true diameter of the planet Saturn?"

Several hours later, with coffee stains covering various pages of *Atlas of the Outer Solar System, Revised Edition, SpaceHome Comprehensive General Survey: 2088*, and with hand calculators hot from overwork (theirs, not mine—I'm more the cerebral type), we had come up with the following additional data:

(A) As near as we could make it, the image of Saturn on the artifact was exactly the equatorial diameter of the planet divided by 6^{12}.

(B) The images of Saturn's moons were enlarged with respect to Saturn's image, presumably for pictorial balance. The expansion factor was exactly six.

(C) If one were to inscribe a circle in the overall hexagonal figure, its diameter would be exactly six times that of the central image of Saturn.

(D) All orbits shown on the image, including those of the ring boundaries, were compressed logarithmically, base six, keyed on Saturn's image diameter.

There was more, but the gist of it was that the number six was overwhelmingly important to the message. And by then, none of us was in any doubt that the picture *was* a message.

"That sixth apex is just begging to be filled," said Buffington plaintively. "Why isn't it?" It was not the cleverest observation in the world; both Grism and I

had been saying that under our breath for over two
hours.

The cryptologist was nicer than I; he answered civ-
illy: "I think that when we get the answer to that one,
Tim, we'll be all finished with our work." He turned to
me. "The paucity of information in the drawing leads
me to believe that the message must be a very simple
one. Do you concur, Whitey?"

I looked up from the *Atlas.* "Yes."

He said: "I'll then assume that everything is as we
believe presently, and that the message says look for the
artifact in the B-Ring; the ones on Titan, Dione and
Enceladus are all identical to the one we're holding."
He tapped the set of circles in the center of the drawing.
"But the fifth one, the one somewhere in the B-Ring,
will show us how to find the sixth one—the real message." He looked wistfully at the diagram. "But *where*
in the B-Ring? Why 48,000 kilometers from the surface,
if we're to believe the scale? And where are the other
artifacts, for that matter?"

"Where indeed, gentlemen?" said Ogumi, bustling in
as if he'd had a full night's sleep, which he hadn't.

I was looking at a photo-image map of Iapetus. I
glanced up at Ogumi. "Where did the I-Base manager
say those men found the artifact?"

The small man elbowed Buffington aside and opened
a desk drawer; he pulled out the message and scanned
it. "About four hundred kilometers from the Base, east
by northeast. Do you have an idea, Whitey?"

"Maybe," I said. "Could you show me where I-Base is
on this photo?"

The SpaceHome president pointed to a spot almost
exactly on the equator, and right at the boundary between the light and dark halves of the moon. I took the
dividers and set them for four hundred kilometers on
the scale at the bottom, then put one point at I-Base
and swung an arc northward from due east. In a second, I stopped the other point in an hourglass-shaped
patch of black. It was surrounded by a large expanse of
pure white; this in turn was bordered by a distinct

band of black. It was a striking feature. I looked at Ogumi with raised eyebrows.

"I believe they call that 'the Bullseye,' Whitey."

I nodded. "Apropos. And I suggest that we'll find the other artifacts centered in similarly distinctive features on Titan, Dione and Enceladus. The artifact that really counts—a different one—will be found at a striking feature in or near the B-Ring, approximately 48,000 kilometers from the planetary surface."

"Excellent, Whitey." If Ogumi was elated, he hid it very well; instead, he appeared worried. "Whitey, I'd like you to do me a big favor. I'm sure you of all people realize the importance of having a trained archaeologist follow up on this find. Now, the regularly scheduled quarterly supply tug leaves tomorrow for I-Base. Would you please take that tug to Iapetus, commandeer a boat, and investigate your deductions? SpaceHome and I would be most grateful."

I demurred strongly. I had classes to teach. He could get someone else. He could wait a few days and send a specially commissioned boat. I was no pilot, and never had any pretensions to being one. If I went on the tug, it would be a dead giveaway, anyway.

Ogumi was forceful. He'd clear my absence with the SHU dean of faculty. Buffington could take over my classes for the remaining three weeks of the quarter. Everyone else who qualified had family responsibilities. Sending a special boat would create unwanted attention. He'd give me authority to commandeer a pilot. A cover story could be arranged to account for my going with the tug; specialists went along occasionally for working visits to the base.

"And," he said, looking into my eyes and reading my soul, "there really won't be any personal danger involved, Whitey. I've talked this over with the board, and we've made arrangements, in case a visit to I-Base was required. We're all agreed that you are the best choice."

I made a final try. "But we need more time to study.

We don't even know where to look for the moon-located artifacts, let alone the one in the B-Ring."

"Time is of the essence, Whitey. You can take along reference materials; you'll have plenty of time on the outbound trip. And if you need more help, the Saturn Orbiting Station will be able to supply all you want. In fact, that is the most likely place to find transportation to the inner system; they have a research boat which they use specifically for that purpose." He smiled. "And SpaceHome Corporation foots all their bills."

I shook my head in a last-ditch effort. "Heather is never going to believe this. . . ."

Ogumi's smile reminded me of a cat which, after some effort, has cornered a small rodent. "I'm sure a personal phone call will handle that aspect of things, Dr. Whitedimple. Your friend seems quite amenable to persuasion from . . . ah . . . shall we say, higher author-ity?"

Out-gunned, out-maneuvered, out-thought, and out-talked. Mutely, I nodded my head. I also stole a glance at Grism and Buffington; they were regarding me with looks combining pity and relief. For a moment, I dis-liked them intensely; it drove me to a hard positive commitment. "Very well, George. You seem to have taken care of all my local worries, so I shall be most happy to go. The thought of making such a find as might be out there is really quite exciting. What time does the tug leave?"

"At noon, Whitey," he replied. "Go home and get a little sleep. Come back here at nine, and I'll have a package of papers and credentials for you to carry with the rest of your luggage."

I nodded and left the office, looking at my watch. It was nearly four in the morning. My shoulders slumped as soon as I left the room. I was tired and depressed. The thrill of deciphering the artifact had worn off for the moment, even though I knew it would return. I felt badgered and bullied into doing something I didn't re-ally want to do. I was mad at Ogumi for taking advan-tage of me, and even madder at myself for capitulating so easily. I wanted to find the artifacts, true, but I wanted to find them right here in 'Home III—not in some godforsaken corner of the solar system. I am definitely not the hero type; the hair on my chest is entirely civilized.

2

She: I don't care *what* Mr. Ogumi said! The fact is, you're going off God knows where—and you won't even tell me, not even *me*—for God knows how long, and probably going to get into God knows *what* kind of trouble! And I'm supposed to just meekly let you go, not ask any questions, and quietly wait for you to come back!

He: I'm afraid that's how it has to be, sweetheart.

She: Don't you "sweetheart" me, Kurious Whitedimple! I'm not feeling at all sweet at the moment.

He: Listen, Heather. If there's anything at all I can do, I will. I'll make this up to you when I get back, I swear it.

She: I doubt you will, Kurious, because I doubt I'll be here! So goodbye!

He: Goodbye, Heather.

And that's how *that* went. Heather is a most attractive woman, and at times a joy to have around; but she

20

can lay down a guilt trip that is hard to believe unless felt in person. And she called me by my first name more than once; she knew I hated that.

So an hour later, bag packed and stuffed with letters of introduction I'd picked up from Ogumi in person ("Good luck, Whitey, and find us a find!"), I climbed into the spoke elevator. It raised me inexorably up past offices in the spoke, past the louvered glass "ceiling" of 'Home III, through a passage in the banks of secondary solar reflector mirrors, and into the hub.

The 'Home III hub is fairly large—about 300 meters in diameter, as I recall. Even so, when I got out on the "ground" floor, gravity was down to a fifth of what I was used to. It had been some time since I'd been up to low G; I didn't particularly like it, especially when I recalled that for at least two or three months I'd have to live in such a condition, or even lighter. But at least it made my kit easier to heft, though it tended to steer me along, rather than vice-versa.

I made my way to the vast locker storage area and found my number. I was half surprised to find my suit still inside. Not only that, the maintenance record showed that earlier in the morning it had been completely inspected, overhauled and freshly charged with supplies. Ogumi was covering all bets; he wasn't about to let me miss the tug because my suit wasn't up to snuff for vacuum travel.

Not that such a thing would have stopped me now. I had made a witnessed commitment, the breaking of which would have cost me an intolerable amount of face. Besides, I found an enthusiasm for the voyage beginning to wax in spite of my reluctance to venture away from the Colonies. The deciphering of the artifact's message had finally done its work. Tired as I was, the excitement of the hunt was stirring.

And it was a fact that, in spite of SpaceHome's industry there, relatively few people had seen the rings from a bird's-eye vantage. And finally, my status in the SHU hierarchy—which had been relatively static for a dozen years—was quite likely to elevate in the event of a successful find. All in all, the balance was tipping.

So with my heart lightening to match the gravity, I strapped my kit on the backpack and began to velcro myself into the micropore suit. By the time I had dogged the helmet down and made the pressure tests, I felt ready for anything. Which, as it turned out, was most fortunate.

Suited, I drifted past more lockers, past one of the freight elevators, and around to another passenger elevator. I noticed that there were remarkably few people, then remembered it was Sunday and still early in the morning.

I got on the elevator and took it up to the inner part of the hub, passing three intermediate levels on which were low-G offices, manufacturing concerns and various entertainment establishments offering everything from multi-wall nerf-pong to discrete sexual encounters. The top floor was where I was headed—the inner hub.

The inner hub originally had been built like a wafer— very fat, very strong, about sixty meters in diameter—to which all six spokes were attached and in which were contained all the 'Home III airlocks. Since the construction of the Pinwheel, that wafer had been partitioned and was now two wafers back-to-back with a strong dividing wall. One of the wafers handled the small volume of direct dockings at the torus. The other one handled ninety-nine-plus percent of 'Home III commerce via the cable system. I went to the latter, of course.

Once inside I took a moment to orient myself; this was necessary because almost all activities use the center dividing wall as a "floor." From my vantage point just coming out of the elevator, I could look up and see across the entire hub diameter. The walkway on which I was standing curved up in both directions and met itself directly overhead; it was the edge of the wafer. Way up on the wall, near zero G, were four cylinders extending to the outer skin of the hub. Two enclosed and hid the personnel cables; and two much larger cylinders enclosed a set of four cables each, on which ran the cargo trolleys.

Even on a Sunday morning, there was some bustle in the dock. I noticed that a trolley had just come in, which was a pity; it wouldn't be returning for a while and I'd wanted to catch a ride if I could. As I watched, the first of the cargo pods came through the airlock. The handlers did their work efficiently, wedging their bodies against the safety rails and horsing the load onto one of the flatcars lined up alongside. When they'd tied the pod down, they released the car's brake and let it drift outward on its rail. It began moving very slowly under the weak centripetal pull of the hub's rotation; it would eventually come to rest on a shock absorber near one of the freight elevators.

Fast as they were going, the crew wouldn't be ready to release the trolley for the return trip for another two hours. I looked at my watch. If I waited, I might have enough time—barely—but I didn't want to arrive at the Iapetus tug late and out of breath. I sighed and made my way around the walkway to a point directly under the inbound personnel airlock which was, here in the 'Home III hub, chauvinistically marked Outbound.

Flimsy-looking ladder rungs ran up the wall to the airlock twenty-five meters overhead. The prospect of such a climb would have scared me to death down at the residence level. But up here, almost floating at about a fiftieth G, I swarmed up easily; by the time I reached the lock I weighed next to nothing. I drifted inside and cycled the chamber.

It had been some time since I'd gone vacuum, and I gave a nervous little cough as the pressure in my helmet dropped along with the outside. But the helmet display reported that its pressure leveled off dutifully at five psi; and the trapped air bubbles in the suit's stretch fabric expanded dutifully to hug the rest of my body at matching pressure, even as the air finished spilling out of the lock. I opened the inner door when pressure zeroed, and stepped into the cable room. This was nothing but a cylinder about eight meters across, with its floor near the center of the 'Home III hub, and its ceiling open to space. I pulled myself into the center using the handholds on the floor. The cable ran dye-straight from a hole in the floor up through the open ceiling. I hooked on with a belt loop and looked up. Through the opening I could see the Pinwheel, looking like a toy five kilometers away.

Remembering my duty, I voice-activated the suit intercom and talked briefly to the computer at the Hub. It didn't matter that it had been several years since I'd taken the cable; the processor called me by name and gave me clearance for the inbound trip. It reported no one else on the line, and informed me in its flat phonemes that I was cleared to proceed at the maximum allowable speed of twenty-five kilometers per hour.

Fat chance. Ten was plenty for my blood, even though the shock absorbers at the inbound end were supposed to keep a person alive coming in at many times that. I tentatively activated my gas thrusters and began to move slowly upward out of the 'Home III hub.

As I passed through the ceiling I experienced a momentary spasm of agoraphobia; it had been a long time.

You must know the difference between the hub and the Hub. The hub—little *h*—is the center of gravity of whichever one of the habitats you happen to be in at the moment. The Hub—big *H*—is the center of the Pinwheel.

The Pinwheel, so they say, is the Engineering Wonder of the Age, and the Hub the strongest structure ever built by man and woman; and the bearings are the strongest and most perfect ever devised; and the controlling computer contains the most complex system ever programmed. And so forth. Get the particulars from your local library; but be prepared for a large printout. Myself, such details bored me and I never bothered to learn them.

I did know that (A) Earth said it could never be done, but that (B) the SpaceHome central economic processor said about twenty years ago that it was time to make the investment, with the way fuel prices were headed.

Ogumi's predecessor finished the project, and Ogumi had to pay the bill. He was still paying, too—with fuel savings and nothing else. About five or six more years would see it in the black, as I seemed to remember from the Sunday supplement article. One thing I knew for sure: Travel from habitat to habitat became a lot easier after it was finished.

Each of the six Colonies was connected to the Hub by ten strong cables. Eight were for the two trolleys which carried almost all commercial traffic; and two were for personnel who didn't wish to wait for the trolleys—which ran synchronously, but somewhat irregularly.

Earth officials claimed that when they got their first equatorial beanstalk up and running, *they* would be able to claim the greatest wonder of the age, and the Pinwheel would descend to second place. But they'd been talking and planning and fighting about it for the past generation. The technology was certainly there, but the politics were something else. Where would the first one be located—Africa? South America? Borneo, Sumatra, the Celebes? And who would foot the bill? Not just the fifteen or twenty billion for the system, but the fifty or hundred billion to clean enough junk from orbit to make the thing a sane investment. Good luck. And in the meantime, Earthers stayed mired in their gravity well, and SpaceHome gained every year in reaping the benefits of the commercially exploitable solar system because of its superior position in the high ground.

In the meantime, I found myself forgetting my initial fears of the wide open spaces and enjoying the view. Earth and Moon were sixty degrees apart, forming a lighted backdrop for the other Colonies strung in an irregular line across my field of view. Immediately to my left was 'Home VI, which was called the Large Cylinder; in about three years it would become the Medium Cylinder—a mediocre name, at best. Directly on my right was the venerable 'Home I—the original Space-Home—which was now ingloriously called the Cube, since its 600 meter length was equalled by its diameter. Further around to the right was 'Home IV, our sister.

We both tended to be called the Hundred-Second Torus because of our rotation periods, but it made for some confusion. 'Home V was invisible behind the Hub. Second on the left was 'Home II, now called the Farm for the obvious reason: We sent it garbage and excess CO_2; it returned food, and oxygen for boat and pliss use.

I looked back into the Hub, then up along the north axis to the old Brayton parabolas fifteen kilometers above it. The enormous array was shrunk to proper size by distance. Below the Pinwheel, but only a couple of kilometers south, was the microgravity manufacturing facility. The MMF was almost as big as the Hub itself, but had absolutely no spin. It was almost totally isolated from the Pinwheel. Even the almost imperceptible disturbances occasionally experienced by the inner Hub were too much for some of the delicate processes which gave us ultra-pure crystals, ultra-pure pharmaceuticals, ultra-round bearings and a bunch of other ultra-perfect things to sell to Earth and ourselves. At ultra-high prices, it goes without saying. I think that it also manufactured the cables, one of which I was currently using. Something to do with the proper setting of the filaments, perhaps; I'm not good at engineering details.

And about ten kilometers south of the MMF 'Home VII was taking shape. It would be the Big Cylinder when it was finished; it would double the available living space of SpaceHome. They said it would even have weather. I wasn't sure I approved; I'd experienced weather on Earth, and thought it a chancy way to condition a habitat. Meanwhile, the girders of the monstrous thing were silhouetted against the gibbous Moon, a promise for three years hence. I could wait. I heard that when they attached it to the Pinwheel, everyone else would be drastically inconvenienced while they rearranged the habitats to balance.

I was about fifteen minutes out, maybe halfway to the Hub, when I felt a sharp tug on the cable. That was unheard of; those cables each had nearly a million kilograms tension. I squinted along its length toward the Hub, but didn't see anything. Uneasy, I twisted around

to look back toward 'Home III. I was starting to slow
down from the extra friction, when I saw a flash in the
sunlight. It was a wave in the cable, coming at me with
great speed.

I suppose I should have been paralyzed, because something inside me knew that I was looking at death. If
that wave didn't shake my intestines loose, what was
coming afterward would be the killer. For an instant I
flashed on a picture—a moment of horror I'd experienced back on Earth two decades ago: We were pulling
a very heavy block of stone from the excavation, when
one of the steel cables from the hoist above snapped.
The stone fell without hitting anyone, but the loose end
of the cable whipped down and struck a worker standing next to me. It all happened so fast no one had time
to react. I heard the sound of the cable end hitting the
man's upper arm; it went right through, breaking the
bone and severing the large artery. We saved his life,
but barely.

By the time I'd finished that one-second daydream,
my hands had miraculously begun to act of their own
accord. They fumbled at the release, finding the two
buttons with maddening slowness, and finally pressing
them simultaneously. As soon as the loop disengaged
from the cable, I hit the buttons to activate my reaction
jets, somehow working the controller to aim my suit at
right angles to the cable line. I headed in the general
direction of 'Home IV.

My suit thrusters had been on for about three seconds
and I was just beginning to get that simultaneous feeling of relief and shakes, when something struck me a
terrific, numbing blow on the right shoulder. I might
have passed out for a second or two; I can't remember.
All I know is that when I was conscious of things again,
I couldn't figure out which was worse, the monstrous
pain in my right shoulder or the feeling of vertigo from
my complex tumbling motion.

My right arm was useless, so I reached my suit controls with my left hand, and at the same time tried to
straighten my legs out from their instinctive doubled-up

position. From many, many years ago, the voice of my old suit instructor whispered into my brain: "Use your eyes in a tumble; try to pick out a stationary reference object in the distance. Move your control experimentally; if the tumbling gets worse, push it in the other direction. Try to work one axis at a time; first roll, then pitch, then yaw. Don't black out or you might get dead."

It was the Hub that first caught my eye, rolling—too fast!—past my field of vision. Concentrating on the pain in my shoulder to avoid throwing up, I somehow managed to do the right things.

Only when I was relatively stabilized and thinking about calling the Hub did I really notice the nature of the sensation in my right upper arm. Not only was there pain, but also a cold, aching feeling. I craned my neck as far to the right as my helmet would allow. Horrified, I saw from the corner of my eye a fine spray. A stray droplet plastered itself on the plastic visor. It was blood.

I had to swallow my gorge again as I frantically dug into my belt kit and fumbled out the tube of Qwik-Patch. I forced it into my right hand, and somehow made the hand function enough to hold it while I found the applicator back in the kit with my left hand. I had it halfway to the tube in my right hand, when I remembered something which made me swear and pee my pants at the same time. I put the applicator back in the belt kit, reached over and unscrewed the cap from the tube. Then my left hand moved back to the kit, put the cap in, and took the applicator back out. I brought the applicator over to the tip of the tube and, with gritted teeth, forced my reluctant right hand to squeeze the sticky stuff onto the tip of the applicator. I didn't know how big the tear in the suit was, so I squeezed out a liberal amount.

The little fifteen-centimeter handle was barely long enough. It was a contortionist's job to wrap my left arm across the front of my body and smear the junk onto the shoulder. I was thankful, in a gruesome sort of way, that the stuff stung violently as it touched my open wound; at least I could tell I was getting it on the right spot.

By the time the cold sensation was gone, my left arm and hand were so cramped I could hardly pull them back around to put everything away. I corrected my residual tumble—it wasn't bad—and looked around again. I was drifting to a spot somewhere between the Hub and 'Home IV.

I'd lined myself up on the Hub, and was just about to activate my thrusters again, when I noticed a group of four cables moving into my vision from the right. Hastily, I changed my mind, and worked hard for a minute to bring myself to rest with respect to them. Gratefully, I hooked up to one with my beltloop and looked back along the line. It was one of the trolley cables strung between the Hub and 'Home I. I looked off further to the right and upward, and spotted one of the personnel cables a few meters away. I suppose I should have transferred to it; but at that moment I was in no mood to give up the security of the cable to which I was now firmly anchored. I looked up and down the line to make sure no trolleys were coming, then activated my suit thrusters once again and began the inward trip to the Hub.

Only then did I finally remember to make a long overdue call to the Hub computer. I gave the emergency code, and was answered by a worried voicecomm operator. I explained what had happened, and that I was coming in on the 'Home I trolley line.

"Can you make it on your own, or do you need some help, over?" Her voice somehow managed to sound worried and impersonal at the same time.

"My condition is groggy but navigable," I replied. "By the time you can get someone suited up and out here, I'll practically be at the airlock anyway, over."

"Very well, Dr. Whitedimple. We'll have a doctor standing by for your arrival."

A technician, suited up, was waiting at the bottom of the line. He helped me through the airlock. As soon as we floated out of the chamber, I was greeted by an M.D.

plus a swarm of about two dozen curious onlookers. I let one of the other technicians take my helmet off, since I didn't feel up to it. As soon as my head was free, the M.D. began: "Now, sir, where—"

"Pardon me a moment, doctor," I turned to the technician and said: "Where's the nearest john?"

He pointed back over his shoulder. "Through the spin door and about twenty meters to the right. I'll show you if you—"

"Thanks." I was already moving away from the group. The doctor still had his mouth open.

Vomiting in microgravity is on a par with all the other bodily waste removal functions—inconvenient. I remembered to do most of the right things, so I didn't have too much of a mess to clean up when it was all over. I emerged white and cold-sweating, but feeling better nonetheless. When I pushed through the exit door, the doctor was waiting to guide me to his office.

Half an hour later I was feeling *much* better. My torn and soiled suit was being cleaned and repaired. I was in fresh clothes from my kit and my wound had been cleaned and bandaged. The only thing sour was my disposition. I had several years of nightmares to look forward to; and losing control of my bladder had been a serious blow to my professorial dignity.

"No fracture," the doctor said, studying the scan hologram from all angles. "And I'd estimate that you lost only about 200 milliliters of blood." He pursed his lips. "Of course, the blow itself and the subsequent exposure to a vacuum environment have produce a massive subdermal haemotoma. . . ."

"I beg your pardon?" I said, suddenly worried.

"A big bruise." He smiled as he said it. He was probably trying to get back at me for rushing off to throw up without a formal greeting. I felt a mild impulse to stuff him out the nearest airlock.

"You'll be sore for a couple of weeks, and stiff for twice that long. I advise you, if you have to hit vacuum again, to wear a full-pressure suit rather than a micropore."

He smiled again. "Of course, the fact that you were in a micropore suit in the first place is what saved your life; a tear that size in a pressure suit would have dumped your air and killed you in no time. In fact, you were also lucky that the cable end didn't hit your helmet. It's quite remarkable that you're alive, Dr. White-dimple."

"Yeah," I gushed. "Lucky. Remarkable."

He looked sharply at me. "In any case, sir, I'd advise you to rest for the remainder of the day. You've undergone quite a physical and emotional trauma."

I thought briefly about using that as an excuse for missing the tug, then decided once again that I'd made too many commitments.

"Sorry, doctor; I've got a tug to catch in less than an hour."

"Very well then, sir. You're fit enough, I suppose. But please, no micropore suit for at least two weeks."

"Thank you, doctor." I was already drifting out the door.

Before I left for Iapetus, there was an itch I had to scratch. I made my way back to the appropriate outer section of the Hub and followed signs to the 'Home III port complex. The surrounding area, which normally would have been bustling with incoming and outgoing traffic, was dead—not a soul around. I drifted over to one of the viewports and looked through to the vacuum of the cable table. The large circular platform was still rotating slowly, matching the hundred-second period of 'Home III; one trolley was in, but the table was empty of personnel. The inbound single cable was missing, and the shock absorber was gone. So was a circular portion of the table, a hatch about two meters in diameter through which the cable normally ran.

I moved away from the window and looked around. There had to be people *somewhere.* I noticed a deck hatchway marked To Cable Tier: Authorized Personnel Only. I drifted over to it and began to fumble with the latch.

"Just a second! What do you think you're doing; that's restricted access!"

I looked at the voice; it was the man who'd removed my helmet when I first came out of the airlock less than an hour ago. We recognized each other at the same time.

"Oh, excuse me, Dr. Whitedimple. Everybody's a little jumpy what with the accident and all. I'm sorry, but we're really busy down there; I'm going to have to ask you to stay here abovedecks."

"I was just trying to find somebody who could tell me what happened. I feel like I have a right to know, since it was my life on the line."

"Damn right," he said with some degree of admiration. "And nine-tenths of the little old ladies around here would've been dead right now if they were in your place. That was pretty fast thinking out there, Dr. White—"

"Call me Whitey, please," I broke in.

"Yeah, okay, Whitey; my name's Frank. Like I was saying, you got a good head on your shoulders, and some guts to boot. Most of the birds around here would've just frozen. And that repair job you did on your suit, with your bum arm and all—you really had to suck it up, pardner."

"Yes, but what happened?" I asked. He was starting to embarrass me. I tended to agree with the doctor; luck had been with me more than anything else. My actions had been governed by fear and panic for the most part.

"Well," he said, "if it wasn't a one-in-a-million shot, it's the closest thing to it I've seen in some time. The safety system components for the cables are triply redundant; but the power supplies for the two backups were accidentally shorted together by some freak accident up on 'Home III. About the same time, before the repairman could get down underneath, the on-line tension sensor went open. That elevated the reading so fast that the cable spooling system couldn't react. So the emergency quick-disconnect activated: 'Home III kicked out the cable, reel and all. And when *that* happened, the Hub safety system automatically kicked its own end out to prevent the 'Home III spool from doing damage down here."

He looked at my damaged shoulder. "So if you had hung around the cable—even if you survived getting wrapped up by the 'Home III end—chances are the Hub end would have finished you off." He shook his head; admiration was still in his eyes. "That was a smart move, heading out at right angles like that. But you got tagged anyway—probably by the 'Home III spool. Just bum luck that it found you." He winked. "But good luck it only gave you a love tap; that thing masses over three tons, not including any cable spooled up on it. Must have hit you a bare glancing blow. That makes you both smart *and* lucky." He laughed. "If you were a jockey, I'd bet on your horse, Whitey!"

His line of talk was bringing things back a little too vividly, and what I felt like at the moment was neither smart nor lucky; it was more like throwing up again. I searched for something to say to take my mind from the grisly and move it back toward the mundane.

"That sounds like an impossibly rare occurrence, Frank. It doesn't sound like I was very lucky at all."

"Listen Whitey," he came back. "I'm a SpaceHome maintenance specialist—been one for twenty-five years. And if there's one thing I've learned, it's to expect the unexpected. We been livin' up here for over fifty years now, and we're still learnin' about the environment— cosmic burst anomalies, vacuum-induced bearing creep, lubricant outgassing, trapped corona discharge, and on and on. Every time we think we've got a problem licked and begin to start congratulating ourselves, it shows up again in a different form, and—bingo!—we got a new long-term environmental phenomenon to worry about."

He was getting warmed up; I pictured a soapbox glued to the bottom of his feet.

"And mark my words, Whitey," he continued. "We're just starting. Next'll come the biological effects. When we get a couple more generations worth of baseline, we're probably gonna find out things that'll make pure physical phenomena seem mundane."

He shook his head. "Oh well, it's not a bad life up here; and it's gettin' better every year. Maybe I shouldn't read so much."

He looked me in the eye. "So in answer to your question, Whitey, I'd say ask me again in a couple of decades, and I'll tell you whether or not it was really a million-to-one."

"Well, Frank, thanks for nothing." I smiled broadly to let him know there was no insult.

"Any time, Tiger," he said, then cocked an ear as the PA system made an urgent demand. "Oops, there's my call; been yakkin' a little too long. We're in the middle of reeling in 'Home III a few hundred meters to ease the strain on the other nine cables; and you know what that means: All the other cables to the other five Colonies gotta be adjusted accordingly. Gotta keep that ol' angular momentum balanced." He was opening the hatch as he finished: "Then, when the retrieval crew gets the loose cable in, checked, and reattached, we gotta do the whole thing again backwards." He was through the hatch and closing it behind him before I had a chance to say thanks or goodbye.

The Hub is built in two pieces. The rotating section, with cables to the six habitats, is a cylinder five hundred meters in diameter and three hundred thick with a hole through the middle. The non-rotating piece, the true Hub, plugs the hole. It's a stubby cylinder three hundred meters in diameter and three hundred thick. That's where I had to go, because all outside commerce to and from the Hub docked with the non-rotating section.

The outer cylinder makes a complete rotation around the true Hub once every four hours, so the interface movement is only a few centimeters a second. The moving seals between the Hub sections make transfer easy. I went in one of the personnel exchange booths and activated the lock, which was more a safety device than anything else. I checked the readouts to make sure the pressures were equal, then opened the inner lock door, moved across into the Hub and reversed the procedure. I didn't even have to wait for an opening to line up, since the booth I started from was currently opposite one of the long freight windows in the Hub.

I had only been in the Hub a few times—which was more than enough for me. The structure was a labyrinth of corridors and cubbyholes, mixed apparently randomly with large office complexes, shops and recreational facilities. The people who worked there swore the Hub was a model of efficient, logical organization; all you had to do was learn a few simple rules.

My rule was to blunder around clumsily until I found a kind soul to direct me to the central shaft. After that, it was only about one hundred and fifty meters until I bumped into the north skin of the Hub.

I made my way to one of the viewing bubbles, and sucked in my breath like any tourist. The long girder structure leading up to the solar parabolas was only a few kilometers long, but seemed to recede forever before blossoming into the gigantic shapes which were the initial *raisons d'etre* of SpaceHome.

Nine-tenths of their output still went to Earth, even though the magnificent array of Brayton engine collectors was now outmoded by CRF reactors. But so long as Earth was too niggardly to spend the billions required to orbit a few large CRF power plants, they'd continue to buy kilowatts from SpaceHome. I guess the computers knew pretty well how much we could charge without driving the Earth-based energy consortia into pooling their resources to make the investment.

I pulled my gaze back down the girder lattice to where the stationary manipulator arms were attached. Only one was in operation; it was hooking external pods to a big, stubby vessel ringed with very large tanks. The process looked almost complete; I realized that I'd better find the pilot. If he was like most I'd heard about, I wouldn't be getting off to a very good start by making him late for his scheduled takeoff.

The tug was about ninety degrees clockwise around

the Hub; I was glad to see that it was hard-docked—
that would save me from having to borrow a full-pressure
suit to go aboard.

I moved around until I guessed I was clocked correctly, then wandered into a likely looking corridor.
Within a few meters I emerged into a large chamber
with an airlock door standing open. Personnel were
hustling into it with arms loaded, and out empty. I
picked out a short, burly man lounging in an out-of-the-
way corner sipping a bottle of coffee. There was no
doubt.

"Hello," I said tentatively. "My name is Kurious
Whitedimple, and I think I'm going to be your passenger."

He looked me up and down, then stuck out a hand.
"Hi. Name's Armand Tellingast, but you'd better call
me Jock. How did you pronounce that name again? I
didn't pick it up."

"Kurious Whitedimple," I said, then added quickly:
"But you'd better call me Whitey."

"Okay, Whitey. Message came in last night, late. Said
I was gonna have an industrial specialist as a passenger. When I read your name I thought it was a typo. So
your name's right; are you sure you're an industrial
specialist?"

"Sure as shootin' Jock." I tried to be nonchalant.
"Productivity is dropping at Iapetus Base and Mr. Ogumi
is concerned. So he volunteered me to come along at the
last minute. Sorry if it's inconveniencing you."

"Mmmm. Well, this scow isn't the regular personnel
carrier that makes the yearly run. It'll be cramped,
especially with the extra provisions. On the other hand,
the company's welcome, Whitey. And we do run an
extra person or two, occasionally." He smiled. "So let's
climb aboard and I'll give you the two-dollar tour."

I followed him up the hatch, pushing my kit in front
of me. Jock showed me where to stow it—a little cubby-
hole about one meter by two by three, which I found
out was to be my bedroom. I quailed, but bravely re-
frained from commenting. There was one tiny john without a shower ("No problem, Whitey; in the Middle Ages

they went for years without bathing."). There was also an equally tiny galley and Jock's bedroom, which was about the same size as mine. The most cheerful feature was a lounge-cum-workroom which must have been all of twenty-five or thirty cubic meters in volume. Only about half of it was used up by desk, workstation and entertainment center. The control cabin was small, but did have left and right seats.

I supposed I was expected to say something when the tour was over. I pulled out a winning phrase:

"It looked bigger from the outside."

He looked at me sourly for a moment before his natural good humor reasserted itself. "Most of the tug body's fuel tanks, Whitey. Lots of CRF reaction mass, with a fair amount of hydrazine for RCS."

I continued to display brilliance: "But aren't all those external tanks for fuel?"

He shook his head in exasperation. "Where you been all your life, man? Yeah, they're for fuel, all right; but at the moment they're empty, except for a few luxury supplies for I-Base. They'll be loaded with fuel and organic tar on the inbound trip—but not for this tug to use. The fuel's for SpaceHome. That's why I-Base exists—remember?"

"Of course, Jock." I was getting seriously nervous and vowed to keep my mouth shut in the future. "But I'm afraid all this is somewhat new to me. My specialty is really in the, uh, Earth industries area."

"Yeah. Well anyway, this is the space we got. Cheer up, Whitey. It's gonna be crowded, but you can take just about anything for a lousy month. Say, do you play cribbage?"

I moaned inwardly and squeezed out a mental fear, thinking about peaceful days teaching at the U and coming home to Heather's meals. "Right, Jock. No problem. I'll bet I can learn quickly; I'm a fast study."

"Right on, buddy," he said, moving up into the pilot's couch. "Come on up here and take the right seat. It's time for us to punch out; we don't wanna keep Traffic Control waiting."

He flipped switches and talked to the onboard computer as I strapped in. "Nav computer checks out," he said to me. "Now I'm giving control over to Traffic." He thumbed a mike. "I-Tug 2 to Traffic Control. Comm check, over."

A smoothly professional voice came back from the speaker: *"Traffic Control here. You're five-by, Jock, and we confirm you on Traffic computer control. We have a ten-minute window opening up in fifteen seconds, over."*

"Reading you five-by, Sam," Jock answered. "Give me a couple of minutes to batten up and green my board here. I'll come back with a thirty-second tick when we're ready, over."

"Confirm, I-Tug 2; we will wait for a thirty-second tick, clear."

As Jock fiddled with the console and spoke code words to the computer, I tentatively moved my shoulder. It was quite stiff, and the wincing pain brought back all the events of the day. I still couldn't quite believe that it had been only nine hours since I'd agreed to go. Suddenly I wondered exactly when Jock had gotten word that I'd be traveling with him to I-Base. I made a resolution to ask him when he had a free moment. Then I thought of something else, and swore under my breath: I'd forgotten to bring the atlas of the Saturn system. It was sitting in a corner of Ogumi's office, where I'd tucked it for safekeeping when I returned home to get some sleep.

My mind came back to the present when I felt the pressure change. By the time I had swallowed to clear my ears, Jock was telling Traffic Control to kick us out in thirty seconds. All of a sudden, the fact that I was leaving my nice warm home behind for who knew how long, beginning a venture I had no real desire to take part in, struck home with the force of a sledgehammer. I felt like a reluctant groom, standing at the altar with only a few seconds until the preacher said "I now pronounce you . . ."

I nearly threw away my dignity completely. My arm made a movement to unstrap myself, and my mouth was actually opening to tell Jock that I'd changed my mind, and to let me out.

Then the pilot looked over at me and said: "What's the matter, Whitey, your shoulder going stiff on you? Wait'll we torch, and you can get up and move around. It'll only be a few minutes. Ah, here we go now."

The last words were in response to the RCS thrusters lighting off and giving us a gentle push away from the Hub. So it was too late. I guess it was all along, ever since Ogumi had shivvied me into accepting the night before. Reality closed in.

". . . out at forty-five degrees to clear both the Colonies and power parabolas," Jock was saying. I began listening to put myself firmly out of 'Home III and into the present. It was a masochistic act.

"There," he finished as the thrusters of the reaction control system cut out and we were floating again. "Done, for a few minutes. But stay buckled in, Whitey. We'll light the CRF as soon as we get out to fifty klicks. In the meantime, I gotta tell my nav 'puter to get us to Saturn."

He turned back to punch more buttons and speak more words to the onboard processors. I looked out my right-side viewport, since there was nothing but blackness in front. The only thing I could see at first was the Cube. It seemed to be shrinking at an alarming rate; that gentle little push from the RCS must have lasted longer than I thought.

Then, all of a sudden, we did a right turn—a yaw—and a little bit of a roll; I could see the entire Pinwheel. It was tiny. I'd never seen it from this far away, since it had been built after I'd come back from Earth. Now I was going much, much farther than Earth. The cables were invisible with distance. I got a lump in my throat. I didn't want to go.

"Here we go." Jock's voice was like the knell of doom. Then the CRF engine lit off.

Earth children are taught the "three R's." Our equivalent in the Colonies is the "three C's"—cosmics, calcium, and CRF. Cosmics, because long-term exposure is unhealthy to individuals and the race. Calcium, because after long exposure to very low G your bones lose high-gravity options. And CRF, because controlled-rate fusion is the keystone of off-Earth civilization. I knew three things about CRF engines: their plumes were dangerously hot plasma; they could go for a long time on a small amount of fuel; and they were almost always run at low G for reasons of efficiency.

In spite of what I knew intellectually, my emotional state was such that I expected us to be whisked away from the Pinwheel at a breathless velocity, pressed relentlessly into our couches by heavy acceleration. What we got was a gentle push that didn't stop—about a third of what I was accustomed to on 'Home III.

"Is this all the weight we're going to feel?" I hated myself as I said it; but I was defenseless at the moment, and my mouth loves to work without direction at such times.

"Hell, Whitey, this is big G's. Point one." He unstrapped after flipping a final switch on the console, blanking a final amber display. "On the return trip with all those external tanks loaded to the gills, this scow makes only a tenth what we got now."

"They told me the trip out takes about a month. Is that right?"

"Yeah," he said drily. "Anywhere from about twenty-seven to thirty-one days, depending on where Saturn and the Sun are in relation to our starting point. We're quartering on this trip, so we don't have to do any dipsy-doodle to miss the solar heat. We'll be out in about twenny-eight days."

He unbuckled and turned to face me fully. "Now, what do you do for a livin', Whitey?"

"Industrial operations, Jock," I answered slowly. I desperately searched for something to say to make it more real: "I guess you could call me kind of a super efficiency expert."

He looked at me hard. "Sure you're not shittin' me, Whitey? Story's out that we had a hullabaloo after we got a long transmission in from I-Base the other day.

Thought your sudden trip out there might have somethin'
to do with that, huh?"

I tried to look ingenuous. "I'm sorry, Jock; I really
don't know what you're talking about. Ogumi gave me
orders to go see what I could recommend to increase
productivity." Hearing it come from my own lips, the
so-called cover story didn't sound nearly as convincing
as when Ogumi and I rehearsed it in the outbriefing. I
swallowed and hoped Jock would change the subject.

He did: "Okay, Whitey, I'll play. Say, how did you get
that name, anyhow—Curious Whitedimple?"

"That's *Kurious*, Jock. *Koor*—ee—us."

"Hm. Well, it's still weird. Your folks come from
Turkey, or somethin'?"

"It's a long, boring story, Jock. You'd fall asleep in
the middle of it."

He grinned. "Well, with nothin' to do for a month
'cept spin yarns and sleep, that's a *curious* thing to say,
heh, heh!" He elbowed me in the ribs.

"Where's your deck of cards?" I sighed.

3

Earth used to charge outrageous prices for shipping organics up to the Lagrangian Colonies. So when the SpaceHome Corporation finally decided it was solvent enough to seek an alternative source, the computers said: Iapetus. Don't ask me why; I'm an archaelogist, not a computer.

I will freely admit that when the Great Architect of Cause and Effect put me on Jock's tug to I-Base—and once I finally got over my homesickness—the excitement of the hunt crept back into my soul. The first few days out I had time to whip up my enthusiasm for the venture and anticipate the exhilaration of solving the mystery of the artifact's story. And after all, holograms notwithstanding, seeing things firsthand was the best reality—and the rings were definitely something to see.

But by the time we finally were nearing our destination, I was too bored to be excited. Twenty-eight days from L5, the last half of it pointed backward. Space travel: big deal.

Jock helped a lot: "Boring! You call this boring? Hell,

man, this is a piece of cake. After I drop off these supplies, I gotta pick up 20,000 tons mass of fuel and smelly organics and wrestle 'em back to the Pinwheel. Three months at a crummy .01 G, with calcium leaching from my bones and no crib games. You wanna talk boring?"

I'd heard the same story, with variations, several times before. An unfortunately timed yawn earned me a mild glare. "Anyway, if you wanna look at Saturn, we'll be orbiting Iapetus for a while before we burn down to base. You can get a good peek before we land and go underground."

An hour later the tug stopped burning. The onset of zero G after fourteen continuous days of acceleration felt funny. When I started to drift to the starboard viewport, Jock held out a hand. "Strap into your couch for a few seconds, Whitey. We'll prolly have to make a little plane change; I'm checking with I-Base computer now for the verdict."

I'd just strapped in when he said: "Okay, we're about two degrees flat. Hang on; I'm gonna let the nav 'puter do its thing." He spoke and punched code. Almost immediately I heard the muted in-cabin hiss of the hydrazine thrusters. My inner ears did a little dance as the tug performed a rotation in two or three axes simultaneously, then abruptly stopped. A small interval, then the CRF engine lit up again and gave us a gentle eight-second shove.

When we stopped, he stared at the readouts for a few seconds, then announced: "That's got it. Twenny-eight degrees with descending node smackdab at I-Base next pass. Hang on another second." One last dance. "Okay, I've got our ass-end pointed down the groove; you can unstrap and take a look."

About three or four times the diameter of the Moon from Earth or the Colonies, Saturn was big enough, but otherwise not that impressive. The cloud belts lacked striking definition and the rings were edge-on. It wasn't enough after a month of waiting. Jock, as usual, put two cents in: "Iapetus is only a day or two from ascending node. Wait three weeks and the rings'll be tilted about fifteen degrees. The Old Man'll look a lot gaudier then." He pushed away from me and drifted to the other side of the cabin. "C'mon over here; you can see where we're gonna land."

When I'd joined him he pointed toward the planetary horizon. "That's looking backwards along our flight path. Right on the horizon is Hamon crater. It's solid red-black except for a cream-colored central peak—looks like a curious white dimple, heh, heh!" He laughed and elbowed me in the ribs, for perhaps the three dozenth time—and hopefully the last.

I grabbed hold of a fitting to keep from drifting away and awarded him with stony silence.

He subsided to a sheepish grin. "Hell, I couldn't resist; you don't have to be so touchy. Anyway, five hundred klicks over the horizon from Hamon is Baligant, then Grandoyne. All three craters are pretty black, and they checked 'em out early as possible base sites. Tar wasn't thick enough in 'em, though—no more'n ten or twenny centimeters—so they just dropped transponders in 'em for nav aids."

He shifted position and angled a finger in the other direction. "Up ahead there you can see the start of the Black Sea. That's where I-Base is—right on the equator at local Greenwich, so it's always got Saturn dead overhead." He now pointed straight out the viewport. "And right below us here is the Bullseye."

It looked just like the map from our orbit: a wide, dark ring hundreds of kilometers in diameter. Inside was the normal white of Iapetus ice, except that in the very center was a dark pattern with a Coke bottle shape.

"Take a close look at it," Jock said. "Because next time around we'll only be a few klicks up and burning down on our tail. Right there in the center—in the middle of the Bathing Beauty—is where they found your precious artifact. You know, it's crazy; they been on Iapetus all these years, and they just get around to exploring somethin' only four-hunnerd klicks away from base. Goes to show ya—"

"Just a minute," I interrupted, registering every gram of incomprehension I could muster. Jock had caught me by surprise; he hadn't brought up the subject of my "occupation" ever since the beginning of the voyage. "What do you mean, 'my precious artifact'?"

He grinned. "No offense, Whitey, but you never fooled me with that story about being some industrial operations specialist. I got a friend in the Hub comm shack; word's out all over the Colonies that I-Base found somethin' in the center of the Bullseye that was artificial, and not put there by humans. A tablet of some kind," he gazed obliquely at me, "that was covered with markings.

"And in case you think you've kept the news from Earth, forget it; they've had our encryption keys for years. So what you've got is the best-known secret in the solar system." He scratched his chest reflectively. "What I'm tryin' to figure out is why Earth isn't screaming about you guys keepin' this thing to yourselves. I guess you might know somethin' about that, eh?"

I did my best to convey candid astonishment in the look I gave him; in the meantime my brain went into high gear. If what Jock said were true, then it was common enough knowledge that Ogumi must know it also. Which meant that he'd sent me out here without telling me everything. Which also meant I had some serious thinking to do. But not at the moment; the pilot was looking expectantly for an answer. I gave it my best shot.

"Just what the devil are you talking about, Jock?" Unfortunately, intrigue is just not my forté. My voice caught, and I'm afraid my tone wasn't very convincing.

He sighed. "Okay, have it your way. But don't think the rest of us are total dummies. And remember, we're on the same side." He turned back to the viewport. "Hey, here's something interesting: the terminator in the Black Sea. Once you get into shadow, it's like bein' at the bottom of a coal mine at midnight. . . ."

We burned down the groove without incident. The computer did the work, while the pilot grumbled under his breath. I asked what was bothering him. His answer sounded like an Earther complaining about taxes: "Regulations. I gotta come in at .25 G to shorten I-Base's exposure to the plume. Good thing organic hydrogen's cheap here; gotta push so much reaction mass through the throat that my I_{sp} goes down to a crummy 10,000. And taking off with a full load's even worse. They oughta outlaw planetary surfaces. If the good lord'd meant us to land on planets, He'd have given us antigrav. . . ."

He continued the monologue all through the landing, although his eyes never ceased their vigilant watch over the readouts. I finally decided that he would *enjoy* the return trip at .01 G, since it would keep his precious eye-ess-pee high, whatever that meant.

After touchdown, I unstrapped and looked out the viewport facing the base. There was precious little to see; the few structures showing above ground appeared to be part of a refinery. Puzzled, I asked Jock where the solar cells were hidden. Me and my brainless mouth.

He grinned at me. "You're pretty ignorant for an industrial specialist, Whitey. Solar power's out of the question here. It's too far from the Sun, and it stays dark forty days at a crack. You'd have to build two solar arrays on opposite sides of the surface, and each one'd have to be a hundred times bigger than in Earth orbit to get the same power. So even though I-Base was built when solar was cheaper than nuclear, they spent the big bucks and built one CRF generator that supplies all the power they need. Now whattaya say, let's get down inside. I got a thirst that won't quit."

We stripped off our coveralls, threw them into our kits and donned micropore suits. I stretched my shoulder experimentally and decided that the suit wouldn't hurt it; the wound had healed entirely, and there was only a hint of stiffness remaining.

By the time we'd debarked, a crew was already unhooking the supply cannisters from the tug and carrying them inside to be emptied of supplies. They would then be refilled with CRF reaction mass and other organics to be differentiated and refined back at Space-

Home. Even without mechanical aids, they were making good time. The surface gravity was only about a tenth of that at 'Home III.

Once inside the airlock, we changed our suits for coveralls again and took the elevator down to base personnel level. Jock immediately headed for the bar; with more reluctant steps I followed the signs to the manager's office.

Informality reigned. The secretary jerked her head toward the inner door before I even got my mouth open. I walked in and the manager rose from his desk to greet me.

"Hello, I'm Bob Reynolds. And you must be Dr., ahh, Curious Whitedimple." He made a valiant effort to hide his smile.

I sighed. Forty years down, maybe a hundred to go. "That's *Kurious*, Mr. Reynolds. Pronounced *Koor—ee—us.*"

He let the smile emerge. "Goodness, that certainly is an unusual name. . . ." He trailed off expectantly. I briefly toyed with the idea of levying heavy sarcasm, then canceled. After all, I had to work with this person. I quickly decided on a "man-to-man" pitch, and spoke as earnestly as possible:

"Kurious, of course, is Greek, after my maternal great-grandfather. Whitedimple is a loose translation of an old Mariachi Indian name; in the original, it's considerably bawdier." I favored him with a sly wink.

Predictably, he leered. "Oh, ho; I understand now, uh, Dr. . . ."

"Dr. Whitedimple is so formal," I cut in smoothly. "Why don't you just call me Whitey."

"Very well, uh, Whitey. I suppose you'd like a run-down on the operation here. As you probably know, Iapetus Base was established in 2067 for the purpose of fulfilling the SpaceHome Corporation's pressing needs for cheap organic compounds. Besides being the solar system's major supplier of organically bound hydrogen for CRF reaction mass, we ship several tons mass of unprocessed organic tar on each of the quarterly tugs.

Among these compounds are the various clathrates of. . ."

This character was wound up and ready to go; I interrupted him fast: "Excuse me, Bob, but I'm not really what the message from SpaceHome said I was. Maybe you'd better read this letter from Mr. Ogumi before you go any further." I dug the one-pager from the president out of my coveralls and handed it to him.

He read it rapidly, then smiled thinly at me. "I didn't think you could really be an industrial specialist, Whitey. Our operation here is practically all robotic, anyway. Well . . . Mr. Ogumi requests that I give you any assistance I possibly can. So what can I do for you?"

"Naturally, I'm eager to see the artifact. But first I'd like a shower." Spending a month living in one's own sweat is guaranteed to re-establish priorities.

His smile was wider this time. "Water is one thing we have plenty of, Whitey. Practically the whole damn satellite is made of it. Here, I'll show you to your quarters. . . ."

An hour later, considerably refreshed and with my scanty gear stowed in the room assigned to me, I walked into Reynolds' office again. He had his big safe open and a pair of heavy gloves on. "Here, Whitey, grab that other pair of gloves and give me a hand with this; the damn thing masses about twenty or thirty kilos, and it's tricky to move around. Must be gold or platinum alloy of some kind."

Two minutes later the slab was sitting flat on the desk and I was staring avidly at it. My old mentor Professor Jensen would have been palpitating with ecstasy, but I was considerably more phlegmatic. I merely kept whispering "Damn, damn," under my breath as I drank it in.

"You're only the fifth person to see it," Reynolds said quietly. "Of course, word is out all over base. . . ."

I barely heard him. I had pored for hours over the transmitted pictures of the artifact, but the cold perfection before me was unnerving in its impact. It was a regular hexagon, just as pictured by Reynolds' transmission. The lines and circles were so hair-fine I had to move my head to get the light right to see them. The surface gleamed with a beauty indescribable. I sat there with horripilations growing on the back of my neck, until Reynolds' voice brought me back to reality. He'd been leaning over my shoulder, and finally queried:

"I recognize all the moons, but why did they leave out Phoebe?"

I replied condescendingly: "Well, I can think of two good reasons, offhand. Either they didn't consider Phoebe part of the system, or else they didn't find it during their visit—or maybe they didn't include it because it would be a waste of platinum; Phoebe is a lot further out than Iapetus, isn't it?"

Reynolds frowned. "That's three reasons."

A nitpicker. "Choose two good ones and go with them."

I tried to sink back into rapt contemplation of the artifact; it felt so *good* just to sit there and gaze at it and reflect on the beings who might have made it. But alas, the manager was under full steam. "What do you SpaceHome experts make of this thing?"

I let out a deep breath. "Okay, just a second while I take one measurement." I reached into my kit and pulled out a set of micrometer calipers with a thirty-centimeter extension bar.

"Watch out you don't cut yourself," he said. "Those corners may only be ninety degrees, but they're *sharp*."

I carefully measured the distance between opposite sides of the hexagon. The reading was one I'd memorized some time ago. Just to be sure, I measured another pair of sides. I pulled the calipers off and showed the cursor to Reynolds. "The magic number: 33.258 centimeters."

His frown came back. "Why is that a magic number?"

"Well," I used my pontifical voice, toned down in recognition of his amateur status, "those digital scans you sent us had good resolution, and we were reasonably confident about the relative dimensions; but we couldn't be sure of the absolute scale. So we made one assumption and some smart guesses." I put the calipers away. "And that one measurement was all I needed to verify our assumption."

I gestured at the gleaming artifact. "The creators of that thing were adamant about the number six; much more so than meets the eye just looking at it. For instance, if you were to inscribe a circle in the hexagon, its diameter would be exactly six times that of Saturn's image in the center. And the image itself is exactly 5.543 centimeters across, which is exactly the equatorial diameter of Saturn divided by 6^{12}. And you'll notice that the moons are drawn to a larger scale to make all of them easily visible. The scale multiplication is exactly six."

I smiled at him. "There's a lot more." I reached into my kit to fish out a reticle magnifier. "All the orbits shown in the etching are spaced logarithmically—base six—keyed on the image diameter of Saturn."

Placing the reticle on a portion of Iapetus' orbital arc, I bent down and squinted at the image. "This is just for my own curiosity." I moved the reticle to one of the symbols in the nearby apex. "The width of these lines, as far as I can judge, doesn't vary one iota." I looked up at him. "Guess what it is."

He looked a bit irritated. "I wouldn't have the slightest idea."

I ignored his frown. "As near as I can measure, it's about .0257 centimeters; but I'm willing to bet it's almost exactly .02565, because that happens to be Saturn's diameter divided by 6^{15}."

He pursed his lips. "What does that mean?"

"That they were consistent devils." I put the reticle away. "And it's one more indicator that the number six is of overriding importance in the message."

"So what do you think the message is?"

"We think it's two things. First, and most obvious, it says: Hey, there's someone else in the universe! Second, we believe it's a road map, a set of directions showing how to find more artifacts, and especially how to find the real cache that could tell us who they are and where they come from—maybe even how to contact them."

His frown must have been glued on. "So you think there are also artifacts on Titan, Dione, Enceladus, and somewhere in the B-Ring?" His finger pointed in turn to the images opposite the apices.

"Yes, we do," I nodded. "And by the way, that 'somewhere' in the B-Ring is about 48,000 kilometers from the planetary surface; and it's probably the important location."

"Why? Because of those marks in the middle of the little hexagon there?" He pointed to one of the three symbols at the apex opposite the B-ring site.

"Exactly," I said.

"So that's where the big cache is," he said, brightening.

"Well, no, we don't think so," I said.

His frown was back quickly. "Now you've lost me again."

The man had no future in cryptology. I was patient. "Well, if their preoccupation with sixes means anything at all, it's that there *must* be a sixth location, a sixth cache." I gestured at the metal slab. "That missing spoke in Saturn's image and that unfilled apex shout the message loud and clear. And as surely as they were here, it's that sixth location which will contain the real find."

Dawn finally broke on his face. "Then the B-Ring site—"

"Will contain the roadmap to that cache," I finished. "Our final analysis of this artifact's message goes something like this: 'You are looking at one of four identical plates we've placed on Enceladus, Dione, Titan and Iapetus. At a certain location in the B-Ring is a fifth artifact; it will contain directions telling you how to find the sixth site, where the ultimate treasure will be located.'"

Reynolds furrowed his brow. "These people, whoever they are, sure seem to like games. Why not just put road maps in all five locations?"

"Good question," I said. "And one we might answer if we knew a little more xeno-psychology. Maybe it's a test of sorts. Maybe they want to put us through the hoops to impress us with their importance," I smiled. "Or maybe you're right, and they just like to play games."

"Do you think this treasure, as you call it, might be on another planet in the solar system?"

He'd missed again. "I doubt it. Saturn is the sixth major planet out from the Sun. What worries me is that the cache might be on Titan, which is Saturn's sixth major moon. I'm told that we don't have a man-rated vessel with the pressure and temperature compensation to handle a Titan landing. My personal hope is that it's orbiting safely at six Saturn radii out from the planet, or some such innocuous thing. But wherever it is, we've got to find it."

"Then I suppose you'll be heading for the B-Ring?"

"Not right away," I said. "First of all, I'm going to look for the artifacts on Dione and Enceladus. Remember, all we have now is a theory; we need a few statistics to back up our thoughts."

"Where are you going to look?"

Now it was my turn to frown. If I'd remembered to bring the atlas along, most likely I'd have an answer for that one. As it was, I had to temporize. "Well, I'm going to search for striking geological or geographical features. You found this one in the middle of the Bullseye; I hope to find something equally obvious on the other satellites."

Reynolds gave me a puzzled look. "It seems to me that you're not very well prepared for this search, Whitey. Why did you hotfoot out here before doing your homework? And why did SpaceHome call after I transmitted the pictures, and tell me to put a lid on communications until I was contacted?"

His questions struck home. I'd done some hurried thinking in the past hour, and had come to the conclusion that there were holes in the story Ogumi had cajoled me with. Jock, bless his hairy heart, had plugged some of them. I didn't question the need to have a field-trained archaeologist on hand before going after the rest of the artifacts; Ogumi had enough common sense to know that amateurs might miss valuable on-site clues or data. But outside of that, the SpaceHome board of directors had to have known that Earth was aware of our find, so speed must be of extreme importance.

Ogumi and his moguls undoubtedly had me pegged as a naive bookworm type (not without reason) and wanted to keep me dumb and happy while racing with Earth to make the crucial find. Lucky me. I wondered anew what I was getting into. For a long, wistful moment—and for the hundredth time since leaving—I wished I were back at 'Home III again, teaching classes to a bunch of sleepy-eyed kids. I'm most definitely not a hairy-chested hero.

Meanwhile, Reynolds was looking at me with raised eyebrows. Ogumi had enjoined me not to discuss the board's economic motivation with anybody; he didn't want loose talk, and didn't want to raise any hopes which might later be dashed. He'd been very adamant about the point in his final briefing to me just before I left. So I dredged up a partial answer that I'd carefully prepared on the outward voyage; it was pieced together from knowledge painstakingly recalled from years of bull sessions with fellow academicians. And to that I added the bombshell Jock had dropped earlier.

"Bob, you must know that for years and years Earth has been strictly second place in astronomy. SpaceHome has all the best useful equipment, both in orbit and on the lunar surface. If Earth scientists want to use it, they pay through the nose—it helps our balance of trade.

"The only field where Earth is still number one is in SETI research, and that only because we won't waste our time on it. They've had a program under way for more than three generations, and have still come up empty. One of their few loud boasts is: If there is a communicating intelligence out there, we'll find it.

"So here turns up the first ever evidence of extraterrestrial life, and who discovers it? A couple of ordinary SpaceHome employees, out on a routine job to repair a broken transponder. How would you feel if you were an Earther?"

I pursed my lips and tried to look hairy-chested. "Now our sources" (I'd promoted Jock) "lead us to believe that Earth was able to receive and decode your original message and picture scan. If so, they'll undoubtedly try to beat us to the cache. So what we have tried to do is act as if we weren't going to follow up the discovery in any great rush. And so I came incognito on the regular Iapetus tug—which unfortunately left only a day or so after we got your transmission.

"Now Earth, in turn, is probably keeping quiet about the discovery while they try to mount an expedition to beat us to the punch. If so, it won't do any harm to keep our activities under cover."

It seemed to satisfy him.

"Well, good luck. So what do you need from me in the way of help?"

"A vessel to take me to Dione, Enceladus, and probably the B-Ring. As soon as possible."

He shook his head definitively. "Nothing doing, Whitey. What I have here are two surface-hoppers and one tug for emergency evacuation. I won't let that go, even if Ogumi himself orders it."

I nodded. "That's what he said you'd tell me. But I understand that the, uh, Saturn Orbiting Station is close by right now, and that they've got an all-purpose vehicle for inner-system travel, besides their supply tug. And SpaceHome pays their bills, too. Could we get a message to them?"

"Better than that. We'll be at ascending node tomorrow, and either Pop or Junior will bring the tug in for supplies; the SOS crosses at the same time we do, about 50,000 klicks down-orbit. They work it that way to save fuel. Their orbit is the same as ours, except they're in polar and we're only tilted fourteen degrees."

While I tried to picture what he was talking about, he glanced at his watch. "Matter of fact, the tug'll be here in about . . . seven hours, give or take. Mom and Pop will be glad to have your company." He wore an indefinable look as he said this, which I figured out later was one of speculation.

4

Barely a day later, with Pop piloting the tug, we were approaching the Saturn Orbiting Station. Pop was Dr. Thomas B. Badille. He was the originally designated team leader of the SOS project—a rather misleading title, since his "team" consisted of only a single colleague, one Dr. Aurica Berry. They'd married themselves the second year alone in space and were now only a few years away from their silver anniversary.

Earth pulled out of the joint project about the time of the marital union. The Badilles volunteered to stay on as permanent managers of the station, even though funding would be drastically reduced. Ever since, they had regularly churned out papers on Saturn's weather system, magnetosphere, rings, satellites, and what-have-you. SpaceHome picked up the tab without too much reluctance; the team performed heroically for their meager salary.

But according to Bob Reynolds, and also Jock, this couple were more than a trifle strange. And as for Junior, I was firmly told that I'd have to form my own opinion.

Pop was a plump man of medium height, with pleasant round-faced features. He had the white hair and wrinkle-free skin common among second and third generation inhabitants of low G, Sun-protected environments. He could have been anywhere from forty to eighty years old. At I-Base he'd been pleasant enough, but with a distracted air. He had been in a tearing hurry to depart and kept urging the ground crew to expedite the loading so he could get back up and "minimize the transfer orbit burn." I'd gotten a wink from one of the grinning stevedores, who later whispered that Pop was much more interested in getting back to Mom than in saving reaction mass. . . .

"There she is!" Pop broke into my reverie with more animation that I'd yet heard from him. He was pointing out the forward observation ports to a stubby cylinder slowly rotating about an axis which seemed to point toward Saturn.

"We dock at the near end of the axis, next to the research boat there; the Saturn end houses all the instruments, of course."

He was happier than he'd been all day. "Our little home isn't so little, really. The drum is more than fifty meters in diameter; of course, the outside three meters is ice for protection from cosmics." He smiled. "Our own little igloo. The experts said it was too confining an environment; they predicted we'd go crazy in less than three years. Mom and I fooled them, though. And Junior likes it, too."

I was beginning to have my doubts. But they *had* continued to publish those scholarly papers, and Pop seemed *almost* normal, anyway. A curious feature of the station caught my eye. "What are those pipes sticking out at all angles?" I asked.

Pop blinked at the rapidly enlarging structure. "Thruster vents. They're insulated, but the ice still melts around them when we have to make orbital or spin correction burns. That doesn't matter, really; in fact the shield is liquid the first few centimeters out from the hull. Excuse me, I must call Momma."

He pushed over to the comm and established contact. "Aurie, it's Tommy. Turn off the scanners, baby; we're going to bump you in a few minutes."

Half an hour later I was in a comfortable looking living room being introduced to Pop's wife. "Aurica, I'd like you to meet Dr. Kurious Whitedimple, from 'Home III. He comes from Mr. Ogumi and needs our help to fly in-system."

She looked like Pop's female clone, except that she was just shy of being plump. She produced a beatific smile and bestowed it on me. "Welcome to our home, Dr. Whitedimple. My, that's an unusual name. . . ."

I launched into a rather involved story about a slave ancestor and an interesting birthmark noticed by his first master in the New World. I was warming to my tale when a high-pitched voice, floating in from the rear, rudely interrupted: "Good! We'll call you 'Dimp.'"

I turned too fast in the light gravity and left the floor for a clumsy moment. Confronting me was a little gnome of a man with sandy hair, big ears and nose, crooked teeth, wrinkled skin—and an almost senile twinkle in his eyes.

"Dimp, this is Junior," said Mom. "He was born almost twenty years ago right here in SOS. We were going to move temporarily to Iapetus Base for the birth, but he came along a few weeks early, so Tom delivered him without help." I turned back around to see her smiling into Pop's eyes.

"Nonsense, Aurie," he retorted. "*You* helped me." He turned back to me. "Maybe you remember, Dimp. He made quite a little splash in the news—'the boy with the accelerating IQ.' What is it this month, Junior?"

"The last time I programmed the computer to check, it was just over 300." The twinkle was still in his eyes, and he put his hand on my arm in mock confidentiality. "Actually, Dimp, it's not accelerating any more; it finally plotted out as an S-curve, and it's beginning to go asymptotic now. It'll level off in about three or four years at something just shy of 400. Of course, I'll probably be dead by then. . . ."

I consider myself urbane, but I'm afraid at that point my mouth was unattractively open. Some words finally stumbled out: "But you look so much older than ninteen—"

"What do you expect," he snapped, "with the equivalent of a sixty-year-old central processor for my body?"

Now Pop broke in: "Actually, Junior's condition is due to the orbit we were following during Aurica's pregnancy and the year afterward. We were in a very tight ellipse with periapse way down inside the G-Ring." He looked a little wistful. "That was when we had plenty of money for reaction mass." He shook his head, then cheered up almost immediately. "Anyway, all those in-system phenomena—magnetic field lines, ring spoke extensions, solar wind bowshock, and so forth—were interacting with our new little bio-system here," he gestured at Junior, "and causing his central nervous system to wire itself a little differently. Much less redundancy, but a lot more efficiency."

Mom smiled proudly. "Junior wrote quite a paper on it when he was six or seven. Of course, we never had it published. You can just imagine the horde of psychologists that would have descended on us, all trying to make geniuses from dogs and rats, or some other silly thing."

My mouth was still flapping. A few more random words spilled out: "Wrote a paper when he was six?"

"Why yes," she said. "As a matter of fact, Junior has written almost all of our papers for the past twelve or thirteen years. In fact, he recently developed a quite convincing model of solar system formation based on ring dynamics. It was very well received by the community. Of course we publish everything under our own names; Junior doesn't have any real credentials."

Junior made a rude noise. "Big deal. I write two, three papers a year. Takes maybe a week total out of my free time. No use getting fancy; those yokels in

Earth orbit wouldn't recognize a good piece of work if it hit 'em in the face."

A vagrant thought kicked my vocal cords back into action before I could stop them. "If Junior has been writing all your papers, then what . . ."

Pop saved me from finishing the embarrassing question: "For the past several years, Momma and I have been collaborating on a book which we believe will be a definitive and important addition to the literature of the Colonies. It will be titled *Human Social Interactions During Long-term Environmental Confinement.*" His arm was around Mom's waist. He smiled at her. "And we must get back to work. Would you care to review what we've done so far, Dimp?"

I swiftly put my conversational wit to work: "Uhhh, well, I, uh, really think I should, uh, get to work on this problem. . . ."

"Yes, of course," Pop said. "Well, just tell Junior what you need; he'll take care of everything and pilot the research boat wherever you want to go. Junior, by the way, is the best pilot in the solar system, only nobody knows it."

I looked questioningly at their son. He was nodding and smiling cynically. I looked back at the Badilles to find them already halfway through the inner door. Mom looked over her shoulder and said: "If you're in a hurry to leave, don't bother to wait for us." Then they were gone and the door shut.

A little bemused, I commenced to bring Junior into the picture. He was quick on the uptake; in a few minutes he was finishing sentences for me. When I handed him a picture of the artifact without interpretation, he studied it briefly, then broke into a grin.

"Playful creatures, aren't they? Well, do we bother with Dione and Enceladus, or head right for the B-Ring?"

I hesitated. "The group consensus is that we get the Dione and Enceladus artifacts first, to double-check our translation of the message. Trouble is, I don't have a clue as to where to look for them. . . ."

Junior was the epitome of tact: "Dimp, you must be a

damned good archaeologist, because you're worthless otherwise. The Enceladus location will be in the middle of the Big Cross. Dione is a little less straightforward, but ten gets you five it's in Amata. The B-Ring cache has to be on the Iron Maiden. The top of Mons Gargantua is the best bet for Titan, but our boat isn't equipped to—"

"Hold on a minute. Just what is the Iron Maiden?"

"Dimp, don't you know anything at all about Saturn?"

"Well, I finished near the top third of my class in solar system geology," (a white lie) "but I don't recall too much about the rings. . . ."

He grimaced and shook his head. "Well, then. An elementary capsule history of the rings, scaled down for present company." He scratched the side of his nose. "Several million years ago Saturn's rings were run of the mill, just like the skimpy things circling the other gas giants. Orbiting Saturn at about one point eight radii was a ten kilometer moon—mostly ice, but with an iron-rich core. Along came a stray meteor about a kilometer in diameter and also rich in iron. Bang! The origin of the ring system as we know it now. Especially the B-Ring, which you might think of as a bunch of snowballs covered with iron dust. And all that's left of the original satellite is—"

"The Iron Maiden!" I felt like a kid at a remedial tutorial.

"Right," said Junior. "The Mother of the B-Ring. And also its destroyer."

Suddenly uneasy, I asked him what he meant.

"Well, Dimp, all those snowballs are highly charged, and the Iron Maiden is busily zapping them out of existence with little lightning bolts." An impish grin emerged on his face. "Too bad we can't wait a few million years; by then, most of the ring would be gone. As it is, retrieving the artifact will probably be a hair-raising experience, ha, ha!"

Dutifully, I laughed too, although it developed more the quality of a croak as it edged past the lump in my throat. Also, sad to relate, my skin blanched to a delicate shade of chalk.

Junior's empathy was monumental. "C'mon, Dimp, where's your spunk? This is going to be great fun." He pulled himself up the wall bars toward the overhead hatch into the axis. "Let's go; we've got supplies to load." He grinned evilly from the ceiling. "Unless you'd rather join Mom and Pop in their study."

I took a deep breath and started up the wall. There were more than a few things Ogumi might have told me.

Two hours later our supplies were in place and we hoisted ourselves into the main cabin. Junior drifted over to the pilot's station and began flipping switches. The subdued hum of the CRF reactor signalled ignition; panel lights and screens came to life. The cabin lights flickered as he switched from umbilical to internal power. The controls seemed quite different from those on the tug. I looked on with interest as the little gnome activated the boat.

"I souped up this scow considerably a few years back," he said as he busied himself at the console. "Managed to increase drive efficiency thirty percent across the board by reconfiguring the magnetic confinement field equations and boosting chamber temperature a few million degrees. The high-G I_{sp}—" He noticed my blank look and broke off. "Never mind. Better strap in; we're going to disconnect and test the RCS in a second."

As I took the right-hand seat and began belting up, Junior flipped a switch and began speaking clearly to no one in particular: "Pandora. Self check of all electrical systems. Pandora."

My dearth of knowledge of computer technology was practically all-embracing. But I did know that voice-controlled processors—especially navigation computers! —were *always* activated by recognition code words. And certainly not by the simple calling out of a pet name. And I was also dimly aware that to perform the implied reprogramming was an exacting, complex task. Either

Junior was unaware of this, or else he misinterpreted
my raised eyebrows.

"I named her that because I had to open her box to
add memory and make a few software changes. That
was seven or eight years ago, back when I was interested in girls. My IQ was down around two—"

He stopped as the speaker came to life: "*Pandora in.
Self-check completed. All electrical systems green. All backup
systems green. Pandora out.*" The voice, though a little
flat, was recognizably Mom's. Before I could pursue
that, Junior spoke again:

"Pandora. Backout and RCS check ten seconds from
mark. Reiterate. Pandora."

"*Pandora in. Reiteration. I will disconnect umbilical,
back five-hundred meters from Station, and conduct a
complete checkout of all reaction control system thrusters.
I will commence this sequence only upon your confirma-
tion and ten seconds after your mark. Pandora out.*"

"Pandora. Confirm. Mark. Pandora."

I looked at the little man and shuddered involuntarily
when I remembered he was not yet twenty years old.
"Junior, do you mean you were only twelve years old
when you, uh, invented Pan—"

"Don't say her name out loud!" It was my first glimpse
of excitement in him. "I didn't bother to program in
voice recognition; you'll confuse her."

Just then the RCS thrusters came to life, giving us a
gentle shove backward. By the time Junior spoke again,
SOS was shrinking visibly in the forward viewports.

"Now what were you saying, Dimp?"

I sighed. "Never mind. It's too late now, anyway."

In a moment we were once more stationary. Then the
boat performed several quick maneuvers in roll, pitch
and yaw—finishing precisely in its original orientation,
but leaving my stomach and inner ears still back on
square three.

"*Pandora in. RCS system green. Backups green. Fuel
remaining in hydrazine tanks: 7238 full-thrust engine-
seconds. Pandora out.*"

Apparently Junior was inured to the checkout procedure. "Well, Dimp, let's figure out a destination. Pandora. 3-D display of inner system. Pandora."

An L-shaped group of three large, flat panels on the control console lit up, displaying what appeared to be standard architectural elevations of the Saturnian system. The planetary bodies were color coded; the top view showed faint circles that seemed to be orbital tracks of the major moons. A blinking white spot in all three screens indicated our boat's position. I asked Junior if the picture came from the computer's memory.

"Naw. We've got seventeen navsats in orbits all over the system. Pandy keeps in touch with four or five at a time and just calculates speed-of-light lag for real-time updates. For closeup work she uses her own stereo odar or radar. But that comes later.

"Now look here." He pointed to the top screen. "At .1 G it's going to take us thirty hours, give or take, to get into a down-system orbit. That'll put Dione about halfway to the eastern limb, right here," he touched the screen, "which is convenient. Enceladus, on the other hand, will just be starting across the far side," he moved his finger, "which is decidedly inconvenient." He looked at me expectantly. "But it's your decision, Admiral."

"Whatever you think best, Junior," I said carefully.

He snorted, then addressed the computer: "Pandora. Establish and display trajectory for a 0.10 G constant acceleration journey, beginning with current state vector and terminating in circular equatorial orbit about Dione at one hundred fifty kilometers mean altitude above surface. Reiterate. Pandora."

As the computer paraphrased Junior's instructions, dotted lines appeared on the screens. Junior listened, looked, and nodded. "Pandora. Confirm as program SD. Perform RCS burn five seconds from mark, to terminate stationary with respect to SOS ten kilometers up-orbit. Mark. Pandora."

As we moved away from the station under RCS, Junior explained: "I always give the SOS plenty of safety margin. That stream of hot ions coming from the CRF drive is nothing to fool around with."

I informed him that I was well aware of the dangers of a CRF exhaust plume. He made me pay for my stuffiness:

"Well I'll be damned, Dimp. And all along I thought you didn't know anything. Boy, was I wrong!"

I wondered where he'd learned sarcasm. Mom and Pop seemed incapable of it.

The SOS was a fly speck on the starboard viewport a few minutes later, when Junior ordered the computer to execute program SD. She counted us down, then we were pressed gently into our seats as the low rumbling of the CRF drive permeated the vessel.

At least it was gentle to me. Junior had a slightly strained look on his face, and said: "Well, Dimp, the best thing to do when starting a high-acceleration trip is to get some shut-eye. So I'll see you in four or five hours." He promptly closed his eyes, and in a couple of minutes was snoring softly.

I closed my eyes, but not to sleep. Pop had mentioned that they maintained .06 G on the SOS to protect from long-term calcium leaching; I-Base was less than half that, but the resident staff only took two-year duty shifts. SpaceHome III was kept at 0.3 G; hence, anything out here felt lightweight to my muscles. So I was stuck with a racing mind and a thousand unanswered questions, being navigated toward a monstrous gravity well by a computer customized by a precocious youngster. I silently cursed Ogumi and company, calling upon several ancient deities they'd probably never heard of. . . .

5

Junior was shaking me awake.

"Dimp, we've got company."

I focussed bleary eyes on the 3-D display. It now showed not one blinking light, but two. I closed my eyes again and tried to ignore the universe, but Junior continued remorselessly:

"Another boat has entered the inner system. It's decelerating at about about .7 G, and will be orbiting Dione in less than four hours. It must be loaded to the gills with fuel, and it almost has to be from Earth. So what now?"

My heart began to pound uncomfortably, and there was a faint taste of bile in my mouth. My immediate impulse was to head for the B-Ring, but that was a decision I needed help in making.

"I suppose we can break radio silence now. Can you contact SpaceHome?"

"With a half-meter antenna? You must be kidding."

"Well, raise I-Base then. Reynolds can relay the message."

"Blow that off, too. I-Base receivers only watch Earth system and SOS, and we're at too much angular separation from either; we couldn't even sneak in on a prayer."

"Raise SOS then and have Mom and Pop relay messages. I've got to talk to Ogumi!"

Junior's smirk was positively evil. "I tried, but no luck. They're probably working on Chapter Fourteen. And even if I could, it would still be hours before you got a reply back—and the situation will need action before them. C'mon Dimp, grow up; whether you like it or not, it's decision time."

At the moment I felt more like shrinking than growing. "Okay," I sighed. "Raise the other ship."

Junior nodded and started broadcasting, while I began to think in earnest. They would surely beat us to the Dione site. If we headed at once for the B-Ring, could we get there first? Probably not—surely not, if they decided to make a race of it. Anyway, if the Dione and Enceladus plates contained unexpected data, going at once to the Iron Maiden could be a mistake. . . .

Junior interrupted my train of thought. "No luck, Dimp. They didn't even answer a call on the emergency hailing frequency. We're being deliberately ignored."

"Do they even know we're here?"

"Sure, the same way we detected them. The navsats can see any CRF plume, and any boat can get information from them, since their activation frequencies are well-published."

I was still trying to assess possibilities; it was a new kind of thinking, and I wasn't sure I would ever be any good at it.

"If we head right for the Iron Maiden, can they beat us there by changing course? And if we head for Enceladus, even if they know where we're going, do you suppose they will keep on toward Dione? I mean—"

Junior broke out laughing. "Dimp, I really like you, but your brain is a morass. Okay, here's the situation as I see it. Assuming that the people and computer on that boat are not dumb, they know we're headed for Dione, and that they'll beat us to the Amata artifact by several hours. If we change course for either Enceladus or the Maiden, they'll calculate time and distance and decide what to do next. If we head right for the Maiden, they'll probably do likewise and beat us there; if we go for Enceladus, they'll figure they have time to pick up the Dione artifact first. They must have a big tug with lots of CRF reaction mass onboard, and they have one-G muscles; so they've got all the advantages."

He scratched his chin. "Now all I know about human nature I got from Mom and Dad, occasional trips to I-Base and a whole bunch of novels I read when I was four or five years old. But I'll bet they think they can beat us to the punch no matter what we decide to do. So, Admiral, what *do* we decide to do?"

I stalled. "Maybe you could try to raise SOS again?"

"C'mon Dimp. Time's a-wasting. Even if you could send a message to Ogumi right now, there'd still be that long time delay. So bite the bullet."

"Okay, let's head for Enceladus."

"Attaboy, Admiral! A decision! The most cowardly option, admittedly, but a decision nonetheless."

He began talking to the computer. Most of it was too technical to follow—phrases like "north polar traverse," "safe minimum distance," "state vector update," and so forth. I spent the time wondering who was in the other tug and what their orders were. I barely noticed the computer counting us down. Then, suddenly the boat slewed and pitched slightly, and my weight grew noticeably.

"Okay Dimp, here's the plan," Junior said. "We've increased acceleration to .15 G and we're going over the top of Saturn." He indicated the new flight path on the display. "Then, we'll slew into Enceladus orbit and finish dead-stopped right above the Big Cross." His face looked strained, but his smirk was evident. "The bad guys'll figure that we'll be orbiting a couple of times to lay a groove for computer landing; but I'm gonna fool 'em and take the boat down on manual. That'll gain us an hour or so if they're sloppy about noticing our state vector at CRF cutoff. If we can find the artifact and get away fast, we might still beat 'em to the Maiden."

It wasn't the increased acceleration that brought the sudden lump to my throat.

"Land on manual?"

His face turned impish. "Sure thing, Dimp. The way I see it, our one advantage is that I can do state vectors real time in my head. We'll have to use that punch if we're gonna try and win this fight. Besides, low-G landings are a snap. Okay?"

My mouth was still in control. "Land on manual?"

"Relax, Dimp. I goose this lady on manual all the time. That's the main reason for having three screens." He yawned and swallowed. "But right now we've got over twenty hours to kill, and this acceleration's more than twice what I'm used to. I'm going to get some more sleep." He promptly conked off again, leaving me to dream up some more curses for Ogumi.

Sleep has a habit of sneaking up. I awoke some hours later to the sounds of Junior preparing a meal. We ate, then talked at length. I taught him some archaeology, and he taught me some Saturn—which we both recognized by then as survival training for a naive traveler. To my surprise I found myself becoming engrossed in the mechanics and the lore of the Old Man and his family. Junior was a latent poet when he forgot to be cynical, and he made each of the moons sing its own song. I stopped regarding them as boring chunks of ice.

Saturn grew slowly in the forward windows until it doubled in size. But distance still blurred the cloud formations, and the rings were tilted only a few degrees, when we flipped end for end and started braking toward the Giant; at that point we were not even down to Hyperion's orbit. I was disappointed; by that time I was eager to see the Old Man at close range.

"Hang on, Dimp," Junior said. "In less than ten hours we'll be going over the top; then you'll have the best seat in the house—and I'll guarantee the sight will suck your gut right up into your throat."

The Earth tug had stopped decelerating before we

reached flip-over. According to Pandora, its state vector at the time of CRF cutoff indicated that it had gone into equatorial orbit about two hundred kilometers above the surface. An hour later it burned for fifteen seconds; Junior said it was a plane change.

"It'll put them over Amata for three consecutive passes. They'll probably use two to lay a groove, then land on the third."

There would be no more information about the tug for some time. It could only be detected by its CRF plume; and it would probably land with RCS thrusters rather than punch a hole in the unprepared surface below it. But Junior was optimistic. "No news is good news, Dimp. Amata's two hundred klicks in diameter and full of junk. Hell, they might be ten, twenty hours searching for the artifact."

We ate lightly, then dozed again. This time the computer woke us both: *"Pandora in. Stand by for seventeen-minute free-fall period for state vector update, five seconds from mark. Mark. Pandora out."* Almost immediately we were floating. Stretching, I asked Junior what a state vector update was.

"The navigation gets hairy from here on," he said. "We're doing about seventeen kilometers a second now, but it's almost all radial with respect to the Saturnian system. We've got to kill that, and at the same time gain about twelve klicks tangential to match Enceladus' orbital velocity. All that time Saturn will be pulling us down toward the ring plane; we encourage that at first, then cancel it as we match orbit with Enceladus. Doing all that at once is tricky, even for Pandy. So she's coasting for a few minutes while she gets some precise data on our position, velocity, and acceleration here at the bottom of the gravity well.

"Meanwhile, since we're only about 20,000 klicks above the clouds, I'm going to tilt us down so you can get a good look at the Old Man from close up."

"Won't that mess up the, uh, fix the computer's trying to get?"

"Naw. Attitude and state vector are completely different things." He spoke briefly to Pandora, and the boat pitched over. "There. Unstrap yourself and take a good look." He gestured to the front viewports.

As a student of cultures and languages I know full well the inadequacies of the written word. But I will tell you that even as I sit here safely at my desk in 'Home III, my heart pounds and my mouth turns dry as I relive that magic, awesome moment.

The Giant filled everything—the viewports, my senses, all of space—so that I had to press my nose to the glass even to see the edge of the rings against the black. The northern cloudbands, with their delicate colors, formed beautiful pale rings around the pole, cut in half by the black knife of the shadow's edge. Sworls, spots, eddies, all were displayed in lovely, exquisite detail. For time unmeasured I stared; then I turned my eyes back out to the rings. The far edge of the A-Ring was opaque pale white, reflecting the Sun's feeble glow from a trillion chips of ice. The Encke Division, a sharp black ribbon near the outer edge, was only a slender cousin to Cassini—that monstrous ebon gap between A and B. A star twinkled there as it was alternately revealed and occluded by the tenuous gap rings. The broad, bright ruddy B-Ring was grooved by a thousand shadings of light and gray; my eyes roved inward across its vast expanse to where the brightness abruptly gave way to the gray translucence of the Crepe Ring, and then on to the bright limb of Saturn. And so once again my eyes feasted on the Old Man, bemused by the whorls and wisps of the gigantic, colder-than-ice weather systems.

I was struck dumb with fear and awe, my heart pounding so hard it seemed ready to burst at every beat. My throat was dry and my tongue clove to the roof of my mouth. My bowels were all but moving of their own accord. I was certain that we were going to be sucked into that pattern—to become a part of it. At the time, somehow, it seemed right; as if it were unfair to behold such beauty and still be allowed to live.

I have no idea how long I gazed before Junior, his voice uncharacteristically husky, finally broke the silence:

"You are now one of only eight members of the human race who have seen this sight. It has changed every one of us."

I nodded, unable to reply, as he continued softly: "When I know I'm dying, I'm going to suit up and have the boat throw me straight down at the Old Man's heart."

My voice returned in a whisper: "I'm coming with you."

He nodded, then shook himself, looked at the mission clock and sighed. "Come on, we'd better strap in; it's almost time to start burning again."

I returned to my couch with enormous reluctance.

Now we were decelerating at almost .2 G. Junior turned his head with mine toward the starboard 'port, where the Giant could now be seen, then dozed off once again. The next four hours seemed only minutes as I stared at the Old Man, first out the side viewport, then the front again as we backed away from the planet and down toward the ring place; then finally out the side again as the boat gradually slewed around to push us into equatorial orbit. By the time the Sun's glare finally dominated the front windows, the rings were once again a thin bright line. Then at last I could see the crescent Enceladus ahead and to the right, and it was time to wake Junior.

Twenty minutes later the boat stopped burning, turned end for end, and gave a last firm push before Pandora announced that Junior was now in control for manual landing. He tested the manual RCS controls, pitched the boat so that the forward viewports pointed down at the surface, and began to unstrap.

"C'mon. I'll show you where we're going."

My confidence in his abilities had increased considerably during the voyage; nevertheless I couldn't entirely quell a momentary twinge of panic. "You mean right now? Don't you have to blast down tail-first, or some such?"

The impish grin returned. "Not for a while, Dimp. The surface gravity is only about nine centimeters—less than .01 G. And up here, at a hundred klicks, it's just half that. So to save hydrazine I'm going to let us fall sixty kilometers; it'll be about twenty-five minutes before we start burning." He gestured out the viewports. "So unstrap and come look."

The view was impressive. I stared while Junior talked me into the picture.

Since its formation, Enceladus has gone through four or five epochs of vast restructuring, the latest as recently as a hundred million years ago. System geologists still don't know for sure what caused the cold-body volcanism which spewed lava in the form of melted ice over half the surface. During these times, the slush was filling craters, and the subsequent surface recooling was generating the magnificent set of fault valleys which still dominate the sphere.

One of those valleys is Daryabar Fossa, a straight gash running east-west for two hundred kilometers, about five degrees above the equator. Several dozen million years ago Daryabar was cut in half by another movement of the crust, which displaced its eastern and western halves by thirteen kilometers along a new fault measuring one hundred forty kilometers, running north-south almost exactly at local Greenwich. The name of this newer valley is Isbanir Fossa. The two, intersecting at right angles, form the Big Cross. . . .

". . . and dollars to doughnuts, Dimp, we'll find the artifact right smack dab in the geologic center—in Isbanir, at the six-and-a-half kilometer point exactly between the split legs of Daryabar."

At the moment, ninety minutes before local sunset, the Cross was spectacular. Isbanir, running as it did north and south, was a dark gash in the smooth landscape. Daryabar, in contrast, was brilliantly illuminated by the rays of the distant Sun. This huge study in black and white dominated the forward viewports. I watched it enlarge, entranced, until my companion told me it was time to strap in and flip the boat for landing.

The three screens at the control console provided orthoginal views of the surface, which Junior used to fly us down. Each screen showed a stylized image of the boat, beside which were numbers displaying distance, velocity and acceleration in the relevant axis. These numbers were calculated with respect to an aim point which Junior established in Isbanir, slightly north of where he expected to find the cache.

The landing was anticlimactic. When we were forty kilometers above the surface and dropping at just over eighty meters a second, Junior activated the thrusters. After some fiddling to get over the aim point, we went down on our tail at a gentle .02 G. In fifteen minutes, the boat was stopped dead one meter above the surface. Junior cut the RCS, and five seconds later we landed with a feathery bump.

I looked over at him. "I think I could do that."

He grinned. "Sure you could, Dimp. Any moron could, with a little practice. Hell, the Apollo pilots did it over a hundred years ago, in a gravity field seventeen times this one. It's the managers and owners who're afraid to trust their precious property to anything but computers. They write regulations about track-laying orbits and computer-controlled landings and all that silly rot. And so we've got ourselves a generation of pantywaist pilots, who are whizzes at punching buttons and not much else. Hmmph!"

He began the task of shutting the operating systems down. "Of course, orbital maneuvers are something else. There isn't a human alive who can work a six-variable state vector in his head to get from orbit to orbit with any efficiency. For that, you do need computers." He glanced sidelong at me. "I'm the exception to that rule—but maybe I'm not quite human."

My heart warmed to that lonesome little gnome of a man as he chuckled at me through crooked teeth. "Okay, we'd better get moving. We've got a job to do."

When we were in our micropore suits and ready for helmets, Junior carefully tipped over the suit box. Four large boot-shaped objects clunked slowly onto the deck. "Here, better put a pair of these on your feet. They're low-gravity crampons."

I hefted one; it must have massed fifteen kilos or more. My legs got tired just thinking about them. "What good will these things do, for God's sake?"

The grin again. "What we've got here is a .01 G ball of hard ice, and we're going to tramp around using high-gravity muscles. You wear these so you don't spend nine-tenths of your time two meters up off the surface, spinning ass-over-teakettle." He pointed to the bottoms. "The spikes give you some traction, and the large mass makes you move carefully. Watch out you don't step on anything valuable once you've got 'em on."

When the airlock opened, Junior took the folded ladder in hand and jumped the eight meters to the surface. I followed, lacking his nonchalance. It was a ten-second drop, and by the time I hit the surface the crampons had already proved their worth; they kept my feet down while I was falling. We extended the ladder and hooked it over the lockframe, then I took time to check out the surroundings.

We were in a valley about five kilometers wide and one or two deep. The visible contours were rounded; no boulders or rough terrain were in sight. In fact, there was no loose surface at all; the ground through the crampons felt more like an ice cube than anything else. Junior explained that micrometeoroids, which help grind regolith on rocky satellites, merely serve to smooth the surface of an ice world.

Isbanir had looked darker than the Black Hole of Calcutta from a hundred kilometers up, but the reality wasn't nearly so bad. Sunlight reflected from the tops of the cliffs to the east, and Saturn at half-phase made a significant contribution to the illumination. We carried flashlights, but they stayed hooked to our belts. Bending backward far enough to see all the Giant overhead was uncomfortable, but I did it anyway. It was stunning—two hundred times the size of Earth from 'Home III, even though we were nearly 200,000 kilometers from the nearest cloud tops. The cloud formations were sharply visible; the ring shadow was a wide black band below the equator, divided by light shining through the

Cassini gap. The ring line was brilliant white and en-
compassed fully half the sky between cliffs. Where it cut
back into the darkness west of the planet's terminator,
it seemed as if some cosmic artist had drawn a die-
straight line of white ink on a black velvet canvas. The
ring was much more brilliant in the center; out loud, I
wondered why.

*"You've got to learn to start doing kitchen arithmetic in
your head, Dimp,"* came Junior's tinny voice in my ear-
speaker. *"The east and west limbs of the rings are a
quarter of a million klicks from here, but the center is only
a hundred thousand."*

He sounded as if he were straining. I looked over and
saw that he, too, was bending backward. Then he
straightened up and sighed. *"I've got to spend more time
in-system. Okay, duty calls. Let's head south."*

We took parallel tracks along the valley floor about a
hundred fifty meters apart. The overhead light from
Saturn was diffuse, but illumination from the cliffs threw
blurred shadows toward the west; any unusual feature
would be easy to spot.

Once again I was glad for the crampons: After a careless movement I found myself a meter and a half off the
surface and starting to tumble head first. The boots did
their work nobly, and my feet were already starting to
pull my head back up by the time I touched. Junior's
only comment was to remind me that hitting the ground
with anything but feet, gloves or helmet was an invitation to frostbite; the thin, shiny material of the micropore
suit was an excellent heat conductor.

Eventually, I learned to let the crampons do the work.
I merely used my leg muscles to pull them up and
forward, and their own momentum did the rest. My
strides were slow and long. I was just starting to enjoy
the rhythm when Junior's voice sounded in my ear: *"Up
ahead there a hundred meters, right between us. Head
toward it and start slowing down right away."*

The insulating case was unmistakable, a hexagon-
shaped hatbox with a brilliant white coating. Its twin
was in Bob Reynolds' safe nearly four million kilome-

ters away. It sat casually on the surface, as if it had been placed there only yesterday. The incredible presence of a precisely engineered object on this barren globe sent shivers down my spine.

Junior seemed to sense my emotion. *"I'm with you, Dimp. It gives me the willies in a way I've never experienced before. It's been us against the universe for a million years or more; but now—company for sure."* He stepped back while I got my camera from a side pouch. *"You know, life has been getting a little boring the past few years, but I have a feeling that's going to change."*

He waited patiently while I took several pictures and spoke appropriate notes into my personal recorder. When I'd put the camera away, he said: *"Ready?"*

"Yeah. Hey Junior, how did you know it would be here?"

"Hey Dimp, I didn't—not for sure, anyway." I could picture that crooked grin on his face. *"It was logical from seeing the picture of the first artifact, and knowing where on Iapetus it was found. The uncertainty came from not knowing whether or not our idea of logic and theirs have enough similarities."* He turned his helmet toward me. *"Which I'm sure you've wondered, too, Dimp; buried somewhere underneath all that fluff and ignorance in your head, you've got more than your share of brains."*

I was startled by Junior's remark; it was uncharacteristically complimentary. But before I had time to formulate an inane reply, he spoke again and saved me: *"Anyway, it's nice to know that they have at least some parallels with us; otherwise this treasure hunt would be impossible. I also think they have some of our wackiness, which is even more interesting to contemplate."*

We returned to the boat and buttoned up in preparation for liftoff. A light was flashing on the console; per Junior, it indicated a message from SOS, relayed through one of the navsats. That was intriguing, but first things first; the hatbox had the highest priority.

The lid came off easily, and we were looking at another plate. It was an exact duplicate of the first. Junior looked on as I checked image sizes, then said: "Well, it's going to be the Iron Maiden, then."

He turned to the console and played the message back. It had been encrypted, taped, and relayed from SpaceHome to I-Base to SOS to navsat-3 to Enceladus, but the voice was still recognizably Ogumi's:

"To Dr. Whitedimple from President Ogumi. It has been brought to our attention that an unidentified vessel is approaching the Saturnian system. This is probably an Earth-sponsored expedition with the same goal as yours. Since time delays make decisions from SpaceHome impractical, you are authorized to use your own judgement in handling the situation. If you deem it necessary, you are empowered to negotiate a joint scientific mission. Your task may be difficult, but we have every confidence in your ability to cope. Good luck. End of message."

Junior snorted. "Bunch of pantywaists! Well, the ball's in your court, Admiral—and God help you if you don't come up with at least a tie score."

I reluctantly took my attention from the hypnotic gleam of the artifact. "Where is the Earth tug now?"

He spoke briefly to Pandora, and the 3-D screens lit up with a close-in set of views of the inner system. After a few seconds' study, he replied: "It's in a minimum-time transfer orbit from Dione to the Maiden, coming around fast from the night side and cutting across the ring plane in a tight curve." He glanced at the screens again. "It's only going to miss the cloud tops by a few thousand klicks. Whoever's piloting that tug is pretty gutsy."

"Can we beat them to the Maiden?"

He stared at the display and furrowed his brow for a long moment. Finally he said: "If we start now and punch at .25 G all the way, it'll be close to a dead heat."

I asked him why he couldn't burn at .3 G and beat them outright.

"Because I wouldn't be worth anything when we got there," he answered candidly. "A quarter G is my maximum for anything over an hour, and this run will be six times that long."

I took a deep breath. Growing hair on the chest at this advanced stage of my career was decidedly painful. But nevertheless:

"So what are we waiting for? Up ship and away!"

Junior threw me a startled look, then relaxed into a grin. "Righto, Admiral."

6

We went straight up for one minute on thrusters, then the CRF drive cut in. The acceleration was still under that at 'Home III, so I wasn't straining; but it was quadruple the little gnome's customary environment. He seemed very drawn, and more wizened than ever.

"Are you okay, Junior?"

"Sure," he smiled weakly. "Just need a little sleep. Wake me ten minutes from rendezvous, or sooner if anything interesting happens. You'd better stay awake, to keep tabs on events." He gestured toward the 3-D. "And to enjoy the ride. Our friends are staying a couple of hundred klicks above the ring plane, but Pandy is going to shave it by eighty. Safe enough, but guaranteed to make you pee your pants. G'night."

He closed his eyes and in less than a minute was sawing logs. His face smoothed out a little, and he looked reassuringly better.

The rendezvous point was almost directly inward from our current position near Enceladus. Even so, the navigation would be complex. Our actual path to the Maiden would be *S*-shaped, but the boat's attitude would make it seem a *C*. So I wasn't too surprised when the vessel slewed radically to the left, pointing well past the dark half of Saturn.

The exertions of our trek on Enceladus, plus the relatively high acceleration, served to weight my eyelids, too. I catnapped as the Giant peered in on us, first from the starboard viewport, then the front, as we gradually changed attitude to point directly toward it. The yaw thrusters, operating briefly at ten-minute intervals, acted to keep me somewhat awake.

Three hours into the trip, the boat suddenly rolled ninety degrees clockwise. My head and stomach reacted violently as Saturn tilted up on end. I was all at once very wide awake and a little frightened.

Junior, stretching and yawning, roused enough to gaze briefly out the front windows, then at the screens and clock—then he closed his eyes again. Before he could get back to sleep, I asked him what the hell.

" 'S okay Dimp," he mumbled. "Part of the thrill ride. . . ." And he was snoring again. I pondered this, then decided that he'd ordered Pandora to roll the boat on its side so I could see the rings out my starboard viewport as they passed by. Maybe he thought I was getting hooked on thrill rides. Maybe I was.

Meanwhile, the now-vertical line of the ring plane was getting quite bright. It forced the illusion that we were going to fly straight into it, to be annihilated by its billions of bullets. Ever brighter it became, without taking on dimension; there was no hint of a clue that we might miss it. Fright bathed me in perspiration—a most undignified condition for a full professor in his forties, and one to which it seemed I had recently been subjected too often. A dozen times the temptation to wake Junior almost overpowered me; his "peeing my pants" prediction was too close to be funny.

Just when my self control was nearly gone, a hair-thin strand separated itself from the ring line and began moving steadily to the right. After some thought, I

decided it must be the F-Ring. Soon it disappeared
from the front 'ports; I leaned over and watched it flash
by on the right. It was thicker in some places than
others, and somehow seemed twisted; it did not con-
form to my idea of a proper ring.

Knowing we should be eighty kilometers from the
ring, I tried to estimate our velocity. My best guess was
between five and ten kilometers per second. If that were
true, it should be only a few minutes until we reached
the edge of the A-Ring.

In the forward viewports the ring line grew even
brighter; though we'd safely missed the F-Ring, my
fears returned unbidden. Banishing them resolutely, I
checked the displays. The Earth tug was west of us, and
just inside the C-Ring. Our own position was at the
outer edge of the A-Ring.

When I peered forward again the ring line had started
to widen. At first barely noticeable, the phenomenon
accelerated as I watched. Then perspective shifted
sharply; instead of flying into the ring, we were going to
pass it on the left. Then with breathtaking suddenness,
the A-Ring was flashing by the right side of the boat.
Our velocity was dizzying. The sunlit half of the Giant
had become only a quarter-circle in the front 'ports; the
right side was obliterated by a white wall that seemed
to extend up and down to infinity.

Once we were past the ring edge, the sense of speed
was provided by the gaps. Gray lines would regularly
materialize from the white wall, then widen and darken
as they moved to the right; they would flash by the
starboard 'port as distinctively thinner bands of ring
material, or even as black gaps through which I could
see occasional stars. For the second time since beginning the trip I was appalled, entranced, and struck
dumb with wonder.

Eventually the Encke Gap allowed me, for a few minutes, to see all of Saturn again out the front viewports;
but I had to lean far forward, because the boat had by
now pitched up so far that the Old Man was almost

below us. The rest of the A-Ring moved past with the bands almost parallel to the boat.

Then suddenly we were traversing Cassini's Division. Space and stars were again visible to starboard, but broken repeatedly by the bands of the gap itself, including four wide white ones. Resonances within resonances, Junior had called them.

By now the boat had pitched so that its nose was pointing slightly backward into the gap, so there was no warning when it ended. One moment we had black space in our view; the next, the ruddy white edge of the B-Ring was rising along the right side like a gigantic slanted curtain. The bands of this ring seemed brighter and more tightly compacted. And since we were killing our inward velocity and picking up orbital speed, they did not flash by with such breathtaking rapidity. I watched as our relative motion became more and more sluggish. By the time the clock showed ten minutes to rendezvous, our apparent motion had almost stopped.

I glanced at the 3-D; our boat and the Earth tug were just touching on the screens when one of the flashing dots disappeared. The other vessel had shut down its CRF drive.

I roused Junior; he brought himself up to date, then tried to contact the Earth tug on universal hailing frequency. He had no success; either they weren't monitoring that frequency—a most unlikely oversight—or else they chose not to answer.

Our own drive now shut down. We spun end-for-end, got a final love tap from the RCS thrusters, then Junior once more had control. He tilted the craft so that the nose pointed at the ring plane. We were above an unusual gap, one with a kink in it: The down-orbit section was visibly closer to Saturn than the up-orbit section. And where the two legs joined was the Iron Maiden. Less than a kilometer across, it was a brown ball which from our distance appeared about the size of the Moon seen from home.

While I gawked, Junior checked the radar. "They're about a hundred sixty klicks up, coming down slowly."

He grinned. "But since we're safely inside them, I don't have to be polite." He called up displays for local maneuvering, then threw a couple of switches. "Hang on; we're going down fast." The CRF cut in.

We dove straight down for a few minutes, then flipped and decelerated for the same interval and came to rest. Now Junior tipped the nose over so that it pointed straight down. We were half a kilometer above the ring plane, even with the leading edge of the Iron Maiden, and directly over the gap.

For the first time I could resolve at least some of the individual particles making up the ring. Most were only tiny white specks against the black, but I could see larger bodies further down in. Junior told me that most of the particles were only a centimeter or two in diameter. The occasional large particles, including a rare boulder now and then, were concentrated near the center of the hundred-meter-thick ring.

Seeing a gap in three dimensions was strange after watching so many flash by the boat in blurs. And this particular gap was strange, indeed. Underneath us, down-orbit from the Maiden, the edge closest to Saturn was sharp, and coincided with the inward edge of the satellite. But the outer edge was ragged, and crept in almost to the Maiden's center. Up-orbit, just beyond the Maiden, the geometry was exactly reversed.

Junior noticed my puzzled look and read my mind. "It's the 'jointer effect,' Dimp. Brought to the attention of the scientific community by yours truly. The Maiden is seven hundred meters wide, and in an orbit 108,000 kilometers from the Old Man's center. That makes the velocity differential between particles at the inner and outer edges about six centimeters a second. So you can think of the Maiden as a giant spinning blade, with the inner and outer edges of the ring gap being fed into it at three centimeters per second in opposite directions. And since there's no gravitational resonance at this particular distance from the primary, the gap tries to heal itself during the eight-hundred-year feed cycle."

He pulled a pair of binoculars from a box by the

control panel. "Does a pretty good job of healing, too; around on the other side the gap narrows to fifty, sixty meters."

He handed me the glasses. "There are seven 'jointer' gaps. In the other six, the little satellite just pushes the ring particles out of its path. But the Maiden's a real bitch; she lures 'em in, then blows 'em out of the sky." He pointed down to where the leading edge of the ball was silhouetted against the gap. "Find a likely looking particle about three or four meters from the Maiden, there, and watch what happens."

"What makes the Iron Maiden different," he continued as I focussed the glasses, "is that she's a conductor—got a very high iron content." I found a small ball of ice about four meters from the edge of the tiny moon, drifting very slowly toward the surface. "The ring particles are coated with iron dust, and pick up pretty healthy charges from the ionized hydrogen in this region. When they get close enough to the old girl, she develops a localized image charge which draws them toward her..."

As I watched, my particular ice chip began to move more rapidly; in a moment it was only two meters away, with collision imminent.

"... then when they get within a meter or so ..."

Suddenly the faintest of purplish-blue lines appeared between the Maiden and the particle, and the latter disappeared with a flash.

"... zap! Scratch one snowball. Some of it converts to energy—enough for a bunch of gigajoules; the rest vaporizes ... hey now! Look what's sitting on the north pole. Damn!"

Startled, I looked over at him. He was staring through another pair of glasses at the top of the Maiden and swearing volubly. I put my own binoculars back to my eyes and looked. Sitting there, casually as you please, was a white hexagon hatbox.

I checked the almost overwhelming urge to whoop and holler, and instead asked Junior why the profanity.

He smiled ruefully. "Two reasons. First one is, I spent

a lot of time studying the Maiden—took lots of pictures, and all that. But it was several years ago." He shook his head sadly. "The rings were sunlit from the other side, so that's where I stayed—only a couple of kilometers from the artifact the whole time. Talk about irony on the grand scale!" He shook his head. "The second reason is, if that box were on the other side of the Maiden, we'd win this race hands down."

"How's that?"

"Because then we'd have to shoot the gap. That's no problem for this boat, because I've modified it specially to handle sudden high skin currents. But going through a narrow gap is nothing that an unequipped boat—like that tug above us—should attempt."

I tried to look politely quizzical; but my expression must have emerged as profound ignorance. Junior continued patiently: "Dimp, that gap may look innocent, but it's loaded with one-micron particles and a few larger snowballs. And every boat in the system has a hull that's an excellent conductor—even more so than our girl friend down there. An ordinary boat navigating a narrow gap like this one has better than a fifty-fifty chance of being on the receiving end of one of those little lightning bolts. It'd blow out every electrical system in the vessel faster than the circuit breakers could react."

I saw the light. "So we could go straight through, and they'd have to go all the way out to the edge of the rings?"

"Well, at least to Cassini's Division, which is eight thousand kilometers out. We'd beat 'em to the hatbox by a couple of hours or more, and be on our way before they could even get back here."

A red light glowed on the control panel, and a beep sounded. Junior grimaced. "Speak of the devil; there's a hail from the baddies." He activated the RCS and pitched the boat so that the nose pointed directly up-orbit. The tug was only a couple of hundred meters away—slightly above us and almost directly over the north pole of the Maiden. A suited person in the open airlock was fiddling with some apparatus whose purpose was not immediately clear. Junior activated the transceiver.

"This is SOS research boat *Panda* responding to your hail. Dr. Whitedimple commanding, pilot Dr. Badille; over."

Their reply was interrupted frequently by interference bursts from the nearby discharges, but the meaning was abundantly clear:

"This is UN tug Discoverer, Dr. Cornwallis comm— SSSS—pilot Mr. Jacobs, assisted by Colonel Jackson. Notification is hereby pro—SSSSS—that this vessel is undertaking—SS—legitimate salvage operation as defined in the United Nat—SSSSS—preme Court decision in Buchwald vs. Vacuum Crystals, Inc., 2047. This vessel will—SSSS—no interference with its operation. You are ordered and required—SS—remove yourselves to a minimum distance of—SSSSS—hundred kilometers from the site of this operation; over."

"Cornwallis!" I exclaimed. "That pompous ass!"

"I take it you know this guy?"

"Yes. His idea of field research is to spend three weeks in the basement of the British Museum. His main claim to fame is his bad temper, which he vents on colleagues who have the temerity to question his findings. Here," I reached out a hand. "Let me have the mike."

I spoke with as much conciliation as I could muster: "Cornwallis, this is Whitedimple. Let's admit that we both got here at the same time, and make a joint expedition out of it. It's too big a find to keep bottled up anyway, no matter what our respective leaders say, over."

"Cornw—SSS—speaking. This is your last warning. We have a high-powered infrared laser train—SS—on you and—SSSSS— use it to disrupt your RCS if you do not leave immediately."

We stared incredulously at the other boat. The man in the airlock was now steadying the apparatus at head level and seemed to be sighting at us along a stubby projection. This was getting serious. I thumbed the mike.

"Now look here, Cornwallis. Don't you think you're carrying this a little too—"

Suddenly there was a green flash in my eyes; the unmistakable retinal image pattern of laser light. Then a buzzer sounded from the overhead speaker. Junior yelped, flipped the boat ninety degrees, and blasted straight up on the thrusters.

A minute later, still accelerating, Junior pressed a reset button on the control panel. The buzzing stopped, only to resume as soon as he removed his finger. He swore. "Check and see if they're still firing at us."

"I've been watching. He stopped as soon as you turned the boat, as far as I could tell."

He nodded, flipped the vessel one-eighty, and continued on RCS for another minute before trying to reset again. This time the buzzer remained off. He breathed a sigh and shut down the thrusters. We were now a kilometer above the tug, drifting upward very slowly. I asked Junior what had happened.

"They were telling the truth," he said shakily. "That green light must have been the frequency-doubled sighting beam for an infrared laser. A second after it came on, I got an overtemp indication in my hydrazine tank cluster. Hydrazine's pretty stable stuff, but it'll boil." He shivered visibly. "From the speed with which that indicator came on, I'd say we were about three seconds away from a pressure explosion."

Looking grimmer than I'd yet seen him, he turned back to check the control panel. Face averted, he said: "Well, what now, Admiral?"

I didn't answer right away. I thought furiously, while fright and anger fought for control. We'd learned the hard way that Earth had no intention of making a friendly race of this affair; they were desperate to reach the cache before SpaceHome, and would apparently go to any lengths to do so.

I was disgusted with Ogumi, and afraid for my life. But most of all, I felt overwhelmingly angry at the execrable Cornwallis. He must have been given the power to negotiate, but had chosen instead a life-threatening act of intimidation. Now the ball was really in my court. Did we slink away, or fight back at the risk of our lives? "What now, Admiral" indeed!

With the exception of Junior's superior piloting, they appeared to have all the advantages: a larger boat, much more accelerative capability, more fuel, presumably more supplies and at least one weapon. If they wanted to, they could chase us all over the system. Except . . . the germ of an idea began to form.

My thoughts were interrupted. "Dimp, a message just came in from SOS. Want to hear it?" I nodded.

It was a followup from Ogumi, asking our current status, reminding me again of my power to negotiate, and professing warm confidence in my ability to handle the situation.

I snapped an irritated reply: "Tell him we're undertaking negotiations!"

Junior raised an eyebrow. "You're the boss, Admiral." He framed the message and fast-taped it back to SOS after encryption. By the time Ogumi received it, I reflected sourly, things would be settled one way or another.

When Junior was finished, I said: "You told me that pilot had guts. Do you think he'd try to navigate that gap down there?"

My little companion rubbed his nose. "I don't think he'd be stupid enough to do it."

"But maybe he doesn't know the danger."

"I'm sure he's got at least a basic knowledge of the hazards. They don't give pilot's licenses for ignorance, Dimp."

"Okay, but what if we . . ." My plan was conceived in anger, based on uncertain assumptions, possibly foolhardy, and certainly illegal. Anger lent me eloquence; as I talked, Junior began to nod. Soon his grin returned, and he was looking at me with a newfound respect. Even through my anger, I found myself enjoying that.

When I finished, he held my eyes with his and asked: "You really willing to take the risks, Admiral?"

I returned his gaze. "Are you the best pilot in the system or not, Junior?"

"Touché!" he cackled. "All right, let's see what they're up to."

We put the binoculars into service. The tug was a trifle over a kilometer below; the laser operator was watching us. Another man had joined him in the airlock and was fiddling with equipment that seemed to include a coiled line.

"They look like they're getting ready to go down," I said. "We'd better get started."

"Buckle up, Admiral; we're on our way." He angled the nose and lit the CRF engine. After a minute of hard acceleration, he did a flipship and blasted back to kill our velocity. We finished less than a kilometer above the gap and some five kilometers down-orbit from the Maiden and the Earth tug.

We pitched over so that our nose pointed straight at the other vessel. Through the binoculars I could just make out the men in the airlock. Both were watching us; the laser operator was also readying his weapon. I swallowed once and told Junior to proceed.

"Into the breech, Admiral." He aligned the boat carefully, then lit the CRF again and blasted directly at the tug for fifteen seconds. I kept the glasses on the man with the laser. He was sighting it as Junior cut the drive. Just as we began the flipship I saw a green flash; then our tail was pointing directly at the Earth vessel and Junior cut in the CRF.

We blasted for thirty seconds at low acceleration, our exhaust aimed precisely at the tug. As he fussed with the controls, Junior remarked: "You really shouldn't look at a laser with binoculars, Admiral—it could be dangerous." The wicked grin was in full display.

"Do you think they kept firing at us?" I asked.

"I didn't get any thermals," Junior replied. "Would *you* go up against a CRF plume with only a micropore suit and a hand-held laser?"

I was still mulling that over when he announced:

"Closest approach, 3.95 kilometers." He angled the nose down and increased power. "Time to shoot the gap."

We were almost stationary with respect to the ring plane; now we picked up speed rapidly as we edged down toward it. Junior was intent on his displays; from time to time he looked up from his 3-D to gauge the approaching gap. Then he cut the drive, made a last-second correction with thrusters, reached to his left, and flipped a switch prominently marked "GS." A loud click echoed through the hull. The 3-D display froze. The lights flickered, but remained lit.

I asked what "GS" stood for. "Gap-shooter," was the reply. "Cuts off all conductive paths from the hull to the interior of the boat."

Even as he was answering we slipped into the gap. There was little time to see anything. I did notice that the individual particles were quite far apart, although through the starboard viewport our velocity merged them into a solid wall. Another phenomenon was the color change. As we dropped through the gut the light grew dimmer, changing from off-white to ruddy, then to dull orange. In a few seconds we were through, and the B-Ring formed a monstrous ceiling above us. I felt as if we were in a huge darkroom, illuminated with the wrong shade of red.

While I caught my breath, Junior flipped off the GS and ordered a systems check. Pandora ran through her routine and pronounced us "green," whereupon we flipshipped again and killed our drift.

I had to resolve something that had been bothering me.

"Junior, you said our closest approach to the tug was about four kilometers. Was that close enough to hurt the men in the airlock?"

"Naw. A .10 G plume from this little boat wouldn't be dangerous for a short time at that distance. The only damage will be wet pants." His crooked grin was eerie in the dim orange light glowing through the rings.

I took a deep breath. "Okay, let's go again."

He glanced up at the screens, then pitched our nose

toward the ring plane and cut in the CRF drive. Shortly, we were drifting once more through the gap; then the ring turned white and we were in sunlight. After a quick systems check Junior swapped ends and killed our drift. We were pointed once more at the tug, which was sitting a few hundred meters above the Maiden, several kilometers up-orbit.

Now the airlock was closed. I wondered what was happening inside—but not for long; a call came in at once on our emergency band. It was Cornwallis, so furious that he was literally spluttering. He shouted that we were in violation of UN and SpaceHome regulations, international and interspace law; that we were furthermore bounders and cads and that he would personally see to it that we suffered a lifetime of imprisonment. He ended with a demand for an explanation of our actions.

"You want to reply, Boss?" Junior asked. "Sounds like he's willing to reopen negotiations."

I told Junior exactly how to reply.

"You're a hard man, Admiral," he cackled. Then he lined up our nose and gunned hard toward the tug. And once more he flipped the boat and blasted back for thirty seconds before tilting us down toward the gap.

"Got to within 3.46 klicks that time," he said with satisfaction. "Close enough to set off a thermal or two and give 'em something to think about."

Halfway through the gap on this pass my hair tried to stand on end, and there was a funny taste in my mouth. Junior was calm. "We just took our first hit," was the terse explanation. I didn't like it, and was apprehensive until Pandora completed a successful systems check.

Once again we hung motionless below the gap in that orange half-light. I asked what would happen if we got zapped without the GS being activated. Junior reached up and tugged an ear. "Well, I've got a fast-reaction auto-tripper wired into it that should theoretically kick it over in time." He showed teeth. "But with the kind of risetimes and currents we're messing with, I'd prefer not to put it to the test."

When we shot the gap again and lined up on the other vessel, it was waiting for us. From six kilometers away we were gazing into the throat of their CRF. The message from Cornwallis was short and nasty: If we tried anything again, they'd roast us.

I swallowed hard. Junior seemed unperturbed, although he kept his hands on the controls.

"Well, Admiral, that gun's bigger than ours. Any ideas?"

From the tone of his voice it was evident that he'd already come up with an answer.

"How far above the Maiden are they?" I asked.

He glanced at the 3-D. "Two hundred sixty meters."

"Okay, let's hit them from straight overhead."

He laughed delightedly. "Anger sure whets your brains, Admiral!"

"I wish it would dry my pants," I said shakily.

Still laughing, he angled the boat upward, then gunned the CRF. After a minute he flipped and blasted back, stopping six or seven kilometers above the tug. Their pilot maneuvered with his RCS to keep his nozzle pointed directly at our boat. I put the binoculars to my eyes and focussed them on the Earth vessel; for the first time I realized how wicked-looking a CRF throat really was. Half to myself I grunted: "The tail's still aimed our way."

"Yeah, but their nose is pointed straight at the Maiden."

"Okay," I said, taking a deep breath, "singe the hell out of them!"

Without a word Junior kicked in the CRF drive and dove us toward the enemy tug. To take my mind off that lethal nozzle, I asked him why the pilot hadn't done more maneuvering during the encounter.

"No matter how good that Jacobs character might be," he grunted, eyes glued to the screens, "he's got to switch over to manual control to play our game. And it's been drilled into him that manual is for emergencies only." He made a tiny course correction. "So it's taking him a while to overcome that computer-programming, button-pushing training." He cut the CRF and flipshipped. "Besides, his displays probably aren't as good as mine." He aligned the boat carefully with the tug, tail to tail. "Okay, here we go."

We poured hot hydrogen at them for almost a minute before Junior finally pitched the boat over and headed for the gap. "That time it was 3.04 klicks," he gloated. "They'll be up to their ears in alarms."

"And Cornwallis will be madder than hell."

"And they've seen us shoot the gap four times now."

We looked at each other and laughed.

Drifting through the gap for the fifth time, I asked Junior why he'd introduced himself as "Dr." Badille.

"Partly one-upsmanship," he answered with a twinkle, "and partly truth. Princeton conferred honorary degrees on Mom and Dad three years ago, for their work on ring resonances. Since I'd done all the research and written all the papers, they held a little ceremony and reconferred the doctorates on me." He winked. "Just between us, of course."

Another systems check, then we flipped and blasted back. Coming through the gap, we took another hit. I liked it even less the second time, but neither Junior nor Pandora were bothered.

This time, when we lined up with the tug at six kilometers, we found ourselves nose to nose. Junior said: "Want to bet we've got a new ballgame this time?"

"Let's wait a bit and see what they do," I said.

So we waited. A full ten minutes. The tug did not move, nor did it call. "Okay, I sighed. "Once more."

As soon as we started accelerating, so did they. The six kilometers began to melt rapidly. Junior immediately pitched the boat up ninety degrees and headed directly away from the ring plane.

"Jacobs is catching on to boat fighting," he said, busy with the controls. "He was probably planning to mirror us. As soon as we flipped, he would have done the same, then blasted us with a one-G plume and wiped us out. Our best bet is to get above him—or at least play like we're trying to. . . . Ahh, here he comes."

The Earth tug, pitching up in turn, was now blasting furiously. Junior immediately flipped us one-eighty and burned at .3 G toward the gap. We passed the tug at a distance of four kilometers; it cut its drive, yawed over so that its tail pointed at us and cut in its CRF at high acceleration. We were only in its wash for a second or two before the pilot lost us; shortly thereafter it was too far away to be effective.

But that second or two had been enough to trip four thermal alarms. I found myself drenched in sweat. Junior swore again as he punched reset buttons while maneuvering to shoot the gap. The last alarm went silent just before he hit the GS switch and coasted us through.

After killing our relative velocity, we looked again for the Earth vessel. It was four or five kilometers above the ring plane, and just coming to rest. Junior edged us up until we were barely under the gap, in plain sight. And there we sat, bait in a trap—I hoped.

We had done the job of raising their hackles. I was counting on their pride not to admit that Junior was the better pilot, their incomplete knowledge of the gap's perils, and their anger to override the small voice of reason. Plus the now-proven fact that we had to be disposed of permanently before they could retrieve the artifact.

We waited, until fears and doubts began to gnaw. Then finally Junior announced: "Here they come!" Now I could see the foreshortened tug silhouetted against the glow of its CRF plume; but it was several seconds before the vessel was noticeably larger. "He's taking it slow and easy," Junior said, glancing at the screens. "Acceleration's only about .1 G."

The tug presently stopped its drive and drifted closer, thrusters cutting in and out as it made course corrections. About three kilometers up, it pitched end-for-end. Junior moved us several hundred kilometers down-orbit, keeping our nose toward the opposition. "I don't think they'll be silly enough to fire the CRF into the gap and roil up the particles," he said, "but it doesn't hurt to be safe."

Sure enough, only the tug's RCS was used to slow it down for shooting the gap; the pitch and yaw thrusters all burned in unison for a long minute, then shut off when the vessel was still a half kilometer above the ring plane.

Junior studied his displays. "He's coming through at about twenty-three meters a second. Not bad for an amateur. But I'll lay heavy money he'll get zapped first time through."

"Why is that?"

"Because he's coming through the radar-indicated center of the gap, instead of hugging the clean wall nearest Saturn. On that course, chances are ten to one he'll take a hit."

I watched fascinated as the tug entered the gap, still making an occasional attitude correction with its thrusters. The vessel was nearly through the passage when I noticed that a yaw burn cut off immediately after its inception.

"Got 'em!" cried Junior. "I saw the spark!"

The tug was now through the gap, drifting downward in the ruddy orange glow. A minute later it was more than a kilometer below us, still on the same course. To all appearances it was a dead ship; not even a running light was showing. My partner turned to me and stuck out his hand.

"War's over, Admiral. You did good."

Numbly I accepted the hand. "Do you think they're all right?"

"Sure. They can hold out in there as long as their supplies last. Might get a little smelly, though." He turned back to his controls. "Let's go say hello."

He accelerated down toward the tug, flipped, and matched velocities—all on RCS. Now that the battle was over he meticulously followed the rules of minimum safe distance and forebore using the CRF drive.

After matching rates, we carefully drifted toward the tug until only a few meters separated our noses. All three men were at the forward viewports. Two were waving wildly; the man at the pilot's position was calmly holding up a large piece of paper, bearing the legend: HELP?

"How about it?" Junior asked.

I was looking at Cornwallis and getting mad all over again. "Let's get the artifact first, dammit!"

Junior developed a wry smile. "You're a hard man, Admiral."

Ordering Pandora to keep station on the tug, he drifted to the back of the cabin, dug out a sheet of white plastic and scrawled on it with a grease pencil. Bringing it forward, he held it up against the viewport. After a second the pilot nodded his head. The other two shook their fists.

Junior handed me the sign and began backing the boat away from the other vessel. I read the message: BACK BEFORE SUNDOWN. Not for the first time, I wondered about his reading habits.

As we headed back up I began having second thoughts. "Junior, are you sure they'll be okay?"

"Yeah. You didn't notice the pilot getting excited, did you? It was just the two groundpounders who panicked. They don't have any cabin heating, but they can wear micropore suits to keep warm if they have to; and it's four hours yet until we enter shadow."

"Let's see . . . by that time they'll be about . . . three hundred fifty kilometers below the gap." I took a modicum of pride in performing the mental arithmetic.

"Good try, Boss, but totally wrong. They'll be about eighty klicks away and heading back up toward us. In fact, if we waited five hours, they'd punch right up through the ring plane." He laughed at my expression. "Admiral, you're one hell of a boat commander, but what you know about orbital mechanics you could write on the head of a pin!"

Since they were undoubtedly watching us with binoculars, shooting the gap again was like a final victory.

We set the boat down twenty meters from the hatbox.

Junior assured me that it was perfectly safe that high up on the surface of the Maiden ("Well, *almost* perfectly safe.") because we were so far out of the ring plane and our boots and gloves were insulated.

Then, for the first time, I saw the Giant really close up in open space, unframed by a viewport. Only the northern half was visible, but even that seemed to fill the sky, rising from the infinite white horizon of the ring plane. I stared, hypnotized by the stunning splendor, until Junior called me back to duty.

We retrieved the box and had it back inside the boat within fifteen minutes. There was a single plate—and it was different from the others. We studied it with utmost concentration. After about fifteen seconds, Junior began to snicker. Within thirty he was laughing out loud. By then I was plenty uneasy about prospects for an immediate find. The artifact contained what appeared to be an oblique view of Saturn, with a wedge cut out to show interior layers. There were curved lines, this time; and also more of the artificial symbols. Junior explained it to me while my heart sank. . . .

7

There is a point on Saturn at 82° 37′ north latitude, and at a longitude which has been defined as "surface" Greenwich for the better part of a century. There, at local noon each day, a kilometric radio pulse is emitted, as if the spot were a clock ticking once every ten hours, thirty-nine minutes and twenty-six seconds. And at that point, under thousands of kilometers of atmosphere and ton upon ton of pressure—and floating somehow on a sea of hot liquid hydrogen—is the promised treasure that the alien race most graciously left for us to retrieve.

"Hot liquid hydrogen?" I said. "I thought that you couldn't liquefy hydrogen without cooling it down a couple of hundred degrees below zero."

Junior rolled his eyes. "Admiral, I know you've got a brain; I've seen it in action."

Then he just looked at me while I cudgeled my memory. High school physics was many years back; I remembered it mainly because I got the lowest C in the class, and emerged shaky but still eligible for college.

Finally a dim recollection of triple points crawled out of the fog. "Something to do with pressure?" I hazarded.

He grinned approvingly. "Something is right. At two thousand kilometers down, where this thing," he pointed to a small symbol on the artifact, "is floating, the pressure is about 5600 Earth sea-level atmospheres, or about 9000 times the pressure we carry in Colony space. The fact that the local temperature at that depth is around 1800 degrees Kelvin is almost irrelevant. What you get is a phase change; the hydrogen stops being a gas and starts being a liquid."

"It'll be pretty tough to get at, won't it?" I asked. "I mean, don't a lot of metals start to melt at that temperature, or something?"

Junior shook his head. "Admiral, you're going to 'something' me to death. But, yeah, it will be an interesting problem."

"Maybe the aliens are trying to test us—test our technological readiness."

"Naw. Given that we've got enough technology in the first place to be kicking around the outer system like we are, putting a retrieval probe together is just a matter of a little time and money. Whoever *they* are can certainly figure that out." He scratched his nose. "No, Dimp, what we're dealing with here is a perverse sense of humor." He glanced at his wristwatch. "Speaking of which, maybe we'd better see about rescuing our panicky brethren." He looked thoughtful. "And maybe we'd better be a bit circumspect about it, while we're at it."

"How's that?" I asked. I was still harboring a healthy anger at Cornwallis—enough to vent some spleen when I saw him. In fact, I had been secretly planning on doing so—in a manner, of course, consonant with my professorial dignity.

"Well," Junior said slowly, "I don't claim to know a lot about Earth-orbit politics, but it seems to me that we might be able to use some high-gravity muscles to help pull that thing," he waved at the drawing on the artifact again, "out of that unhealthy gravity well. And we might need some high-gravity money, too. It's not going to be cheap, you know."

I scratched my head. "I thought you just said 'a little time and money.'"

He laughed. "A quibble, Dimp. I was speaking from the aliens' viewpoint. From ours, it's going to be quite an undertaking. We'll probably be in it for a couple of hundred million before we're done."

He was putting gloves on as he spoke, so I followed suit; soon we had the artifact back in its box, and the box stowed safely in my aft cabin.

As Junior goosed the boat gently and headed for the gap, he said: "One request, Admiral. I'd rather you not say anything about Pandy. She's the only navigation computer this boat has, and I'd rather keep her presence to ourselves." He looked at me hard. "Just in case—I'm not saying they'll try anything—but just in case they get ideas, it'll give us a lot of leverage. If they think about taking the boat, it might make them change their minds if they have to wrestle it home on manual. Figuring orbital trajectories without a computer is a job tough enough to make even a good pilot think twice."

I nodded. Then we shot the gap. We took a hit going through. I didn't like it again.

When we got back to the Earth tug, there were still two hours before it was due to shoot back up through the gap. They were *very* glad to see us. Looking back with a small degree of empathy, which I certainly did not possess at the time, I begin to understand. It must have been rather lonely and frightening, in orbit around the Giant, in the darkening glow, with no power, and no hope at all if we didn't come back for them.

So we didn't have any trouble with them right away. Cornwallis was almost whimpering with gratitude as he came aboard. The Colonel was a bit winded from helping Jacobs work the emergency airlock bleed, but he was still white. Even Jacobs wasn't quite so phlegmatic, and smiled shakily as he emerged from our airlock into the dayroom. But he had enough moxie left to salute me as he came in:

"Dr. Badille?" He stuck his hand out in my direction

as soon as he got his helmet off. "I want to tell you that was some shit-hot piloting! You—"

"I'm Dr. Whitedimple," I said hurriedly, pulling my hand out of his grip (my fingers stuck together for five minutes thereafter). "This," I waved to Junior, "is Dr. Badille, the shit-hot pilot. I'm merely the shit-hot passenger."

Jacobs shook his head ruefully. "Seems like I can't do anything right today." He turned to face Junior. "Sir, I've never seen a boat handled like that. Where did you do your training?"

"Self-taught," Junior snapped. "Where did you learn your manners, firing on a harmless research boat with a deadly weapon?"

"Believe me, mister, if I'd've known it was going to happen, I would have wrecked that damned laser with a crowbar. I was sittin' up in the left seat during the whole thing. The Colonel and the blowhard, here," he waved a hand at the frowning Cornwallis, "assured me they were only going to scare you off with it—said they'd just use the sighting beam to frighten you into backing off. I didn't know they'd actually turn on the heat until I saw the power drain." He smiled again. "After that, we were fighting for our lives and all bets were off."

He was shaking his head. "You guys suckered us four ways from Sunday. Gotta hand it to you." He furrowed his brow. "But how'd you manage to punch through that gap so many times without gettin' zapped?"

"I imagine you'll find out soon," Junior said. His voice had mellowed slightly. "In fact," he glanced at his watch, "maybe too soon. We'd better jury-rig these two boats together so we can give you a little nudge." He waved in the direction of the 3-D display. "We have about an hour and a half until we punch back up through the ring plane; and on this course, we're going to miss the gap by a couple of hundred meters."

Jacobs nodded. "I'll give you a hand. Where's your towing magnets?"

Junior looked at me with a question in his eyes. "Admiral?"

"It's okay, Junior; I'd only be in your way. I'll stay here and keep our other guests company."

He nodded and went aft to don his suit. Jacobs followed. We'd both reached the same conclusion silently: Jacobs seemed okay, but the other two weren't to be quite trusted.

By the time they'd finally cycled through the airlock and begun clanking around on the hull, Cornwallis had recovered most of his aplomb. His first words to me were typical of his behavior to date:

"Whitedimple, in turning your fusion plume on our boat, you broke one of the fundamental rules of pilotry. When I get back to Earth, I will personally see to it that you are incarcerated along with that withered dwarf of a partner."

The man's effrontery astounded me. I'd rehearsed a dignified-but-triumphant little tete-a-tete between us, in which I would let it be known that his professional reputation was now ruined, and he'd be persona-non-grata anywhere off Earth. I'd known that he was wont to attack when challenged; but I had no idea that this situation could mean anything but remorse to him. His words turned me ice cold.

"*Doctor* Cornwallis,"—I labored diligently to make the title an insult—"I do not know what you hope to gain by your accusations, but I must inform you that this entire episode has been put on tape—including your threats, and our instrument readings when your laser fired on us—and sent by encrypted datafax to SpaceHome Headquarters. I don't know whether or not SpaceHome will make it available to authorities on Earth," (if I'd been telling the truth, this would have been a quibble—since I was quite sure by then that Earth would be perfectly capable of deciphering such a transmission) "but if you return with such a lie to try to save face, I assure you that I will make *my* copy public knowledge."

Without waiting for him to answer, I turned to the Colonel. "And what is your capacity on this expedition, sir?"

He'd regained some color, and spoke calmly. "I was sent by the British government as an observer."

"As an observer," I said acidly, "you took a rather active role."

"I was obeying the needs and orders of the vessel's commanding officer," he stated firmly.

"Ah, I see," I said. "And did, by any chance, this man," I indicated Cornwallis without the courtesy of naming him, "have something to do with your selection for this expedition? Perhaps you had been previously acquainted?"

"I've known Dr. Cornwallis for some years," he replied stiffly. "And yes, I do believe that he had some input to the selection process."

"I understand perfectly," I said. The heavy irony was undoubtedly lost on the Colonel, but Cornwallis-the-manipulator could be counted upon to pick it up.

"Now see here, Whitedimple," he said. "I advise you to keep a civil tongue in your head. Remember you *are* outnumbered, and civilization is indeed a long way off."

I looked at him with contempt. "You must really be hungry for success, Corny. What's the matter—have they run out of unopened crates in the basement of the museum?" It was a cheap shot, and really not within the bounds of dignity. But it caught Cornwallis in a sensitive mood; perhaps he was thinking of the consequences of his failure when he returned home. His face turned red and his brow clouded even further. He moved toward me and began to shout:

"You've gone too far, Whitedimple! I intend to make you sorry for what—"

"Oh, grow up, Cornwallis," I interrupted him without bothering to move. "Why don't you ask the Colonel here to give you some advice on the current tactical situation. In the first place, I doubt that Jacobs would go along with anything you're likely to try. In the second place, this boat has no navigation computer, and yours probably can't be fixed until we get back to I-Base. Even if the Colonel is a good pilot, which I doubt, I don't think he'd be willing to try to fly this thing all the way back to Earth—or even to I-Base—on manual control.

I turned my eyes full on those of the Colonel, who already had a restraining hand on Cornwallis. "How about it, Colonel? You willing to try? Going to blast now, kill off Junior and Jacobs, and try to make it back to base?"

He shook his head without speaking. I could tell from his expression that he was somewhat embarrassed at Cornwallis' actions.

I looked back at the still-fuming archaeologist. "Sorry, Corny. One despicable act per day is all you're going to be allowed." I half turned back to the desk at which I was starting to work. "Now, if you gentlemen will excuse me, I'd like to get busy on this followup report to SpaceHome."

The two fell back and positioned themselves at the small table across the dayroom from the computer console at which I was working. The room was much too tiny to suit me; I'm afraid they were still close enough to see that I was trembling. I could only hope that they took it for anger, whereas it was—sad to admit—really compounded of fear and shakes. I hate confrontations, and it had been many years since I'd engaged in one. I could smell the stink of my own pheromones and hoped the cabin circulation wasn't wafting my air in their direction.

After what seemed like ten hours, but was really only one, Junior and Jacobs cycled back into the boat. I had composed two and a half sentences during the entire interval.

"Okay, we're going to give it a shot," Junior announced, moving straight to the pilot's seat after getting his helmet off. He began to flip switches while Jacobs looked on with interest.

"Disabling two, six and eight?" the big man asked. Junior nodded, then tentatively tried a low-power RCS burn with several other thrusters, mumbling under his breath and watching the numbers on the 3-D change as a result of each firing. The display showed just a portion of the rings; our position looked alarmingly close to the ring plane. I moved forward and looked out the front viewports for reassurance. They were still comfortably far away; the gap was the thinnest of black threads in the dark orange sky.

"I didn't see you entering those trial RCS data in the computer, Junior," Jacobs said nervously. "What the hell do you use to do your thruster calculations?"

"Those," Junior pointed to the 3-D displays, "and Kentucky windage, old son." His grin was eerie in the backlit ring glow.

"Jesus," said the big man. "You mean you horse this thing all the time on man—"

"Better hang on to something!" Junior interrupted, making his voice loud enough for all of us to hear. "I'm going to commence RCS maneuvering almost immediately." I buckled into the right seat, while Jacobs slipped into some foot restraints and held on to the back of my chair. Cornwallis and the Colonel stayed seated at the table in the dayroom in back of us.

Junior pressed buttons and we began a slow yaw. He stopped it after we'd done about ninety degrees; then we were pushed gently down into our seats for about five seconds. Then the little man reversed the procedure by turning us one-eighty and thrusting back again for a brief period. When we'd stopped, he looked carefully at the 3-D, yawed just a few degrees, and hit the RCS for about half a second. Another careful scrutiny of the screens, then he announced: "That does it. Okay Jake, let's go back out and get those safety lines off and release the magnets. We're going through in single file."

Jacobs had had his mouth open throughout the whole performance. Finally he closed it, swallowed, then shook his head. "Jesus, old timer; you've got one hell of a touch. No wonder I didn't stand a chance!"

Junior happened to be looking in my direction; he caught my eye and raised his eyebrows minutely. I shook my head just as minutely. It would be better for Jacobs' digestion if we broke the news gently—when we were alone—that Junior was still a teenager. Besides, I didn't know to what nefarious purposes Cornwallis and the Colonel might put the information if they possessed it.

Junior blinked assent and released himself from the pilot's couch. "Well, you're not so bad yourself, Jake. You came around pretty tight from Dione; and then damn near fried us on our final pass. . . ."

They moved aft, donning their helmets, and I was left to mull over Jacobs' reactions. His awe of Junior generated a certain respect that I hadn't possessed before. Not knowing anything about piloting, I'd only had a vague uneasiness at first about Junior's handling of the boat—and that had vanished some time ago. Now, after what Jacobs had to say, I was glad for my previous ignorance. If I'd been more knowledgeable, I might have demurred much more strongly about heading toward the Giant alone with the youngster. And that would have been much to my embarrassment and detriment. I'd really come to admire and respect the little gnome. I *liked* him. And I realized that he liked me, even if I could not put my finger on exactly why. I'd never thought of myself as having many likeable traits, as far as men were concerned; in fact I hadn't made any close friends since college days.

But I felt a bond with Junior. Perhaps it was because he seemed to be able to see right through whatever front I happened to be putting on at the moment, and didn't really care—but liked whatever it was he saw underneath. All in all, I felt lucky to have found him. So maybe it was a blessing that I knew precious little about navigation and its difficulties.

But, at the same time, I felt helpless in my ignorance. I should have been able to help Junior during this difficult time; but I could contribute nothing. He had to rely on the skills of a man who was nominally the enemy, even though it appeared that Jacobs was rapidly turning into a friend. I felt an internal embarrassment with my ignorance—another new emotion, since for more than twenty years I'd been content to confine my knowledge to the narrow niche I'd carved for myself at SHU.

But now something was stirring in me. I wasn't sure what it was, and I most certainly was not sure I liked it; but stirring it was. I felt as if I were being forced down on Procrusteus' bed—but that he was going to stretch my head instead of my legs.

I sighed and looked back at Cornwallis and the Colonel. They were still at the table in the dayroom, leaning together and talking quietly with their heads together. The Colonel looked up and saw me; he leaned back and I turned away. They still made either of them uneasy, but I didn't want either of them to see that in my face.

Presently the two pilots cycled back through the airlock. Junior went right to the console and released the electromagnets holding the boats together. The release springs were so gentle that I could barely feel the pushoff. But Junior wasn't satisfied until he studied the 3-D. "Relative velocity 9.3 centimeters per second," he announced. "And three-fourths of it is ours, since that monster of yours is so massy." He looked at his watch. "And only fifteen minutes to the gap. The tug'll go through clean."

He began flipping switches. "Hang on, everyone. We're moving up to lead this parade." The boat moved as he spoke and we accelerated away from the lifeless Earth tug. When we were about to shoot the gap, Junior reached up and threw the GS switch.

Jacobs laughed. "I begin to understand," he said. "That was quite a plan you concocted, old timer!"

As we drifted up into sunlight, Junior hooked a thumb at me. "It was the Admiral here who made the plan," he said. "You got suckered by his brains and guts."

I began to turn beet red, but Junior was relentless: "He doesn't talk much, but when it comes to the nub, he's got what it takes."

"So?" Jacobs looked at me with respect. "Remind me not to play poker with you, Dr. Whitedimple."

"Call me Whitey," I mumbled. I was furious with Junior. I realized that he was constitutionally incapable of taking the credit for the plan, but he was deliberately laying it on much too thickly. I glared daggers at him while stammering with embarrassment.

The gnome looked at my flushed face and cackled. "Take your due like a man, Admiral; you earned it!"

The Earth tug came up through the gap, after which Junior and Jacobs spent considerable time reconnecting the two vessels; they rigged an umbilical so we could supply power to the other boat. There wasn't room for all of us in Junior's vessel, and it was a long trip back—nearly two days, since Junior wouldn't push the connected boats over .05 G.

The first thing I did when we were finally alone and accelerating was to ask Junior if we had recorded all that had happened, including voices and hydrazine tank temperature readouts. He said yes, then asked me why. I admitted what I'd told Cornwallis and the Colonel.

The little man's eyes twinkled as he looked at me. "I think that maybe I'd avoid a poker game with you, too, Dimp," he said. "Okay, we'll fix up a tape and send it off first thing." We did the deed, along with a quick summary of what we'd accomplished and our current status, and squealed it in code to Ogumi. I didn't even care that Earth authorities would be able to decode the message. If Ogumi wanted to keep me in the dark to string me along, he'd have to bear the consequences.

We then slept until Ogumi's reply came back to us. It was a very long message in code, with detailed instructions. The essence of it was that we were no longer constrained to keep the story of the artifacts a secret, but that the true story of the battle of the Iron Maiden was to be kept a private matter. The official version was to be that the Earth vessel had run into trouble—electrical power system malfunction, naturally!—and that we had saved them with a tow back to I-Base. I guess Ogumi might have been harboring the same kind of thoughts as Junior: that it might be necessary to let Earth in on our action.

I was satisfied. There was no doubt in my mind that Earth powers had also read my report; and I had made it quite clear that the acts of Cornwallis and the Colonel were sufficiently heinous to effectively blacklist them in any ensuing joint venture. I'd gotten over the worst of my anger and was left with only a very cold feeling toward the two.

Mike Jacobs was another matter; he was smart, friendly as a puppy and apparently felt not a whit of resentment at being had in the Iron Maiden affair. He was almost insistent about offering his services in helping to pilot the boats back to I-Base.

"We've got a long ways to go, Junior, and you're only one man—begging your pardon Whitey, but you're no pilot—and you've got to get sleep like anybody else."

Finally, Junior and I invited him over to "our side" during the mid-trip turnover hiatus, and told him about Pandora. I also told him about Junior's real age.

"Jesus," he said, after floating there, blinking, for about fifteen seconds. "You guys got any other surprises up your sleeves before I go shooting off my mouth any more?"

"I don't think so," I said. "Except that you must trust the fact that Junior is a higher-level genius than anybody realizes, except for we three and his parents. We'd prefer that this, and the other facts, be kept to yourself. For obvious reasons." I smiled.

"Don't worry," he said. "I'm not one to go shooting off my mouth to curry favor." He grinned that friendly grin. "Which you two must've already figured out, or else you wouldn't be telling me all this in the first place." Then he got serious for a moment. "But I would like to ask a favor."

I raised my eyebrows a fraction of a centimeter. We'd also decided that Jacobs wasn't one to beg favors, and this was a bit surprising.

"What can we do for you?" I asked, trying to keep the worry out of my voice. Now that we'd told him a few things, he had a tentative blackmail hold on us. It was an uneasy feeling.

But if Jacobs noticed the catch in my voice, or Junior's frown, he didn't show it. "Well," he acted almost

embarrassed, "I figure that after those two," he pointed
a finger in the general direction of the attached Earth
tug, "get through puttin' a bug in the ears of the authorities back home, my name might not be held in too
much esteem any more—even though they told me I
was the best pilot they had when they asked me to
skipper that tug out here."

He got a wistful look in his eyes. "And that's a dirty
shame, because I figure that this artifact discovery is
going to throw an interesting hunk of business in the
way of a good pilot."

The gnome and I both nodded. "You've got the nub of
it, old son," Junior said. "Afraid you're going to miss
your piece of the action?"

"Yeah," the burly pilot said, looking more wistful
than ever. But he didn't say any more. When it came
right down to it, he was too proud to ask us to help him
out—after all, he'd been engaged in a life-and-death
struggle with us less than a day and a half ago.

Junior and I exchanged rapid glances, in which Jacobs was saved by mutual consent. Junior liked and
trusted him, and I had a great respect for Junior's judg-
ment. And I'd come to like Jacobs, too, even in the few
minutes total I'd spent with him. He didn't have a
vindictive bone in his body.

"Mike," I said, "I'm not sure what kind of or how
much influence Junior and I will have in this coming
show out here; but for whatever it's worth, you have
our backing." I pursed my lips as I thought of something else. "Is it possible that it would be better if you
didn't have to return to Earth at all?"

"Yeah." Jacobs was so red faced that he almost choked
on the single word. Then he had to continue. "But I
don't think that'll be possible. There really isn't anybody else that can pilot those two 'hogs back to Earth
orbit."

"Well, we'll see what happens, Jake," I said.

He nodded thanks, still embarrassed, then Junior suggested a game of cribbage—truly an heroic gesture since
I knew positively that the game bored him to tears. I

lost four dollars in the three-handed melee. I really play quite a good game, but somehow always get dealt miserable cards. Pandora did her job, while Junior and Jake split my money between them.

Less than twenty-four hours later, we nudged the double craft into orbit around Iapetus; and almost immediately the surface-hopper was up with tools, materiel and technicians to set the Earth tug to rights.

After we'd orbited, and travel between the two boats was safe, Cornwallis came humbly, hat in hand—a sight I thought I'd never live to see!—and asked to view the artifact we found on the Maiden. His appeal was emotional, colleague to colleague, and most difficult to refuse on those grounds. Ogumi's message hadn't mentioned this possibility one way or another; I interpreted that to mean that it was up to my discretion. I thought about the implications if I didn't let him see it—especially after an honest, humble request—and decided in Cornwallis' favor. And if the small truth be known, perhaps I couldn't resist the temptation of having the man twice indebted to me.

He studied it for a long time; his memory was well-known in the profession and I was sure he was engraving every line and symbol in his brain. When he asked me what my interpretation was, I demurred. I saw no point in carrying my help that far; so I told him I didn't feel right about making any statements at that early point in time. He nodded, perhaps remembering my reputation for academic conservatism. By the time I hustled him out of the boat, he was quite ready to go; there was no doubt that he could reproduce the drawing well enough, especially with hypnotic techniques, for Earth to locate the aliens' cache.

When it came down to it, neither Junior nor I could do anything right away for Jacobs. He had no choice, after three days of repairs and tests in which the Earth tug checked out perfectly, but to bid us a cheerful adieu and herd the two Earthers back to the home planet.

"I'll see you guys again, I hope," he said with that puppy grin.

"We hope, too, Mike," I said, shaking his hand solemnly. "We'll do everything we can to get you back out here."

"You planning on coming back yourself, Whitey?" he asked with mild surprise. By then he knew my profession, and my inclinations to be away from where the action was.

"Well," I said, "I may not be back out here, but that doesn't mean that I won't be trying to do a little politicking."

Jacobs nodded and turned to Junior. "It's been a pleasure, little buddy," he said, "whether or not we get together again."

Then he was gone, crossing over to the Earth tug. Junior backed our boat off as soon as Jacobs was in the hatch of the other vessel. Ten minutes later, from ten kilometers away, it sprouted brightness and warped out on its big CRF plume.

Junior took me back to SOS as soon as the Earth tug cleared orbit. This was a decision I'd made some time ago. My detailed report to Ogumi was finished and sent, and I was to return to SpaceHome on the next scheduled inbound boat. But that was three weeks away. I'd professed a strong desire to wait at SOS rather than at I-Base, if Pop, Mom and Junior would put me up. They'd seemed genuinely delighted at the prospect.

The three weeks went quickly enough. I learned the SOS operation, peered through telescopes, and took pictures with various instruments; at night I played bridge with Mom, Pop and Junior. And the little gnome began to teach me the rudiments of piloting and orbital dynamics. I was pleasantly surprised at how quickly I picked it up—even though Junior was wont to wax sarcastic when I forgot some obscure detail of lore from a previous session. By the third week, he'd rigged Pandora as a simulator, and had me landing on RCS and CRF in every size of gravity well from Hyperion to Earth. After learning the art, I only "bent the boat" a few times.

One of those times was in a simulated one-G field.

"Well," said Junior with an appraising twinkle in his eye, "it wasn't *too* bad. You could've walked away from it, anyway—which is more than *I* could have done." He flexed a nonexistent arm muscle.

I locked the board and looked at him. "So why don't you come live in the Colonies, Junior? You can start in one of the spokes in 'Home III and work your way slowly down to .3 G—develop some real muscles to match your brain."

He looked out the viewport where the Old Man was hanging, a toy right next to the window—or a giant millions of kilometers away. "Naw. I'm not cut out to be a city boy, Dimp. I'd probably go crazy from people-phobia inside a month." He looked away from the 'port and back into my eyes. "Why don't *you* come live out *here*? Enjoy the wide open spaces for a change." I sensed hope in his voice, a hunger for companionship that I'm sure he didn't even realize he was projecting. Reluctantly, I shook my head.

"I can't, Junior. I don't have any skills to pay my way out here. I'd just be a hanger-on."

"Who cares?"

"I do. I'm not very much a man of the world, but I have a little bit of pride. I could never live as a charity case."

He nodded slowly. "Yeah. I know that. A man with your depth . . . guess I'll have to wait a while."

Now he was talking in riddles. "Depth?" I said incredulously. "You're blowing smoke rings, Junior. Depth is one thing that I seem to have a sad lack of, or I wouldn't be out here in the first place."

"Doesn't matter what got you out here in the first place, Admiral. Fact is, you've got more character in your little finger than most people show their whole lives. And that's what'll return you here, and make you itch to cast around and see what there is to see. You're going to go back to the Colonies and find 'em just a little too small for you now."

He had me totally bemused. "How can you know all that when I don't know it myself, Wonder Boy?"

He smiled. "I just do, Whitey. You'll be back. C'mon, let's take Pandy in; it's almost supper time."

When he said "you'll be back," there was confidence in his voice—but it was laced with wistfulness. I was definitely in sympathy with that. I didn't know what made Junior take to me so strongly, but whatever it was went in both directions. He was the first human being I'd met in many, many years who I could call "friend" without reservation.

The pleasant hours with Junior were interspersed occasionally with darker ones spent alone—usually lying in bed before falling asleep at night. Sometimes the mental processes were of such force as to keep me awake longer than I wished. During that hiatus between one life and another, I came to some pretty grim conclusions. Ogumi, and probably Buffington—and come to think of it, probably everyone else involved—knew exactly what they were sending me into. It struck me forcefully that my prime qualification for being sent on the mission wasn't my unattached status, but rather my ignorance of many facets of Earth-SpaceHome antagonism—and of the potential danger to my person. And it also occurred to me, one self-flagellating night, that another prime consideration might have been that I was rather amenable to high-level persuasion; I'd been easily maneuvered into making the commitment to undertake the venture.

My thinking also led me to the inevitable conclusion that the "accident" of the cable separation was almost certainly not that at all. It had been a deliberate attempt to prevent my departure on the scheduled tug, so as to gain Earth the time to mount an expedition. That chain also led to the inexorable deduction that someone high in Ogumi's counsels—presumably on the Space-Home board of directors—was an informer being paid, or in sympathy with, at least one of the giant Earth cartels. I was vaguely aware that encrypted commercial data flowed at all hours between the Colonies and various Earth concerns; so messages and instructions could have passed back and forth in short order between the time my morning departure for the Hub was set up, and the time I actually began the cable traverse.

I am very fond of my life and I shuddered again at the memory of that awful quarter-hour in which I'd battled fear and panic. I suppose it didn't matter to the saboteur whether or not I was killed—as long as I was prevented from leaving with the tug. Looking back on it, I wondered at my own naiveté that I could pass it off as an accident. The events in which I was involved were simply too important, too far-reaching, to admit of coincidence as a factor in that "accident."

All ruminations along these lines served to fuel my anger at Ogumi. True, even he couldn't foresee that Cornwallis would be in charge of the Earth expedition and would threaten our lives so callously—but I could see now that he certainly must have considered the possibility. In my own eyes, Ogumi was perhaps just as villainous an actor in the drama as Cornwallis—and perhaps worse. The SpaceHome president had been aware of my character and took advantage of it to the full; whereas Cornwallis' act was relatively straightforward—execrable, but straightforward. But now Cornwallis was paying, and would continue to pay, for his actions. So what about Ogumi? Could he be made to atone for using me as he did?

The evening before leaving SOS to head back to I-Base, I aired some of these thoughts to the Badilles and put forth the idea that I might have a knock-down drag-out with the president when I returned to 'Home III.

Pop looked sad, with a faraway expression, as he slowly shook his head. "I met Mr. Ogumi once, Dimp. I'd been chosen as the SOS team leader, and he was the junior SpaceHome board member in charge of administering the project. He gave me a going-away party and was there to see me off." He smiled at Mom. "That was two days after I'd chosen you as my associate, Aurie—remember?"

She nodded as he continued: "He struck me as being a very forceful man, and one I'd hate to get on the bad side of. Since then I've followed his career with some interest." It was my turn to nod understanding. Life was serene but lonely on SOS; and the bi-weekly news summary squealed in from I-Base was read word-by-word by all three—all four since I'd been there. Pop continued:

"He seems to be all the bad things that you call him: sneaky, self-serving, and apt to use others coldly to gain his ends." He carefully took a sip of orange juice from the open-ended glass he insisted on using instead of the universal low-G squeeze bottle (I'd tried it once, and spent half an hour cleaning up the mess). "But there are two things you must keep in mind before making up your mind to act rashly. First, Mr. Ogumi's principal priority is the independence of the SpaceHome Colonies. As far as I can discern, every act he's performed in office has been toward that end, no matter how its immediate purpose is construed. He's done well; perhaps his single-mindedness is the best thing the Space-Home Corporation could have found during this generation."

He blinked mild eyes at me. "And, however distasteful his behavior might seem to you, the chances approach certainty that this episode has forwarded his cause—and therefore that of the Colonies."

"Yes, but what if I'd failed?" I asked. "Failure could just as easily have been the outcome of the expedition. Junior's a superb pilot—and I'll even grant that Ogumi might know of his skills—but the fact that we prevailed nevertheless is due to a rather low probability sequence of events."

Pop smiled at me. "Perhaps you think less of yourself than does the president, Dimp," he said. "And you might consider this: It is quite possible that Mr. Ogumi could have used your very defeat, somehow, to advantage. As a matter of fact, it would be very unlike the man not to have thought out both sides of such a situation—no matter how distasteful you might find that personally."

I shook my head, unable to speak. Pop continued, gently but remorselessly: "And the second thing, Dimp, is that Mr. Ogumi is a master at handling confrontation. He prefers to charm adversaries into submission; but if you approach him antagonistically, he will certainly attempt to put you down without mercy. He is quite well versed in both techniques and you will find him very difficult to deal with." He looked quite seriously into my eyes. "Do you think you can handle such an adversary?"

I glanced over to Junior. By that time I could read his face well enough to know when he disagreed with something Pop had said. But that *just so* smile and that certain eyebrow set were not in evidence. Instead, the little man floated himself across the conversation pit, stood directly in front of me, and peered carefully into my eyes.

"It's not there yet," he announced, shaking his head.

"What the devil are you talking about, Junior?" I asked.

He didn't answer; he merely added a smile to the head shake. "Listen, Admiral, you're a good man—and you've come a long way in a month or so. And Ogumi might not chew you into little pieces—but he'll sure as hell take a couple of very large chunks out of your hide. Maybe you ought to sleep on it some more. . . ."

The next day we left for I-Base. During my three-week stay at SOS we'd gone "over the top" of Saturn (watching through the telescope from three and a half million kilometers somehow wasn't quite the same) and were now only about a week from passing behind Iapetus as it spun through its descending node. I did some rough figuring on a slate while the SOS tug went through stomach-wrenching checkouts.

"Thirty hours at one-tenth?" I asked.

Junior cackled. "Close enough, Admiral. Add a couple for the Kentucky slew factor and you're right on the money. We'll teach you some arithmetic yet."

We landed at I-Base and Junior stayed to see to the loading of the provisions needed at SOS while I went to beg a shower from Reynolds. By the time I finished and made it back to the staging area, Junior was waiting, ready to go. He was suited with helmet off.

"Gotta pull up stakes, Admiral."

"Sure you don't want to stay until I leave, Junior? It's only another day."

"Naw. Long goodbyes suck canal water." He looked hard into my eyes a final time. "Besides, you'll be back."

"I don't know, Junior. I'm not the adventuresome type. Comforts of home, and all that."

"Rot. You're going to find that 'home' got a little more cramped while you were gone."

"Well . . ."

"Anyway, you've got a standing invitation at SOS. And next time we'll do a south polar traverse. Seeing those backlit rings, with the shadows on the Old Man, is worth stretching your legs for."

I smiled around a sudden lump in my throat. "Maybe I will, Junior. But God knows when; tourists are rare out here, and the round trip fare is heavy."

"Quit shovelin' cow patties, Dimp," he said. "Won't be any time at all before they'll be needing good men out here to wrestle with the Giant—and you're a qualifier." He reached up with a gloved hand and rubbed his generous nose. "All you have to do is decide to come. The rest'll take care of itself." He took my hand; his grip was that of a child. "So long, Admiral."

And then he was into the airlock, sealing his helmet as he drifted through the hatch. The lump was still in my throat. I wondered if I'd ever see him again.

8

The yearly personnel carrier arrived from the Hub
twelve hours later. It brought fifty-six rookies; the smiles
on their faces were undoubtedly due to the new experience of the low-G surface—and perhaps due to the fat
bonus check freshly deposited in their bank accounts
back in Earth system. The vessel also brought a brand
new encryption key under very tight security. I followed
the frowning messenger right into Reynolds' office, and
as soon as the I-Base manager signed for the software I
urged him to get it processed through the comm shack.
I had a message I wanted to get off to Ogumi before I
left for Earth.

The message was a long one, but the communications
specialist sent it off without complaint. It seemed most
of I-Base had learned the real story of the Iron Maiden
affair, and to my embarrassment I was regarded as
something of a hero among the local personnel.

In the message, I urged Ogumi to use what negotiating powers he had to get one Michael Jacobs transferred to SpaceHome on the pilot's roster. I explained that

he was an excellent pilot capable of withstanding high-gravity maneuvering, and that he was quite disenchanted with Earth and willing to emigrate. I also detailed some of Junior's virtues—as a potential research team member, not pilot. It was important to me to get that message off as soon as possible, because I figured Ogumi would act right away if he thought it was in Space-Home's best interest. But after I got back and had it out with him, my word might not carry too much weight anymore.

That done, I went down to the bar and joined the party being thrown for themselves by the fifty-three personnel whose two-year hitch was up and were heading back to Earth system. The rookies were already being instructed in their new jobs by the other half of the contingent who still had a year to go on their hitch. I was welcomed as one of the "oldtimers." True, my tenure hadn't been anywhere near two years; but my accomplishments apparently counted for a lot. Besides, these people were so happy they would have let *anybody* join. I had a few things I wanted to forget, so I really got into it. By the time I'd managed to half-drown my sorrow at leaving Junior, I'd listened to enough what-I'm-going-to-do-when-I-get-back stories to pick up the homesick bug. I was glad to be returning. The dull-but-safe life was made to order for me.

I was lucky to have picked up the personnel carrier for the inbound return; the quarterly supply tug would have taken three months. This boat was much speedier; it started at point one-G and would work up to point three by the time we hit Earth orbit. This flight regime avoided end-of-journey fatigue problems; and it meant that the voyage would be only about three weeks.

But when we punched out the next morning, I was thinking only about how much my head hurt. The on-board PA system didn't help; every few minutes it called out another name to report to the doctor's office. When it came my turn, I got a lot of sympathy:

"Headache? You and half the cargo. It'll go away. Bare your arm."

The nurse took blood, after which the doctor gave me a bottle of large pills. "Calcium," he said to my raised eyebrows. "Didn't you get the outbriefing?"

"No, you see I was—"

"Well, never mind," he said. "Just take one a day until we dock at the Pinwheel. If you need special attention, your blood test will show it. Call in the next one, Dorothy."

I shrugged. It couldn't hurt to take the pills.

Three weeks. I lost seventeen dollars and sixty-five cents. I *never* get good cards at cribbage.

When we finally docked at the Hub, I was more than eager to get back to my routine. I'd had enough excitement to last me for three decades—and by *that* time, I expected to be a venerated sage, beyond mere physical adventure. I'd contacted the university and had received both congratulations and an eager query from my department head. He'd asked me urgently if I'd be able to teach next quarter; Buffington was doing a mediocre job. I accepted with dignity, especially when I found there was a modest increase in salary involved.

Within five minutes after the airlock was attached, the personnel carrier was empty, or at least so I presume. I was one of the first off her and into the Hub.

There were eight of us heading for 'Home III. The trolley wasn't available, so we hooked up to the outbound personnel cable and scooted across in our suits. Seeing and using the now-repaired line brought back bad memories, as expected—but, strangely enough, no shudders of fear. Perhaps time was healing the terror of that day. But the memories did strengthen my resolve to have a showdown with Ogumi. I made up my mind to see him as soon as I got unpacked and freshened up.

But just inside the door of my apartment I was met by a short-term fate-changer. As soon as I'd turned on the lights and put down my kit, I had an armful of woman, with generous breasts and lips crushing into mine. After a generous fifteen seconds, I broke free and stepped back. "Heather! What the hell. Last I knew you were mad enough to roast my hide."

Her eyes spoke volumes in a language I'd never seen her use before. "Whitey. The story's out all over the Colonies about what you did at Saturn—both the official version, and the real one about how you fought the Earthers and beat them out of being the first to reach the artifact, or whatever it was. Oh, Whitey, I'm so proud of you!" The eyes intensified, if that were possible. "And when I found out, I understood why you couldn't say anything before. Please forgive me, darling. I know I was a bitch, but I was so worried!"

I had to smile. She was so eager to win my acceptance, and so afraid that I wouldn't let her.

And from the looks of the negligee she was almost wearing, she was also eager for something else. In spite of the incongruity of the moment, I felt a strong stirring. Uneasily, I reflected that there'd been a hiatus of some eleven or twelve weeks in relieving that certain biological urge.

But apparently relief was only a moment away. Heather had no trouble deciphering my reactions. She lowered her eyelids and glanced toward the bedroom, then back into my eyes. "May I offer you a hero's welcome, sir?"

I took her hand and headed toward the magic place, reflecting that Ogumi could bloody well wait half an hour longer. A hero's welcome, indeed!

I surprised myself. It was more like two hours later when Heather, half guiltily, half impishly, handed me a sealed envelope from the president of the SpaceHome Corporation.

"This came for you about an hour before you got here." She was suddenly coy—another trait which was new to her. "But I thought that if you read it as soon as you got home, you might have neglected some . . . ah . . . more important business."

The note was short and cordial:

Dear Whitey,

As soon as you've settled in, I would appreciate it if you could drop over for an hour or two. Please give my secretary a call when you are coming, and I'll arrange to be free. Hoping to see you soon.

Ogumi

I showered, dressed, called Ogumi's secretary, and headed cross-torus. Heather promised me a feast when I returned. I hoped limply that she was talking about something to eat.

The details of Ogumi's suite were the same, right down to the secretary talking into her voicewriter—but somehow it wasn't quite so imposing. I felt heartened by the realization. And there *was* one slight difference in detail; I noticed it when the secretary looked up and recognized me.

"Dr. Whitedimple!" she gushed. "It's *so* good to see you again! Mr. Ogumi is waiting. Here, let me do that for you." She brushed by me and opened the door. Her voice, eyes, and unnecessary body contact all told me that my reputation had preceded me here, too. The smile she flashed at me promised more than I could accept; I reddened slightly as I walked into the inner office.

Ogumi came out from behind his desk and held out a hand. "Congratulations, Whitey. The artifacts are tucked away in the safe here. That was a brilliant job of . . . ah . . . negotiating." He smiled and winked, then went back around the desk and flipped the intercom switch.

"Andrea, you can call the reporters and photographers up now." Then the smile at me again. "You've really done us proud, Whitey; I'm only sorry that we can't tell the whole story; but it's one that we wouldn't dare try to shove down the throats of the Earth authorities—they'd have to tell lies to the people in order to vindicate their actions."

He was smooth, and it was a great temptation to let it all happen as he wanted. It would be the easiest course, and perhaps even pleasant, if I could get over the embarrassment. But the smile was the slightest shade too calculated, the wink aimed at a younger, more naive Whitedimple. And that thought brought the cable incident and the Iron Maiden battle flooding back into my mind. I gulped once for luck and threw out my first words:

"I'd appreciate it if you would forget the newsmen, Ogumi. I do not wish to be fashioned into a political football."

He gave me that penetrating look. It didn't take him long to decide I was serious; whereupon an extremely annoyed expression settled itself on his face. He flipped the intercom switch again. "Andrea, there's been a change of plans. Try to head off the reporters. Tell them that Dr. Whitedimple wishes to remain out of the spotlight for the moment, and that I'll give them a statement as soon as possible—perhaps half an hour from now."

That was the first time I'd ever seen him peevish. It gave me heart to know I could get through his guard, even though I was apprehensive about what must come. And it wasn't long in coming.

"Well, Dr. Whitedimple, it seems that you and I have different reasons for your being here. Suppose you tell me what's on your mind."

"That cable malfunction was no accident," I began. "I didn't think about it at first, when the technician told me it was a million-to-one shot; but in light of later events, it had to have been deliberate sabotage. And given the timing, that can only mean there's a paid informer or Earth sympathizer on your board of directors. That person notified Earth, and received orders in return to take action to slow the retrieval effort down so Earth could get to Saturn first. I believe you knew this, or at least strongly suspected it—yet you did not recall me from my commitment to go to I-Base, or even inform me of the facts."

He opened his mouth to speak, but I continued firmly; I was working up steam now, and didn't want to be stopped.

"So you let me carry on, dumb and innocent. You *must* have known that Earth was probably mounting an expedition of their own, and that they were fully aware of our own plans and schedule; whereas I was in total ignorance of their intentions.

"So you sent me out there with no useful instructions, to try to resolve a situation which was nearly hopeless. The Earth tug was armed and dangerous, and we came within a hair of losing our lives. If it hadn't been for a fluke" (I didn't mention Junior's name) "we would have come home with nothing and been a laughing stock—or worse, been killed and listed as missing without anybody important caring one damn for our carcasses."

I had to stop for a moment, then, to take a breath or two. My volume had been increasing, and loud talk saps the wind. Besides, I'd just about gotten it off my chest. I was sweating, but my voice hadn't broken.

"Are you through now, Dr. Whitedimple?" asked Ogumi. "Good," he continued without waiting for me to reply. "Because now I have a few things to say. First of all, yes, most of the things you said were correct. I had suspected for some time that there was an informer for Earth on the SpaceHome board of directors. And the incident of the cable pinpointed her. She had to move a little too quickly to set it up, and was careless."

I opened my mouth, but he held up a hand. "It was nothing that could be proven. That reprehensible act against your person was crafted—and most cleverly so, I must admit—to make it appear accidental. Given a reasonably competent defense attorney, no jury would ever pronounce guilt on either the esteemed former member of the board or her accomplice."

He fixed my eye. "Yes, I said 'former.' Both are enjoying a heavy schedule of exercises in the one-G centrifuge and will be shipped to Earth within the week. I suspect they will live out short, uncomfortable lives there."

He put his fingertips together. "So what was I to do then? Admit that Earth had scared us and call the whole thing off?"

"Well," I said, "you might have postponed my departure and sent me later on a better-equipped expedition. Perhaps even an armed one, since the Earthers had made clear their intentions."

"To what purpose, Dr. Whitedimple? Any such expedition would have taken weeks to organize. By the time it would have arrived at Saturn, Earth would have been there before us and snatched the prize. In fact, I'm sure that's exactly what they were hoping we would decide to do after the cable sabotage." He shook his head. "No, Dr. Whitedimple; I had no real choice but to go on with the original plan. And, after some thought, I decided not to worry you unnecessarily with my deductions. It was not very polite of me, I know; but given your reluctance to go in the first place, and knowing our time constraint, what else could I do?"

I cleared my throat. "Well, I think—"

He butted back in before I could get half a sentence out: "I haven't finished yet, Dr. Whitedimple. That was a rhetorical question, and it had only one answer. I had many factors to consider, the principal one of which was that you were the only candidate whatsoever with *any* reasonable qualifications for the job. Another was that you were quite likely to have backed out if told the whole truth—so I couldn't afford the luxury of telling you. One does not sit in this chair by sparing the rod and spoiling the child."

The insult wasn't very well concealed, and I stiffened. "I still think you might have announced the find publicly and offered a joint expedition from the start."

"Dr. Whitedimple, are you fully aware of the economic implications of this series of artifacts and what they might lead to?" The hand came up again. "Don't answer; that was another rhetorical question. I know I talked to you briefly about the subject before, but I doubt that it sunk in very deeply." Another insult. I reddened, but he didn't give me an opportunity to retort.

"I ask you now to consider the economic position of the SpaceHome Colonies with respect to Earth. We have fundamental resources, but they are few in number compared to those available Earthside. And until we undertake considerably more development of the riches the solar system has to offer, we will be relatively poor in many substances needed to guarantee our independent survival and quality of life.

"We are also woven with complex entanglements with Earth combines and cartels. These form a Gordian knot we dare not cut in the fashion of young Alexander; we must unravel it cleanly to extricate ourselves. Nevertheless, we must do it rapidly, because of the growing estrangement between ourselves and the Earthers."

He fixed me with the ten-kilovolt stare. "I cannot be sure we will win clear in time, Whitey. In fact, I cannot even venture to make book on our chances for success. Perhaps fifty-fifty. If things go badly enough, if feelings grow strong enough for several governments or cartels Earthside to combine forces against us, our tale will be done. The economic bases of SpaceHome will be split like a pie in the sky. Almost all of the major operations will be a hundred percent automated—our computers and robots are quite sophisticated enough to do that—and most of the colonists will be shipped to Earth to live out their lives. Earth will give up the long-term advantages of the Colonies for short-term economic gain, and they will do it with a vengeance.

"Fifty-fifty are not odds that I enjoy contemplating, Whitey. Anything to give us an edge must be welcomed with open arms. And that certainly describes this incredible series of finds. Any new technology described, or even hinted at, by the aliens who left those artifacts could mean the difference in SpaceHome's survival. And all of my actions have flowed from that consideration since the discovery on Iapetus."

He let his face relax into a smile. "And besides, Whitey, you passed the tests that mattered; two times you came through in the pinch. I must admit that I'm pleased and gratified, even though I'd noticed a potential in you—a potential which apparently even you did not realize you possessed."

I almost took the bait; Ogumi held it in front of me *so* enticingly. Then I remembered Pop's words about how the SpaceHome president preferred to charm his adversaries into submission. I stiffened, and Ogumi's smile slowly melted as I replied:

"However gratifying your words, the fact remains that you deliberately put my life into danger without my knowledge or consent. That is an act which cannot be forgiven or dismissed with words. I think you are self-serving and underhanded, and I shall never support your manipulation of me to your own ends."

"So?" he said through tight lips. "Very well. I accept your opinion of me, Dr. Whitedimple. I will make every effort to insure that you do not have to come into contact with me again. Your further involvement in the current aspects of this affair shall be downplayed as you wish, and you shall take no part in events yet to transpire. Go back to your teaching and be as happy as you can. Good day, sir."

He flipped the intercom switch and began talking to his secretary, forcing me to retreat without a further word.

On the breezeway across to the elevator, I took stock. My objectives for the interview, which I suppose were to vent my spleen on Ogumi and have him beg forgiveness, were only half accomplished. And the half was poorly done, at that: If my condemnations bothered Ogumi at all, he didn't show it. My major victory was to make him look slightly bad in the reporters' eyes. The cost for that was burning all bridges behind me; I had an uneasy feeling in the pit of my stomach about being so completely severed from the artifact retrieval effort.

Heather helped for a while. When I got home she was putting the finishing touches on a sumptuous-smelling dinner. "Oh, Whitey; I'm glad you're back so soon. Now we can have a leisurely meal before I have to report to the hospital."

Over beef (*expensive* beef) Bourguignon and broccoli, I told Heather about the interview. Edited tastefully, of course, to make Ogumi look *slightly* worse and myself *slightly* better—I admit to a modicum of emotional vanity. Nevertheless, all the facts came out. And Heather was totally gratified with the results.

"Oh, Whitey, I'm *so* glad you won't be leaving again! You've got the best of everything right now; you're famous among your friends, and even throughout the Colonies. And you get to live on that glory—and you've earned it!—without having to risk your neck on those long-distance trips any more. I'd be worried *sick* if you had to go away again, now that I know what it's all about, with those awful Earthers trying to do you in and all. I think I'd just curl up and die!"

She kept it up, ebullient, even while putting on her uniform and makeup for work. My mind was wandering by the time I kissed her goodbye. After she left I stood by the door, staring at nothing in particular. My mind was 20,000 miles above the north polar cloudtops of the Old Man. I wondered if the memory of that sight would be enough to last a lifetime.

The next day I dropped into the office of Dr. Abbot Theodore Smith—head of the SHU department of history, and my once and future boss.

"Hello, Ted."

"Whitey!" he shouted joyfully, coming around the desk and grabbing my hand. "The prodigal returns. Martha! Bring out that fatted calf we've been saving!" His secretary leaned around the doorway and blew me a second kiss. The first had been on the lips, thirty seconds previously.

"I must tell you, Whitey," the man continued after we'd sat down to business, "that I was a little upset about you leaving so suddenly and having Buffington sit in for you for the final three weeks of the quarter." He smiled. "Then I got an invitation from Ogumi himself to come to his office. He told me in strict confidence that you were off on extremely important SpaceHome business and asked me to forgive the interruption of your services to the university."

I smiled and bet to myself that Ogumi'd layed it on thick.

"Then, when we got the news a month and a half ago about what had happened out at Saturn, it all came together." He shot a shrewd glance at me. "Say, what really did happen? The official version is in all the papers and newscasts, but you wouldn't believe some of the word-of-mouth stories going around. Did you really have to fight 'em off?"

I thinned my smile. "I'm afraid we'll have to stick with the official version, Ted."

He looked disappointed, but nodded. "I thought you'd have to say that, Whitey, and I understand. But if there's ever a time when you feel like talking, I'd sure like to be there to listen.

"Anyway," he continued, "we're damned glad to have you back. Buffington's a good teacher, but he's out of his depth when he gets away from anthropology." He looked at me somewhat sharply. "You aren't planning any followups to this, I hope?"

I shook my head. "No plans. None whatsoever."

"Good," he said, relaxing. Then, ingenuously: "Do you have any plans for training a successor?—not that you'll need one for twenty years or so, Whitey—but I'd hate to have to take archaeology off the curriculum in case something happened. We'd lose points with the certification authority. Besides," he continued, "if you could find someone in the next year or so to share your teaching duties, I could use you as assistant department head to take some of this load off me."

I looked at him carefully. He was serious; I was gratified. I constructed my answer slowly: "That's very generous of you, Ted. Unfortunately, the colony kids seem to take no lasting interest in archaeology, since it's so Earth-oriented." I smiled. "Which is not a new subject with us, is it?"

He nodded. "Yes, we've used up a few beers moaning about that one, haven't we? But is there an answer?"

"Maybe we could recruit a youngster from Earth," I

said. "Surely there must be someone down there—even in my field—who has an itch for the high ground."

He nodded. "See what you can do for us, would you Whitey?" Then he visibly relaxed. "Okay, so tell me what Iapetus Base was really like. . . ."

I left an hour later. A pleasant hour. I was to start teaching again at the beginning of next quarter, with a seven percent increase in honorarium. My professional affairs were firmly back on track.

9

"... thus, to summarize—wake up Mr. Bach! You're going to need this for the exam—the Minoan civilization was named for King Minos of Crete, and flourished through the Bronze Age from 3000 to 1200 BC. Nearly the sum total of our archaeological knowledge of the Minoan has been derived from the palace at Cnossus. The evidence is that it developed from a simple culture with pictograph writing into a very complex one with linear writing. During its final century it declined rapidly, as the Aegean cultural torch passed to Troy and the Greek mainland. That's all, class. Remember, the finals will be in the history lecture hall on Wednesday. Good luck."

I sighed as the large class filed out of the room. I thought the quarter would never end. I'd been gratified at first to find that enrollment had nearly doubled for Archaeology 101. Normally, the students put it off until junior or senior year; but when my name had appeared as instructor, I found that freshmen and sophomores signed up in droves. I'd expanded from two classes to four and still had to turn applicants away.

But, naturally, the students weren't there to learn archaeology. They wanted to know about the battle of the Iron Maiden, and when we would find the Hexies—as the alien depositors of the artifacts were coming to be called. When the kids found out that I wasn't going to turn my classroom into storytelling hour, interest waned to the normal level of boredom.

I'd relented from this policy once, about a month into the term, and described the race from Enceladus to the Iron Maiden across the north surface of the ring plane. The class was spellbound for the entire half hour I took to tell the story. Those youngsters were really a group of starry-eyed romantics. I wondered what they'd have thought of me if I'd told them about my fears and vacillations during the episode—or if I'd told them about the generalized boredom of space travel.

Absent-mindedly, I packed my briefcase and wandered to my office; I was mentally comparing the boredom of planetary travel with the interspersed moments of fear and wonder. Quite without thinking about it, when I got back to the office I punched my bank code to check the balance in my account. Eight thousand six hundred thirty-four dollars plus change, which included a generous bonus from SpaceHome Corporation "for special services." (Ogumi was no piker, whatever else his faults.) Enough for two people to spend a week in a lunar tourist resort. Big deal.

Then I punched up the commercial phone directory and found "Pilot Training Courses." There were only two listings. I punched in the first one.

"Lomax School."

"Hello, I'm interested in finding out your rates for training for a license."

"One moment please. I'll connect you with Mr. Lomax."

"This is Lomax. What can I do for you?"

"Hello, this is Dr. Whitedimple, and I'm interested in finding out how long and how much it would take to obtain a pilot's license."

"We can have you through in about three months, Dr. Flytimple. Our standard fee is twelve hundred dollars; that

takes you through soloing and certifies you for unlimited travel within the three-hundred-kilometer radius of Colony space."

"Do you have a more complete program with CRF instruction, planetary landings, and so forth?"

"Sorry, buddy. We aren't licensed for deep-space teaching. But we do have a special this week for the local license. Twenty percent off, which gets you through the course for one thousand dollars."

"Thank you anyway; I'm not interested. Goodbye."

I dialed the other number.

"Sam Sebastian."

"Hello, this is Dr. Kurious Whitedimple. I'm interested in finding out if you can give licenses for deep-space pilots."

"You sure you don't mean a local license? Qualifies you for Colony space. It's one thousand and seventy-five dollars. Includes twenty hours of solo time."

"I'm really interested in an unlimited license."

"Say, did I catch your name right? Aren't you the guy who—"

"That's me."

"Why don't you come over to the office, and we'll talk about it over a beer?"

Sam Sebastian was a small man with blond-white hair and a generous moustache. He didn't look anything at all like Mike Jacobs—yet somehow he reminded me of him. I think it was the air of self-possession, the confidence in his ability to take in stride anything that life had to offer. I liked him almost immediately, which was unusual for me. A first beer blended into a second.

". . . because CRF time is so expensive, Whitey. Nine out of ten people who start through here are SpaceHome Corporation sponsorees. I run 'em through class and flight training in about a year, and use SpaceHome boats for CRF training. I charge 'em six thousand dollars a head." He took a swallow. "But for the occasional freelancer who comes through, I've got to pay rent to SpaceHome for CRF time, buy the fuel and pay the delta insurance costs. So I've got to charge ten thousand five hundred. You still interested?"

"Maybe. Sam, I'll be frank. I've got less than nine thousand dollars on hand. How do you feel about time payments?"

He looked at me; I think he liked me, too. "I'll tell you how it works, Whitey. We've got five washout points: navigation computer class finals; traffic regulations and procedures finals; onboard maintenance and repair; RCS piloting; and CRF piloting. Each class we lose fifty, sixty percent who can't make it through all five checkpoints. I'll start you through; what you do is pay me in advance to the next checkpoint. That'll be one thousand a shot for the three ground classes, two thousand for RCS and five for CRF."

"Bad arithmetic, Sam. That only adds up to ten thousand."

"Whitey, if you make it through to CRF, I'll kick in the last five hundred for saving our bacon out there on the Iron Maiden."

"What are you talking about, Sam?"

"Listen, pal. Charlie Broughton's a good friend of mine. I got him pie-faced last New Year's Eve and he told me the whole thing."

"Who's Charlie Broughton?"

"The guy who was working the Hub comm shack when Ogumi began sending messages to you. He coded the outbounds and decoded yours coming back. Already knew about the artifact, since he'd been on duty when the original find came in from I-Base."

He grinned. "By the time your preliminary report finally came in, he'd been over thirty hours in the hole, but he wouldn't let his shift-relief take over until the situation was decided one way or the other." He took another pull. "Everybody who had encryption clearances was hanging around in the shack by then. Somebody—must have been the director of communications, since he's the only one with enough pull—had put through a coded link to I-Base and they were getting updates every ten minutes from the Saturn navsats.

Had the whole thing up on the big screen, with computers plotting the movements of the two boats—just like a damn war room! When you took off from Enceladus . . ."

As Sam talked, I got seriously red. He was opening up a brand new bag of emotional worms for me. I'd supposed that only two or three people, at the most, outside of the SpaceHome board had direct positive knowledge of the Iron Maiden events. And now, months after the fact, I was learning a larger truth. But if Sam noticed I was blushing, he probably attributed it to the second beer I was drinking.

". . . all taking bets on the outcome. Most of the money was against you and Badille, since the Earth boat had high-G capability. But when the final story came in, the losers cheered just as loud as the winners." He shook his head. "Boy, that Junior Badille guy must be some kind of pilot! Wish I could meet him."

"You'll have to go to Saturn to do that, Sam. But you're right about him being some kind of pilot."

"Too bad," he said. "But there's just Joe and me to run this school; and Joe doesn't have a teaching certification for CRF. And I got two kids to put through college—hell, they'll probably have you for a teacher in a couple of years."

"They'll be bored," I said. "My classes are even starting to bore *me*."

"Boy, you must have it bad, Whitey," he said.

"Beg pardon?"

"The itch. You've got a bad case. Bored with life at home. Willing to put out ten grand for a license. Faraway look in your eye whenever you mention the outer system. Classic case." He tossed back the remains in his glass. "So. You want to start with the next class? Begins in two weeks and runs a year and a month. Lots of hard work, and no mercy if you screw up. We don't give licenses to anybody who doesn't earn 'em."

"I guess I will, Sam. At least I've got to find out how far I can go."

"Yep," he nodded. "You got it all right. Okay, Whitey. Bring the first thousand in on the first night you report.

Here's the schedule for the nav classes. See you two weeks from Monday."

"Thanks," I said. "And you did say something about maintenance and repair classes. I'll learn how to, uh, tinker with the engines and such?"

"Old man, by the time Joe and I are through with you, you'll be able to take a CRF boat apart and put it back together again, in zero G, in the dark—or else you'll be washed out. . . ."

"Whitey. You're two hours late." She kissed me perfunctorily. "And there's alcohol on your breath."

I told her what I'd done.

"I thought you were saving that money to make a down payment on a plot of land on 'Home VII. You told me just last month it would be much more lively living over there!"

"I'm making a better salary now, Heather. I can replace the money almost as fast as I make the installments."

"But why in the world would you want a pilot's license?" she pouted. "You know Mr. Ogumi will never let you hire on as a pilot, and SpaceHome Corporation is the only outfit who needs deep-space pilots. It seems like a waste of money!"

"Learning something new is never a waste, Heather."

"But this . . . say, you *are* still on the outs with Mr. Ogumi, aren't you?" She fixed me with her "lie detector" look. "Is there something you're not telling me?"

"No, Heather," I said. "There's no hidden purpose, and no agreement with Ogumi. I just want very badly to learn a new skill. I'm over forty years old and I can feel my brain rusting."

"But still, ten thousand dollars. . . ."

I finally quieted her down by emphasizing that the first three series of classes were only a thousand apiece, and that there was a possibility that I could flunk any one of them and have to quit, anyway. I let her think I was more interested in the academic portion of the course and would probably not get into the actual piloting, which came much later. Cowardice, of course—but you have to know Heather.

I was dragging and elated. Dragging because archaeology during the day and navigation classes at night made somewhat of a dent in my energy. Elated because the results of the finals were posted and I'd scored highest in the class of twelve; two flunked out.

Heather met me at the door with a worried look. "A letter came in from the Hub." I suppose that could only have meant trouble as far as she was concerned. I didn't know what it meant, so I merely assumed a studied, puzzled look and accepted the sealed envelope.

I opened it, looked immediately at the printed signature, and smiled. "It's from Junior Badille," I said.

"Oh, that little man who was your pilot during the battle?"

"Yes," I said, scanning the message. "He's joined SART. Working for the engineering design group. Having a good time."

"How nice of him to write," she said, losing interest and heading for the bedroom to don her uniform.

I'd read everything I could about the Saturn Artifact Retrieval Team, so I was aware of what Junior had walked into. It had started as a joint Earth-SpaceHome venture; then Earth had pulled out, citing economic reasons. Speculation was that the gambit had been intended to split the SpaceHome board and cause its financial backing to dissolve, while several Earth interests had pooled resources and were mounting an expedition of their own. Ogumi had somehow staved off disaster, replaced the two board members who'd walked out and continued SART with corporation R&D funds. The SART had collected resources at I-Base for about three months, then set up permanent operations on Mimas a few weeks ago.

I read the message three times. It was edited, as all things coming from Saturn, to omit any indication of how far along the work was. But Junior's style came through clearly enough to make me homesick to see him.

Apparently Ogumi hadn't name-requested him to join the SART project; so about a week after they'd set up operations on Mimas, he just took his boat and dropped in on them. I could imagine their surprise—and, given the caliber of talent that must be aggregated on Mimas, I could also imagine that it hadn't taken too much time for them to recognize Junior's worth as a team member. He knew as much about Saturn as any man alive and could probably function brilliantly in any discipline he put his mind to. I wondered fondly how long it would be until he had them all under his thumb.

I made a resolution to get friendly with someone in the Hub comm shack. I felt a need, perhaps at some future date, to be able to communicate freely with Junior. Nothing definite, just a vague feeling.

"Hey, Heather, let's go over to the gym today and work up a good sweat. We're both getting soft."

"I know a better way than going to the gym," she said archly, and waggled her eyebrows at me.

"C'mon, it'll be good for us."

"So will the other," she said. Then, rubbing my too-soft stomach, "Besides, I *like* you this way."

"Yeah, but *I* don't like me this way."

She stepped back and looked at me appraisingly. "Well, you go ahead if you want to. Alice invited me to go shopping, anyway, and I need a new purse."

I took the elevator up to the hub, then suited up and used the personnel cable to zip down to the Hub. Out of habit, during the traverse I visually checked on the construction of 'Home VII. The SART effort had slowed progress of the Monster, as it was coming to be called; but it was far enough along now that Earth investors had begun to help foot the bill. It had maybe two and a half years to completion. It was almost a commercial enterprise, now; about one-third of the vast acreage had been bought up by Earth speculators and they were reselling it to individual Earthers—medium rich ones, of course—for retirement or summer homes. "Your 'Home Away from Home" was the way the Earther advertising

slogans billed it. And even though anti-Colony senti-
ment was building higher on Earth, there were still
plenty of starry-eyed folks down there willing to pay
three hundred thousand for a tenth-hectare and a two-
hundred-square-meter house.

The Cube was right next to 'Home III in the Pinwheel,
so once in the HUB it was just a couple of hundred
meters to the 'Home I cable table. I'd fortuitously
timed my trip to coincide with that of an outbound
trolley, so I climbed aboard and shared the ride with
a dozen passengers and about two tons of fresh fruit
and vegetables.

All of the other passengers, with the exception of the
cargo master, were Earthers. Their medical insurance
companies required them to live in the lower levels of
the Cube if they were going to visit here for over six
months. Reason: The Cube was the only one of the
Colonies that could provide high G.

The Cube was the first of the Lagrangian colonies to
be built, over two generations ago. It was originally
designed to be spun up to one G at the outer skin. But
by the time they were ready to "bend metal" on the
project, the long-term medical data were finally in:
Man didn't really need a one-G environment to function
and survive indefinitely—a third was plenty. But they
went ahead and built it to the original specs anyway.
You'd understand if you had ever been involved in a
massive DDT&E operation; it was cheaper to throw the
extra weight into orbit and overbuild it than to go
through the labor-intensive process of redesign, development, test and evaluation.

So it was overbuilt and spun up at .3 G. Then, a
generation later when 'Homes II, III and IV had been
built, it was spun further up to one G to accommodate
the short-timers. By definition, a short-timer is a person
who comes to SpaceHome for any reason and intends to
eventually return to Earth. By this standard, even ten
years is a short time; intentions are everything.

"Short-timer" worked the other way around, too. If,
for any reason, a colonist intended to visit Earth, it was

a smart idea—especially if that person wanted medical insurance coverage to extend throughout the visit and for several years thereafter—to live in the Cube for at least several months beforehand, gradually moving his apartment from the inner layers to the outer skin. I was familiar with this process, since I'd been through it some twenty years ago. I'd hated it, and had hated Earth even more. When my researches were over and I came back to 'Home III, I'd vowed never to darken the Cube's airlock again.

Well, I lied. But it *had* been a long time.

The Cube had fifty-two levels, beginning at about ninety meters from the center of the hub—.3 G—and working out to within a few meters of the skin, whose radius was three hundred. It wasn't the most pleasant of facilities; there were apartments, shops, and entertainments, but little greenery. It sold CO_2 and bought O_2 from the Farm. But it had one facility which drew many of the Colonists: the Gym.

The Gym was a twenty-meter-square plug punching down through all fifty-two levels. Like the rest of the Cube, it also had fifty-two floors. Each floor had some equipment, but the major facilities were located at every seventh or eighth level. There was an elevator which stopped at every level. There was also a stairwell reaching all the way to the bottom. A prominent sign at the head of the stairs proclaimed:

LEVEL 1: ACCELERATION 0.3000 G
If you mass 60 kilograms, every step down adds 40 grams to your weight. If you don't think you can make it back up from where you are going, *take the elevator.* DON'T BE A DEAD HERO!

I looked down the stairwell to the next landing, four meters below. A smaller sign there read: LEVEL 2: ACCELERATION 0.3133 G. I decided not to go down this time. In fact, I began to wonder what I was really trying to prove here. I *loathed* exercise for the sake of exercise.

But just so the trip over wouldn't be wasted, I worked up a good sweat before showering and heading back.

"*. . . current administration has an established position of concurring with the Lagrangian Colonies' SpaceHome Corporation determination to retrieve the Saturn artifact on its own. In fact, fellow Americans, Ms. Penfield is an admitted supporter of the UN decision to back out of the SART project! I ask you to think about what this means. It means that a privately owned company will be heir to a treasure that belongs to all mankind!*

"*And where is the SpaceHome Corporation finding the hundreds of millions of dollars to foot the bill for this adventure? I'll tell you friends—from YOU! They will charge higher prices for their power, fuels and medicines, and YOU will pay! And yet what benefits will you reap? Perhaps none, friends, perhaps none. Wouldn't it be better, even at some cost, to be a part of this adventure? Wouldn't the interests of the country, and of mankind, be better served by making this a universal effort?*

"*And this is not the only mistake the current administration has made in its space policy. Consider our present stand with regard to the construction of the orbiting CRF power reactor. We have provided not one penny of funding—*"

I turned off the holovision. Heather was yawning.

"I wonder how much of that garbage the Earthers swallow?" I said, shaking my head. "I can't believe the general public is ignorant of the fact that at least seven countries and cartels have joined in the so-called 'secret SART' to beat us to the Saturn surface. Hell, the bits and pieces have been leaving Earth orbit for more than a year now, and all bound for the Jovian system—and it sure as hell isn't a coincidence that Jupiter and Saturn will be at conjunction next year. The Earthers have put enough materiel on Callisto to form a major—"

Then I turned *myself* off. Heather was asleep. I couldn't blame her; politics is like baseball: boring unless you know the players and can root for a team.

Sam knocked back the top three fingers of beer in his

glass. "Whitey, I've got to admit, I don't know what to make of it. Old fart like you, coming in all starry-eyed, willing to put up ten grand on a lark—then you totally ace out all those young kids in the ground classes. Then Joe takes you out for your first RCS ride and says you got the best potential of anybody who's come through in the last ten years." He shook his head with grudging admiration. "Says you handled that old tug like a maestro."

"Who's an old fart? Want to arm wrestle for the next beer?"

He looked at me carefully. "Hmm, you do seem to have toughened up a bit. Been going over to the Cube?"

I admitted that I was a regular habitué of the bottom level.

"What in hell for?" he asked.

"Damned if I know, Sam. I just went over one Saturday, then it got to be a regular thing. Some muscle toner stuff, but mostly cardiovascular. Makes me feel good. I get back up here and seem to float around."

He fixed my eyes. "Charlie Broughton says you owe him ten, eleven bucks worth of crib losses. You been hanging around the comm shack bar?"

"Yeah, I usually go there on the way back from the Gym for a beer. Charlie gets good cards, so he likes to find a sucker."

"I understand you and that Badille guy exchange messages every once in a while. So how's the SART thing going?"

"Mostly what you read on the news, plus a few extras Charlie lets me read before editing. They're wrestling with how to make a combination submarine and balloon out of a spaceship, or vice-versa. Junior's right in the thick of it—one of the key designers, in fact. Little guy's got a brain."

Sam's look was friendly, but appraising nonetheless. "You really like that fellow, don't you?"

Now I looked Sam in the eye. "I was with him for about a month. I think he's about the best friend I ever made."

He nodded, then began to talk crisply: "I'm going to come clean with you, Whitey. I've been doin' some nosing around. I've got some connections here and there, so it wasn't too hard for me to find out about the falling out you had with Ogumi. And I think I understand that itch you've got." He poured a second glass for himself and raised his eyebrows at me; I shook my head and showed him my half-full tumbler.

"Now I'm going to tell you my position. I wouldn't be in business without SpaceHome; it supplies me with ninety-five percent of my students. So, theoretically, I shouldn't mess with you and get on the wrong side of Ogumi.

"On the other hand, Ogumi needs me, too. It'd cost him a pretty penny to set up his own school, and it wouldn't begin to pay for itself for eight or nine years—and SpaceHome cash flow's a little tight right now. Besides, Ogumi's not a small man; he wouldn't begrudge me making a buck or two off you."

He wiped a bit of foam off his moustache with a finger. "And on the third hand, Whitey, you've got motivation, and you could be the best pilot we've ever turned out. So it would be a personal crime for me to kick you out. So, what Joe and I are going to do, is accelerate you. If you're willing to spend more evenings at it, Joe can finish you up in two weeks, then I'll certify you for CRF and planetary landings a month after that—presuming you don't wash out, of course."

He looked at me across the rim of his mug. "But I've seen your scores on the simulators, and I don't think you're going to have any trouble. You've paid your two thousand for the RCS work. I'm cutting the charge for CRF to wholesale—four thousand. Can you come up with it in a couple of weeks?"

"Sure Sam, but I've got plenty—"

"Can it, Whitey. The thousand dollars is guilt money, for debating about whether or not to keep you on. Besides, I'm trying to get on your good side. I don't know what you've got in mind, but if it doesn't work out, I'm going to try to recruit you as an instructor pilot. . . ."

* * *

"Dr. John Poingreve, I'd like to introduce you to Dr. Ted Smith. He's our department head and will be your reporting official when you start teaching classes next quarter."

"How do you do, sir. Whit—uh, Dr. Whitedimple has told me a lot about you."

"All bad, I presume? Don't answer that; it was an unfair question. Are you all settled in? Good. Why don't you let Martha get you started with the paperwork, and we'll be out in a moment to take you around. I've got half a minute of business with Whitey."

Martha came in, collected the young man and shut the door behind her on the way out. Smith turned to me: "Think he'll work out?"

"Yes. He's bright, eager, and knows his stuff."

"Good." He looked at me hard. I'd been used to getting hard looks from people recently, so it didn't bother me. "You know, Whitey, it's a good thing that he's here. I thought that after that flurry of early enrollments, archaeology attendance would drop off. Well, it did for a while, then picked up again. 'Fact, I've had reports of more than one student wanting to take more classes in the subject. Been thinking of approaching you to expand the curriculum. So what do you think?"

"Well, yes, I've had a student or two come to me. I figured it was a statistical anomaly. There's bound to be a few pupils in every generation who take a fancy to learning about the hand that held the cuneiform chisel; maybe they're just clustering right now."

"Mmph. Well, I've taken the liberty of eavesdropping on a few of your sessions and I've got a slightly different theory. The fact is, you've actually been making archaeology *interesting*. Been relating past civilizations to present day. Been linking past and current events. Been putting the SpaceHome Colonies into historical perspective—and you've been doing it better than most of the so-called modern history professors I'm blessed with."

"Well, it seems the kids can hold onto the facts better if they can tie them to something in their own environment. But I certainly haven't been trying to step on anyone's—"

"Please, Whitey. I did not mean those remarks to be criticisms of your work. Just the opposite, in fact. I always thought archaeology was a rather dull subject, myself; I'm all for any trick to gin up a little interest."

He fixed me with another stare. "But that's not the whole story, either. Part of it is your own personality. You're reading lectures much better than you used to, if you'll excuse me. You're not as ... well ... *stiff* as you used to be. I'm really looking forward to having you occupy the assistant's chair. Speaking of which, perhaps you'd like to attend the president's dinner for department heads with me next Sunday? It'll probably be a dull affair as usual, and it wouldn't hurt to introduce a little new blood into the group."

"Damn, Ted, now you've embarrassed me. I'm scheduled to solo on CRF tomorrow. The instructor pilot went through hell to get me that time slot."

A moment of silence—just a very brief one—then: "No problem, Whitey; there'll be plenty of time to insert you into SHU politics. Y'know, I didn't realize you were still in that pilot training program. Don't tell me you're changing specialties at this late date?" The worried undertone was obvious.

"Well, Ted, I started it as just an intellectual exercise, to stretch the old brain; then it got to be a matter of pride to try and finish the whole course—turned into one of those things." I smiled as ingenuously as I could. "Anyway, the brain-stretching did seem to have some beneficial spinoffs, if what you said about the caliber of my teaching is true. . . ."

She: [anxiously] C'mon, Whitey, you've got to get ready to go to the show; it starts at eight thirty, and you *promised!*

He: [distractedly] Just a second, Heather; I'm catching the end of this speech. It's the director of the Chino-Arab Power Consortium.

She: [agitatedly, switching off holovision] Kurious

Whitedimple, what is it with you? Pilot training, exercising over to the Cube every day, hanging around the Hub comm shack, depleting your savings sending messages to that Junior fellow way out at Saturn, reading books on the outer planets and mooning with a faraway look in your eyes, grumbling about Ogumi all the time! It's not that you don't pay any attention to me any more—it's that you've *changed*. You don't seem to *need* me any more! So what is it with you?

He: [laconically] Mid-life crisis, I guess.

She: [coolly] I'm leaving you, Whitey. This is not a threat; it is a statement. Goodbye.

And that's how *that* went. She packed up and left for her own dusty apartment, maintaining a grim "more in sorrow than in anger" countenance the whole time.

And, if the truth be known, I was more than a little relieved. It was time for Heather to go. She was a nice lady for the most part, except for her tendency towards using emotional blackmail; but she was becoming terribly unhappy with me. She'd hit the hammer square on the thumb: I didn't need her any more. Heather was a woman who needed someone to mother; and I was a man who no longer wanted mothering.

That got me to thinking. Really thinking. For over a year now, I'd been *doing*, with no particular direction except that "inner itch" Sam Sebastian kept harping about. Now I thought. All night.

"No particular direction" my ass. The individual behaviors were all individually subject to rationalization. But the sum of behaviors was impressive, and pointed. Figuring that much out took me all of five minutes. The remainder was spent weighing my ammunition. I needed to go to Ogumi again, and I'd better be ready.

I was staring out my apartment window at the 'Home III night. The darkness was relieved only by the string of lights along the "main drag"—the circumference road. Then seven A.M. happened, and the secondary mirrors were rotated to mark the beginning of day. Brilliant sunlight crept through the louvers and down the inner walls of the torus, and finally came to rest flooding the greenery of the residence level. I rubbed blinking eyes and went in to take a shower.

Charlie Broughton worked the day shift that weekend, for which I was glad. I was eager to get started. I could hardly wait to get to the Hub comm shack.

I hung around the break room, drinking the horrible brew they call coffee, waiting until Charlie came in for his twenty minutes. I used the time to compose a message: NEED A SOUTH POLAR TRAVERSE IMMEDIATELY. CAN FLY IT MYSELF. WHINE AND PINE WITHOUT ME. CONFIRM UPON EXECUTION; I'LL CALCULATE THE STEW TIME. LOVE AND KISSES, THE ADMIRALTY.

"Whitey! Haven't seen you in a while. Whereya been keepin' yourself?"

"Hi, Charlie. Had a hard month of flight time. Damn Sam's a slave driver. How's business?"

"Slow, but we got a coded one comin' in from M-Base right now."

"Going to be sending a reply?"

" 'Ja ever hear of a coded from Mimas that didn't need a reply?" He went over to the machine and punched a bottle of coffee.

"Say, when you encrypt the message back, could you tack on a note to Junior for me?"

"What, a non-paying customer? How many words?"

"Couple of dozen."

"Lemme see it."

I handed him the scrap of paper I'd used to pencil the message.

"Jesus, no wonder you didn't want to send it commercial. Editors would figure you're hatchin' some kind of plot and disallow the whole thing. Probably have you in for questioning, too." He took a sip of the coffee and grimaced. "Damn burgoo gets worse every day. Whitey, it's a hell of a risk, shootin' something like that to M-Base. They caught me, they'd have my ass."

"Charlie, I promise you the message is harmless, and that it won't compromise SART in any way. And if you send it, I'll pay off my back debts for crib losses."

"Includin' the game you're about to lose right now?"
He was setting up the board.

"This one'll lower the debt. I'm going to cheat and win for a change. . . ."

Junior played it cool. His reply came back by commercial mail about twenty hours later: TO DR. KURIOUS WHITEDIMPLE, SPACEHOME III. PLEASE RECONSIDER YOUR PREVIOUS REFUSAL TO JOIN SART PROJECT. HAVE MISSED YOU TERRIBLY AND AM BECOMING DEPRESSED. CANNOT CONTINUE MY EFFORTS WITHOUT YOU AND HAVE INFORMED AUTHORITIES OF THIS CONDITION. J. BADILLE.

That afternoon, after classes, I dropped in on the department chairman.

"Ted, I only think it's fair to warn you. I'm expecting a summons from Ogumi within the next few days; I think he'll want me to travel to Mimas."

"You're planning on refusing, of course."

"No, Ted. In fact, I'm afraid I must confess that I'm anxious to go."

"Hmmm. Well, I can't really say I'm surprised, Whitey. But I wish you'd given me a little more notice." He held up a hand. "I know, I know. The quarter's over tomorrow and your contract's up for renewal. But that's an automatic. And you know I had plans for you."

"I appreciate the politicking you've done for me, Ted; believe me I do. And I'm truly sorry I couldn't give you more warning. This bug crept up and bit me in the back without too much warning of its own."

"You sure you don't want to renew your contract? I can set it up so you just take a leave of absence. That way you'll be covered if the bug goes away."

"I've thought about that, too, Ted, and I can't tell you how grateful I am for the offer. But before I meet Ogumi I've got to burn my bridges behind me. I know it's the right thing for me to do, even though it seems illogical. I can't even explain it to myself. All I know is I have to make a complete break with my life on 'Home III.'"

"Well, young John is working out well, so we can get by all right. But you know you're going to leave a hole."

"Yeah, and sometimes I still think I'm crazy for doing it. Thanks, Ted. Thanks for everything."

I packed up my books and papers and left my office at SHU, feeling more than a bit empty. SHU was like Heather: a comfortable habit and a way of life. Breaking away was physically and symbolically necessary. The emptiness left me in need of action; I was very tempted to call Ogumi to satisfy that need. But that would be a mistake, even though Ogumi must have known by then that I was the key to his retention of a critical member of SART. He must call me. I wasn't going to give up a scrap of advantage to a man who excelled at in-fighting.

So I lolled around my apartment, exercised in the Cube and made a few other phone calls to set up my play. The most important one was to Jock Tellingast. We'd become good friends over the past year, and I knew he'd been switched from the quarterly I-Base tug to the Mimas run. The work was irregular, but paid more; senior pilots got first crack at it. Jock was scheduled for the right-seat position on the next flight. I talked to him earnestly for ten minutes, after which he agreed to my request. I hung up light-hearted.

Two days passed. With the pressure that must be on him, Ogumi held out for an impressive length of time. But the summons did come, as I knew it must. Junior is not a person to underrate.

"Dr. Whitedimple? This is Mr. Ogumi's secretary. Would it be possible for you to see the president for a few minutes? He asked me to tell you it is a matter of some importance."

"I'm busy at the moment. How about in two hours, if that's not too inconvenient?"

"Just a minute, please. . . . Yes, Mr. Ogumi says that will be quite all right. We'll see you at four, then?"

"I'll be there. Goodbye."

I used the two hours to take a long, hot bath, and hang the expense.

Cross-torus. Up the elevator. Slowly through the breezeway to make sure of being five minutes late. Take stock before going in. Last time, it was in like a lion, out like a lamb. This time: some fears, but no sweaty armpits.

The outer office was timeless. Same furnishings, same secretary dictating a letter to her computer. She flipped the "pause," then rose with a smile to escort me to the door of the inner office. Before she touched the handle I held her arm for a moment.

"Tell me—Andrea, isn't it?—Andrea, do you ever do anything but write letters and usher people into the Presence?"

"Sometimes I wonder, Dr. Whitedimple. Just a second." She opened the door a crack and announced me to the man inside. I heard a grim "Send him in!" before she turned back to me.

"Good luck," she whispered. "I think you're going to need it."

I winked at her—sheer bravado—and stepped into the Presence. The door clicked solidly behind me. Ogumi didn't rise, but just waved me to a chair. I sat and waited patiently. He did nothing but stare at me for half a minute. I looked at a point one centimeter below his left eye and thought about the mechanics of a manual landing in the Big Cross on Enceladus. *Pandora* would be a sweet boat to fly, after herding around the junk that Joe and Sam used for flight training.

"Dr. Whitedimple, I am in possession of a message from the SART project leader. She says her fair-haired boy with the brains, one Junior Badille, has gone into a depression. Needs his friend Kurious Whitedimple by his side in order to become his normal, nasty genius self again. She asks urgently that I send you by the next available transportation."

I awarded him a nod.

"Now, I'd like to ask you two questions. One is, why do you want to go; and the other is, why should I even consider sending you?"

"I'd like to go because I miss Junior, too. The reasons you should send me are obvious, or else I wouldn't be here in this office. Earth is wasting no time, and sparing no expense on Callisto, to beat SpaceHome down to the artifact. And the Earthers started with a much greater depth of expertise in high-pressure technology than we did. Junior is a big factor in offsetting those advantages. We both know that without him our timelines would be pushed way out to the right, and Earth would probably win its gamble to go it alone."

"Mmm, yes. I see you've cultivated some intelligence sources, Dr. Whitedimple. But the fact remains that your opinion of Mr. Badille's worth is somewhat judgemental. And in the final analysis it is *my* judgement which must prevail."

"Emotional considerations aside," I said, "there is very little complexity involved in such a judgement, sir. It seems to be a rather simple matter of weighing the cost of establishing me on Mimas, against the risk of losing the services of Mr. Badille. Surely your office generates such decisions as a matter of routine."

He looked at me for another fifteen seconds before replying. This time I concentrated on the spot a centimeter below his right eye.

"You are correct in essence, Dr. Whitedimple. Now, assuming I decide to accede to this blackmail—no, let us not mince our words, sir; blackmail it is—I remain with two problems. The first is, under what pretext should I send you? Supernumeraries are not tolerated easily by the people who I must persuade to fund this effort.

"The second one is a matter of timing. Along with the request for your person, the SART director sent a legitimate and urgent draft for five skilled specialists. They have been located and a personnel boat and pilot are available. But, unfortunately, the person who was to be backup pilot developed a stomach virus late last night."

He smiled tightly. "And now, rather ironically, I'm strapped by my own safety regulations. I cannot send a personnel carrier out-system without a certified backup pilot. So perhaps—if we can come up with a solution to the first problem—you can persuade your friend to call off his act by assuring him we're doing everything we can?" He finished with acid.

"Perhaps we won't need to, Mr. Ogumi. I believe both of your problems can be handled at once. I can act as the personnel carrier backup; and you can send me as a trial SART pilot. They need a third one since Ballantine washed out."

He looked quite intently at me. "You *do* have your sources, don't you?"

"The data are available, sir, if one is willing to expend some effort to uncover them. As I once found out the hard way, it's difficult to keep secrets in the Colonies."

"Yes. Well, my own sources tell me that the pilot training class in which you are enrolled will not graduate until next month. Am I to understand that you wish me to break another regulation and waive your certification on my own cognizance? I assure you, that would be quite impossible."

"Certainly not, sir. I accelerated ahead of the class and received my certification two weeks ago. Unlimited. Three days ago, after further testing, I obtained a rider for sustained high-G acceleration and maneuvering."

He looked me up and down. "Dr. Whitedimple, I do believe you've changed some of that baby fat into muscle during the past year or so." He shook his head. "And at your age, too. Very well, sir, I'll see to it that the proper arrangements are made at once—after I've checked your qualifications, of course. You'll probably hear from my office sometime later tonight. Since you seem to have all your ducks in a row, I presume you've made arrangements for a leave of absence from your duties at the university?"

"Actually, Mr. Ogumi, what I've done is to sever my ties with that institution. Good day, sir."

I was at the door when he stopped me with a final word: "And this time, Dr. Whitedimple, whatever happens out-system is on your own head. I'll bear no moral responsibility for any pass/fail situation in which you might find yourself."

I turned around. "As you said, Mr. Ogumi, I've lost some of my baby fat."

He nodded. The look he gave me as I was turning to leave was more one of speculation than of rancor. I went out thoughtfully.

"How did it go? Or would you rather not talk about it?"

"Well, Andrea, I'd say he took about a kilo from me. But I picked up about one and a half from him."

"That's not bad, for an amateur." Her appraising look was entirely different from Ogumi's. "I suppose you're currently attached," she said with a gratifying touch of wistfulness.

"Actually, I'm not. And I think it would be nice. But, unfortunately, I'm not very available, either." I pointed to her intercom, which as if by magic began buzzing immediately. "You'll see what I mean in a second." I walked out of the office as she was answering Ogumi's summons. I wondered idly if I'd ever be back.

10

The personnel boat pilot was Jacqueline ("Jackie") Caras. She looked to be in her early sixties, hard and stocky. But most of her wrinkles were squint and smile lines. She had a firm handshake.

"Kurious Whitedimple? I don't—"

"Call me Whitey."

"Okay, Whitey. I know most of the pilots on the list by sight, but you're something of a newcomer. . . ."

"Raw rookie is the word, Jackie. Ink's still wet on my certificate."

"Mind if I see it, Whitey? It's not that I don't trust you, believe me—and you've got official sanction from SpaceHome—but I'm under strict instructions not to trust *anything* involving a Mimas run."

"Sure. They said you'd ask. Here." I handed her my certification holo. It had my picture and fingertips embedded in it and was extremely difficult to counterfeit.

The pilot looked it over carefully, then looked at me just as carefully. Finally, she nodded. "I guess you're you." She tapped the document. "And if half of what

155

Sam says about you is true, you were one shit-hot student. Even a high-G rider. Sam still like his beer?"

"I've never seen him stop at just one. Every time I visit his office, I put on five pounds."

She looked me up and down. It was part professional, part personal. "The weight seems to go right to muscle. I usually hang out at level 15. Where do you keep yourself?"

"Down at 50. With the Earthers and masochists."

She nodded. "Figures. Well, Whitey, you want to take her out?"

"If you'll look over my shoulder."

"I wouldn't dream of doing anything else." She smiled evilly. "In case you didn't know it, this is a test. I got strong requests from SpaceHome *and* Jake and Willie at M-Base to find out what you've got."

"That figures," I said casually. But suddenly my palms oozed a bit of moisture. I suppose I knew it had to come, but I wasn't familiar enough with the pilots' informal guild structure to be ready for it quite so soon. I still had a lot to learn about my new profession and the people who plied it.

I moved toward the right seat, but Jackie said: "You might as well take the pilot's chair, Whitey. I intend to relax all the way to Mimas."

I nodded, moved over and strapped into the left seat. As I flipped the mike switch, my hands were pleasantly dry again.

"MP-8 to Hub Control, over."

"Hub Control over." Traffic control was being handled by Marge Simpson; I recognized her voice, but kept it formal:

"Request vector and window for RCS burn to fifty kilometers for CRF maneuvering, over."

"One moment, please . . . Vector fifty-two at one hundred thirty-five degrees. You have a thirty-seven minute window open in forty seconds. CRF window opens in ten minutes for indefinite period. Please advise, over."

I didn't have to think very hard; the RCS maneuver away from the Hub was standard stuff.

"MP-8 to Hub. RCS maneuvering. Confirm vector fifty-two at rotation angle one hundred thirty-five degrees. Will commence two minutes from my mark. CRF maneuvering will commence beginning forty-five minutes plus-or-minus five minutes from my mark. Mark, over." I punched the timer as I said the word.

"*Confirm your mark, MP-8, at ZULU 1543:32:58. No further communication necessary except for deviations. Ten-ten. Good luck, Whitey.*"

"Thanks, Margaret. MP-8 going ten-ten."

I asked Jackie to warn the five technicians in the back cabin, while I spoke to the navigation computer and moved its mouse around. On the two-minute mark, the navigation processor took us ten meters off the surface of the Hub, moved us over to the one hundred thirty-five degree stripe, pitched the nose up to fifty-two degrees, and gently accelerated us out on RCS. We stopped burning when our relative velocity was twenty-five meters a second.

"Why didn't you do an RCS checkout?" snapped the pilot. I looked at her. "You took it up and did the checkout about ten minutes before I came onboard. Your log was on the screen when I sat down."

"You sure you had time to read all that, Whitey?" she said. "You erased that display almost as soon as you sat down."

She hadn't missed a thing. I answered slowly, visualizing the screen as I recited: "You did a full RCS and computer/instrument checkout at 1517 ZULU. All primaries and backups were green. You have a full CRF tank and just over twelve thousand full-thrust engine-seconds worth of fuel in the hydrazine tanks."

She raised one eyebrow. (I'd never learned to do that.) "Wow. You're pretty fast for a rookie."

"Sam Sebastian had a new theory he tried out on me. Said anybody who had half a brain should be able to remember ninety-five percent of the information on a thirty-centimeter display after a three-second glance." I smiled. "He made me prove it."

I turned back to the navigation computer and began

to set up the Saturn run. Our beginning solar system state vector was complex. The L5 point runs sixty degrees behind the Moon in its orbit, so theoretically the Hub simply sums the Earth and lunar revolution vectors. But actually, we were travelling in a large, irregular ellipse around L5. This orbit is completely stable—the Pinwheel never needed to do a correction burn—but our position at any time depended on everything from sunspots to the current locations of Venus and Jupiter.

Luckily, the Hub kept good track of its own position and vector with respect to the Sun. I could just plug in the fifty-kilometer offset to the running state vector broadcast by the Hub. I set up for a Hub-to-Saturn calculation in less than thirty seconds, then turned to the older woman.

"You're the Captain, lady. How do you want to get there: fast, slow, or in-between?"

"Let's set up for decremental G's starting at point three and finishing at Mimas orbit with point one. Equal time deltas of point oh two five G."

I nodded and turned back to the console. I suspected she'd give me a problem with two kinds of iteration; it was the hardest type to program. But still not all that difficult. The onboard computer was quite intelligent; all I had to do was encourage it once in a while. When it spewed out the arrival time and gave me a graph of the orbit I looked it over, coded the burn schedule as "Pantywaist," and reran the problem with a constant burn at point three G.

That one turned out to be messier because the flight path cut too far inside the orbit of Venus. I had to instruct the computer to miss the Sun by a hundred million kilometers, which kinked the flight path and added a few million kilometers. When the results came back, I coded them as "Hairychest." After that I looked at the clock, just as we got the computer's warning for RCS deceleration. The boat slewed around, then thrust for fifteen seconds to bring us to a standstill relative to the Hub, now fifty kilometers away.

Well, almost a standstill. We had a residual relative

velocity of about six centimeters per second. As was good form, I performed a manual correction with a gentle pair of hunderdth-power burns, then turned toward the right seat.

"Jackie, would you have a terrible hangup if we did the whole trip at point three G? It'll save about three and a half days, and I figure to lose about six dollars less playing cribbage."

"Hell, Whitey, I never had any intention of doing anything else. Orders from Ogumi: Get there as quickly as possible. I just gave you that other problem for practice."

"Well, perhaps we can do it at point four, then."

"Now that's going a little too far. I'm not going to start wearing arch supports and a bra to save a couple of days' flight time!"

I nodded; it had been a forlorn hope. "Point three it is." I looked at the timer; forty-one minutes had elapsed. We could leave any time.

I instructed the computer to execute "Hairychest" five minutes from my mark, slapped the event key and turned to the shipboard intercom to tell the cargo to batten down for high G—but a flashing message on the screen caught my eye: *The flight regime you have chosen involves sustained high acceleration and a longer-than-necessary flight path. Suggest you consider reprogramming to conserve SpaceHome resources.*

"What the hell!" I said. Jackie was leaning over to look at the console and laughing loudly. She calmed down enough to say: "Well, Whitey, your reaction to *that* would mark you as a rookie if nothing else. That message is built into all of SpaceHome's CRF vessels. Ignore it; it'll go away in a few seconds."

"There oughta be a law against corporate policy software," I grumbled, then turned back to the comm and made the announcement.

When I'd warned the passengers and was stuffing loose papers into their proper cubbyholes, the woman said: "Y'know, Whitey, I'm glad Jock got that stomach bug. I think this is going to be a non-dull trip."

I looked at her. She had a quirky smile on her face.

"I guess you know."

"Yeah. Jock and I are pretty good friends. He's a little slow and crude, but a heart of gold."

"Uh-huh. And he was perfectly willing to give me my chance when my chance came along." I winked at her. "Besides, he owed me a favor; I motivated his oldest boy into starting college."

The seventeen day flight cost me only $12.87 in crib losses; I got better cards than usual. I tried to get a bridge game going, but to no avail; they all recognized an easy mark when they saw one. The time went by quickly, though; the company was bright, and the last half of the voyage was punctuated with increasingly frequent messages to and from I-Base.

A Mimas approach is nothing to get cute with; the little satellite is much too close to a very large gravity well. I coaxed the vessel into Mimas' orbital plane—one and a half degrees tilted with respect to the ring plane—before final approach, then eased it into Mimas equatorial for one pass before the de-orbit burn. Junior was in the M-Base comm shack most of the time and made a few acerbic comments about pansy piloting.

He was right. Mimas' surface gravity is only about three-fourths that of Enceladus—call it seven thousandths G—and I could have set the boat down with all but three of the RCS thrusters out of commission. But I wasn't about to contravene SpaceHome regulations on my maiden flight. So I orbited and directed the computer to plot and control the landing, using the navigational transponder grid which had been laid down on Mimas' surface.

During orbit, I finally had time to look at Saturn again. Since Mimas is the closest moon of any size, the Old Man was a monster, dominating the sky. I stared for a quarter of an hour, remembering. It stretched across even more of the heavens than from Enceladus, and the rings drew their thin, bright lines across its face and into the black past the western limb. The Giant itself was more than three-quarters full. I stared at the

weather patterns, hypnotized. The Old Man's lure had a
new urgency: If I didn't wash out, there was an excellent chance that I would go down there. I pictured
myself sliding into those monstrous storms, being buried by hundreds of kilometers of atmosphere. I shuddered involuntarily, remembering the sharing of Junior's
death wish during the north polar traverse.

"Kind of gets to you, doesn't it?" Jackie was looking
over my shoulder.

"You just don't know."

"Oh, that's right," she said. "You get to fly down into
that, don't you? Well, better you than me, Gunga Din."

I nodded. Her point was well taken. I broke my eyes
away from the sight and looked down at the surface of
the little iceball which was to be my new home.

11

Christiaan Huygens was able to see Titan, even with his crude glass, in 1655. Cassini, with a state-of-the-art Campini refractor half a generation later, found Iapetus and Rhea; a dozen years after that he hung a big unwieldy lens from the side of a building, turned it toward Saturn, stood back forty meters with an eyepiece, and saw Dione and Tethys.

But it wasn't until Herschel polished his 122-cm speculum and pointed it outward in 1789 that the smaller and closer Mimas and Enceladus were discovered. A few hundred million years before, a large hunk of rock had almost destroyed Mimas, which would have robbed Herschel of one of his discoveries; as it is, it left a crater a hundred and thirty kilometers across—one-third of the little moon's diameter—which eventually got his name.

In addition to Herschel Crater, with its prominent central peak almost exactly on the equator, there were a few other major features with relatively mundane names: Pelion, Ossa, Tristam and Iseult, and so forth.

But the main theme of Mimas was the Arthurian legend. We floated over Percivale, Bedivere, Modred, Launcelot and Gwynevere; and the spirits of Arthur, Pellinore, Galahad, Morgan, Kay, Merlin and others called to us out of their craters over the horizons.

When we passed eastward over the Herschel Mountain transponder, we were only one hundred four degrees west of the sub-Saturn point at which M-Base was located. The nav computer pitched the boat up and began a series of short de-orbit burns. I hovered over the console, ready to take over, but the processor performed its job flawlessly. We were down within half an hour.

There was a plastic walkway from the landing area to the M-Base personnel lock, so we didn't need crampons. Jackie instructed the newcomers, however, not to wander off the artificial surface, unless they were eager to invite falls and frostbite. She and I were last off because we had to shut all systems down and batten the vessel. I knew better than to jump down to the surface, so I carefully walked down the side of the boat, using the edge of the ladder as a handhold.

M-Base looked a lot like I-Base from the surface: uninhabited. Even though cosmics were much less fluxy there, because of the proximity to the primary, there were still good reasons for building most of the facilities underground. Some were economical, some architectural and some psychological.

The technicians were clustered together, looking around and up at the overwhelming spectacle of the Old Man—agog, as was proper to newcomers in Saturn's system. Jackie and I herded them into the personnel airlock. The primitiveness of the facilities here would have them bored in a very short time; that I knew from experience.

Junior was waiting right outside the locker room. As soon as I emerged in my coveralls, I ran into his crooked grin.

"Junior! I've missed—" "—issed you, Admiral Dimp!" We looked at each other, then we were pounding backs and laughing, our feet leaving the floor like those of any rookies. I felt at home for the first time since leaving Earth orbit.

After we got our feet back down, the first thing Junior did was to look carefully into my eyes.

"Not quite, Admiral," he said, shaking his head minutely. "But, boy, I'll tell you it's close to being there. Maybe a few more weeks, huh?"

"What the hell are you talking about, Junior?"

"Later, Dimp. C'mon, I'll introduce you to the bar."

"Don't you think I should report to Ms. O'Malley first? I do have appearances to maintain, you know."

"Naw. Maggie told me to take you in tow while she gives the standard pep talk to the rookies. We've got half an hour."

On the way to the bar, Junior gave me a quick rundown on Mimas Base—something we hadn't wasted message words on. M-Base wasn't quite as primitive as I'd thought, after all. There were a hundred fifty full-time personnel, plus a few dozen specialist transients at any given time. There was a concentration of talent there—design, structures, propulsion, materials and processes, computer, communications—that would make any team leader's mouth water. And there were a few amenities to coddle this high-powered group: a nice rec room, complete medical facilities, exercise centrifuge, bar and theater. And something I was to come to know more intimately: a well-equipped hyperbaric medicine lab, complete with a specialist from Earth who'd decided to stick it out with SpaceHome when Earth pulled out.

"The only thing we really don't have enough of is living quarters," Junior said with that crooked grin. "You'll be finding that out the hard way when you doss. You'll share a four-by-five room with the other two pilots; and that includes beds and computer terminals. Bathroom down the hall, of course."

The grin broadened. "Plenty of water though, just like in I-Base; so I have it better than at home. A bath a day is almost mandatory because of the cramped space;

makes it easier for the air conditioning to handle all those pheromones. Here we are."

We'd arrived at the bar. The thing had honest-to-goodness swinging doors, which I'd only seen in movies. Over them hung a large sign painted gaudily in old English style, which stated: "Pendragon Pub and Grille."

"Zounds," I said.

"Right," said Junior. "Here we go." He pushed the swinging doors open authoritatively, even though his head came barely to their tops. He led me to a couple of open seats at the bar and ordered two vodka-rocks.

"They tell me this joint is an approximate cross between Murphy's on 'Home V and Bergman's at I-Base," Junior said while the night's volunteer bartender brought us the clear liquid. "So I'd advise you not to drink that stuff too fast—"

Junior's presence had taken away my sense of caution. I squeezed back a medium-sized slug of the watery-looking libation, then coughed immodestly while trying to breathe again. The stuff burned like crazy.

The gnome's cackle was totally unsympathetic; at least that part of him hadn't changed. "As I was about to say," he laughed, "I understand they all serve the same old rotgut—fermented kitchen garbage distilled in a low-pressure boiler." He took a tiny sip. "This crop's been aged half a week or so; it's better than usual."

We chatted about how the research and development was going (pretty well) and our chances for beating the Earth team on Callisto. I found out that even though they got some information from the Hub about the race, they were still hungry for more. SpaceHome was reluctant to discuss what little it knew over a data link, even though the encryption keys were now changed with every boat.

"Maggie'll probably grill you the first chance she gets," said Junior. "She's a hell of a team leader, but even she needs realistic timelines. She's got to push as hard as she can but still keep something in reserve for a sustained peak effort."

He finished his drink and I offered to spring for a

second round. After all, there was no charge for the liquor.

"No thanks, Dimp," he said. "One drink every other day is my limit."

"Orders from Mom?" I smirked.

"Nah. I like alcohol well enough, but my brain doesn't. When *you* have one too many, it doesn't matter too much; you kill a few thousand cells, okay. Your brain just rewires around the dead ones. Good software. Me, I'm hardwired. Every time I lose a few cells, something goes."

He pulled at his ear. "First time we threw a party here, I got more than a little tipsy—didn't take much, either, since I'm so small. When I woke up next morning, I found I'd lost six pages of twelve-place logarithms I'd memorized when I was three. Had to have 'em printed out by my computer so I could memorize them again."

"But can't you calculate a logarithm anyway, any time you need it?"

"Sure, but it takes me about a second and a half to figure a twelve-place log, whereas I can remember one in about two hundred milliseconds."

I shook my head with mock seriousness. "That's pathetic, Junior. I should have your problems."

"You're a hard man, Admiral," he said chuckling. "Let's go see Maggie; it's time."

The project leader's secretary was a model of formality as he announced us to his boss: "Maggie, you free? The star boarder's here with his new playmate."

"Send 'em in, Hank!"

Margaret O'Malley was slightly plump, and white-haired; but she didn't have a line on her face, except minute crow-foot crinkles at the corners of her eyes. Her smile displayed humanity but was backed by a hint of steel which let you know she wasn't one to be pushed around.

"Ms. O'Malley," Junior said. "I'd like you to meet Dr. Kurious Whitedimple. And don't ask him how he got the name. He'll spend half the day telling you an elaborate lie."

Her handshake was firm and warm. "Hello, Whitey; heard a lot about you, both past and present. And you might as well call me Maggie."

"Don't be taken in by her smile, Admiral," Junior said. "She's a slave driver at heart." He looked at his watch. "Speaking of which, I'd better get back to work myself. Greg's middle names are 'Simon' and 'Legree.' " He threw us both a parting salute as he wafted out the door.

The woman smiled after Junior and said, half under her breath: "God help me but I love that nasty little runt."

I looked at her appraisingly; she seemed to mean it. "Well," I said, "that makes at least two of us. But I'm curious about something. I'd have thought that he'd be in charge of whatever section he's in, by now. His knowledge of Saturn, CRF engines, boat design . . ."

She smiled. "Have you met his boss, Greg Simpson?"

"Not yet."

"Well, you'll be impressed when you do; he's got dedication, intelligence, and common sense enough for three men. I know. He headed up the design team for me when we were doing DDT&E for 'Home VII.

"He's not selfish or self-serving, either. Two days after he first met Junior, he came to me and said that the little man should be put in charge; had a brain none of us could match and could learn and integrate facts with phenomenal speed.

"So we called in Junior and put it to him." She shook her head and the smile turned rueful. "That was the only time I've ever seen fear in his eyes. He flatly refused; said he definitely wasn't the leader type. Then he laughed that evil laugh and said he'd rather someone else make the decisions, so he could criticize at will.

"Of course, there wasn't any choice but to honor his wishes; hell, he's not even on the payroll—says he's got no use for either money or employment contracts."

She laughed softly; it had a warm quality which I liked. "So Greg stayed design team leader. Junior does most of the hard thinking and Greg takes the ideas and shuffles them off to the rest of his gang; and they work out the engineering and economics to test for feasibility. And when Greg calls Junior in to consult about a problem, he makes sure he's got the tape recorder going; says he needs to go over the tape two or three times to figure out what the runt's talking about, most of the time." She grinned. "Then Greg comes to me and I talk to him about how he shouldn't get an inferiority problem."

I nodded. "That I understand completely."

"But," she continued, "you can't help but feel sorry for the little guy. Even with his sarcasm and cutting humor, he's eager to please and hungry for acceptance. Emotionally, he's about at the level of a homeless puppy. And he doesn't seem to be able to make close friends easily—which is very bad. In a Godforsaken hole of an outpost like this one, a close friend can sometimes make the difference between coping satisfactorily and a depression of medical proportions."

All of a sudden, she was very serious. "Something you don't know, Whitey. Junior was, in the jargon, beginning to 'take the nosedive.' His productivity was beginning to go downhill, and he was exhibiting signs which would shortly have forced me to take him off the SART and send him back to the bosom of his family on SOS.

"Then he got your message," she smiled broadly, "and lit up like a Christmas tree. You must be something very special to him."

"That works both ways, Maggie. A large part of the motivation for my, uh, extracurricular activities of the past year was to get a chance to see Junior again. But surely he's made friends here?"

"Oh, yes, I suppose so," she said. "He likes Jacobs and Williams well enough, and seems to get along well with Greg and me. But there's a difference with you. You're not constantly in awe of him. You've shared danger together. You've proved yourself to him under pressure—gained his respect—in ways which can't easily be duplicated. I strongly suspect that you're the only person to whom he'd ever admit being afraid—or cry with.

"Anyway," she continued, seeing that I was becoming embarrassed, "when we concocted those messages to you and Ogumi, there was a strong element of truth in them.

"But that's now a problem we'll pretend we can forget." Her eyes got a trifle harder. "So let's talk about you. I've got reports on you from Sam Sebastian, and now from Jackie, of course. They both say you've got what it takes. But, to fill that third SART pilot position, it takes even more than that. We need a seat-of-the-pants person, one with really good spatial feeling, as well as a competent computer operator." A fleeting, mischievous smile crossed her face. "I understand from one who should know—Jake—that Junior himself is just such a pilot."

I nodded acquiescence as she continued: "Unfortunately, Junior's acceleration tolerance is simply too low; he can't take any sustained loads over a quarter G because of his frail condition. Besides which, he absolutely refuses to work out—says it disturbs his *Wa*, whatever that means."

"Junior would say something like that."

"Yes. Well, anyway, we've got Jake, who's good, and has nice high-gravity muscles. And we've got Colin Williams, who's got a good touch and is busily building up muscles, even though he detests the centrifuge. And we've washed out four other candidates who thought they had it, but didn't."

She looked me in the eyes. "Junior says you can do anything you want to and that you really want to do this. Is he right?"

I answered slowly: "I suppose you'll have to decide that for yourself—which you intend to do anyway."

"You are correct, Whitey." She gave me a hard smile, then looked me up and down. "You seem to be very fit. Are you willing to spend time on the centrifuge to keep yourself that way? Lifting weights on a small wheel, tossing your cookies if you move your head too fast?"

"Yeah. One G's no stranger. But cookies don't get tossed in the Gym in 'Home I. I'll be careful."

"Do you still have high-G muscles? How long has it been since your last workout?"

"Less than three weeks."

"Good, then you're ready for your checkout flight. It'll be down to Mons Gargantua; we want to get the Titan artifact. Ogumi has three of the five—from Iapetus, Enceladus, and the Iron Maiden; he'd like to have the one from Titan to complete his collection. At least as much as possible," she grinned, "since you let the Earthers keep the one they picked up on Dione."

"They found it; worked hard for it. I'm no thief, no matter how I feel about them personally."

"Agreed. And even Ogumi agrees with your decision—publicly. Privately, I think he'd like to choke you." She winked. "Maybe, when we tell him that you got the Titan artifact for him, he'll mellow a bit."

"Why do I doubt that?" I replied, grinning. But my smile stopped a lump in my throat. I'd read about the surface of Titan. The retrieval was going to be no picnic.

12

"No need to introduce you to Whitey, Jake," Junior grinned as I shook hands with the former Earther pilot. His grip still felt like an iron maw, but I was able to return it a little better than last time.

"Well, you've put on a little muscle to add to that conniving brain, Whitey," he said, finally releasing my bruised fingers. "Here, say hello to Colin Williams; you two have something in common: you both hate your first names."

"Hello, old chap," he said, pumping my hand. "Welcome to the ranks of the high-G masochists." I was ready for the thick British accent; Junior had briefed me. Williams had emigrated to 'Home VI with his parents when he was fifteen; everybody suspected that his speech was affected, but no one had ever caught him slipping out of it.

"How do you do, Willie," I said. "I understand that you, too, wasted a good education to herd junk around the system." Williams had degrees in economics and philosophy.

171

"Quite so," he agreed. "Found out that doing something was ever so much better than thinking about it. I was even willing to put up with those horrible workouts for a spot of adventure." His muscles seemed larger than mine, but also, somehow, a little softer. I had a hunch that he did as little work as possible to keep in shape and relied heavily on his Earth-bred frame to get him by.

"So," said Jacobs. "Let's get ourselves busy. Whitey, go ahead and doss yourself down—the far bunk over there; the far left set of drawers is yours. You tired, or ready to get started right away?"

"I'm pretty pumped up; I can sleep next week."

"Good. Maggie wants to find out as soon as possible whether or not you've got what it takes. We're gettin' down to the short strokes, and if she's got to send for another pilot she wants to be able to do it right away."

"Thanks, Jake; you really know how to make a fellow feel right at home." I'd finished unpacking my kit and stowing the gear. I tossed my toothbrush back into it, along with a couple of pairs of clean coveralls. I looked at my bed, wondering how often I'd sleep there—if ever. "Okay. Lead me to the wars."

On the way to the topside airlock, Jacobs briefed me. The tug we were going to use was officially called the Saturn Expeditionary Retrieval Vessel. Nobody bothered to remember it as anything but the Catcher. It was built big and strong, with a large airlock and hold into which the actual atmospheric descent vessels would fit. It was designed to take off and land only on CRF. It had been built in a surface shed, then towed to a prepared pad ten kilometers from base for checkout.

Before traveling to the Catcher we went to the suit room, where I was fitted for a full-pressure suit. It looked like a standard model, except it had an extra large pliss and was every bit as shiny as a micropore suit.

"Going to be bloody cold up on that mountain," Williams commented when he saw my raised eyebrows.

"So we used reflective outer cloth, and put extra batteries in the pliss to help heat everything toasty warm."

I nodded, then noticed something else. There was a very small suit included in the group hanging on the rack. I turned to Junior. "Don't tell me you're coming with us."

"Wouldn't miss it for the world, Admiral. Besides, I'm one of the pilot selection panel members. Your pass/fail's got to have my vote, along with Jake's and Willie's." His smirk was typically evil.

"Yeah," I said, "but Titan G's are more than twice what you were raised on, and twenty times what you have on this iceball."

"No sweat, Dimp. Just don't cowboy the landing and I'll be fine."

"So why the suit? Once we hit the surface you should be doing nothing but resting."

"Well, Admiral, we'll see when we get down. I went through a great deal to get this suit made, and I'm going to give it a workout if I can."

"What he did," Jacobs said, "was to go crying to Greg and Maggie—threatened 'em with a hunger strike, or some damn thing, if they didn't coddle him."

"Indeed," Williams chipped in, "I understand that his histrionics were quite impressive."

I looked at Junior. "I'd really feel better if you didn't come. Can't you take the word of these two yahoos," I waved at Jacobs and Williams, "on how well I do?"

"No way, Admiral. You're my special project. Raised you from a baby. Want to see you graduate."

I nodded. "Okay, but I might tie you down to your chair when we hit the surface."

"You and which platoon of marines?"

We put on micropore suits for the trip to the Catcher, then caught the final supply truck and swung aboard. The road was smooth—it had been cut by the simple process of melting surface ice—and the vehicle's tires were covered with short spikes.

The Catcher was over a hill from the base proper and completely hidden from sight. As we topped the rise, about half of it came into view; the bottom was still under the horizon. We were almost up to it before my perspective shifted and its true size became apparent. I was intellectually prepared, but not emotionally. It was a leviathan they were asking me to fly. The cargo lock was closed, but I could see from its outline, standing and looking up at it, that it was large enough to swallow two small houses at the same time.

Junior must have noticed my open mouth. His nasty grin was in the voice that came over the four-way intercom: *"Don't let it scare you, Admiral. It handles pretty sweet for a damn truck."*

For all of its height, the tug was squatty; the enormous girth was necessary to contain all the CRF reaction mass needed to hold the vessel stationary above Saturn's cloud tops. While performing its primary function, it would be hovering, rather than orbiting. Its four landing jacks were presumably for the sole purpose of setting it down on Mimas—or Titan. But even considering the tug's size, those jacks seemed excessively strong. I thought about that as we floated up the thirty meters of ladder into the personnel and small cargo lock. The supply crew had already cycled it and were getting ready to load food and oxygen bottles.

Before settling down in the control room, I demanded an inspection trip. For all its cargo space and tankage requirements, its conveniences were ample. It would accommodate several people on an extended voyage. The crew were finishing the storage of supplies in a generous-sized locker. After they left with waves and messages of good luck, I reinspected their stowage job to make sure everything was tight. The others allowed me to do this without comment; but I knew three sharp brains were taking notes. Everything counted from now on.

We closed the tug airtight and established pressure, then doffed our micropore suits and hung them up in the locker alongside the pressure suits which the crew had stowed there. Then we went up to the control room.

The instrument panel was standard plus. A Pandora-style 3-D was in prominent evidence, a sight I hadn't seen for nearly two years. There were also programmable flat panels and switches for extra radars. I looked at my diminutive friend; he was grinning with a glint in his eyes.

"Okay, Junior," I said ticking off points on my fingers: "We've got landing jacks heavy enough to set down almost anywhere in the solar system, we've got accommodations for a dozen people for several months or more, and we've got a 3-D to play with. Is this another one of your little projects?"

"You might say that." He rubbed his nose. "I persuaded Maggie that the Catcher would be just so much scrap after the retrieval unless we scarred it for useful work later on. I pointed out that there was a lot of system left to explore and that we might be going God-knows-where after we got the Hexie artifact."

I estimated the cost of the frills at ten to fifteen million dollars, and reflected briefly on Ogumi's financial situation. "C'mon, Wonder Boy. Are you going to tell the whole story, or not?"

"Well, I did kind of sweeten the pot by promising to show them how to boost the CRF drive efficiency by twenty or thirty percent." There was no apology in his smirk.

"Junior, your amorality is frightening."

Jacobs took me through the controls. Besides the 3-D and good surface landing odar and radar, there was an extremely sophisticated laser-radar capture-control computer, which could be switched to take over the vessel's navigation.

"Damn thing'll do everything but poach eggs," he said. "Floater gets within a hundred kilometers—ten, if the transponder isn't working—you give control over to the capture navigator, then sit back and relax. Navigator maneuvers the Catcher so that the Floater enters right through the cargo door, gentle as a maid's kiss."

"What if there's a malfunction?" (I remembered a practice landing on the Moon that Sam had taken me through. We did two orbits to lay a track. I put the nav computer on auto landing per regulations; then, about thirty kilometers from touchdown, the malfunction alarm sounded. I nearly jumped out of my skin, then took over the landing on manual with Sam standing by on the duplicate controls, ready to cut me out and take over. After I'd brought it down, he said that navigation computers were almost foolproof and I'd just passed an illegal gut check. But I never forgot the word "almost.")

"Whichever one of us is skippering this tub finishes the job on manual, then we go beat the hell out of the builders." He grinned at me. "We just gotta make sure that any one of us can finish the job on manual."

"Think you could do it if you had to, old chap?" Williams asked on cue.

I turned to him. "Yes. But we might fall a long way while I was doing it."

"That's alright, Admiral," Junior said. "This tub's got enough juice to float the Ark. She'll make three G for sixty hours; and at one and a half G she'll run all year. If you make the pickup, you'll get back out okay."

"I noticed heavy buttressing throughout the boat," I said. "Can I infer that she can stand a little plunge into Saturn's atmosphere?"

"Yeah," said Jacobs. "She's rated down to a hundred kilometers, which is farther than you'd fall if you made a pickup under the worst conditions, completing just before hitting the cloud tops."

"Ah, so," I said. "Which is why she is also eminently qualified to brave the atmospheric rigors of our estimable brother Titan."

"Speaking of which, let's get this show on the road," said Jacobs.

I spent the next hour thoroughly checking out all the boat systems under the tutelage of Jake and Willie. I let the navigation computer take it off the surface; I wanted to get the feel of the vessel before going on manual near a planetary surface—even such a low-gravity one as Mimas.

I programmed the computer to put us in a polar orbit, after studying large-scale terrain maps of Mimas and Mons Gargantua. I intended to make my practice run down into Camelot Chasma, one of the fault valleys formed in the surface ice when Herschel Crater came into being. The southernmost tip of Camelot was three hundred kilometers due south of M-Base, and it wended northwestward for about two hundred. Two passes would map it perfectly and I could land on the third.

"Good choice," Jacobs said grudgingly. "But why didn't you go after Herschel Peak? It's a regular Mons Gargantua in miniature." The central peak of Herschel Crater was a distinctive cone rising six kilometers from the crater floor.

"Yes," I said, "except for the slope. Near the peak of Mons Gargantua, where we're going to have to land," I pointed at the radar map of Titan, "the slope'll be about ten degrees. Now, you've told me that the landing jacks on this tug are rated to fifteen degrees' slope, and can handle anything up to twenty with an empty hold.

"But these contour lines," I put my finger on the Mimas mountain, "seem to indicate that even twenty is a rarity on Herschel. It's a very regular peak with an average slope of twenty-five to thirty degrees." I smiled. Junior was grinning evilly, for some reason. "And I need practice landing on a ten-degree slope, more than I need to find a mountain."

"Pay up, turkeys," Junior said, cackling like a mother hen. "And that'll teach you to bet against the Admiral."

I let the computer calculate the de-orbit burn while we were making our mapping passes. I also pre computed a special acceleration burn I wanted to make for my own benefit. When the time came to de-orbit, I fired the CRF on manual, keeping the vessel in the calculated groove with the 6-DOF hand controller.

Junior was right; the boat handled sweetly. The hand controller had just the perfect amount of tactile feedback: that hard-to-find middle ground between too much slop and too much stiffness. And the thrust vector control of the CRF worked so smoothly with the RCS system that I couldn't discern, except by instrument readouts, whether the attitude control was using one or the other, or blending them.

I finished dead in the groove, two hundred kilometers above my chosen spot in Camelot Chasma, with zero relative velocity. We began to fall with excruciating slowness.

I pointed the nose straight down at the surface and used the mouse to mark my landing point on the 3-D screens; it was a smooth area of about half a square kilometer, where the valley floor started to rise to become wall; the slope was eight or nine degrees with no surprises.

"I say, Whitey, why all this altitude?"

"I like to get a running start," I answered. "Everybody strap in. CRF maneuvers coming up."

With nose still pointed directly at the surface, I lit the CRF, still on manual. I watched the 3-D readouts and the timing clock at the same time with four of my eyes, while holding the boat in the groove I'd laid for myself. An alarm began sounding almost immediately; I reached over with my free hand and slapped the cutoff. The annoying clamor ceased, but not Williams.

"What the devil are you doing, Whitey?"

"Tell him, Junior," I said. "I'm a little busy right now." I noticed that Jacobs was calm, but had his hands near the right-seat controls, ready to take over.

"I'd say offhand," Junior grunted from the back couch, "that the Admiral wishes to practice something a little more challenging than a fiftieth-G landing. Which will have the added benefit of cutting our time-to-touchdown from an hour down to ten or fifteen minutes, depending on how strong his kamikaze urges are."

"Not all that strong," I said, cutting off the drive and pitching the tug end-for-end. We now began a five-minute period of free fall. "Average G's for this run will be about point one. Just want to get the feel of the landing system under some reasonable acceleration."

Executing a manual CRF landing on an unprepared surface is not routine. The engine creates worrisome side effects, like throwing up surface junk and digging a hole you have to miss with the landing jacks. The proper method is to lay a tight vertical groove and lock the stereo odar—laser optical radar—onto a small landing area so you can keep a maximum-resolution sweep. The reason for this is to paint as good a picture as possible of the landing site before the CRF plume kicks up enough steam or dust to confuse the optical scan—usually somewhere between two and ten kilometers off the surface. After that, the nav computer continues to update the display map with inertial data; it supplements this whenever possible with partial visual scans during random moments of clear viewing. While this may seem haphazard compared with using radar all the way down, it's not. The stereo resolution of the odar at ten kilometers is better than that of the radar at twenty meters.

But if you drift more than a few meters from the original landing spot, all bets are off. You've got to baby it in using the best information you can get—usually a combination of low-resolution odar and radar—and pray you don't put a landing jack into the trench your CRF is digging. You've also got to hope you don't set down on any large rocks or slope irregularities your scans didn't give you time to react to.

This particular touchdown was without incident, though for me it was five minutes of medium nervousness. The landing-jack proximity radars all functioned perfectly, and all four telescoping legs were well outside the melt circle cut by the plume. Even though I stayed tight in the original groove, I used split screens on the 3-D because I wanted to calibrate the radar against the odar. When we touched down, the odar read an altitude of minus point seven centimeters; the radar claimed we were still four tenths of a meter off the surface.

"Nice professional job, Whitey," Jacobs said. His eyes hadn't missed anything. "Now let's see how smooth you are under a real G field. Head this bucket up and out of here."

I programmed the journey out to Titan for positive G increments of .025, beginning with .05 and ending with .15 before falling into orbit around the Old Man's largest child. Junior was acid; he said he was perfectly capable of sustaining .15 G all the way, and that we were just wasting several hours in a misguided attempt to coddle him.

I pointed out to Junior that as long as I was skippering the boat he had advisory capacity only, and that he would either shut up or take steps to remove me from command.

He shut up, then retaliated by beating me out of my shirt in high-stakes gin rummy. Gin was the game onboard, not cribbage. The trip took less than eighteen hours, of which I spent nine in sleep and eating and three or four more studying Titan and Mons Gargantua maps and setting up trial computer programs. During the remainder, I lost a total of one hundred twenty-eight dollars and some cents at gin. Call it half a buck a minute. I never realized how expensive space travel really was until I started doing it.

"You've got to learn to come in when you're down to ten or below, Whitey," Jake lectured. "Most of the time, sticking it out for a gin is a sucker play. But if you want to keep with your style, well, SART pilots get fat bonuses. Maybe you can cover your losses."

On our final approach to the dirty orange ball, I swung us into a thirty-degree orbit such that our first pass would take us thirty kilometers southeast of Mons Gargantua; our next pass, about three hours later, would be thirty kilometers to the northwest of the objective. I planned to bring us down on the third, after those two very careful radar fixes.

In the meantime, we had hours to kill. We all knew something about Titan, but Junior's lore was encyclopaedic; I cajoled him into a discourse filled with his charming mixture of cynicism and poetry. It saved me maybe fifty or sixty dollars in gin losses.

Titan is the only satellite in the solar system with any atmosphere to speak of. Its nature is this: Although it's predominantly nitrogen like that of Earth, there is a significant percentage of methane; the reaction between these two gases, fueled by the solar effluvium, creates traces of many other compounds, including all kinds of acetylenes.

The weakness of Titan's gravity allows formation of these compounds, significant amounts of them, very high above the surface—up to three hundred kilometers or more. The result is a high-floating, very thick layer of aerosols which prevent all optical viewing of the surface from space.

"Of course," Junior said, "aerosols is the polite name for the stuff. What it is, is smog. Smog thicker than the worst junk that ever plagued Tokyo before they outlawed hydrocarbon burning."

The ironic twist to all this is that the thickest part of the aerosol layer is concentrated at two hundred kilometers above the surface. Below that it thins out dramatically, so that at fifty kilometers the viewing would be excellent. But an optical probe had never been sent down through Titan's atmosphere—it was simply one of seven or eight million interesting things in the solar system we hadn't got around to doing. However, there are sensors other than optical, and in the early 21st century the first orbiting probe package let us know what the surface was like.

When we found out, it was, for the most part, what had been speculated for some time: lots of liquid and solid methane forming oceans and icebergs, continents of rocky crust overlaying a water-ice mantle—and one thing that hadn't been expected: shield volcanoes of pure ice. They were all long extinct, products of Titan's warm-core and meteor-bombarded adolescence; the last of them had stopped vomiting its slushy magma before the first trilobites started scrabbling over the surface of Earth.

There were twenty-two of notable size, ranging from

six to nineteen kilometers in altitude. And there was also Mons Gargantua.

Picture Mount Fuji, one of the most beautiful of Earth's creations. Now pull and stretch its perfect cone up ten, eleven times its already-perfect height; stretch its magnificent base out and around until it measures six hundred kilometers in diameter. Now you've transformed the beautiful into the frighteningly awesome; you've built Mons Gargantua. With the exception of the Old Man's rings, it may rank as the number one wonder of the solar system.

And yet its awesome slopes and peak had never been seen, never even been photographed in the optical spectrum. And never would, for that matter—at least not in their entirety—because Mons Gargantua is so high that its final seven or eight kilometers sticks up above the top of the thick belt of clouds hovering over almost the entire planetary surface.

"And a good thing, too," added the little gnome. "Otherwise, we'd never be able to get that artifact with these jury-rigged suits, even though the tug might be able to stand up under the surface conditions for a while."

"How's that?" asked Jacobs, who hadn't taken too much interest in planetography, except for that of the Old Man himself.

"Surface temperature runs tight at ninety to ninety-five Kelvin," replied Junior. "Right around the triple point of methane. Those thick clouds covering the lower thirty kilometers of the atmosphere are methane. And they drizzle methane rain and sleet everywhere and every season." He scratched his nose. "So in addition to a very cold nitrogen atmosphere at one and a half times Earth surface pressure, you get a continuous bath at a couple of hundred degrees below freezing. Not recommended for a Sunday outing."

Junior was right. So right that it made me a little uneasy, even about the current undertaking. At thirty-nine kilometers above the surface, where we'd be, there was still enough pressure—about a fifth of an Earth atmosphere—and cold nitrogen breezes to give our suit heaters a workout. And we'd be in full pressure suits, which were always uncomfortable. And we'd be in crampons and breathing hard. I firmly put apprehensions out of mind.

Now the time of truth was approaching. There were only a few minutes until the start of the de-orbit burn. The next hour would probably decide whether I'd be a real working member of the SART effort, or just useless deadwood kept around as Junior's pet. I stared at the orange murk below.

Junior noticed my mild funk and provided welcome sympathy: "That's okay, Admiral—just remember that your whole future rests on this landing, and try not to be nervous."

"Thanks, buddy. You're always so helpful in times of trouble." I looked at the mission clock. "All right, troops. Time to strap in for de-orbit and landing. We're going down at .25 G in two minutes."

Junior looked at me hard, but didn't say anything. Normally, to avoid a long ride through the atmosphere, such a landing approach would be at about half a G. Junior knew I was taking it easy for his sake; he also knew it would do no good to argue about it.

The CRF rumbled to life. We were going down. Six hundred kilometers away our objective loomed, just over the horizon. In a minute or so, we began to be buffeted by the optical haze layer. Of the four of us, Jacobs was the only one with experience in atmospheric navigation; he appeared quite unconcerned. I envied him his phlegmatism, while wondering if Junior's and Williams' hands were damp like mine.

Then we hit the top of the aerosol layer and were backing down through a darkening orange haze. The Sun's light diffused and dimmed dramatically; I was unaccountably reminded of shooting the gap through the rings. I watched our approach carefully on the 3-D. Suddenly, the pictures and numbers changed slightly and the computer made an announcement: We were within line-of-sight radar contact with Mons Gargantua.

Jacobs leaned over as far as he could and pressed his

nose against the starboard viewport, trying to see backward. "Can't pick out a damned thing," he said. "But it seems like the murk is thinning out—hard to tell for sure, though, because it's so featureless."

I didn't pay much attention; my eyes and mind were glued on the 3-D and the mission clock. I noted absently that we were close enough for Jake to be able to see the peak quite clearly if angle and visibility permitted. The mission timer was sweeping inexorably toward the handoff point. At minus one minute, the nav computer announced itself and gave me the option of changing my mind and letting it land itself—or of aborting the landing altogether and accelerating back to escape velocity. Almost casually, I reached over and chose the manual landing; the default was to abort. Once I was committed, I wondered fleetingly whether or not any of the other pilot candidates had got this far and chose to abort.

But my attention was still mainlined on the graphs and readouts. At thirty seconds to handoff, the stick came to life electronically; it still wouldn't control the ship, but the simulated readouts from my manipulation of it were displayed adjacent to the real ones, in a different color. I matched the navigation computer's readings to get the feel of the controller once again. Now it was just a few seconds to handoff. We were about twenty-five kilometers from the top of Mons Gargantua and coming down at three hundred fifty meters a second, right in the groove. Our projected landing point was a spot of ten-degree slope half a kilometer outside the rim of the crater.

I—we all—would have preferred to land inside the crater itself, because it measured seven kilometers across and getting to the center would be a chore. But just inside the rim the slope was too great; and further down was a jumbled mess, with no obvious landing spots. The resolution of the radar maps simply wasn't good enough to chance finding a suitable site inside. Even on the relatively smooth slope outside the rim, I hoped the landing radars wouldn't spot any irregularities once we got closer in; if I had to hunt for a spot, it would make my job much more difficult.

My thoughts were all flashing—fragmented by my need to concentrate on the pictures and figures on the screens. By then, I was already flying the vessel in my own mind; I barely noticed when the computer handed over control. Shortly after that, Jake announced quietly that he could see the mountain, now; the atmosphere was quite clear down where we were. He was being quiet in recognition of my need to concentrate, but he could have shouted it and it wouldn't have made any difference; I was locked into the job.

Down in the groove. At ten kilometers up I switched off the odar and swore under my breath as I did so. A surface anomaly appeared to be forming in the screens. But it had frozen without resolving fully, at the moment I switched off the laser update. I went to split screen to bring up the radar picture. When we were down to five kilometers, the radar began to show significant detail. I increased acceleration to .28 G. The fact that this would take us up out of the groove was not important; getting a longer look at the surface features was critical. Almost annoyedly, I slapped the switch to turn off the navigation alarm as I continued to keep one eye on the readouts and the other on the terrain below.

At three kilometers it became clear; the spot I'd grooved for the landing was a rather narrow shelf—certainly too narrow to accommodate the width of the vessel. Both up- and down-slope the terrain became considerably steeper, then shelved off into terraces of their own. The terraces had slopes of seven or eight degrees; the risers between them had slopes of thirty or so. The average slope of the whole region was about ten degrees, sure enough—but none of it was fit to land on. The vessel was too wide to fit on a single terrace, but did not set up high enough on its landing jacks to safely chance straddling a riser between two terraces. I had to find an area which had either broader terraces, or lower risers.

I unsplit the 3-D screens and went to straight stereo

radar readouts. "Tighten your seatbelts, please," I said out loud to no one in particular. "We're going to take the scenic route."

We were now at about two kilometers' altitude. I increased acceleration briefly until we were stationary with respect to the surface, then cut it to .14 G, hovering. I wanted to take a moment to orient the boat carefully. I intended to move laterally along the face of the mountain and the CRF plume would dig a trench in the ice. I had to make sure that the landing jacks would straddle the trench when we finally landed and that the exit port would be facing upslope. I'd already programmed the port for an upslope orientation, but it was much more critical now. I looked minutely at the instruments, then rolled the boat a few degrees and locked the roll axis.

"Can't see a damn thing," Jacobs muttered from the right side. "Steam's risen up past the viewports."

"Cheer up Jake," I said distractedly. "We'll be down in a minute or two—I hope."

I expanded the radar sweep pattern, yawed the boat twelve degrees to port and increased thrust to .16 G. This served the dual purpose of putting us in a constant-altitude traverse and letting me get a glimpse out my portside window of where we were going. The radar would provide a barely adequate picture of downrange conditions; I wanted to *see* the terrain ahead of our flight path. I gave the 3-D a final inspection; we were traversing and gaining altitude at the rate of about one meter per second. I locked in the controller settings, then turned to the left and leaned over to peer out of the viewport.

The mountain was stunningly large, a fact which I noted in passing only. I was looking sideways at the slope profile in the direction of our travel. The terracing was depressingly uniform out to the edge of my vision and up and down the slope. I was beginning to toy with the idea of taking us up over the rim to try our luck in the caldera, when I saw our landing spot—three kilometers ahead and a hundred meters downslope. Three or four of the terraces had fused together to form an irregularly shaped area of smooth slope. I quickly turned back to the 3-D, found the spot on the screens and locked the radar onto it with a tight beam. It was suitable. I took over control of the stick and rapidly moved us downslope so that we would be on the same level as the landing area, then resumed the traverse.

When we were almost over the smooth patch, I yawed us back thirty degrees in the other direction and increased acceleration to .2 G; this quickly killed our lateral. When the numbers showed zero velocity in the Y-axis, we were 2200 meters above the surface. I yawed back to vertical and cut acceleration to .05 G; we began to drop straight down toward the slope. It would be another minute before I needed to take action again. I locked the controls once more, then studied the radar picture of the terrain below us very carefully.

The slope averaged nine degrees, but was somewhat uneven; I didn't trust the radar to properly set the lengths of the landing jacks. And odar was out of the question; steam was billowing up, freezing almost immediately and falling as powder—all in the way of the laser rangers. I expanded the scale on the 3-D, froze the image, and manually moused the boat's image down to the surface. I adjusted landing jack lengths by eye and hand, to compensate for the terrain irregularities.

While I was performing the operation, the collision alarm went off. I was busy with both hands. "Jake, would you get that for me, please?" I said without looking up. Shortly, it cut off. I finished and switched the 3-D back to real time, glancing at the mission clock. About fifteen seconds. I cut in automatics to freeze our attitude at vertical.

We were six hundred twelve meters up and dropping at fifty-two meters per second. I took control and pushed acceleration up to .35 G. Twenty-five seconds later we were dead-stopped relative to the surface, with the radar indicating our altitude at .45 meters. I cut the CRF. Almost instantly I felt the gentle multiple thump as the landing jacks touched down and drove their power spikes into the ice. Mons Gargantua was under our feet.

I let out my breath, wondering how long I'd been holding it. Then, remembering, switched on the radio and let the antenna search for the nearest navsat. When contact was established, I sent a brief message to M-Base: "Whitedimple to O'Malley at Mimas Base. We've landed on target with no complications. Estimate retrieval and return in six hours, but don't be surprised if we're gone for eight. Whitedimple out."

I got up from my couch and looked at the others for the first time in several minutes; it seemed like hours. My legs were the tiniest bit shaky—no doubt due to the switchover from acceleration to planetary gravity—but my voice was working all right:

"Well, folks, did I pass your little test, or should I go back up and try it over?"

Jake was mopping hands and forehead with a handkerchief. He looked back at Williams and raised his eyebrows. Williams was just getting up from his seat; his legs seemed a bit shakier than mine. Junior was grinning at both of them. Williams broke the silence:

"Well, I'd say it was rather, uh, *smooth*, wouldn't you, Jacobs?"

Jake was busy forming a smile. "Yeah, Willie, *smooth* is about right. What do you say, Badille?"

"Definitely, *smooth*." Junior was smothering his grin and trying his best to be officious. He looked me in the eye, cleared his throat, and said: "Dr. Whitedimple, we've decided that your landing was *smooth*."

"Assholes," I said, and turned back to the console to shut down the boat's nav systems.

An eleven-percent grade is relatively mild. But when it's pure ice at seventy degrees Kelvin (it was colder up there than on the surface), it must be classed as more than mildly dangerous. If one were to slip, he might keep on slipping—down forty kilometers to the bottom.

Jake had been elected by acclaim to solve this minor problem. He was to go first and string a line up over the rim of the caldera. This chore required him to carry fifteen hundred meters of low-temperature line and a dozen or so power pitons, plus about twenty kilograms of extra battery to heat the spikes of his special crampons. That ice was hard and we weren't taking any chances.

When he was all suited up, he looked like a small mountain himself.

"Well, off to do a man's work," he said as Williams lifted his helmet into place.

"Better you than me, old boy," Williams said. "And if you fall, do try not to bump the boat on your way down the mountain; you might disturb my beauty sleep."

I didn't say anything but was glad that Jake was doing this work. The batteries, line spool, sack of pitons, ice axe and extra-heavy crampons made quite a burden to add to the already-large pliss on his back.

Helmet on, pressure test, radio check—then he was into the airlock, cycled and down the ladder. He anchored one end of the line to a piton driven into the ice near its foot. We watched him from the viewport in the dayroom as he slowly made his way up the terraced slope, driving a new piton and attaching the line every hundred meters or so. The dark orange overcast lent an alien flavor to the scene. Within an hour, Jacobs announced that he'd reached the rim. We asked him what it was like inside.

"Like the detailed radar pictures," his voice came back clearly. *"Except in burnt orange. Smooth slope near the rim, but more'n twice as steep as on your side. About a kilometer of that, then it levels off where the junk starts. It's buckled and folded ice. Large hunks and small. You'll have to wade through a couple of kilometers of that stuff, but I can see plenty of pathways, even in this dim light. Don't think you'll have any trouble."*

"Copy, Jake," I said into the mike. "Now get the rest of it done and get back here before your batteries run dry."

"Yes, Mother," he answered. Then, *"Okay, going over. See you in an hour or so."*

Through the binoculars I watched him back over the

edge, hanging onto the line as he disappeared from sight. The suit radios weren't powerful enough to raise the navsats, so he'd be out of radio contact until he reappeared.

"Down for one," Willie said, spreading his hand. I looked at his sets; I didn't have any play cards.

"Seven," I said, spreading four tens, six-seven-eight of clubs, and a leftover pair of deuces and a trey.

"Tough luck, old fellow," he said. "That puts me over the top again." He began scribbling figures on the score sheet, then looked up. "I say, Whitey, why didn't you come in with that seven? I was holding two nines, an eight and an ace, until I picked up the third nine. You'd have caught me with twenty-seven."

"Well," I said lamely, "I had a four-way hit for a gin and I needed the points."

"Mmmm, yes. Well, that makes a total of, ah, twenty-four sixty-two so far. Care to try your—"

"Jacobs to Catcher. Hey, you guys awake in there?"

I switched on the mike. "We're reading you, Jake. Only Junior's asleep. Willie and I are playing gin and waiting for the sound of your charming voice."

"Well, save some of your bankroll. I'm over the top and coming down. Be there in about fifteen minutes."

He sounded a bit winded, and when he finally stomped in through the airlock, we could see that he'd done a day's work.

"Okay you guys," he said as soon as I got his helmet off. "I've done the hard part. It's your turn to go grab the glory."

"Did your crampon heaters hold out?" I asked, helping him out of the cumbersome suit.

"Long enough," he said. "They didn't run out of juice until I finished the back side and was on the way back up. Didn't matter by then; I was hooked onto the line, and the going was safe and easy. You won't have any problems, unless you try to run downslope." He was out of the suit and stretching hugely. "Junior going with you?"

"Well," said Williams, "if he doesn't awaken, I'm for letting the little fellow stay behind. Might be a bit of a scratch for him, even with the line strung."

"If you want to try to leave me behind," Junior said entering the suiting room, "you'll have to produce that platoon of marines."

I helped the gnome into his suit, checked the pliss and heating circuit while Jake levered Williams into his own suit. Before I put Junior's helmet in place, I looked searchingly into his eyes.

"Just button me up and don't worry, Admiral. This is going to be a piece of cake. Besides, there's no way I'm going to miss looking down into that caldera, after all these years of stale glimpses on radar." He smiled, but it was short of his normal evil grin. "And if I'm too tuckered when we get to the rim, I'll stay and be your comm link while you and Willie descend the depths."

Jacobs helped me into my suit, and after checkout we all put on our crampons (much lighter than Jake's). Then it was out the lock, down the ladder, and hook onto the line. I led the way and kept the pace deliberately slow. Going up the risers between terraces, I felt much safer pulling myself up on the line; the crampons just didn't have enough bite to hold well on the steeper slopes. We hooked across each piton with a second suit line before disconnecting the first.

Even going slowly, we were at the rim in under an hour. For the first time, I stopped and took a truly comprehensive look at our surroundings. They were impressive for a SpaceHome boy who hadn't seen a true planetary vista in over twenty years. Down past the tug, which was now small in the distance, the slope dropped steeper and steeper—falling finally out of sight to the cloud tops eight or nine kilometers below. The clouds stretched seemingly unbroken from horizon to horizon; they were a fluffy brown blanket hiding the frigid world underneath. As the others came toiling up to the summit, I turned and looked down into the caldera. It was as Jake had described—a tumbled and broken mess, surrounded by the smooth, steep inner wall running around the rim at the top. The entire bowl was six or seven kilometers in diameter, with the central ice field occupying a rough circle over four kilometers across.

The others had now reached the top; Williams was setting up the tripod for the inertial guide, and Junior was standing and panting hard. I let Junior pant and moved to help Williams. I extended the tripod legs, while he readied the laser ranger/computer and hooked it up to the inertial guider. We attached the ranger to the tripod after its legs were firmly seated, then Willie bent to the instrument and successively sighted various points around the rim. When he got ten or so, he looked at the inertial unit and announced over the comm:

"Well chaps, the approximate centroid of revolution of this delightful ditch is three thousand two hundred twenty-seven meters in that direction." His arm was pointed down into the center of the ice field. *"So, shall we be off into the depths?"*

I peered at Junior; his chest was still heaving and his face looked drawn through the helmet plastic. "You're not looking real great, pardner. Why don't you stay here and talk to Jake and us?"

His helmet moved weakly from side to side, but his voice was definitive in the speaker: *"Not on your tintype, Dimp. I'll get my breath in a moment. I got a bet on with Willie and I want to be around to make sure he doesn't cheat."*

(Eight hundred kilometers away, almost exactly at the sub-Saturn point, was a very distinct formation of four large volcanoes. Looking at the Titan geographical maps during the voyage out, Williams had become convinced that the Hexie artifact was not in Mons Gargantua, but down under that cloud layer, in the geometrical center of that formation. He had gone so far as to make a small wager with Junior on the matter, even though Junior by now had a reputation for never losing a bet.)

"Okay," I said reluctantly. "We'll rest here a while longer, then all go down in. Don't bother to pack the tripod and ranger, Willie; we'll pick it up on the way back."

"Copy that, old chap," Williams said gratefully, disconnecting the inertial guider from the computer umbilical and stuffing it into a pouch on his chest.

"Okay, I'm ready now. Let's get this clambake into gear." Junior was straightening up and looking down the descent line into the crater.

I called Jacobs, while hooking my suit line to the other side of the summit piton. "Keep 'em burning, Jake. With luck, we'll be back up in three or four hours."

"Take your time, Whitey. I'm gonna enjoy a long nap. If you're not back by sundown, I'll come looking for you."

"Right." The brighter patch of orange hiding the distant Sun was almost due overhead; local sunset was four days hence. We had air and suit heater batteries for nine hours.

We backed carefully down the nine hundred meters of line Jake had laid into the caldera. When we hit the level, folded area at the bottom, Williams was breathing a little heavily and Junior needed a rest. I half-unfolded a shiny insulating blanket I'd brought along and spread it on an up-jutting table of ice. Junior thankfully sat down on it, put his hands on his knees and tried to catch his breath.

Williams was peering at the guider which he'd pulled out of its pouch, and pointing into the caldera. *"Twenty-four hundred meters, Whitey. How much line do you have?"*

"Two and a half kilometers," I replied. "So try to guide us straight. Otherwise, I'll have to start dropping bread crumbs. Here, hand me the end of it, would you?"

He reached over to my backpack, unreeled a few meters of line from the spool and hooked the carabiner on the end to Jake's final piton. *"There you are, old fellow. Now every meter you step off, your load will be lightened by several grams."*

"Unending thanks." I looked over to Junior. I was beginning to be quite concerned about him. The little man's cardiovascular conditioning could only be described as pathetic.

"Well, how about it, Wonder Boy? You going to wait here for us? It'd be a lot safer for you."

"Naw." He was still breathing hard. *"We'll be on . . . level ground the rest . . . of the way . . . I'll . . . be all right . . . Admiral."*

Five minutes to rest, then we started off with Williams leading with the inertial unit and me trailing with the line spooling out behind. A Junior sandwich.

Slow but steady. The going was thankfully easy. Williams picked his way with alacrity along the folded terrain, finding level footing with one eye and keeping the other on the inertial guider. The load on my back grew lighter at a gratifying rate. We had two or three hundred meters to go when we traversed a rather large open area with a nearly level floor. I looked at it appraisingly. We *might* have set the tug down there, but I was glad we hadn't tried. It would have been an awfully tight fit.

After another ten minutes Williams announced: *"By the dial on my boy scout wristwatch, we ought to be in the immediate vicinity of the artifact. Everyone please keep his eyes peeled."*

Junior's chest was heaving. Nevertheless, he scrambled up an outcropping of ice—a dangerous thing to do—and stood with his head two meters above ours and scanned the area. After about ten seconds he pointed off at an angle about thirty degrees from our present course.

"There it is . . . the hatbox . . . sitting up on a slab . . . twenty meters . . . over there . . . Pay up Willie . . . you owe me."

While Williams went to get the artifact, Junior climbed down on shaking legs. I had a hand on him the whole time to make sure he didn't fall. His breathing was very fast and deep, as if he would never catch his wind. I spread the blanket for him to sit down on. He sat, then continued to crumple.

"Gotta . . . lay down for a second . . . Admiral . . . take a little . . . nap . . . wake me up . . . when it's . . . time to start . . . back."

I hastily pulled the blanket under him as he collapsed to the ground. If he touched the ice, it would frostbite him in short order—full pressure suit and heated underwear notwithstanding. He lay on the shiny blanket, breathing fast and shallow but not moving otherwise.

"Willie," I said quietly over the intercom. "You got that damned box yet? We've got trouble here." I was trying to talk with a dry mouth and a lump of apprehension in my throat. I was so afraid for Junior, and in such a need to do something in a hurry, that the urge to urinate was almost overpowering.

"On my way back, Whitey."

"Good. Listen: I'll stay here with Junior. You get back up to the ridge and radio Jacobs. Have him bring the boat to that clearing two hundred meters back."

"You're not thinking clearly, old boy, which proves there's a first time for everything. I shall stay here with our small friend, while you go all the way back to the Catcher. Take the inertial guider with you; when you reach the center of the clearing, press the reset button twice. It will then home on the clearing. Once you get back to the tug, Jacobs can hold the guide while you bring the vessel back to the clearing."

"You're not making any sense, Willie. In the first place, your muscles are bigger than mine, so you can probably get back to get in touch with Jake faster than I can. And in the second, I'm just a raw rookie of a pilot. I'd feel a lot better with you or Jake at the controls—we all would, for that matter."

Williams had arrived back by then. He was breathing hard, but put down the familiar hexagon hatbox and immediately began unfastening the spool from my pliss.

"You are currently in a state of ignorance, old chap. Allow me to enlighten you. In the first place, my muscles may be larger than yours, but they are decidedly softer; I am a notorious slacker when it comes to doing my exercises. Therefore you can most probably make the best progress back to the tug."

He finished unhooking the spool and threw it on the ground next to the hatbox. *"In the second place, you are the best pilot of the three of us, rookie or no. You have demonstrated a touch and control which neither Jacobs nor I can currently match. And if either of us were sitting here a paltry two hundred meters from a CRF plume, we would choose you to be controlling that plume. In addition, that clearing is not much larger than the landing jack spread of the tug; putting it down there is going to be a dicey proposition. And, by the same reasoning, you stand the best chance of doing it without damaging the vessel and stranding us all on this lovely orange freezer."*

He thrust the inertial unit into my hands; I accepted it numbly. *"So you see, old boy, the mantle of responsibility is thrust upon you by inexorable logic. Accept it and waste no further moments with modest protestations. And please do hurry; I don't believe our heater batteries will be amenable to an extended stay."*

Dumbfounded, I looked at him, then down at Junior. Then I stuffed the inertial unit into my chest pouch and departed without another word.

I was an hour and a half getting to the top of the rim, and another half gingerly edging backwards down to the Catcher, arguing with Jacobs instead of conserving my wind. Jacobs won:

"You're no judge of your own ability, Whitey, so just shaddup and save your breath. I'll take it up if you want, but you're going to fly it down."

The second I stepped through the airlock he was helping me off with the suit, while I caught my breath. Then we were poring over the radar scans of the caldera. I marked our approximate position on the southwest part of the rim, then cut a line to the center of the crater. I didn't see anything that gave me a warm feeling; those scans simply didn't have enough resolution.

"It's no good, Jake; we're going to have to take it up a few kilometers and map it real time."

"I suspected as much. Okay, no problem. We'll go up to twenty klicks and look at it with the odar."

I was still breathing hard, so Jake took it up from the right seat. He did it correctly—got us all the way up to altitude before drifting us over the caldera, then stopped, hovering, about halfway between the lip and the center and let the odar paint its picture. We both saw it almost immediately; the position and size were just right.

Jacobs looked at the scale of the 3-D, then again at the picture of the clearing. "Jesus, Whitey! You think you can shoehorn this tub into that little ice patch?"

"Good question," I said, thinking hard. "I'll let you know when we get down. Listen: I think you'd better lock the landing jacks at equal lengths; I'm pretty sure I'll be rotating it all the way into the caldera. We might land on a tilt, but it won't be too bad; that spot was pretty level."

He nodded and did the deed, then asked me if I was ready to take command. I took a deep breath and said yes.

"Okay, switching control over to the left side, now."

I kept acceleration locked to leave us high, then used the RCS to put us over the clearing, making sure that we approached from the rim rather than the center. The plume at twenty kilometers shouldn't be a danger to Junior and Willie, but it would be bad form to take any chances at all.

When the 3-D indicated us over the center of the clearing, I asked Jake to check the inertial guider. "This thing says it's 19,987 meters straight down," he said.

I nodded, then carefully aligned our burn axis with the gravity gradient and set the RCS on automatic, to keep pitch and yaw at zero. I took manual control of the roll axis, then cut the CRF. We began to fall. I reached over and switched off an alarm just as it began to sound off.

"Do me a favor, Jake. Take care of the alarms. I'm going to be busy for the next couple of minutes lining up our landing jacks as the odar resolution gets better."

"Sure, Whitey. How long you gonna leave it falling?"

"Down to five kilometers. I need to keep scanning on laser as long as I can. That'll also put the CRF plume tight into the landing area."

"I'll cinch up my chinstrap."

"C'mon, Jake; it'll be less than .6 G. And you're the one who's had the nap."

It was a sweaty time. If I had to abort and go back,

Willie and Junior might run out of battery juice and freeze before we could get them back over the rim. If I broke the boat, we'd likely all buy the farm; the nearest possible rescue vessel was probably on Callisto.

During the two minutes it took to fall the first ten kilometers, I watched nervously as the odar scan grew in resolution. I concentrated on the overhead view, erasing the boat silhouette and projecting the landing jack footprints in true dimensions on the terrain picture. At first it looked like I'd be able to squeeze us in; then, as the smaller ice boulders came into focus at the edge of the clearing, I saw that it was going to be a near miss. I rolled us this way and that, but could only put three of the four jacks on clear ground.

Another alarm began to clamor, then cut off almost immediately as Jake pounced on it. Eight kilometers from the surface; going down at a hundred thirty-two meters per second. I rubbed sweat off my face with a sleeve.

A gap between two boulders on the clearing's edge began to resolve. I didn't know how wide it would be, but rolled the boat so that one jack was on top of it; the other three were clear by a meter or more. Six kilometers up; one hundred ninety-six meters per second. My left eye stung as sweat siphoned into it. The picture resolved a hair more; the gap would be about a meter and a half wide—barely enough. I used two precious seconds to vernier the jack footprint into the exact center of the tiny opening, then locked the roll axis while mumbling a prayer.

Time was out; we were at 5100 meters and coming down at two hundred meters a second. I cut in the CRF at .55 G; the breath I'd been holding whooshed out of my lungs as the acceleration jammed us into the couch.

I kept it on manual all the way down, ready to abort if it looked like I was going to wreck the tug. The last ten meters I was on a hair trigger; but no bumping or scraping gave any clue that this was anything but a routine landing. We touched down with a quadruple love tap which left us less than two degrees from vertical.

I threw six switches and was heading down to the suiting room almost before the plume died out. Jacobs was right behind me and stopped me with a vise-like hand on my upper arm. "Cool it, Whitey, and help me on with my suit. You'll be of more use plotting us up and out of here, while I go out and get the runt. You might also get in touch with the doctor at M-Base and have him standing by. We might need to take some action before we get back."

He cycled through the airlock, and within half an hour was back. Junior was leaning heavily on him; Williams was carrying the artifact. Junior's voice was weak and had little of its normal bite; he was obviously suffering from an acute case of an uncharacteristic disease: embarrassment.

Once they cycled in, I helped get Junior unsuited and onto an acceleration couch, first thing. The doctor at M-Base talked to him with long-distance pauses, and tentatively confirmed his preliminary diagnosis of acute exhaustion.

"You were a damned fool to be running around out there, Badille," came the tinny voice, *"without preparatory cardiovascular conditioning. Next time you pull a stunt like that, I'll have you evicted from M-Base for advanced stupidity. And when you get back here, report at once to the dispensary for a complete checkup. That's an order. Over and out, or whatever I'm supposed to say."*

While Junior slept once again, we opened the hatbox; the artifact was identical to the ones from Iapetus and Enceladus. Somehow, it didn't seem worth the effort.

As I was preparing for takeoff, Williams had a droll comment: "I say, old chap, better make sure you take it straight up; the clearance on your number two landing jack is something less than fifteen centimeters on either side."

I looked back, to catch him finishing an elaborate wink to Jacobs. The big man was grinning. "Assholes," I said again, turning back to the console.

Junior stayed asleep through my initial maneuvers, which consisted of a computer-controlled takeoff at a miserly .18 G. Once in orbit, I plotted a course back to M-Base at a sedate .05 G. Junior was awake; I dared him with my eyes as I spoke the number to the navigation computer. He smiled, but didn't say anything. I mentally estimated my gin losses at four hundred dollars for the long return trip. I vowed to sleep as much as I could.

13

Twenty-six hours later we touched down at M-Base. We hustled Junior, protesting, to the clinic and left him in the clutches of the merciless doctor, there to be ensconced for an indeterminate period with a minimum value of twenty-four hours.

The reason I only lost fifty-six dollars on the return trip was that I'd been doing some serious thinking while Junior was sleeping. It wasn't just the little gnome who was out of shape; it was all of us. I could see that living at M-Base meant little more than living in a zero-G field; and that would make for rapid deterioration, even with centrifuge workouts. I went in to talk to Maggie about it as soon as I'd cleaned up and changed clothes.

But it turned out that Maggie was ready with a surprise of her own.

"Congratulations, Whitey. Now that I know Junior's going to be all right, I feel a lot better about offering you the chief pilot's job." She grinned—I'd never seen her grin before—and it was a ghost of Junior's, evil glint and all. "Apparently, you put on quite a show out there."

"Are you out of your mind, Maggie?" I was taken totally aback. "You can't put me in that position. I'm just a raw rookie; you don't put a raw rookie in charge of two savvy boat commanders. And besides," I added, thinking of something else, "you simply can't do such a thing without the concurrence of the other two. I know for a fact that Jake's a damned good pilot, and he's a much better leader-figure for us than I would be."

She got serious, but there was still an imp in her eyes as she replied: "Whitey, why do you think Ogumi chose me for this job?"

"Well, uh . . ."

"Never mind; it was an unfair question. So I'll tell you the answer. It's because I'm not dumb, and I know what makes people tick. And I know how to get top performance out of them in difficult circumstances." She smiled. "Now, let's go back to the first qualification: Maggie's not dumb. Do you think I'd be doing this without the knowledge and consent of Jake and Willie?"

"But we just got back an hour ago."

"You slept for seven hours after you got the Catcher headed back for Mimas. First thing Jacobs did after you started snoring was to give me a call. He and Williams and I held a two-hour round-robin discussion of your sterling merits. The final conclusion was that, not only were you the best pilot of the three, but that you had the moxie to make tough decisions under pressure.

"And I know a little about you, myself." She put the smile back on her face again. "Apparently your main fault is that you keep bleating to the world about how you're just a raw rookie, and couldn't possibly do this or that. You'll have to stop that now—it'll ruin your image."

"Not stating the fact won't make it go away, Maggie."

"You'd be surprised. The fact is, you've never *acted* like a rookie, even though you say it a lot. So all you have to do is stop saying it, and you'll be an old hand in no time."

"But I—"

"Case dismissed, Whitey. But I'll tell you what. I'm

going to make you chief pilot, acting, for now. You go back and talk it over with the other two. If you can persuade them that you're not the man for the job, then you all come back to me and we'll talk it over again. And," she finished, showing a centimeter of steel, "if nothing happens within three days, the 'acting' part goes away."

The steel left. "Now, I'll bet you came here for some other reason than to have the chief pilot's job dumped on you. What is it?"

I had to switch tracks. "Uh, well, I was going to talk with you about being out of shape . . ." I told her of my deductions.

"So, do you have a suggestion?" she said after I was finished.

"Well, maybe. The main problem is that the centrifuge is so constraining on movement. Essentially, you're limited to isometrics on it; that builds up muscle, but not cardiovascular endurance. And there's not much incentive because of the nauseating nature and the general boredom of the whole routine. The bottom-line result is that there's little motivation to spend anything but a minimum daily workout on the thing."

She nodded, but waited for me to continue.

"So how often do you send boats to Iapetus Base for fuel and other supplies?"

She had a quick mind; it only took her about half a second to smile. "Right now, about twice a month for one reason or another. I take it you're suggesting we make the trip considerably more often—and at considerably higher acceleration?"

"Yes," I said. "At least twice a week if possible. With at least two of us aboard—preferably all three. We could fit the dayroom of the Catcher up as an exercise room; and the cargo hold is more than large enough to carry fuel supplies or anything else we might wish to take to or from I-Base." The supply tugs traveling the Earth/I-Base run had increased from quarterly to bi-monthly in order to supply both Saturn system bases; but they still docked only at I-Base. I-Base had also been increased in scope to supply the extra fuel for the effort—and, if the fact be known, to sell extra fuel to Earth for their own retrieval effort. Ogumi wasn't about to lose a fat profit just for the sake of forcing the Earthers to manufacture and ship their own fuel into orbit.

But increasing by fourfold our number of trips to I-Base was a significant investment in fuel, a fact which was quickly pointed out by the SART director.

"Well, Maggie," I countered, "fuel's cheaper here than any other place in the solar system. And you can just call them dual-purpose training trips, if all else fails. I can make a strong argument that all of us pilots need extensive high-G maneuvering practice in the Catcher if we're going to be ready to perform adequately in the Saturnian gravity well."

She was smiling. "Okay, Whitey. You've made your point. And it's only a few extra bucks out of Ogumi's pocket anyway, since it won't be too much longer before we're ready to make the grab. So work out a training schedule for my official approval." She held up a hand as I turned to go. "And by the way, son, you've just proved *my* point about your being the man for the chief pilot's job. Think about it."

"And this is the monster that's caused us most of our development time and bucks." Junior, three days out of the dispensary, was his old nasty self again, but undergoing a forced routine of low-gravity treadmill exercises to strengthen his cardiovascular system.

I'd been spending most of my time on paperwork, including working out a high-G trip schedule with the Catcher; and now Jacobs and Williams were off on the first junket to Iapetus. I had to stay back because I urgently needed training in the rest of the retrieval operation.

This tour was part of it. Also the simulators to follow and hyperbaric acclimatization in the chamber. Junior had just ushered me into the Lander construction facility and was pointing to what could only be described as a *thing*. It was a huge cluster of dull black spheres, supported from an overhead crane by thin netting; the spheres ranged from one to three meters in diameter. They were definitely made of metal. And their combined volume was enormous. It was so overwhelming that I almost didn't notice the three-meter-diameter open framework hung on the bottom. A second glance, however, showed that this was the business end of the apparatus. There were three antennae, various other small devices—all spherical in shape—and a large space at the bottom which was obviously meant to carry the artifact. The bottom was open, but there was some kind of double-fork arrangement which could apparently rotate down and close it off. There were also smaller metal balls attached all over the outside of the framework.

"Egad," I said.

"Now you know one of the reasons why the Catcher's hold has to be so big," said the little gnome.

"But still," I said, "outside of the balloons, it doesn't look like too much." I made the statement partly to bait my friend, and partly out of ignorance. Junior had pretty much stuck to SpaceHome policy and not written me too much concerning details.

"Speaks the voice of monumental ignorance," he snorted caustically. "Pressures of 5600 Earth atmospheres are five times what you find in the deepest ocean trenches. Added to that you've got eighteen, nineteen hundred degrees Kelvin trying to soften everything. You see those three antennae?"

He pointed and I nodded. "Three complete sets of electronics. They're for different depths and temperatures. Hell, two of 'em won't even work at normal temperature and pressure. We tested the mid-range one in the high-pressure/temperature hydrogen chamber, and it works all right. But the one for fifteen hundred kilometers and below can't even be tried out until we drop way down into the soup."

He scratched his nose. "So many things we're not really sure of until the fat's in the fire. Radar. Sonar.

Communications. Bearings. Guidance and control. Motors. Batteries. You name it. It's all new technology. Even the metals and electronics are heavily doped with high-temperature elements: osmium, rhenium, tantalum, tungst—"

"Hold it right there, Wonder Boy," I interrupted. "You're loading me with data I can't use; wasting breath."

"Damn amateur."

"Right. Now give me something I can work with. What are the chances that this kluge is going to work?"

The gnome reached up and pulled an earlobe, chewed for a second on the inside of his cheek. "Pretty good, actually. Overall chances about ninety-three percent. Except for that." He was pointing to a twenty-centimeter sphere near the top center of the framework. A small wire bundle ran from it to one of the strange looking spherical electronics clusters attached to the frame lower down.

"It's the inertial measurement unit. Laser gyros have to run in a vacuum. Can't get power in and signal out without wires. They're tight-sealed through a tapered plug. We've tested it as far down in the chamber as we can get it, and it seems to work okay. But it'll crap out at three, four hundred feet above sea level." He laughed evilly.

I raised my eyebrows. "Which gives you a special glee?"

"No," he cackled. "Which wins me a bet with the chief of materials and processes. Then we go to the backup system: Junior Badille's brute force insurance policy. All three antennae have transponders folded in. Remember that when we go back up and look over the Floater."

"Okay, but before we leave, you've got to tell me about that huge cluster of overgrown grapes. You told me you were wrestling with balloons, but this is overwhelming. I've done most of my reading on submarines."

He snorted. "Submarines work in water; that stuff stays the same density no matter how deep you go.

What we got on the Old Man is a compressible gas. Lots of pressure, sure; but even at the bottom, density's only about half that of water—hydrogen's the lightweight champ of the universe."

He pulled at an ear. "But down at sea level isn't the problem. It's trying to get it to float back up to where the Floater is waiting to grab it. That'll be way, way up—pressure only seventy or eighty atmospheres. To get neutral buoyancy there, you have to wrap a vacuum around a cubic meter for every five or six kilograms you want to lift. That set of balloons," he pointed up to the huge array, "makes about four hundred cubic meters. The whole apparatus, balloons and all, masses around seventeen hundred kilos, batteries included."

"Which means," I said, "that the artifact had better not mass more than four or five hundred kilograms, or we'll never get it up to the Floater."

"Keep your fingers crossed," agreed the little man.

"Wait a minute." I'd thought of something else. "If it floats up at the higher levels, how do we get it down to—" Then I looked at the smaller metal spheres attached around the lower framework. "Oh," I pointed. "Then those must be our sandbags. Lead weights, or something."

"Better go with the 'or something,'" he said drily. "Lead would melt less than halfway down. It's a thousand kilograms of one of those high-temperature alloys you didn't want to hear about."

"Okay, I asked for that. So here we go: The Lander sinks to the bottom, drops weights to achieve neutral buoyancy, motors around hunting for the artifact, finds it and scoops it up, releases the rest of the weights, and rises back up to the Floater; whereupon the Floater snags it and takes it out of the atmosphere to the waiting Catcher."

"Close enough, Admiral. 'Big fleas have little fleas.' Of course you'll have to do lots of practicing on the simulator; the guy in the Floater has to control all that on manual."

"Seems like a simple enough operation. Be easy to program a smart processor to do most of the work."

Junior grinned wryly. "Yeah, except for one problem: the environment. There's no way we can shield from the heat and pressure without excessive weight penalties. That IMU is a prime example: weighs a hundred kilograms and it's still going to be a worthless piece of junk, because those wires have to run out of it. If we tried to build a small protected computer to control it, I'd run the mission success projections down to less than ten percent. 'Fact, if mission success depended on that IMU, I'd do the same thing. In writing, to Greg."

"I believe it, Wonder Boy," I said. "But you've got other high-temperature high-pressure electronics built there," I pointed to the various spheres attached to the inside of the framework, "so why not just build a computer the same way?"

He snorted again. "Those are dumb circuits. Just route electrons through large pathways, amplify signals, and perform switching functions. To build a smart computer you have to jam millions of functions into a very small space. Temperature doesn't let you do that. I did some calculations on high-temperature computer requirements; turned out that to send a workable smart processor down to sea level, we'd have to add well over three thousand kilograms to the Lander mass. Added about sixty million dollars to the cost of the project— extra large Catcher, more R&D and so forth. I even worked out a scenario where we took the computer down, then abandoned it to get the Lander back topside. The dollars turned out even worse, because of the expected value of having to abort a mission and build a twin. I even tried to work another scenario in which—"

"Enough!" I cried. "I understand. The simpler the better. Consider me enlightened, and lead me to the Floater."

He moved across the room toward a large door, muttering under his breath. I followed complacently.

The Floater was as small as possible for a vessel which had to carry a CRF engine and a pressure shell inside its hull. Fifteen meters long, streamlined, with a gouge in one side into which the Lander would eventually fit. The double fork to clamp over the Lander was retracted; it looked strong. I could see the attach points clustered near the top of the vessel—but no balloons.

"Where's the cluster of black grapes?"

"In that mountain of boxes along the north and west walls, there. And, in this case, there are seven clusters. Dimp, you wouldn't believe the volume of balloons we have to attach to the Floater to get it to live up to its name; barely fits into the cargo lock of the Catcher when it's assembled."

"Then where does that leave the Lander?"

"You carry the Floater, Lander and balloons as separate tight-packed cargo. Once you're in orbit around Saturn, you take the Lander out of the hold, attach it to a special arm on the Catcher's hull, and attach the balloons. You do the same thing to the Floater inside the cargo bay. Then the Catcher does its de-orbit burn, dumps the Lander, and pushes the Floater out after it. A triumph of brute force operations design."

"How big is the pressure vessel?"

"Big enough. Unless you have a tendency towards claustrophobia—then it's way too small. Want to take a look?"

We walked up the side of the boat and through the hatch and into the heart of the thing. It was a sphere, of course, and all of 1.8 meters inside diameter. Junior, the acceleration couch and I were a severe strain on its capacity. Claustrophobic, indeed!

"Weight was the primary consideration, naturally," Junior said. "So the smaller we could build the pressure vessel, the better. Materials are lightweight and don't have to be fanatically temperature-resistant; at Floater depth you only run about 540 Kelvin."

"I take it we run hyperbaric to conserve weight."

"Damn right, Dimp. We save five, six hundred kilograms by making you pop your ears during the descent. If you'll take a look, you'll also see the sphere's only broken in four places: hatch, wire bundle, pressure dump valve and air conditioning. Seventy bars is no problem for a water submarine; but we had to be as skimpy as we could with weight, so we pushed technology. Biggest weight drivers are the CRF engine, heliox bottles and refrigerator, and the heavy forks to grab the *Lander* and hold it in place while you accelerate up out of the atmosphere."

"I take it the Lander releases its balloons when we grab it?"

"Yeah. And the Floater releases its own balloons at the same time you light off the CRF. You might bump into one or two of 'em on the way up, but what the hell."

"There has to be a way to descend a moderate amount if necessary."

"Yes, of course. Your computer, here, has a model atmosphere in databank, and the hull has sensors of all kinds hung over it. You tell your nav processor how far down you need to go and it'll release the appropriate balloon or two." A glint entered his eyes. "Of course, since this is a kluge operation, once you go down you're stuck until you release a sandbag. Got plenty of those—until you pick the Lander up and have to drop a bunch. After that, who knows? We could only guess at the artifact's mass."

I levered myself into the acceleration couch. It was in a central position with access to viewscreens, computer controls, switches, et cetera. From the seat, I could dust all the walls with my fingertips. I pictured myself locked into the little spheroid, falling into the Old Man's coat of hydrogen, down, down, into 70,000 millibars and a hundred degrees hotter than the proper boiling point of water.

"Junior, why can't this whole operation be controlled by a smart computer?"

He not only read my mind, but must have been looking into my soul, too; it was the first time I'd ever seen a sympathetic smile on his face.

"Admiral, for the first four months we were in business, the SART did nothing but tradeoff analyses. We collected our talent, collected a database and worked our butts off. First thing we did was to scope seventeen different retrieval scenarios, from single-stage unmanned to four-stage manned. You want the whole printout?"

"Just give me the high points."

"Okay. The high-sensitivity drivers were time, money, temperature, pressure, gas permeability, and slow data transmission rate because of the compressed hydrogen medium limiting us to low-frequency bands. The place we had to use the most Kentucky windage was in determining how much inventiveness we'd have to use in grabbing the artifact. We could program a smart computer to cope with every variation in the actual retrieval maneuver we could dream up—then, sure as hell, the real situation would turn up a problem we hadn't thought of. And the transmission data rate simply isn't enough for us to reprogram in real time if we run a cropper and need to take original fast action."

He scratched his nose. "So our final decision was to send a man down into the transmission medium and let him make decisions real time with the simple stereo sonar data from the Lander. Old Russian tradition: throw Ivan into the soup and see what happens."

He smiled again—and it wasn't evil! "If it makes you feel any better, we threw out all options that showed less than a 99.7 percent chance of getting the Floater operator out alive, no matter what happened. That was a lot easier to quantify."

"It *does* make me feel better. Especially if *you* were the one to make the calculations for this tub."

"Damn right. I knew *you* were going to be flying it," he said smugly. "Knew as soon as you started ground training classes with Sam Sebastian."

"That's very interesting, Junior, seeing as how I haven't made the decision yet about who's going down."

"Maybe not publicly; but deep down inside, you have. Willie's a good pilot—I've seen him work—but he's not in your league, or even Jake's. Strictly backup material, even if he gets his muscles toned up. Jake's damn good. He'll make a great Catcher pilot; he can sit up above the atmosphere all day at 1.3 G and still juggle eggs at sundown. But when it comes to figuring what to do—and how to do it—when the chips are down, you're the only Admiral on the team, Admiral."

He peered into my face and looked from eye to eye. "Besides, you're afraid to go down in this thing, so there's no way you'd ask anyone else to do it."

"You might be right. But you've got no call to know more about myself than I do." I changed the subject. "Okay, you were going to tell me about your 'brute force' transponder system?"

"That I was, Dimp. Right behind you there is the twin to that IMU you saw on the Lander, only this one will keep on working in your relatively benign environment."

"A light dawns," I said. "You get Floater position with this one, bounce a signal off the Lander's transponder, then use vector addition to calculate Lander position." I blinked twice while my brain worked. "But what do you do about attitude? Compass readings aren't that accurate, are they?"

"Dimp, you're gettin' pretty smart for a no-neck pilot. The reason it's brute force is that, for the best accuracy, you've got to position the Floater exactly over the artifact using your own IMU, and maneuver the Lander so that the return signal comes straight back up the gravity gradient. Greatest uncertainty is in the computer's atmospheric speed-of-transmission model. But while the other IMU is still working, you use it to let the computer update its model."

I nodded, then went off on another tangent. "Junior, what do you think the Earthers are going to do?"

He stood there for ten seconds while scratching his neck with one finger. "Good question. We've taken all the data we have, including those from your trance session with Maggie and the psychiatrist—by the way, did you know you were a gold mine of information? You must have followed every blessed thing that came over the air, and stolen everything that didn't."

"Yeah," I said drily. "So they told me."

"Anyway, we fed all that data into the smartest computer we've got, then added our own gamut of possible scenarios, and a Kentucky windage factor or two. Main drivers seem to be that Earth has a little more money to play with and better high-pressure technology going in. Another is that they started behind us, but got some benefit from the early teaming before they pulled out of SART.

"Given all that, the computer comes up with a sixty-forty solution: The Earthers will probably go with a two-stage scenario. Catcher drops a lander. Lander goes all the way down, grabs the artifact, and blasts all the way back out on CRF. If they can maintain a pressure vessel all the way down, that simplifies their problem considerably. Balloons don't have to be nearly as big, either—only an eightieth of the volume per unit mass to achieve neutral buoyancy, compared to our *Floater's* depth."

He stopped scratching his neck to pull at his earlobe for a moment. "Question is, if they go two-stage, will their lander be manned or computer operated? Greg says computer; I'm inclined to believe they'll go manned—but I'm not sure enough about *anything* to take bets."

I chewed a lip for a moment. "Got any idea when they're coming?"

He grinned. "We ask that question all the time. We monitor flights to Callisto and calculate supply and personnel tonnage. Then we use Ogumi's computers and our own. Then we make what we think are educated guesses. Current estimates range from three weeks to a year and a half. Maggie's betting on three months, based on the new stuff you brought in—including a lot of political speeches Earthside that Ogumi hadn't bothered to send us tapes of. She's planned our shot for ten weeks from now. I think she's come up with a pretty good guess."

As we elbowed ourselves out of the pressure vessel, I noticed something mildly disturbing. "Hey, Junior. This thing doesn't have an airlock."

"Nope." The grin. "Just a double hatch. Inner one

won't open if you're pressurized in vacuum; outer won't open down in the atmosphere. Internal and external pressures have to be nearly equal to get 'em both undone at the same time."

He laughed evilly at my dubious expression. "Cheer up, Admiral. If the Catcher doesn't pick you up, you're probably dead anyway."

14

"Advise pressure is now 6000 millibars, Dr. Whitedimple."

"Acknowledge," I said, swallowing once more for a final ear pop. I was wondering what the computer would have in store for me on this run. Last time I'd just picked up the artifact and was beginning to float the "lander" back up when I'd lost half my balloons. I had to abort the mission and get out of there quick on CRF before the "floater" sank too far.

I continued to perform now, guiding the lander so that it fell straight down beneath me, keeping myself exactly over the artifact location using my IMU readouts. This part of the task was nearly mindless, and I found my thoughts straying.

I'd now undergone—along with Jacobs and Williams—two months of intense training in the simulators, including Catcher mission profiles on computer and manual in the centrifuge. We'd also taken several high-G runs to I-Base, the last two at 1.3 G, much to Williams' chagrin. We'd also practiced manual "catches" with the monster boat at high-G, letting the computer simulate the Floater.

And of all those sweaty, spine-grinding exercises, I hated this one—the hyperbaric chamber—the most. Which really should not have been the case. Physically, it was certainly the easiest—just sitting there with a phony Floater pressure vessel wrapped around me and performing a relatively routine task. But I hated the Valsalva-ing and ear-popping, hated the feeling of claustrophobia, and hated my own helium-filled Munchkin-sounding voice.

But this was to be the final trial; the next time I felt the claustrophobic pressure it would be the real thing. There was only a week to go until we made the retrieval attempt. That brought me back to the task at hand; I concentrated diligently in a vain, emotional attempt to speed up events and get back out of the chamber.

The computer-generated Lander was now at the gas-liquid interface—"sea level." I search-patterned for a while, found the bogey, and picked it up; the sonar painted it as a thick hexagonal plate. This time, it was too heavy to lift all the way up to my "depth" of 550 kilometers below the cloud tops; it strained up to 600 kilometers and floated there, waiting.

I talked Munchkin-talk: "Advise Lander inability to ascend to Floater depth. I will descend fifty kilometers to complete pickup."

I instructed the computer to do the deed, flipping off an alarm as the boat dropped through its maximum safe limit of 72 bars. At 600 kilometers down, 83 bars, and 585 Kelvin, I made the snatch—then released everything and lit the CRF. I was "picked up" and walked out of the chamber fifteen minutes later.

The technician was frowning, which was unusual; he was generally all smiles after I'd finished a simulation. The hyperbaric medicine doctor had a thoughtful look on his face. A puzzling pair of reactions. I decided on a frontal attack on the tech:

"What's the matter, Hal? You look like the early worm who got bird-bit."

"Dr. Whitedimple, I'm afraid that I must score a *fail* for you on this simulation." He was red-faced and flustered; he hadn't gotten much practice at failing people and didn't really know how to go about it.

"What's the matter, Hal; was I supposed to leave the Lander down there and save myself?"

"Uh, yes sir. And I'm afraid that Ms. O'Malley called and asked for you to come to her office." Then, because he couldn't bear to leave me without softening the blow: "But your mechanical performance was totally optimum as usual, sir."

"Thanks Hal," I smiled. "That's a comfort." I turned to the doctor; I could guess what he was thinking and needed his professional opinion.

"Doctor, when I went down that extra fifty kilometers, I could have increased cabin pressure and brought the vessel back to a more favorable margin of safety. What would have been the consequences?"

"Well, Dr. Whitedimple, you would have had to inject with Curabend...." Curabend was the rather sophomoric brand name for a compound which prevented dissolved gases in the blood from coming out of solution too quickly upon depressurization; it acted much like a chemical hyperbaric chamber, while giving a diver time to get to a real one. It had saved many lives down on Earth, but had lost some, too. It was tricky stuff to use; you had to gauge the dosage carefully. The actual chemical name was alka-hemo-something-something-something-something. If we ever had to pressurize the Floater over 8000 millibars (about 7.9 Earth atmospheres), God forbid, we'd be required to self-inject. Reason: The Floater was built to take lots of pressure from the outside, but could only handle about two atmospheres on the inside with vacuum surrounding it. Once the CRF was lit off and the Floater headed for space, the pressure vessel decompressed automatically to keep pace—no choice. I understand that helium bends is a rather agonizing way to go, and it was a long way from Catcher pickup back to the M-Base hyperbaric chamber.

"... would have to make the judgement based on the degree of pressurization and the requisite dosage of

Curabend. The human risk increases strongly with dosage, even when the diver has had his metabolism calibrated in the laboratory. For instance, if you were to go down to 10,000 millibars and take a five-milligram dosage, the literature shows that your survival chances would be approximately—"

"Thank you, Doctor; you've given me the information I need." Which was a blatant lie, but I didn't have time to sit through the half hour that he would take to get to the answer.

"Sorry," he said. "I suppose I was getting a little too involved."

I felt sorry for him. He'd stayed behind when Earth pulled out and now had no one to talk shop with. He was de facto committed to SpaceHome and would have to specialize in another field in the Colonies, or go into general practice. I gave him as warm a smile as I could.

"Well, I really am interested in the answer—Carl, isn't it?—because my life might depend on it. But, unfortunately, I've got a date to get chewed out by Maggie O'Malley; so let's save it for tomorrow."

Not only was the SART director in the office, but Junior was there, too. That was something of a relief because Maggie was too good a leader to give me a thorough reaming in front of someone else—unless she wanted a witness present as she fired me from the project.

Junior had a subdued grin on his face. A good trick.

Maggie looked stern, which she could do very well when the occasion demanded. When she spoke there was more than a hint of steel in her voice:

"Whitey, you know the strict injunction against taking the Lander below its safety limit of 570 kilometers. Yet you dove to 600 without hesitation to make the pickup. Why?"

"It was a combination of factors, Maggie. It would have most likely been a permanent abort to lower it back down to sea level, because even if we juiced up the backup Lander to make the pickup and get it up to 550, the original Lander would still have to drop the artifact before the backup could get it—and the thing would probably sink for good. Also, the fact that the Floater design limit is 126 bars, and I only had to go down to 83. And it would have been an overwhelming defeat if we got that close and then had to give up. It all added up to 'now or never.'"

She nodded and handed a dollar bill to Junior. He took it without comment. His grin widened imperceptibly. As he stuffed it into a pocket, the woman continued:

"Tell me, what do you think the other two pilots would have done in that situation?"

I pondered a moment before replying: "Jacobs would have thought about it for a while, then gone down and got it. Willie would have thought about it even longer, then aborted."

She nodded again. "Well, I can't fault your judgement about your fellow pilots. That's exactly what they did."

I raised my eyebrows.

"Yes, Whitey. We didn't let the computer pick the anomaly for that particular situation. Jacobs ran it four days ago, Williams two. I asked both of them not to talk about it until you finished your own run today. The other two did exactly as you guessed, except Williams thought about it for an *extremely* long time, then was sorry afterward that he aborted."

She was quite careful to look me in the eye as she continued: "Whitey, I got Jake's and Willie's word on this, and I want yours, too—it's especially important because you're probably going to be the Floater pilot: Promise me that *under no circumstances* will you exceed the safety limits of the Floater."

"No, Maggie; I can't promise that. I love my skin very dearly, but I am a human and must make human decisions. If you want preprogrammed behavior in response to unpredictable situations, then send a computer down to do the pickup."

She looked over every square millimeter of my face. "You feel quite strongly about that, don't you?"

"Yes. You can prevent me from going down, but you

can't stop me from making my own estimates of the situation once I'm in control. That's my *job*."

Silence for fifteen seconds while her eyes flickered over my face again. Then she glanced at the wall calendar.

"You may not have realized it, Whitey, but you've just attempted to make a policy decision—and that's *my* job. We have six days until liftoff for Saturn. In three days we'll talk again to see if either of us has changed our mind. If not, I shall have to give the Lander pilot's position to Jacobs."

I nodded with a heavy heart. I knew that I wouldn't change my mind, and the consequences of that were more than just the loss of the Lander pilot's job. Maggie would also have to remove me from the chief pilot position—not that that would mean anything if the retrieval attempt were successful. But I didn't want to send either of the others into that murk. All I had to do to prevent it was to make the promise. I would be lying, but the chances were 99-plus percent that the situation to prove the lie would never come up. A pretty problem in ethics; just the thing to ruin my week.

Junior followed me out the door. I headed for the bar; I felt like libating. On the way, I asked the gnome why he'd been in the office.

"To collect my bet, of course; and have a drink with you afterward. I don't think Maggie expected a confrontation—you caught her by surprise."

"Junior, how do *you* feel about it?"

"I agree with Maggie. We've got along for quite a while without the Hexies, and can probably muddle along a while longer without their help. On the other hand, there's only one Admiral Dimp. The future would be a bleak place without you, pardner. Here we are."

He pushed through the French doors and led the way to a pair of empty seats at the bar. The tender brought us "vodka" without comment.

"Your health, Wonder Boy." I raised the squeeze bottle and took a cautious sip. Same old stuff; it reamed out my sinuses. "Speaking of which," I continued with fiery breath, "how're you doing lately?"

He knew what I meant. "Okay, I guess. SART's been good for me. A challenge. Probably added two, three years to my life; I figure I've still got four or five left."

I couldn't stand it. "Dammit, Junior, that's a bunch of crap! You're barely twenty-one."

He chuckled. "All the crap in the universe won't make entropy spin backwards, Dimp. My IQ's just about leveled off, and there's nowhere to go but downhill."

"Entropy may not spin backwards, but you sure as hell can encourage it to spin slower. The solar system has a huge database you could tap: longevity research, geriatrics, cloning, causes of premature aging—"

"Premature aging's a hormonal condition, Dimp. My problem lies squarely in the central nervous system."

I looked carefully at him. He was hedging, evading the issue. I wondered why.

"Quit trying to blow smoke rings through me, Wonder Boy. This is your buddy the Admiral speaking. You've got twice the brain God ever graced anybody else with; don't tell me you can't make a good stab at holding off the grim reaper—probably benefit the rest of mankind while you're at it."

He swirled the remaining liquid in his bottle for a long time before answering. "Dimp, I'm not sure mankind is ready for a breakthrough in geriatrics, even assuming I could provide it. We've added just three or four decades to the average lifespan of the human beast during the past couple of centuries and it seems to have brought us nothing but grief."

He sipped. "Yes, I've thought about it. I might do something—I've even gone so far as to work out a tentative schedule of preliminary research. But would it really 'benefit' the human condition? I've got strong doubts, Dimp old friend. Strong doubts."

He smiled in self-deprecation—an event of the first magnitude for the cocky little man—then added: "And there's another thing. I think I'm afraid of failing."

That I understood. The little gnome had succeeded in every venture he'd attempted. The thought that he might

take too big a bite even for his prodigious intellect
might be frightening, indeed.

"I'm with you on both counts, Junior. But I'm selfish;
I think the world would be a bleak place without you,
too."

I ordered a second vodka, still thinking. Junior had a
soft drink—some artificial lemon concoction.

"Junior, there isn't too much doubt that the Hexies
have star travel."

"True."

"If we make contact with them, it's possible that the
universe is going to become a radically smaller place
for us."

"True."

"It may be just a pipe dream, but it could be that
within just a few years—or even months—we might be
thinking seriously about things never before possible:
interstellar commerce, colonization of other planets. I
don't know what all."

"Possible."

"Well, I'd like you to make *me* a promise. If the pipe
dream seems like it's going to come true—if we retrieve
the artifact and the message is promising—tell me you'll
go after that longevity problem, doubts and all. I frankly
couldn't care less about the rest of mankind; but if
there's fun and frolic to be had out there, I need *you* to
help me do it up right."

He stared down at the bar for a long time, then
looked up and grinned.

"Okay, Admiral."

I started on my third drink, and we began to swap
stories. In two hours, I was feeling very little pain. He
helped me into bed and tucked me in. The last thing I
remember before dropping off was that crooked-toothed
smile wishing me a happy dream.

15

There was a blinding light in my eyes and a monster was shaking my whole body until my teeth rattled. I squeezed my eyes shut tighter and hunched my shoulders to make everything go away, but light and monster were remorseless. I squinted my eyes open a crack.

The blinding light was the austere 500 lux at bed level in my room. The monster was Jake, gently shaking my shoulder.

"Whitey, you've got to wake up."

"Go 'way and turn out the light."

"Whitey. The Earthers are nearly in-system. There's a powwow in Maggie's conference room. You've got to come."

I sat up on the bunk. Even at .007 G it was a magnificent achievement. My heart was pounding right up into my head. My tongue felt rusted in place, but I ruthlessly forced it to form words: "How far out are they?"

"Eleven hours. They're at ten million kilometers and braking in at 1.32 G."

"Got any coffee?"

"Here." The big man handed me an insulated squeeze bottle. I took a sip. The stuff was probably the second rottenest concoction I'd ever tasted.

"Good God. What did you put in this?"

"Things to unparalyze your stomach and brain, Chief. Doc's prescription. We need you alert; Junior warned us."

Even the first sip had done some good. My mind was groggy, but working. "When's the next SKP due?" From the start of the project, we knew we'd have to make the retrieval during the ten-and-a-half hour interval between the kilometric radio pulses emanating from the surface. Those pulses were so strong they could ruin our electronics.

"Five minutes from now," Jacobs said. "They've timed it almost perfectly; they'll be on site to make their drop just fifteen minutes after the following pulse."

My brain was up to three-quarters by then. "Damn; they've beat us, then." Loading the Catcher with Floater, Lander and balloons was a minimum seven-hour job. Two hours to establish a polar orbit around Saturn, even at 1.3 G from Mimas. At least three hours in orbit to get the Lander out of the Catcher, attach all balloons and check out all systems. Another half hour for de-orbit and drop. There was no way.

"Relax, Whitey. We spotted 'em six hours ago—just a few minutes after you went unconscious. We didn't wake you on Junior's strong advice, but we've been working. The balloons and Floater are already tucked away in the cargo bay and they're almost ready to start loading the Lander. We'll be ready to lift in an hour or so."

He frowned. "But that's not the main problem. The big hassle is whether to even make the attempt or not. They weren't scheduled to finish final checkout of the system for another two days; then there were two more days of on-orbit tests before the drop—all of which you know very well."

I nodded, then excused myself and went down the hall to the john. The quick lukewarm shower worked wonders. I came back, put coveralls on, then Jake and I left for the headshed.

The conference room was filled with people and voices. Maggie, the eight division chiefs, Junior, and five or six of the brightest horse-holders were there, as well as Williams. Voices were heated. As we came in, Maggie and Willie nodded, and Junior grinned and winked. The others barely had time to notice us; they were much too busy wrangling. I stood for a few minutes, wincing slightly whenever the noise went over 120 decibels, and collected data.

The "go" and "no-go" factions seemed to be of equal strength. The "go" people were saying that many checkouts had already been finished, and that the remainder were just icing on the cake; and that there was no way we should let Earth beat us to the artifact and waste the whole effort. The "no-go" faction said that eliminating the final tests would significantly reduce the 99.7 percent *Floater* survival figure; and that there was a chance that Earth would fail in the mission—in which event we might build on their failure data and give ourselves an even better chance of making the pickup.

The SART director was listening politely with a serious expression on her face. I got the impression she had cotton in her ears and was doing her own thinking. Junior was sitting on a corner of the conference table near his boss; he wore a permanent wry smile. Neither he nor Greg had said a word since I'd arrived. Williams was also silent; he'd come over to the door to greet us, made a cynical comment about the "ballyhoo," then proceeded to slouch against a nearby wall.

Margaret let the conversation continue for six or seven minutes after Jake and I arrived. Every half minute or so there was a statistical fluctuation of the noise level down to fifty or sixty decibels. Into one of these pools of relative silence, she finally said:

"Ladies and gentlemen, let me have your attention, please!" The donnybrook stopped. "I would like to hear from the chief pilot. Dr. Whitedimple?"

A small sea of eyes turned in my direction; my adam's apple bobbed minutely. My tongue was still a little thick, so I spoke slowly: "Before I add my own comments, for whatever they're worth, I need one data point. Junior, if we go now, how far do the Floater survival percentages drop?"

"Down to 99.3," he said crisply, "plus or minus point three percent. That assumes you do a complete on-orbit systems check while the technicians are attaching balloons to the two vessels."

"How about overall mission success chances?" I asked.

"A negligible change. It's lost in the noise."

I nodded. The uncertainty of the artifact's size, mass and means of staying in place was very large. The 84 percent mission success figure was more an educated guess than anything else. I looked back to the director.

"Ms. O'Malley, I think this team has put together one hell of a system, and that it would be a bad mistake just to stand by and not use it while the Earthers took their best shot. I haven't had time to poll the other two pilots, but based on what I've heard during the last several minutes I believe that we're just wasting time here."

She smiled. It was medium thin. "It's not been *quite* the waste you think, Whitey. The major issues had to be brought out, and we do have nearly another hour yet until the Catcher will be ready to go. But if it makes you feel any better, both of your fellows," she nodded at Jacobs and Williams, "expressed identical opinions some time ago."

The smile vanished as she addressed the room in general: "Ladies and gentlemen, I have heard your arguments and opinions and it is my decision to carry on with the attempt. There will be another decision point after completion of the on-orbit systems checks. You are all on standby until then, and throughout the remainder of the mission, should we proceed. Thank you for your inputs. Dr. Whitedimple, will you please remain after the others leave?"

They cleared out quickly, even Junior. Maggie cast a

mean die. There was no smile on her face when she spoke to me:

"Whitey, your last report had yourself listed as primary Floater pilot with Jake as backup; primary Catcher pilot was Jake, with Willie as backup. Given that Willie was the only one who didn't flunk that last chamber exercise, is that still your lineup?"

"Did you look at the mechanical efficiency scores of that run, disregarding the judgement call?"

"Yes. Jake had a 98.8, you got 99.6, and Willie had a 96.2. I also know that your scores for previous runs with Catcher and Floater line up the same way. My question still remains."

"The answer is yes, Margaret."

"Whitey, I have no wish to undermine your considerable authority over the other two pilots, but I must have that promise before I can okay your lineup."

We both knew what she was talking about.

"I promise, Maggie." Ever try to relax your face and hold it rigid at the same time? It's hard. She looked over my efforts very carefully, then reached her own decision. She smiled warmly, put an arm around me, pulled my head down and kissed me quite tenderly on the cheek.

"All our hopes go with you, son; and our main hope is that you come back to us. There's more than one of us who loves you."

I left for breakfast with a red face, a lumpy throat and guilt in my heart.

16

"We are now in Saturn polar orbit. De-orbit burn will commence in four hours, twenty-three minutes. You all know your jobs; let's get to it!" Jake's poppa-bear voice over the Catcher's intercom was a warm, gruff command. After nearly five hours at .3 G from Mimas, the return to weightlessness was relaxing. I stayed strapped into my couch for an extra stolen moment. The volunteer crew of six technicians was already in action, headed aft to suit up for their three hours-plus of arduous free-fall work.

The reason they were "volunteers" was that we had to make the Mimas-to-Saturn run at almost a third of a G to get here in time to make preparations. This was pretty high acceleration for anybody who'd spent the past year or more in Mimas' feeble field. Of course, everybody on base had volunteered, so the operations chief had simply picked the six best.

Junior would be along shortly in Pandora. He'd left a little before us, but was making the voyage at a quarter G. He would take the crew back at a more sedate pace after the retrieval.

The Earth vessel had changed neither course nor acceleration—nor would they. Their progress had been carefully monitored and plotted by the big computer on the Catcher, using continuous update data from the Saturn navsats. They were decelerating at 1.34 G on a course exquisitely calculated to place them dead stopped with respect to the correct drop point, just above cloud top level, exactly fourteen minutes after the next Saturn kilometric pulse. Which was—I checked my watch—four hours and forty minutes away.

I unstrapped and made my way forward. Jake and Willie were just finishing buttoning down the control board.

"Whitey, old bean. So nice you could tear yourself away from bed to join us. How are you feeling?"

"A lot better, thanks, Willie. I got two hours' sleep once the crew settled down. I wonder how Junior's doing?"

"Pandy to Catcher. Anybody awake in that whale, over?"

"Speak of the devil," Jacobs grunted, then thumbed the mike. "Catcher to Pandy. We've got you five by, Badille. Got anything interesting we should wake up for, over?"

"Not in particular. I've cut the CRF and will be matching you on RCS in about eight minutes, over."

I did some quick calculations and took the mike from Jake. "Junior, you must have been pushing it past .25 to make that kind of time. Who do you think you are, Superman or something?"

"Hello, the Admiral. Took it in at .28. No problem. I'm in a lot better shape since I started doing my treadmills. Not even breathing hard. See you in a few minutes. Out."

I worked my way back to the suiting room, donned my micropore, and cycled through to the now evacuated cargo hold. The technicians were working heroically; they already had the Lander out and were attaching it to the specially installed offset arm jutting out of the Catcher's hull near the cargo door. The arm would hold it firmly, upside down and balloons trailing aft, during the de-orbit burn. At release point the arm would let go and drop the Floater into the Old Man's cloud tops.

I had to check out the Lander's systems from the Floater, beginning with the balloon release solenoids, so they could get on with attaching the spheres to the smaller vehicle. I switched to their suit frequency and checked progress; they'd have it attached to the arm in five minutes and I could begin while they were readying the balloons.

I opened the hatches of the Floater, drifted in and set myself in the couch. I activated the Floater's systems and began checkout of the communications equipment. Soon I got word that the Lander was attached. I activated its low-pressure electronics and began subsystem checkouts—at least on the low-pressure mechanisms. The few I could test, including the balloon releases, worked perfectly. I called the technician crew chief after climbing out of the cargo hold and establishing line-of-sight contact.

"Ken, you can string 'em up now; I'm finished."

"Roger, Whitey. Some kind of scenery out here, eh?"

"You can say that again."

We were orbiting just a bare 5000 kilometers above the planetary cloud tops, in order to miss even the tenuous D-Ring when we passed through the ring plane in another hour. We were on the sunlit half of the planet, below the ring shadow. The backlit rings were partially cut off by the Old Man's bright limb, but nevertheless stretched across an enormous horizon; they stunned the senses, even from tens of thousands of kilometers. I was sorry that I'd be in the Floater performing checkouts when we passed through the ring plane; at 24 kilometers a second, it would be quite a sensation.

I shook my head and ducked back into the cargo hatch. Some of the crew were already unshipping clusters of balloons. They were now white, covered with shock-insulating foam which would sublimate away at 465 degrees Kelvin, leaving only the black spheres. By then, the vessel would be almost 500 kilometers down and long finished with any buffeting from the initial drop.

Those balloons needed shock protection. When I found out how thin they were, and still able to survive the environment to which they'd be subjected, I was astounded.

The secret was their composition and perfect sphericity. They were not only formed in free fall, but the little manufacturing facility was way out at Iapetus, so that Saturn's gravity gradient wouldn't mar their perfection during forming. A spherical mold, which was a polymer bubble of some kind, was formed first; then the lightweight alloy was deposited on, lovingly, molecule by molecule, until a thickness of half a millimeter was achieved. Then a holographic spherometer checked the perfection—half of them were rejected—before the process was allowed to continue. The molecular deposition then continued on a computer-controlled regime to build up stress ribs to distribute the loads from the attach points.

Down at 70,000 millibars, a two-meter balloon formed by this method could lift about twice its mass of 12 kilograms. Four-meter balloons had slightly thicker skins and massed 60 kilograms, but could lift well over three times that weight.

I watched while the technicians built up the balloon structure on the Lander. Junior was docked by then and swarmed into the cargo hatch. I waved a hand.

"Why aren't you inside checking out the Floater?" I could see him grinning through the clear plastic helmet.

"Just lolligagging," I replied. "Eating a last hearty meal with my eyes."

"Old Man puts on quite a show from here, doesn't he?"

"Roger that. And back to work."

I made my way into the cargo hatch and into the little pressure vessel of the Floater, there to begin the tedious job of subsystem and system checks necessary to insure the health of the system. Willie would be the communicator, so he acted as Catcher voice during the procedure. We let the computers do much of the work, but there were still stereo television, radar, sonar, communications channels and backups to occupy our attention. Junior and Jake came back out to help the crew tie the immense volume of balloons onto the Floater, and install and fill the enormous bag which wrapped the entire package. They went outside during passage through the ring plane and gave us a two-minute account of the spectacle. I was determined to see it myself some day.

We finished over an hour before de-orbit burn. By then all other operations had also been completed, and the cargo hatch had been sealed and pressurized again. I climbed out and looked at my vehicle. The entire top half of the Floater—and three-fourths of the immense hold—was occupied by the white bag. I shook my head at the size of the bloated monstrosity and exited to the suiting room.

The half-dozen technicians were suiting up to cycle through the personnel lock and transfer over to Pandora. The Catcher would be no place for them in the maneuvers to follow: Junior would keep his little research vessel in polar orbit and rendezvous with the Catcher after it made pickup. I shook hands with all of them and thanked them for favors rendered. They wished me luck one by one, each more sincere than the last. Each of them had that unspoken "better you than me" look in his eyes. I didn't blame them. The Old Man was awesome from there, and not one of us could escape the irrational notion that to dive down into him was permanent. I knew it was irrational, because that's what I kept telling myself.

When I got up to the control cabin, Jake and Junior were busy listening to Willie debrief Maggie on the checkout.

"... lived up to its pedigree, old girl. Neither the computers, nor Whitey or I, could turn up a single anomaly, over."

We weren't in line-of-sight with Mimas, so there was a four-second pause for the double relay through the nearest navsat.

"*Very good. While we're waiting for Whitey, I have some more news on the Earth vessel. It's close enough to esti-*"

mate the mass being pushed out in the CRF plume. Our computers here say it's got almost twice the mass of the Catcher, which seems excessive even for as rich a project as we'd calculated. Is Whitey back to the control room yet, over?"

I took the mike. "I'm here, Maggie, over."

Pause.

"How do you feel, Whitey, over?"

"I feel ready, over."

Pause.

"Are you afraid, over?"

"Yes, over."

Pause.

"In that case you may proceed. And may God go with you, Whitey. You have the best wishes and the backing of all of us who are stuck back here at Mimas. And with this transmission we shall sign off, but be standing by. Out."

"Thank you, Maggie, and thank the whole gang for me, out."

We were all digesting the news about the size of the Earth vessel. A two-stage scenario would have their catcher being somewhat smaller than ours. Junior seemed to think so, too.

"Well, so much for our predictions about the Earth SART. Looks like they had to put together a three-stage mission, just like us poor folk."

"Then why is their catcher so much larger than ours?"

I could guess at that one. "Two reasons, Jake. First one is simple: they have to carry more fuel. Second, they probably have both floater and lander tucked away in the cargo hold."

The big man looked at Junior, who was nodding. "The Admiral has the right of it. Which is very good for us. We're going to beat them to the drop by four minutes; and, everything else being equal, that means we have a better chance of getting to the artifact first."

"I say, chaps, isn't there a chance they might try some funny business like they did at the Iron Maiden— begging your pardon, old boy."

The last was addressed to Jake, who waved it off.

"I don't think so, Willie," I said. "We're beaming everything on open transmission, both to Mimas and I-Base, for Earth-orbit consumption. Maggie and Ogumi made that decision some time ago, just to preclude such an event."

Junior was looking at the mission clock. "Time for me to get over to Pandora and back off. Dimp, could you come aft and help me suit up?"

I tagged along and assisted the little gnome in silence. We both knew how the other felt; neither of us really wanted to separate at the moment of truth. When I started the helmet toward his head, he put a restraining hand on my arm.

"Admiral, I want you to come back without any fuss. If you have to drop the Lander, do it without hesitation. We've got a backup. And then get the hell out of there. I'll see you in five or six hours."

I nodded, unable to speak. He gave my arm a little squeeze before pulling his hand away. I locked his helmet in place, then he was gone, cycling through the lock. If everything went right, he'd be back around just about the time the Catcher picked me up and accelerated to orbital speed. Part of the technicians' payment for their arduous effort would be to have a first crack at viewing the artifact. If everything went right. I was scared and had an irrational feeling that everything would not go right.

When I got back forward, Jacobs turned around long enough to say: "Time to go strap in, Whitey. Thirty minutes to de-orbit burn."

I nodded again; it was getting harder and harder for me to force words out of my mouth. But as Willie unstrapped to escort me back to the cargo hold, I did manage to mumble a goodbye to Jake. He replied cheerfully:

"Same to you, Chief. And listen: You get that little tin can to within fifty miles of the cloud tops, and I'll pick you up, you hear me?"

"Thanks, Jake. Be seeing you."

Willie kept up a line of chatter as we made our way

back to the Floater. I listened to him in an almost mindless state, wishing there was some way I could back out of doing this, even at the last moment. What I was experiencing was pure fear; it was a primitive, emasculating thing.

We entered the cargo hold. To provide a proper acceleration environment for the Floater-balloon system, the Floater was held firmly in place against the forward bulkhead of the large chamber, with the balloons trailing aft. When acceleration was applied, the Floater would be hanging upside down with the balloons trailing below—the same orientation as the Lander outside the hull. The balloon cables and attach rings were stress-designed to withstand this environment, and no other orientation would do.

But that meant I would have to be upside down in the Floater, hanging by the chair straps, during the full half hour while Jake killed our orbital velocity. And acceleration would be a grinding 1.4 G—a tenth higher than I'd feel right side up once I was dangling comfortably in the atmosphere.

The straps were very strong, wide and padded. It was almost like being wrapped in a cocoon with only my arms dangling out—and there were even pockets for those. Before he left, Willie made sure I could find the quick-disconnects on at least the nearby buckles. Then he put his hand on my shoulder and said: "We'll keep in touch, old top." Then he dogged both hatches and I was in the coffin alone.

"Floater to Catcher. Radio check, over."

"We got you with fives, Whitey. Willie's strapping in now, and he'll take over the comm in a minute, over."

"Thanks, Jake; and you're five by. Willie, give me an update for deceleration burn start, over."

"We now have three minutes ten seconds from my mark . . . mark."

"Thanks, Willie." I wouldn't be signing "out" from now on, since voice comm would be automatic from my end; all swearing and cursing would be recorded for posterity. I prayed that if I screwed any pooches, I would screw in style.

I reached out and set internal atmosphere at 1100 millibars, then flipped the "pressurize" switch. My ears popped as heliox began to hiss into the pressure vessel.

"The chipmunk special is now in operation," I said, my voice already rising in pitch. "Pressurization system checks healthy." Another mission "go" point.

"*Copy, Floater,*" Williams' voice came back. "*Two minutes to burn.*"

They went by very slowly. I had time to relive my life several times over. I noted that the first forty years were generally mundane; most of the joy, terror and triumph were crammed into the last two.

"*Begin deceleration profile.*"

Jake did it by the book, starting off with .05 G and taking three minutes to work up to maximum; this was to make sure the balloons settled properly into place. By the time we'd achieved 1.4 G my breathing was labored; it was like lying on my stomach in bed with a large person standing on my back. I survived.

For something to do, I activated the stereo TV hanging near the Floater's pickup forks and turned it toward the big door. After about ten minutes I heard the muffled sounds of the cargo bay being depressurized; then the hatch opened—the huge door splitting and the halves sliding back into their recesses in the Catcher's double hull. Through the open door, I could see part of the Lander, and just a glimpse of the rings. We were backing up away from the ring plane and the viewing angle wasn't the greatest.

"*SKP due in fifteen seconds, old boy. Cutting communications for thirty seconds, out.*"

They went by slowly.

"*Catcher to Floater. Radio check, over.*"

"You're five by, Willie. Switching to batteries now. Switched. Battery power nominal. All systems functioning. Disconnect the umbilical, Willie."

"*Umbilical disconnected. Seven minutes to free fall. We're right on profile.*"

"How's the Earth ship doing, over?"

"Maintaining profile. Coming in from seventy degrees west of us. Since we're going to get to the drop point first, the blighters will have to stand off a few kilometers to maintain the niceties."

By then we were down into the optical haze layer, standing almost vertically on our tail. Jake did the whole drill smooth as butter; he'd practiced it more than any of us, and this was indeed a virtuoso performance. I wished my heart weren't pounding so hard— and that I could enjoy it from a distance.

By the time he'd achieved zero velocity with respect to the upper-latitude circulation system, we were actually down into the uppermost layer of ammonia clouds. He cut acceleration down to .03 G, released the Lander from its holding arm, then cut the CRF completely and moved north on RCS. The atmosphere turned the little vessel right side up and began to push up against the balloons, so the Catcher fell faster than the Lander. Once we were a safe distance away, the big pilot cut the CRF back in, gradually building up acceleration again to settle my own balloons while the Lander dropped away beneath us to the south.

Jake then pulled us up out of the clouds at 1.4 G, and back over the SKP point where the Lander was now falling many kilometers below.

"Our friends the Earthers have arrived on the scene. They're maneuvering seven kilometers west of us. They've just dropped their lander."

"Could you pick up its size on the radar, over?"

"Appears to be about the same size as ours; at least, the balloon volumes are equal. Stand by for your drop."

I had a brief moment to be glad the Earth vessel was observing the proprieties. Then it was dipsy doodle time. Jake had stopped us again, right in the top of the highest cloud layer. He cut the CRF, then yawed 90 degrees so that the Catcher was falling on its back with the cargo door on top. Then he released the latches holding the Floater in the cargo bay and gunned the RCS again to fall right out from under me, fast, before maneuvering to the north and cutting in the CRF once more.

In the meantime, I was busy being a pendulum; it was a race between damping and throwing up. I won the fight to hold down my gorge, barely. Down I went through the layers: ammonia, ammonium sulfate, water, phosphine, blending finally into molecular hydrogen.

"Floater to Catcher. Radio check, over."

"We read you five by, chap. How's the ride, over?"

"Rough but manageable. Damped out now. Almost no side buffeting. Just passed through max velocity. I peaked at 460 meters per second; am now slowing down through 430. My IMU says no more lateral velocity with respect to the SKP point. You may tell Junior that his models are essentially correct; I appear to have achieved System III rotational velocity after falling only a couple of hundred kilometers. How are things on top, over?"

"We've achieved hovering altitude and are holding just above the optical haze layer. We shall be here all summer if necessary, old chap. So you may get on with your job, over."

"Thanks, Willie."

The high latitude of the SKP had two advantages. First, since it was northern summer, we'd be in sunlight the whole time. The second was the weather systems. Down in the System I circulation, from the equator to 55 degrees latitude, the zonal velocities could reach 500 meters per second—three-fourths of the local speed of sound. The System II weather of the high latitudes had four zonal velocity peaks of decreasing magnitude; the final one was down at latitude 79, almost four degrees south of us—and it was only 50 meters per second. Up where we were, the zonal velocity was effectively zero, and one didn't have to drop very far into the hydrogen below the top cloud layers to achieve the true Saturn rotational velocity—the System III figure. That was where I was now.

But I was about eight kilometers east of the SKP

point, according to the computer's figures calculated from the IMU and the onboard compass. I instructed the nav computer to correct this condition, and it promptly activated the warm-gas hydrogen thrusters and began moving the vessel sluggishly westward as it continued falling.

In the meantime, I established contact with the Lander, cranked its IMU and transponder signals into my onboard processors, and began to run the atmospheric model update program. The Lander had a lot more negative buoyancy than the Floater; it was now almost 300 kilometers below me, nearly a third of the way down to sea level. As the atmospheric density increased, its terminal velocity would decrease. It would be something over two hours before it was all the way down and I could begin the search pattern.

"Floater to Catcher. Am correcting an eight-kilometer deviation eastward from SKP point. Have activated Lander and—"

"MIDDLE BOY TO HIGH BOY. MIDDLE BOY TO HIGH BOY. RADIO CHECK, OVER."

"WE READ YOU FIVE BY, MIDDLE BOY. REPORT YOUR POSITION AS SOON AS YOU HAVE STABILIZED, OVER."

"What the. . . . SpaceHome vessel to Earth vessel! SpaceHome vessel to Earth vessel! Respond, please!"

"THIS IS UNITED CONSORTIUM VESSEL HIGH BOY. PLEASE SWITCH OFF THIS FREQUENCY, OVER."

"We were on the air first on this frequency. You do not have the right to—"

"THIS IS THE ONLY FREQUENCY ON WHICH OUR EXPEDITION CAN BROADCAST. IT IS ESSENTIAL TO THE SAFETY OF THE VESSEL NOW IN SATURN'S ATMOSPHERE THAT WE CONTINUE TO BROADCAST ON THIS FREQUENCY. WE REGRET ANY INCONVENIENCE THIS MAY CAUSE YOUR VESSEL, BUT WE ARE HELPLESS TO DO ANYTHING ABOUT IT. OVER AND OUT."

"Floater to Catcher. Willie, it looks like we'll have to—"

"MIDDLE BOY TO HIGH BOY. MIDDLE BOY TO HIGH BOY. NOW STABILIZED AT—"

Savagely, I flipped the comm switch to backup frequency.

"Floater to Catcher. Willie, you switched over to back-up yet, over?"

"Indubitably, old chap. I read you four by, over." His voice was just the slightest bit hashed, but still coming through well enough.

"Likewise, Willie; except you're at four and a half. Listen; I'd like to talk to Jake. You there, Big Bear?"

"I'm listening, Whitey, over."

"Did Earth know our broadcast frequencies before they dropped out of the project, over?"

"Come to think of it, yes. That was one of the first things we decided on, because so many of the electronic and antenna designs depended on it. We didn't worry about it too much, though; it didn't seem like a big item to keep secret, over."

"Did they know we had a backup frequency, over?"

"Come to think of it, it wasn't decided to go with a backup frequency until a lot later. We finally needed it to push the Floater survival number up over 99 percent . . . oh, I see what you're gettin' at. Those bastards!"

"Right. Bastards." I stopped for a moment to do a Valsalva; I was down below 450 kilometers now and cabin pressure was up to 4000 millibars. "They can claim they used optimum design just like we did, and had no idea we'd both be trying for the artifact at the same time. And then, for an insurance policy, they made sure to build in about twice as much power as necessary. They would have . . . oops, just thought of something else; did they also know our Floater-to-Lander command frequency?"

"Afraid so, Whitey."

"Stand by one." I looked at the running computation of the Lander's position. It was moving erratically off course. Hurriedly, I sent the signal to deactivate the command channel. The readouts steadied down gratifyingly; the Lander would now fall without disturbance all the way to sea level—and right into the liquid phase layer, if I couldn't issue a command to drop a sandbag or two at the appropriate time.

"Whitey old boy, are you all right, over?"

"Yes, Willie. Stand by one again; I want to monitor their frequency for a moment." I switched over.

"—RESPONDS PERFECTLY TO COMMANDS. I WILL NOW MOVE LOW BOY TO A POSITION ESTIMATED AS DIRECTLY OVER THE—"

I switched back. I suppose I should have been grateful that they hadn't accidentally released any of the balloons or sandbags. But somehow, "grateful" had departed from my working vocabulary.

"Willie, this is Whitey. Unless we can figure something out in the next couple of hours, I think we've had it. They're staying lily-white in the eyes of the solar system, and it's just our tough luck that they outpower us."

"Roger that, Whitey. Jake's been monitoring the primary frequency on our backup communicator. Apparently they've even got an excuse for outpowering us: their floater is going down to 750 kilometers, over."

I thought about that for a second. Given enough money . . . they'd have a heavily built floater—more strength, bigger air conditioner and so forth. But it also implied that the receiver electronics on their lander weren't as efficient as ours. Apparently Junior had come up with better high-pressure and high-temperature designs than the Earthers. But it was small consolation to have saved money through better design, and lost the war thereby.

I popped my ears again and looked at the outside sensor readings. Down to 494 kilometers; 480 Kelvin; pressure 59 bars. I felt considerable more weight on me now; the Floater was falling noticeably more slowly. I heard a strange creaking as the surrounding pressure forced my vessel into a slightly more perfect sphere. I was sweating a little.

"Floater to Catcher. Willie, see if you can get hold of Junior on a coded link. Ask him if he can come up with any bright ideas, over."

"We're way ahead of you, old top. Jake has been dis-cussing the problem with the little fellow. Unfortunately, Badille is now offering five for three that the Earth vessel will succeed in lieu of us—that is, provided either of us succeeds, over."

"Tell him I'll take three dollars' worth of that ac-tion." I was beginning to formulate, dimly, a plan in which I'd monitor the Earthers' transmissions, and sneak Lander commands in between commands from their own floater. I didn't hold out very much hope for it, but it was worth three dollars, anyway.

The pressure vessel creaked again, sending a nervous shiver down my spine. I checked the readouts again: 520 kilometers down; 506 Kelvin, 64 bars. Internal pres-sure was 5500 millibars.

"The little man took your money, Whitey. What are your plans, over?"

"I'd rather not say right now. We're in the open and might be monitored, no matter what the Earthers say about only having single-frequency capability. Status report: I'm down at 524 kilometers now; the plotted curve has me going neutral buoyancy at 544. That's close enough so I won't bother to slide down the re-maining six. Level off in fourteen minutes. Still taking readings from the Lander: it's down to 894 kilometers. And I'm still pulsing the transponder to check and up-date the model atmosphere, over."

"Copy. And suggest you might like to turn your radar on to take a look at the Earth floater; it's less than a hundred kilometers below you and its balloon cluster ought to be easy to spot, over."

"Wilco." I snapped on the radar, and found the return almost immediately. "They're 88 kilometers below and still falling pretty fast." I punched buttons and let my computer collect data for a time plot. "Looks like they'll level off at about 745 kilometers below cloud tops, over."

"Copy. Better them than us, eh what?"

I chuckled at his parody of what everyone had been saying about us three pilots for the past month; we'd been getting pretty tired of hearing it. But it was true.

The temperature down there wasn't too bad—the Floater could handle anything up to about 800 Kelvin without developing any soft spots, even though the air conditioner might overload. But the pressure down there was 136 bars—10 over our absolute design limit. I'd be breathing 720-degree hydrogen instead of heliox. Certainly an unpleasant thing to contemplate.

I checked the radar again; they were now 102 kilometers below, and still going rapidly.

"Floater here. Down to 540 kilometers; just about leveled off. Lander down to 1016; I've got it eight klicks northeast of optimum. Taking no action, over."

"Copy you leveled off. We—stand by one."

Pause.

"Whitey, we've got good news. It appears that the Earth floater has developed some trouble with their lander command and control system. Listen in for a moment and see what you think, over."

"Wilco. Switching over." I flipped back to primary frequency.

"—FIND OUT WHO DID THE QUALITY CONTROL ON THOSE DAMN BATTERIES, I'M GONNA CHEW HIS DAMN HEAD OFF, OVER."

"MIDDLE BOY, PLEASE GIVE US A STATUS CHECK ON THE REST OF YOUR BATTERIES, OVER."

"HELL, THEY'RE OKAY, JOHN. OPTIMUM READINGS ON ALL OF THEM."

"MIDDLE BOY, STRONGLY ADVISE YOU CONSIDER ABORTING THE MISSION. CAPPIE, WE THINK IT'S TIME TO CUT AND RUN. IT'S QUITE POSSIBLE THAT THE SPACERS WILL FAIL, TOO, AND WE CAN HAVE ANOTHER MISSION OUT HERE INSIDE TWO WEEKS, OVER."

"NEGATIVE JOHN. I'VE GOT NO INDICATION THAT THIS IS ANYTHING BUT A CHANCE ANOMALY: THAT COMMAND AND CONTROL BUS MIGHT COME BACK ON LINE ANY MINUTE. I'LL BE DAMNED IF I'M GOING TO GIVE THE WHOLE THING UP NOW, WHEN WE'VE CLEARLY GOT THEM BEAT. THINK OF THE

TIME AND MONEY THAT'S GONE INTO THIS PROJ-
ECT. THAT OLD ARAB WOULD HAVE A FIT IF—"
    I switched to backup frequency.
    "Catcher, Floater. You read me, over?"
    "Receiving, over."
    "Instructions. I'm going to activate the Lander again
and get it back under me where it belongs. Have Jake
keep monitoring the Earthers and let me know the instant anything develops, especially if they're able to
establish their lander command channel again. I also
need to know the moment they sound like they're going
to abort; I'm going to station myself three kilometers
north of their position, but I'd like to have some warning if they're coming up. Final item: Advise Mimas
coded about the Earthers' two-week turnaround capability; and while you're at it, ask Junior to cover another three dollars on that bet, over."
    "Copy, Whitey. Advise that we're recording the Earthers'
communications and coding them on-line to M-Base. Also
advise that Badille radio'ed that he will not, repeat will
not, cover any more money on his original offer. Looks
like you're going to be the first one ever to take the little
man to the cleaners. Congratulations, old boy, if I may be
so bold as to project an upset victory, over."
    "We'll see, Willie. Keep me advised. Ten-ten."
    I checked the radar again. The Earth vessel was now
at 715 kilometers and slowing dramatically; it would
level in another quarter hour.
    My own vessel creaked once more. I shuddered; that
sound gave me the creeps. I wished they'd included it in
the training tapes so I could have gotten used to it. I
looked at my readings: 544 kilometers down. I'd been
level for over two minutes. When I activated the thrusters to move north, the Floater creaked again. I sweated
and felt closed in. Hell, I *was* closed in. Hot hydrogen at
68 Earth atmospheres was doing its physical damned-
est to crumple the lightweight pressure vessel around
me. I goose-bumped through my sweat and coded the
activation frequency of the Lander on my command
channel.

Nothing. I panicked for an instant, then slapped myself in the head and activated the intermediate-range electronics. The Lander responded promptly with the ready signal and I ran a quick systems check. All okay.

The Lander was 1288 kilometers below cloud tops; still quite a ways to go, but it had made considerable progress. And now I had to get it back where it belonged. I'd reached my new hover point, three kilometers north of the Earther vessel. I stopped the thrusters and let my motion die out completely; the Floater creaked around me to remind me once again of the awful pressure on the hull, then settled into stillness.

I activated the delicate gravity gradient apparatus—a "laser plumb-bob," Junior had called it—and let the Floater's nav computer go to work to bring the Lander directly beneath me; I could do this directly with the paired IMUs, but I also wanted to calibrate Junior's brute-force system for possible later use.

The IMUs had me laterally displaced 3245 meters from a line through the artifact point, and the Lander displaced 8615 meters. The plumb-bob/transponder system had the Lander displaced 5107 meters laterally from the Floater; cranking in my compass reading put me almost due north of the SKP, and the Lander just north of northeast. The plumb-bob was nearly perfect.

I ordered the navigation computer to bring the Lander to a point directly underneath the Floater. The indicated position began to creep slowly as the small propeller-and-rudder system started to perform, 750 kilometers below. I hoped there would be enough juice to do the job; the intermediate-depth batteries were quite limited in wattage. But I intended to waste them completely if I had to, to save the high-pressure system for its work at the bottom.

"Catcher to Floater. You busy old chap, over?"

"Floater here. What's the news, over?"

"Nothing new with the Earther situation. But I thought you might like to know that Ogumi sent us a pleasant little missive. Wished us luck. Said he was glad you are in command and that he knows you'll do your best for SpaceHome. All that rot. I say, are you all right?"

"Yes, Willie. I was just laughing. Did Junior receive the message too, over?"

"I believe so; it was in the clear. And speaking of the diminutive genius, he says to tell you 'Just like old times, Admiral.' Bit of a cryptic note, what?"

I laughed again. "We'll explain it when we get back to Pendragon, Willie. Takes a couple of drinks to tell right."

"I'll hold you to that, old boy. Ten-ten."

Another hour went by. A long one. I felt like I was in a three-way tug-of-war with the Earthers, the Lander and my own private apprehensions. Whenever I had a few moments to think of the heat and depth around me, I began fear-sweating again. Time and again I checked the cabin temperature readout, only to have it mock me with an unchanging 23 degrees.

In the meantime, the Lander passed through the final electronics changeover depth. At about 1400 kilometers down, the readings from the intermediate system began to get mushy. At 1450, I activated the high-temperature high-pressure system. The signals were hashed at first, then sharpened dramatically as the vessel passed through 1480 kilometers. I did a complete systems checkout, including the double-fork mechanism which would do the hard part; its bearings would function only in that hellacious environment. When I pronounced the Lander operable, it was the final mission "go" point.

Shortly after that, the Lander IMU began to show anomalous readings; within seconds, its signal froze on an impossible number. I instructed the computers to ignore the previous 60 seconds of data and proceed on the transponder system only. Then I called Willie to have him tell Junior that he'd won his bet with the chief of materials and processes.

Sea level on Saturn is the depth at which the enormous pressure overpowers the high temperature to force the hydrogen atmosphere into a liquid state. If we could somehow see this interface it would be very uninteresting: a featureless plain covering the entire planet. Our best models predicted sea level in this vicinity to be 1949 kilometers below the cloud tops.

Now the Lander was 120 kilometers from this depth and slowing dramatically as it approached its neutral buoyancy altitude. I'd kept it directly beneath me during the descent, so it would have to do a three-kilometer southward traverse before starting the search pattern. I wasn't too unhappy about that; the RMS error of the navigation system was almost five kilometers, anyway. The sweep sonar had a range of about four kilometers; the little stereo sonar was good only for extreme closeups—100 meters or less—and would provide the precise detail needed to make the pickup.

I looked at the mission clock. Two hours, seven minutes since the drop. I seemed like I'd been down there half my life.

I started to get a weak return on the sweep sonar; it looked like a bottom signal from the simulations. If that were the case, it was many kilometers closer than predicted. And if the density models were correct, that meant the temperature predictions for sea level were somewhat off on the high side. There was no way to check that, since we hadn't taken the time or money to build the appropriate sensors into the little vessel. Either the Lander worked, or it didn't.

Right now, it was working. The bottom return was getting stronger. I looked at the nav readouts. The Lander was down 1883 kilometers from cloud tops—1340 directly beneath me. If that sonar reading was correct, I had only 3.7 kilometers of fall during which to take some kind of action. I checked the rate of descent; it had slowed to 47 meters per second. Plenty of time, actually.

I instructed my onboard Lander navigator to achieve neutral buoyancy thirty meters above sonar-indicated sea level. It obligingly caused the Lander to release a small sandbag; the rate of descent slowed to 23 meters per second, decreasing.

"Willie, Whitey. Tell Junior and his clever model builders that sea level was 62 kilometers above their predictions, over."

"*Smashing news, chappie. That saves you several min-utes of breathing that foul stuff you call air. And we continue to hear encouragingly depressed reports from your counterpart in the Earthers' so-called Middle Boy. You might want to tune in on them; it will gladden your heart's cockles, over.*"

"I'm rather busy right now. Just give me the gist of it, over."

"*Well, it seems their lander—Low Boy, I believe they call it—is gaily falling out of control; and in just a few more minutes will take the plunge, so to speak. A small bit of power has returned to their command and control unit, but not enough to reach even halfway down to sea level. As soon as their lander is immersed, they will give up trying and abort their mission, leaving you a free hand to snatch the prize.*"

"I'm liking it." The Lander was just about leveled off: forty meters above the surface, descending at just a few centimeters per second and slowing. "Do you have any idea of their lander's position, over?" The Earth vehicle would only sink until the balloons hit the liquid hydro-gen; they might set up a sonar return which I should be on the lookout for. A mountain of balloons was some-thing I didn't want to run into, especially if I were to accidentally implode one or two.

"*Good news on that, also. Its planing tendencies were apparently worse than ours; it's been drifting in a gener-ally westward direction a hundred meters for every ten kilometers of fall since they lost control.*" I nodded to myself. Our Lander's design was calculated to zero out the net lateral lifting forces—but nothing was perfect. I'd had to make drift corrections every once in a while during descent.

"*—ought to splash down at least fifteen kilometers from the SKP point, and perhaps even twenty.*"

"Good news, Willie. Okay, it's leveled off now. Thirty point one meters off the liquid interface. I'm going to work. Keep me posted. Ten-ten."

I started moving the Lander laterally. Any direction would do until I could get an offset reading; the simple machine didn't have a compass. It turned out I'd headed it about 120 degrees off course. I let the navigation computer gather data for about fifteen seconds, then instructed it to move the Lander to a point three kilometers south of the vertical line between the Floater and the planet's center of gravity. Obligingly, the little vehicle slewed around and began the slow southward trek.

"Earth lander Low Boy just splashed into the drink. The fellow in Middle Boy is now beginning system checks preparatory to lifting out of the atmosphere. Perhaps you should move a bit further north, Whitey, over."

"Wilco; moving north." It didn't matter now, since the Lander was being navigated toward a fixed reading; the computer would automatically compensate for any Floater movement. I gave my computer the necessary instructions, then glued my attention back to the sweep sonar return signal. A small anomaly was developing on the horizon; a lump of excitement formed in my chest.

"Floater to Catcher. I think I've got it on sonar. Yes, that must be it. Range 2.7 kilometers; the return is too small to be a balloon cluster, over."

"Congratulations, old—stand by one."

I was glad to wait; my attention was completely focused on the sonar return. Although it was too small to be the Earther lander's balloon cluster, it also seemed way too large to fit into our own Lander. Then, as the image tightened, I saw a smaller, more solid-looking nucleus.

"Catcher, I believe that the artifact is sitting in the middle of a temperature anomaly, a region of cooled hydrogen. The sea level seems to rise several meters to meet it, over."

"Copy, Whitey. I think we've got some troubles with the Earthers; they've got more batteries going out."

"Just keep me informed, Willie. I've got manual control of Lander now. I'm going to move in closer for a good look with the stereo sonar. Ten-ten."

"Old boy, I think you'd better switch to primary frequency and have a listen. The Earther in Middle Boy seems to be in serious trouble, over."

Biting back an angry retort, I deactivated the Lander systems and switched.

"—*IGURE IT OUT. THOSE BATTERIES WERE SHOWING FULL CHARGE RIGHT UP TO THE MOMENT WHEN I HIT THE CRF STARTUP: THEN THE JUICE WAS GONE. SO HERE'S THE SITUATION: COMMAND AND CONTROL BUS GONE FOR THE PAST TWO HOURS: AIR REVITALIZATION GONE. I CAN HOLD PRESSURE, BUT CO_2 SCRUBBING IS OUT. I'LL BE AT DANGER LEVEL IN ABOUT TWENTY-FIVE MINUTES. I'VE STILL GOT COMMUNICATIONS: THANK GOD THE BALLOON RELEASE IS ON THAT BUS. CO_2 POISONING IS A BAD WAY TO GO. I THINK WHAT I'LL DO IS JUST RELEASE—*"

"KNOCK THAT OFF, CAPPIE! THERE'S GOTTA BE SOMETHING WE CAN DO. WE'LL GET IN TOUCH WITH THE SPACER TEAM AND SEE IF THEY CAN—"

"BULLSHIT, JOHN! THAT LITTLE TIN CAN OF THEIRS IS SITTING UP AT 550 KILOMETERS. YOU KNOW DAMN WELL THEY'LL PROBABLY CAVE IN IF THEY TRY TO BRING IT BELOW 650. AND EVEN IF THEY GOT DOWN HERE, WHAT AM I SUPPOSED TO DO—SWIM OVER? I TELL YOU . . ."

As I listened my emotions went from annoyance to chagrin. Then, when I realized that there might be a slim chance to rescue the stranded Earther, I went through a crisis of the spirit. It was brief, but enormous; it centered on the fact that there was a good chance that I would die. And I didn't want to die.

". . . *MARY A KISS GOODBYE FOR ME . . .*"

I looked longingly at the emergency abort switch. All I had to do was throw it; the CRF would light off, the sandbags and balloons would release, and I'd punch out of there at two G and keep going until I was in polar orbit around Saturn. I could even "accidentally" brush against it, say I was reaching for something else and screwed the pooch. The Lander was practically on top of the artifact; there'd be no trouble with the retrieval now, even if they had to send the backup down. I'd done enough; it was Jake's turn now, anyway. Let *him* experience this pressure for a while. My hand reached for the toggle.

"*. . . OKAY, HITTING BALLOON RELEASE—*"

"Wait!"

That was my own voice. It surprised me.

"Middle Boy! This is SpaceHome's Floater. You read me, over?"

"*I READ YOU, FLOATER. DID YOU CALL TO SAY GOODBYE?*"

"Shut your damn mouth and listen to me!" The anger was impractical, but good for my soul. "You've already ruined my day, and I don't want to hear any more of your whining. I'm coming down to get you, but I've got to know a couple of things first. Do you have any juice at all that you can use to release your weights?"

"*NEGATIVE, OVER.*" The voice became gratifyingly businesslike, but the news was terrible.

"I'd sure like to know who designed your crummy power—never mind. What do you have left that works, over?"

"*COMMUNICATIONS AND BALLOON RELEASE; THEY'RE ON THE SAME BUS. BUT THERE SEEMS TO BE A CHARGE LEAK DEVELOPING IN THOSE BATTERIES, ALSO. MAY LAST ANOTHER FIFTEEN MINUTES OR SO BEFORE THEY'RE DEAD. AIR CONDITIONING'S GONE, AND IT'S STARTING TO GET A BIT WARM. BUT THAT'S NOT THE CRITICAL—*"

"Get off the air!"

Silence.

"Good. I'm going to be very busy for the next several minutes and you are going to do nothing but sit there and conserve battery power—because when I get there, you've *got* to have enough juice to let go of your balloons. So after your acknowledgement of this transmission, I want you to go on standby and just monitor my voice. When I get down to you and give you my mark, I want you to release your balloons immediately and hang on. Okay, let me have your acknowledgement, over."

"*ACKNOWLEDGE.*"

"Good. SpaceHome Floater to High Boy, over."

"HIGH BOY HERE, OVER."

"Floater. I'm going to have to grapple onto Middle Boy with my pickup forks. . . ." I described the Floater's double tines, and asked where the best spot to grab their floater was.

"THERE'S A PAIR OF RINGS 180 DEGREES AROUND THE VESSEL FROM OUR OWN PICKUP FORKS. THEY ARE THE ATTACH RINGS WE USED TO HOLD IT IN THE CARGO BAY DURING PASSAGE FROM CALLISTO. THEY ARE A HUNDRED AND FIFTY CENTIMETERS APART AND CLEAR THE HULL BY THIRTY-THREE CENTIMETERS AT MAXIMUM SEPARATION. WILL THOSE DO, OVER?"

"Affirmative." I'd been busy while talking. I now had out the meager medical kit and was inventorying the Curabend supplies. There were four auto-injectors containing five milligrams each, and three containing two milligrams each.

"Floater to Catcher. Willie, you monitoring, over?"

"Yes, over."

"Advise I'm now beginning a dive to Middle Boy; will elevate internal pressure to compensate. I've got to go down below 740 kilometers to find him, then we're likely to fall a considerable distance between the time we drop our balloons and the time I can hook my forks into him and light the CRF. After that, we'll do more falling before our negative velocity zeroes out."

While talking I began to dump heliox into the pressure vessel, swallowing to pop my ears, and instructed Floater's nav computer to home on the radar indication of the Earth vessel. I had to be firm about it, overriding two alarms and a positive control message from the computer.

"So I need you to contact our hyperbaric medicine man at M-Base. Tell him I'm going to pressurize to 35,000 millibars, and ask him what my Curabend dosage should be." I glanced at the nav readouts: 650 kilometers down; 630 Kelvin and 98 bars. "Second. I know Junior's got this thing wired so that if outside pressure exceeds 130 bars, the emergency abort cuts in. I want to take that circuit out without disturbing the normal emergency abort function. Give him a call and find out how to do it, over."

"*Wilco. Ten-ten.*"

I looked at my internal pressure; cabin was at 18,000 millibars and heading down, down, down. I choked back a feeling of panic.

"High Boy, Floater, over."

"*HIGH BOY HERE, OVER.*"

"Listen, I know you guys are shit-hot pilots and can catch an egg in a teacup, and your cargo hold is bigger than ours—but I want you to back off thirty kilometers and let my boy Mike Jacobs do the work. Our cargo doors are plenty big enough, and we're tuned to my transponder, over."

Pause.

"*WILCO. MOVING COMPASS INDICATED WEST BY TWENTY KILOMETERS ON RCS. WILL CONTINUE TO STAND BY, AND WILL MATCH PICKUP MANEUVERS KEEPING THIS OFFSET. IF JACOBS FAILS, WE'LL BACK HIM UP, OVER.*"

I gave him the ten kilometers without comment; I was in no mood to argue, and twenty was far enough. I looked at my readouts: 700 kilometers down; 675 Kelvin; outside pressure 115 bars; inside 25,000 millibars. The gauge pressure was now 18 bars beyond the safe limit.

"*Floater, Catcher, over.*"

"Report, over."

"*The doctor says that under no circumstances should you go below 20,000 millibars, because he doesn't have your metabolism calibrated yet; that was one of the things we were going to do in the final week of prepara—*"

"Willie, dammit! I want answers, not words!" The Catcher's signal was getting worse as I descended and I was getting panicky.

"*Doctor says maybe 22 milligrams, but it's just a guess. Junior says flatly he won't give you an answer. Wants you back alive, over.*"

"Tell Junior if he doesn't come up with the information in fifteen seconds, I'm going to just open the whole damn circuit up. I want the answer *now!*"

I had the wiring panel open and was looking at a mass of multicolored spaghetti. Three wires came off each side of the emergency abort switch. I held a little pair of wire cutters I'd fished from the tiny onboard repair kit; I sweated and prepared to cut all three wires off one side. I'd rather not have to fly the Floater up on manual if I got into trouble, but I would if I had to. I reached the dikes toward the nearest terminal of the switch.

"—oater, Catcher. Badille says cut the yellow— —ire on the near side of the sw— —ver."

"Repeat, over!"

"— —ille says cu— —ellow and black wire nearest to you— —ver."

"Understood." There was a yellow and black striped wire right in front of the dikes. I reached up and snipped it, then bent the bottom part down to make sure it wouldn't touch anything and closed up the panel.

I looked at my readouts: 720 kilometers down; 126 bars external pressure; 693 Kelvin. Pressure vessel was leveling off at 33,000 millibars. So much for 35,000; this was all I was going to get. I was sweating and lightheaded and scared down to my core. I looked at the cabin temperature; it was 28 degrees. The number changed to 29 as I looked at it.

"Floater to Catcher. Your signal is breaking up and this will be my final transmission. I've got to move fast, before Middle Boy runs out of juice and I roast. If I'm not back up in twenty minutes, tell Junior to remember his promise, out."

I took manual control of the navigation system and checked readouts. I was only 300 meters north of the Earth vessel, but still 20 kilometers up, with descent slowing down. This was no time to conserve resources, so I released three of the four-meter balloons; my rate of descent picked up from 48 to 180 meters per second. That was better.

"HIGH BOY TO FLOATER. CATCHER ASKS ME TO

*RELAY THIS TO YOU: YOUR FINAL TRANSMISSION
WAS RECEIVED AND THEY WILL COMPLY. GOING
ON STANDBY AND GOOD LUCK FROM ALL OF US,
OUT."*

The pressure vessel around me was giving out with a
tortured groaning the likes of which I'd never heard. I
sweated and shook in fear, wet my pants and cried out
loud; I was ashamed, but couldn't help myself. It was
entirely unfair of the universe to give me this much
time to contemplate my fate.

I watched readouts, nevertheless. At 740 kilometers
down I was nearly on top of the other vessel; less than
five kilometers to go. I dropped 300 kilograms of weights;
my descent slowed to 120 meters per second. Half a
minute. I reached into the medical kit and grabbed an
auto-injector, and squirted five milligrams of Curabend
into my thigh through the coveralls. Then another. Then
a third, and a fourth. Then a fifth injection of two
milligrams. Every one of them stung like crazy; I cried
at the pain.

While I was crying, I checked the readouts again and
hurriedly released another 500 kilograms. My vessel
shook and swayed and bobbed, and creaked like a hundred violins playing different notes. I quivered with fear
and looked at the radar; the mass of balloons of the
Earth vessel were level with me and slowly moving
upward with relative motion. I was still falling ten
meters a second. I released 20 kilograms; the descent
slowed, stopped and reversed. I bobbed back perhaps
five meters then leveled off. I snuffled, cleared my voice,
and spoke:

"Okay, Cappie, I'm down. Stand by."

I switched on the stereo TV and looked in the direction of the radar return. Fuzzy murk with a darker blob
in the middle. I switched on the floodlights, praying
they'd work. They did. I was looking into a fork-covered
retrieval hold similar to the one on my groaning vessel.

"Shit, Cappie! I've gotta go all the way around you! I
wish you'd've been more cooperative and been turned
the right way when I came down!"

Drying a tear on my sleeve, I put the thrusters in operation and sidled around the other vessel until I could see the two retaining rings that *High Boy* had told me about. They were about four meters above my forks. I pouted and released a one-kilogram weight. I inched up half a meter too high. That would have to do.

Gently, with sweaty hands, I activated the thrusters to push myself in toward the other vessel. Before long, I heard a *clunk*, and hastily cut the thruster. Another *clunk*, then silence. Our balloon clusters were butting against each other. I peered closely at the TV monitor; we were thirty or forty meters apart. That would have to do, too.

I kept one hand on the thruster control and with the other activated my grabbing forks. What was that separation distance, anyway? I cudgeled my brain, but could not come up with the number.

"Dammit!" I shouted. "How can I set my pickup forks if I can't remember how far apart the damn rings are!"

"*ONE HUNDRED FIFTY CENTIMETERS, FLOATER. REPEAT, ONE HUNDRED FIFTY CENTIMETERS.*"

"Okay, okay! I got it the first time!"

I set the tines for a two-meter opening and tried to wipe sweat from my eyes; my sleeve was soaked, too, so it didn't work very well. I blinked and squeezed painful salt from between the lids. Cabin temperature was 45 degrees; as I looked, the number jumped to 47.

I looked once more at my sensor readouts: 744 kilometers down; 714 Kelvin outside; pressure 135 bars. Internal pressure was 33 bars. We could fall maybe 30 or 40 kilometers before imploding. I wondered how much time that gave me to hook him and light the CRF. I shook my head and called the man 40 meters away:

"Cappie, listen up. It's time. Get your finger over that balloon release switch. Three-second countdown: three, two, one, mark!" I jabbed my balloon release as I shouted. There was a little jerk, and I was almost weightless.

I focused my eyes on the TV. The other vessel was still there—his balloon release had worked. But he was falling faster than me. The two rings slipped down one meter, two, four. I sobbed and jammed my thruster control to push me down faster; at the same time I moved myself toward the other hull.

I was thirty meters away, then twenty, ten, five; I eased up on the lateral control—I didn't want to bump him too hard. As I got closer, the rings moved out of sight of the TV cameras, then back in again as I began to overtake him. Now the rings were coming into sight again. Now the top one was even with the bottom fork tine. A meter and a half to go. I edged in to three meters, then two, one. The bottom ring was now just even with the bottom tine. I got ready to close the jaws—then his vessel started to yaw. I cursed and sobbed again, and used my own thruster to match his rate while my heart pounded against my chest wall. I was sweating so hard I had to squint to see the TV screen. I matched him, finally, and then—miraculously—could see a few centimeters' clearance between his bottom ring and my bottom tine. I pushed my thruster lever forward, and as soon as I felt the bump I squeezed the fork closure as hard as I could. The big tines moved together and there was a crunching of metal on metal.

"Gotcha!" I twisted the lock, released the thruster control, reached over and slapped the emergency abort.

I knew it wouldn't work; but it did. The CRF rumbled to life, and I lay back in the acceleration couch crying with relief. I felt even better when I saw that we'd fallen only about six kilometers; I tried to do figures in my head and gave it up. My heart was pounding too fast. Maybe I'd taken thirty seconds.

Fear returned almost immediately. The Floater navigator's instructions for emergency abort were to accelerate the vessel to two G, and achieve close polar orbit about Saturn. But, of course, we'd never counted on dragging another floater along with us. The simple processor moved the plume on thrust-vector control to compensate for the unbalanced load, and poured fuel into the thermonuclear reactor. I wiped both eyes with a wet sleeve and focused on the accelerometer: 1.28 G . . .

1.3, 1.35, 1.4, 1.45 ... 1.47 ... 1.49 ... 1.50 ... 1.51 G. And there it stopped.

The Floater was vibrating unhealthily; I was afraid we'd come apart. I tried to do simple figures in my head to figure out when we'd turn around, but failed. Maybe three or four minutes.

So I watched the sensor readouts and sweated and cried. Down we went, our negative velocity decreasing with agonizing slowness, the vibration decreasing by imperceptible increments as we canceled the backward speed. Down 350 meters per second, then 300, then 240, then 150. Quailing, I looked at the other readouts as we began to near the turnaround point.

Depth 770 kilometers, 145 bars; 778 ... 782 ... 785 kilometers, 159 bars. I shuddered and waited for the implosion. Internal pressure was only 33 bars; we'd reached the design limit of 126 gauge. We were descending much more slowly now, but still going down: 787 kilometers, then 788. The reading froze there for a thousand years, then changed to 787 ... 786 ... 784 ... 782 ... 779 ... 775 ... 770. We were climbing up out of danger. I wept for joy, for life.

"Floater to whoever can hear me. Rescue data. Earth floater attached to this vessel; have been accelerating at full power for about four minutes. Hit bottom at 788 kilometers, and are coming up at 1.51 G. I've got to get some sleep, now." I closed my eyes and let the weight on my chest press me down, down ...

"Mister, I don't know if we're going to get out of this or not, but I'd like to say that you're one hell of a man."

I could have sworn I heard something. But that was impossible, because I knew I was unconscious. Blackness washed me clean.

17

A long time later, over drinks in Pendragon, I heard the rest of the story. The fuel lasted just over seventeen minutes. The Floater flamed out while we were still 90 kilometers below the cloud tops; at the time, we were moving upward at just under 1700 meters per second. We punched out of the uppermost clouds and coasted up a scant 20 kilometers before coming to rest and starting the fall back down.

But Junior knew his Floater. He got mass figures from the Earthers' High Boy, and had already calculated when we'd burn out. He radioed directions to Jake, and the big pilot was already matching our upward fall rate when we came into radar range. By the time we reached the top of the roller coaster, he was only a hundred meters away. He didn't trust the auto system—he had a double vessel to pick up, and not much time to do it—so he gunned the Catcher on manual. He cradled us in gently as you please, shut the cargo doors and applied acceleration so gradually that he was well down into the atmosphere himself before he reached his own turn-around point.

Then, on doctor's orders, he got us back to M-Base *fast*. One point six G. He left Junior cursing behind.

I sure wish I could have seen the pickup; it must have been one sweet bit of piloting to watch.

But that, and the following four days, are lost from my life—except for brief snatches of consciousness I wish I could forget. Floating and vomiting. High-G and trying to vomit. Waking up briefly in a pressurized stretcher with unbearable claustrophobia, screaming, and going black again. The hated hiss of heliox pouring into the hyperbaric chamber—I remember that one more than once; I think I woke up briefly whenever it happened and cursed whoever was doing it. And I remember feeling *very* bad. Hot and cold; wet and dry; acid and alkaline; and indescribable things.

Then the blackness went fuzzy, shrunk to a pinpoint, and I was looking at Junior's crooked grin from a meter away.

"Howdy, Admiral."

"Junior. What are you doing here?" I was disoriented.

"Doc'll be here in a second. I asked if I could be in the room when they stopped pumping you with sleepystuff, and they said okay because of my sterling record of cooperation."

"Junior, you've got bags under your eyes. You been riding the centrifuge?"

"Naw. Just missed my beauty sleep for a night or two. I'll be okay."

"What's happening?"

"Well, they just voted you the Hero-of-the-Quarter Award. First unanimous polling in history. You'll get three extra gold stars on your efficiency ratings."

"How long have I been out of it?"

"A few days. From what I can understand, you were a metabolic mess. Here's the doc; I'll let him explain—he slings that crap better than I do." He let go of my hand—I hadn't even realized he'd been holding it—and stood back as the hyperbaric specialist bustled in.

"Hello, Carl. I guess I didn't learn quite enough about your trade before I had to go, did I?"

"Enough to get you out alive—albeit just barely. Turned out you overdosed with Curabend, and that damned stuff is just like nerve gas antidote—you've got to take just the right amount for the exposure or the medicine can be just as bad as what it's supposed to counteract.

"And you had other problems: You were fatigued to start with from the extended high-G regime; you were subjected to a very hot environment—*that* caused a speedup of the metabolic processes which almost did you in before we got you back here to the clinic. Also, you were sweating, driving sodium and potassium out of your extracellular fluid; and the high-G was driving down your blood calcium too fast, trying to get it back into the bone tissue."

He'd been taking my pulse. Then he attached a pressure cuff to my arm and flipped a switch beside my bed. The machine pumped it up and released the air slowly; the doctor noted the readout on his clipboard. Then he bent over, peeled back my eyelids one by one, and shined a pencil beam into my eyes.

"I also deduced, after the fact, that when you went to maximum cabin pressure, the heliox mixture was slightly unbalanced, so you had some oxygen poisoning to add to everything else."

He finished, straightened up, and smiled. "In short, you were a chemical basket case. First day and a half, I had to pop you in and out of the hyperbaric chamber four times because you couldn't decide whether or not to desorb the helium in your bloodstream. Then your body went on a general strike and chose to ignore three or four of its more important feedback mechanisms. You kept us hopping to stabilize your blood pressure, pH, fluid balance, and a couple of other things."

He walked over to Junior, looked into his eyes and said sternly: "*You* will now get some sleep, young man." Then he turned back to me and said: "You're out of danger now, Whitey; have been, really, for half a day.

You'll be up and around soon—but for the moment you'll leave that infusion pump hooked into your IV and not move out of that bed without my permission. Five minutes, Badille." He bustled out, taking half the air in the room with him.

"So what about the artifact?"

"Jake'll make the first try tomorrow. You can listen on the repeater. See how it feels to be left out of it."

"First try?"

"Yeah. We're hoping the original Lander's still got juice enough and the parts all work. Jake'll take the Floater down and do a systems check. If it's a go, he'll make the pickup right away. If not, we'll go down again with the backup Lander."

"I didn't think the Floater would be in much shape to do anything for a while; I was awfully hard on it."

"Well, the construction crews have been working around the clock while you were relaxing here in bed. Completely replaced the pressure vessel in three days—had a spare on the shelf, you know. Bonuses from Ogumi; he knows about the Callisto turnaround time. They're finishing checkouts now. Oh, and they also had to replace the forks; you bent the hell out of them."

He was peering at me closely as he finished. He put his face half a meter from mine, and looked intently into my eyes.

"Yep, I thought so. It's finally there. Right out in the open for everyone to see."

"There you go again. What in the world *are* you talking about?"

"The Look of Eagles."

I swatted him up alongside the head with my free hand. There was enough force in the blow to maybe put a two-millimeter dent in a pat of soft butter.

He laughed and laughed, but finished with a strange-sounding catch in his voice. When he looked back into my eyes, there were tears streaming down his face. The catch was still there when he spoke:

"Admiral, I was . . . I was in a bad way when you were having all that fun down there, getting ready to

... to buy your farm." He leaned over and kissed my brow. "Don't you ever, *ever* do anything like that again without me along."

He went out the door without another word.

I just lay there with a lump in my throat; I didn't know what to do. So I fell asleep.

18

The pickup went without a hitch; it was a short mission, because the Lander was already down at sea level. Maggie and Greg came into my room to listen with me. So did the Earther pilot of Middle Boy, at his own urgent request. Junior played his same role with the technicians, so he was in orbit again during the drama.

I'd met the other pilot—Frank "Cappie" Hodgkins III—the day before, after I'd woken up again. He made me uneasy; it just wasn't *right*, the way he fawned over me.

I hadn't seen Maggie yet, although I understood she'd been into my room briefly a couple of times while I was sleeping. She had been very busy talking business with Ogumi and making "go" "no-go" decisions. This was the first chance she'd really had to visit with me; she apologized. I looked at her eyes; they had even more bags than Junior's. But I had to tell her something after she hugged me.

"Maggie, I lied to you."

"Unique emergency circumstances, Whitey." She

waved it off, then indicated the other pilot nearby. "I'm sure this gentleman is quite glad you did what you did."

"No, Maggie. I mean I was lying even when I made the promise."

She sighed. "I know that too, son. You sacrificed your principles so Jake or Willie wouldn't have to drop down into that muck. It was quite a sacrifice; the struggle was written all over your face." She smiled. "So I made an on-the-spot decision to sacrifice mine, too. I do have occasional lapses."

We settled down to listen. There was a suspenseful moment when Jake activated the Lander's systems, but they were all still functioning; the SART built well. He cranked up the sonar and confirmed what I'd thought before: There appeared to be a sizeable temperature anomaly associated with the artifact. The sea actually rose up to meet the device. The artifact itself appeared to be spherical, about a meter and a half in diameter, and simply resting on the elevated liquid surface.

The actual retrieval was a snap; the computer had even given us similar shapes during our trial runs.

Floating it up was also quite easy—in fact, much easier than expected. *"Damn thing appears to weigh only a few kilos,"* Jacobs reported in his Munchkin-bear voice. But then, later, when he had to make a lateral course correction of the Lander: *"Hey! This thing's harder'n hell to move sideways. Acts like it's several hundred kilos mass. This is one for Badille to figure out!"*

I could hear the little gnome's brain clicking all the way from the other side of the Old Man. His eventual comment to Willie in the Catcher was cryptic: *"When you grab the Floater, pressurize the cargo hold and apply acceleration, be sure to crank the heating system up to max. And don't touch the thing with your bare hands unless you like to nurse a frostbite."*

The trickiest part of the operation was snagging the Lander with the Floater; the larger vessel had to be yawed ninety degrees onto its back with the balloons still attached. But extra-large push-pull thrusters were attached to the Floater for exactly that purpose. Jake performed the exercise without a flaw, grabbed the Lander, released its balloons, then dropped his sandbags. A minute later he lit the Floater's CRF, released his own balloons, and half an hour later was safely ensconced in the cargo bay of the Catcher.

Then the Earth catcher, High Boy, which had been standing by on backup, headed back for M-Base. Seven hours later, Jake and Willie, Junior and the technicians were all at base. Junior dropped in to see me briefly, before going back to help supervise the emplacement of the artifact in the largest of the labs.

"I think we may be done with sixes, Dimp. The thing is a perfect dodecahedron—pentagonal faces. Maybe the Hexies have five fingers after all." He exited cackling; the next part of the show would be his, and he knew it.

Jake also came in. What he had to say was a little different.

"Once in a while, it got pretty lonely down there."

I smiled sympathetically.

"And once in a while, the pressure vessel would make a weird creaking sound. It was a little scary." He tousled my hair gently and left.

19

Junior figured out how to open the artifact within sixteen hours; but it wasn't until two days later that the deed was done. They were waiting so that I could be there, up and fully alert.

So SpaceHome fumed while the doctor put me through a series of tests and exercises. The exercises began with simply walking around the bedroom, but near the end had developed into some rather strenuous isometric-isotonic routines, with him taking lung gas and blood samples for analysis.

And during those days I had a constant stream of visitors; everybody on the SART came to see me at one time or another. That included the Earthers. They were being harbored politely by M-Base personnel—but coolly. A matter of frequency theft. Official protests had been sent, in the open, to the inner system; presumably Ogumi milked the incident for all its political worth—especially considering the subsequent rescue. He radioed us, in the open, that the three Earthers had permission to remain and witness the opening of the artifact. Ogumi and SpaceHome undoubtedly also benefited from this magnanimous gesture.

If Ogumi was worried about the Earthers being able to decipher the artifact's message on the spot, he didn't show it. I tended to agree with him; whatever the message was, it was bound to be complex and not amenable to instant memorization or analysis. And the Earthers were barred from taking photos.

In the meantime, Ogumi was burning the coded airways with demands that the SART director get on with the opening of the artifact, Whitedimple or no. Maggie held him off—politely at first, then not so politely. Finally the SpaceHome president sent Maggie notification that she was relieved of her position, that the new director was Gregory Simpson—effective immediately—and that Simpson would stand by to receive the next message.

It was another directive to open the artifact immediately. Greg's reply didn't even make any pretentions of politeness; it told Ogumi what to do in his hat to see how he looked in brown curls, and that the box would not be opened in Whitedimple's absence, and that the division chiefs backed him 100 percent in this matter. Upon which Ogumi relented with whatever good graces he had remaining and reinstated Maggie.

All of this took time; so I was ready, ironically, just after Ogumi's final message arrived. The doctor obviously wanted to perform more tests, but finally succumbed to pressures from the SART personnel and sarcastic barbs from Junior and me. I was pronounced provisionally fit, but sternly commanded to report back for an extended series of outpatient tests over the next three months. I grinned and nodded, perhaps lying.

During the wait, Junior had been with me much of the time. He'd given me the news—slanted and salted, of course—and kept me abreast of the Ogumi/SART/Earth tangle. He'd also explained the artifact in as much detail as he thought I could absorb.

"The thing masses about 700 kilos. But it *weighs* 26 kilograms—no matter what kind of gravitational field it's in. Even in zero G, it exerts a 26-kilogram force through its 'bottom' facet."

"Antigravity?" I'd asked, blithely.

"Nah. They've just got a better handle on quantum mechanics than we do. I think they can generate a field to non-randomize molecular motion in a given mass. Needs energy to work on, though; it sucks heat out of its surrounding medium to do the job."

He'd scratched an ear. "Ran some tests just to check the theory. Took it topside to one of the hangers, set up a scale with a half-meter of good insulation on top, then set the artifact carefully on the insulation. Twenty-six kilograms. Then turned out all the lights and evacuated the place. Thing started to lose weight right away. Eventually it fell off to about five kilos, which is just about right for a 700-kilogram mass on Mimas."

He'd then grinned. "That is, before the scale got too cold and went dead, and the insulation got brittle and crumpled. Damn thing sucks heat out of *anything* when it's unhappy about its weight."

I'd then asked him what he'd meant by "bottom" facet.

"Just that," he'd said. "When it's in a gravitational field, it'll roll over until that facet is down. When it's in zero G, it exerts the 26-kilogram force exactly at right angles to that facet's face. That's the only face with no markings on it. Even the top face has a mark—the strike point."

He'd also explained briefly how to open the thing, by applying sudden pressure to the five surrounding facets in a certain sequence, then to the top facet. The pattern was complicated enough so that it was highly unlikely to be performed by random forces; but simple enough to be described graphically, building on symbols already found on the other artifacts.

The lower five facets were jammed with complex markings that would undoubtedly need the help of whatever documents were inside to decipher.

I played back all of this to myself as Junior and I made our way in silence to the "coming out" party waiting for us in the large laboratory. There were only forty people in the lab itself, because of the limited space. The bigwigs were there, plus one Earther and another thirty who'd drawn lots. The rest—a gang twice as large—were out in the hallway, waiting their turn to file in and look at whatever we pulled out of the twelve-sided box.

Junior and I elbowed our way through the crowd, amidst cheers (and boos) from the elbowees. We pushed our way into the room and to the front of the ring of people surrounding the object; they'd kept a clear space of about three meters, as if they were apprehensive about what might happen when Junior did his thing. Maggie and Greg were up front talking quietly together about something. I could guess what.

Junior had the honor by dint of having been the one to crack the opening code. Maggie waved him to the center of attention; he grinned and swaggered (it's extremely difficult to swagger at .007 G, but he managed) up to the artifact. The battery of surrounding lights cast his multiple shadow on the thing.

Without hesitation the little man pulled a thick plastic rod from a pocket and struck one of the facets three times. Then he moved around and struck a non-adjoining facet five times. Then another two times, a fourth facet six times, and a fifth four times. Then he struck the top facet once and said loudly: "Open, Sesame!" before moving back toward me. "That was just for effect," he stage-whispered. It got a laugh from the assemblage.

It also worked. The top facet hinged on one of its edges and opened straight up. Everyone sucked in breath and strained forward, beginning to move in and take a look.

Then the damndest thing happened: A little birdlike monster, squeaking and squalling, flew straight up out of the opening and proceeded to buzz everybody in the lab. There were shouts and screams, and a mad scramble for the door or other protection. It scared the hell out of all of us.

I didn't move—maybe I was *too* scared. I also noticed

that Junior was standing his ground; a look of understanding was rapidly developing on his face. Then it
struck me. Just as Junior began to open his mouth, I
yelled at the top of my lungs:

"*Quiet, everybody!* Someone get a holographic recording setup in here, quick!"

Then Junior added: "We also need an audio frequency
recorder, and a wide-spectrum electromagnetic receiver/
recorder—and make it snappy!"

Light dawned on various people. Technicians rushed
off purposefully, and were soon back with apparatus.
By this time, the "bird" had apparently finished what
might have been a sizing up of the room, and was
settled into a complex regime of flight. It made patterns
in the air, circling, swooping, performing intricate angular maneuvers, and often diving down to touch spots
on various facets of the artifact. It continuously emitted
chirping and squeaking sounds that seemed to run the
gamut of the audio spectrum, but were grouped about a
frequency which was rather high for the human ear.

Its shape was not precisely like anything known on
Earth, but so obviously biological that it couldn't be
mistaken for anything but a representation of a life
form. It was hideous, but somehow comical at the same
time. One of the Earthers later remarked that it looked
something like a baby barn owl with its feathers ruffled.

Within half an hour there were lenses, antennae and
microphones practically filling the boundaries of the
sphere of operation of the little robot. Junior asked
occasional questions, but rarely took his eyes off the
alien performance.

"I'm getting signals on five frequencies," one of the
techs said in response to a query from the gnome. "Everything from kilohertz to gigahertz."

"Audio's being modulated on a wide band," another
added. "Twenty hertz all the way up through 87 kilohertz."

"Are our voices bothering you?" I asked.

"No sir. I'm subtracting all voice conversations from
the signal."

Junior looked for somebody in particular, and found him. "George, you got a common clock pulse on all these recorders?"

"No." The man looked shamefaced.

"You've got five minutes; set it up so there's not even a phemptosec lag between instruments, or I'll have your hide. And I want another holographic recording set up. One that shows at all times the spatial relationship between the bird and every instrument that's focused on it."

The tech ran out of the room, bumping his head on the ceiling like a rookie. I'd never heard Junior give orders in that tone of voice before; I think he was serious.

It took more like ten minutes, but all was finally done. Then the little man seemed finally to relax. I remarked that I hoped we hadn't lost too much information on the front end.

"Nah. The pattern'll repeat. I'll lay ten against that five spot you took off me."

"But will it do five reps or six?"

He grinned. "Good question. Five, I'd say—but no bets. And by the way, Admiral, you were pretty quick on the uptake after that thing popped out of its shell."

"Yeah, but I didn't think of everything, like you did."

"But not bad, for an amateur. You stood there and figured it out, while everyone else was panicking." He chuckled. "A funny sight—all those intellectual hotshots scurrying for cover like a bunch of startled rabbits."

A memory flashed, and I began to laugh out loud.

"Jesus, Dimp, it wasn't *that* funny."

"Maybe it was. Junior, I've got a cousin. Three years older than me. Lives on the Farm, now. For my eighth birthday he gave me a can of peanut brittle. Imported from Earth; very expensive. I'd tasted peanut brittle once before in my life and absolutely loved it. I remember my mouth actually watering as I opened that can. As soon as I got the lid off, a two-meter papier-maché snake popped out of the thing and scared me half to death. I screamed, and cried afterwards. My cousin laughed and laughed until I socked him on the nose."

The gnome looked thoughtful. "You might have a point." He waved a hand at the bird. "This whole business smacks of something more than just communication. If they wanted to leave a message, that is gross inefficiency at its worst." He then grinned again and winked conspiratorily. "But let's keep this opinion to ourselves. We're going to have to be good, sober little boys to get chosen to go meet the Hexies."

"You think it'll come to that?"

"Let's play like it will."

We turned our attention back to the bird's flight. There were now only about a dozen people in the room at one time; the recording equipment took up a lot of space. New people would come in for a while, gaze at the performance, then leave and make room for others. The flight pattern was hypnotic. Finally, after watching it for over two hours, Junior announced:

"It's flown that particular sequence before. We're in a repeat." He glanced at his watch. "The answer to your question is five reps, Dimp. Total time of flight will be ten hours, thirty-nine minutes and twenty-six seconds, give or take."

I nodded; that was the length of Saturn's SKP-derived day. "Well, I suppose we ought to be glad it's not going to be 29 years." I leaned against the wall and closed my eyes. "Wake me up for the finale, would you? I'm going to grab a few."

Walls are quite comfortable beds on Mimas. When Junior elbowed me awake, many hours had passed. "About half a minute, Admiral."

I focused my eyes and got a fleeting sense of déjà vu on seeing the bird; it might have been only seconds since I'd looked at it last. It was still swooping and diving and chirping as pertly as ever.

"End of fifth pass," said one of the techs to no one in particular. "Get ready for the sixth—not that there's going to be one."

There wasn't. The bird made a final pointing dive, flew to a spot about a meter above the artifact, buzzed a small, complex pattern for about ten seconds, chirped up and down the scale three or four times, then dropped straight into the open top of the dodecahedron. Whereupon the lid closed rapidly and a muffled *thump* came from inside. We felt it through the floor, more than heard it.

Junior cackled. "We are now in possession of a dead artifact. We had our chance, and took it."

Bert Congdon, who had worked with Junior during the cracking of the opening code—and was the nearest thing to a cryptologist that M-Base could boast—walked over to the artifact.

"It doesn't feel cold anymore," he said, holding his open palms ten centimeters from one of the facets. He then used his elbow to thump the same patterns Junior had nearly eleven hours ago. Nothing happened. He pushed, straining, against one of the upper facets. The polyhedron slowly tipped over and came to rest on another facet, showing us the blank bottom.

Junior was grinning. "Bert, I don't know if we'll ever get that thing opened up again or not—but if we do, I'll bet that we find nothing but ruined garbage inside."

Maggie O'Malley had come back for the finale, and now spoke up. "But as you say, Junior, we've got everything in the cans. President Ogumi has a team ready to receive the data and begin the decoding work. But I'd kind of like to beat him to the punch; I've still got some mad saved up from yesterday."

She looked at my grinning compatriot and raised her eyebrows. "How about it, Junior? You want to form a team and take a crack at it?"

"Naw. Let Bert here handle it. I'll just look over his shoulder once in a while. . . ."

20

Ogumi wanted no transmission, even encrypted, of the records of the bird's flight. He wanted the artifact and the original tapes sent back post haste, via the fast personnel carrier which he'd dispatched immediately upon learning of our early attempt to beat the Earthers. It would be arriving at M-Base in less than two weeks. (Junior bet it would be armed. I didn't cover.)

Maggie cheerfully replied that all would be sent as ordered, then immediately made copies of the tapes and careful photos of the artifact's outside markings. Bert's team got to work.

Ogumi also ordered the dismantling of SART. What saved us was that it was too big an operation, with too much capital invested, to just abandon. There would be a phase-out of at least six months, with transport of materiel, specialized equipment, and so forth. Maggie was in charge of the whole thing and made sure that Bert's team stayed together and had facilities with which to work.

The "team" was Junior—with a little help from Bert

and me and a couple of brighter folks, including Willie.
The facilities were M-Base's two largest computers. Junior completely changed the machine language architecture of one of them during the first week, promising
Maggie that he'd put it back to rights before she had to
ship it back home.

The job was complex. It took the team eleven weeks
to learn the Hexies' language, then four more to translate the message into four thousand words of careful
English. The language the Hexies chose to use in the
message smacked of artificiality; it was all scientific,
containing nothing of their daily life, culture, emotions—
the very things *I* would have been interested in as an
archaeologist.

Well, by now you all know the main message of the
artifact: The Hexies have left a starship for us in orbit
around the Sun.

Multiply the number of sides in a pentagon by the
number of faces in a dodecahedron; then multiply that
by the mean distance of Saturn from its primary. It's a
pretty big number, whether you call it centimeters,
meters, or kilometers. About ten times the distance from
Sol to Pluto.

The Hexies have placed a vessel out there for us to
find. They put it in an orbit of 13,704 years. Then they
placed an artifact on Saturn to tell us how to find it.
Much of the message was devoted to *when* they put it in
orbit. The solar system planets were in such-and-such
an orientation—and at the same time the moons of
Saturn were in such-and-such an arrangement.

A computer with a carefully calculated model of the
solar system told us that the time was 3,947.0653 years
ago. A short time, even in our history—the Hexies might
still be around!

At that particular instant (well, hour), draw a line
through the center of the Sun perpendicular to the plane
of Saturn's orbit; also draw a perpendicular through
Saturn itself. Let these two lines form a plane. Place in
orbit in this plane the Hexie vessel. Start it on its merry
way at the instant (well, hour) in question, from the

southern side of Sol's line. Start it going in the direction of the line you drew through Saturn. Then wait patiently, as the vessel counts its leisurely turns.

Only we're going to find it before it completes even its first third of a revolution!

Well, maybe.

The distance isn't really all *that* far: 85 billion kilometers. Call it 68 days at one G, or 125 days at point three G. But that's part of the problem: do we go there at Earth acceleration, or SpaceHome acceleration? Believe it or not, a serious offer by the Earth negotiation team suggested .65 G as a "reasonable" compromise!

Yes, the Earthers are coming with us. They threatened to gang up on Ogumi if he didn't let them in on the context of the message. (By the way, the M-Base team had it solved before the SpaceHome team even figured out how to set up their computers. Ogumi said "thanks," and took the translation.) The SpaceHome president agreed, upon extraction of certain concessions: an agreement to roll over all the SpaceHome debts at lower interest rates; bonded promises that Earth would not attempt to mount a solo expedition; bonded assurances that the eventual joint mission would be set up so that Earth and SpaceHome personnel would have equal onboard voice in policy decisions. That "onboard" part was recognized as a necessity, since the round-trip message time from out there would be nearly a week.

But nothing else was recognized by either negotiating team. Who would be leader of the expedition, and who would be captain of the ship? Who would pay what portion of the considerable investment required to mount the expedition? How big would be our contact vessel? How many personnel? What should we take along as examples of our civilization? And on and on.

So maybe it'll take a year or two or three to finish the negotiating and build the expedition—so what? The Hexie vessel will still be there. And, personally, I think it will take whoever wants to go to the Hexie home system.

Right now I'm doing odds and ends, waiting for the wrangling to wind down. Ogumi has already offered me a position with the expedition—especially since Earth did also, under the extraordinary auspices of the largest power consortium's president, one Frank Hodgkins Jr., who just happens to be Cappie's father—and I've graciously accepted. Ogumi's offer, not Earth's. After all, I have to *live* here.

While I'm waiting, I consult a little for the SpaceHome negotiating team, help Sam Sebastian teach young kids how to herd his junk and give a guest lecture or two at SHU. It's a living. And of course I'm also writing these memoirs, which I plan either to burn, or sell for an exorbitant fee to the communications media. I suppose I'll flip a coin.

Junior. Little runt actually came back to SpaceHome with me for a visit. Stayed in an apartment up on one of the Home III spokes—even came down once or twice to have a nap in my place. Ogumi presented him with a commendation certificate and a handsome honorarium, "for services rendered." Junior peered carefully through Ogumi's glasses into his eyes and said: "Nope. It's not quite there."

One thing the gnome did before going back to SOS was to copy a large number of Earth and SpaceHome research data tapes from the SHU library. Subject: geriatrics and longevity. He took maybe a hundred gigabytes back to SOS with him. Said he'd be busy for a while. But when it comes time to form the expedition, he'll be back. I'll lay you ten to one.

Here is an excerpt from Fred Saberhagen's newest novel, coming in February 1986 from Baen Books:

FRED SABERHAGEN
THE FRANKENSTEIN PAPERS

Chapter 1

May? 1782?

I bite the bear.

I bit the bear.

I have bitten the white bear, and the taste of its blood has given me strength. Not physical strength—that I have never lacked—but the confidence to manage my own destiny, insofar as I am able.

With this confidence, my life begins anew. That I may think anew, and act anew, from this time on I will write in English, here on this English ship. For it seems, now that I try to use that language, that my command of it is more than adequate. Though how that ever came to be, God alone can know.

How *I* have come to be, God perhaps does not know. It may be that that knowledge is, or was, reserved to one other, who has—or had—more right than God to be called my Creator.

My first object in beginning this journal is to cling to the fierce sense of purpose that has been reborn in me. My second is to try to keep myself sane. Or to restore myself to sanity, if, as sometimes seems to me likely, madness is indeed the true explanation of the situation, or condition, in which I find myself—in which I believe myself to be.

But I verge on babbling. If I am to write at all—and I must write—let me do so coherently.

I have bitten the white bear, and the blood of the bear has given me life. True enough. But if anyone who reads is to understand then I must write of other matters first.

Yes, if I am to assume this task—or therapy—of journal-keeping, then let me at least be methodical about it. A good way to make a beginning, I must believe, would be to give an objective, calm description of myself, my condition, and my surroundings. All else, I believe—I must hope—can be built from that.

As for my surroundings, I am writing this aboard a ship, using what were undoubtedly once the captain's notebook and his pencils. The captain was wise not to trust that ink would remain unfrozen.

I am quite alone, and on such a voyage as I am sure was never contemplated by the captain, or the owners, or the builders of this stout vessel, *Mary Goode*. (The bows are crusted a foot thick with ice, an accumulation perhaps of decades; but the name is plain on many of the papers in this cabin.)

A fire burns in the captain's little stove, warms my fingers as I write, but I see by a small sullen glow of sunlight emanating from the south—a direction that here encompasses most of the horizon. Little enough of that sunlight finds its way in through the cabin windows, though one of the windows is now free of glass, sealed only with a thin panel of clear ice.

In every direction lie fields of ice, a world of white unmarked by any work of man except this frozen hulk. What fate may have befallen the particular man on the floor of whose cabin I now sleep—the berth is hopelessly small—or the rest of the crew of the *Mary Goode*, I can only guess. There is no clue, or if a clue exists I am too concerned with my own condition and my own fate to look for it or think about it. I can imagine them all bound in by ice aboard this ship, until they chose, over the certainty of starvation, the desperate alternative of committing themselves to the ice.

Patience. Write calmly.

I have lost count of how many timeless days I have been aboard this otherwise forsaken hulk. There is, of course, almost no night here at present. And there are times when my memory is confused. I have written above that it is May, because the daylight is still waxing steadily—and perhaps because I am afraid it is already June, with the beginning of the months of darkness soon to come.

I have triumphed over the white bear. What, then, do I need to fear?

Only the discovery of the truth, perhaps?

I said that I should begin with a description of myself, but now I see that so far I have avoided that unpleasant task. Forward, then. There is a small mirror in this cabin, frost-glued to the wall, but I have not crouched before it. No matter. I know quite well what I should see. A shape manlike but gigantic, an integument unlike that of any other being, animal or human, that I can remember seeing. Neither Asiatic, African, nor European, mine is a yellow skin that, though thick and tough, seems to lack its proper base, revealing in outline the networked veins and nerves and muscles underneath. White teeth, that in another face would be thought beautiful, in mine surrounded by thin blackish lips, are hideous in the sight of men. Hair, straight, black, and luxuriant; a scanty beard.

My physical proportions are in general those of the race of men. My size, alas, is not. Victor Frankenstein, half proud and half horrified at the work of his own hands, has more than once told me that I am eight feet tall. Not that I have ever measured. Certainly this cabin's overhead is much too low for me to stand erect. Nor, I think, has my weight ever been accurately determined—not since I rose from my creator's work table—but it must approximate that of two ordinary men. No human's clothing that I have ever tried has been big enough, nor has any human's chair or bed. Fortunately I still have my own boots, handmade for me at my creator's—I had almost said my master's—order, and I have such furs and wraps, gathered here and there across Europe, as can be wrapped and tied around my body to protect me from the cold.

Sometimes, naked here in the heated cabin, washing myself and my wrappings as best I can in melted snow, I take a closer inventory. What I see forces me to respect my maker's handiwork; his skill, however hideous its product, left no scars, no visible joinings anywhere.

February 1986 • 65550-7 • 320 pp. • $3.50

A giant space station orbiting the Earth can be a scientific boon ... or a terrible sword of Damocles hanging over our heads. In Martin Caidin's *Killer Station*, one brief moment of sabotage transforms Station *Pleiades* into an instrument of death and destruction for millions of people. The massive space station is heading relentlessly toward Earth, and its point of impact is New York City, where it will strike with the impact of the Hiroshima Bomb. Station Commander Rush Cantrell must battle impossible odds to save his station and his crew, and put his life on the line that millions may live.

This high-tech tale of the near future is written in the tradition of Caidin's *Marooned* (which inspired the Soviet-American Apollo/Soyuz Project and became a film classic) and *Cyborg* (the basis for the hit TV series "The Six Million Dollar Man"). Barely fictional, *Killer Station* is an intensely *real* moment of the future, packed with excitement, human drama, and adventure.

Caidin's record for forecasting (and inspiring) developments in space is well-known. *Killer Station* provides another glimpse of what *may* happen with and to all of us in the next few years.

Available December 1985 from Baen Books
55996-6 • 384 pp. • $3.50